To:
Hor .

CHRISTINE COFER

Untamed Desire

A Chloe Pierson Series

This book is for a dear friend of mine—DL Hegal. I wish I was able to tell her how much she impacted my life. She was a great mentor, a martial art instructor, and a writer. I miss our conversations during class. She helped inspire me to keep writing and to never give up in achieving my goals. I know she would have been proud to see me succeed. I will remember her always.

CHAPTER 1 Chloe

I sat at my desk in the bedroom, writing about the crazy events that happened a few weeks ago. I had since quit my job at the cosmetic surgeon's office to pursue my dream of writing. Now, I was working with my dad at his company, *Dark World Magazine*. My story would make its debut in next month's issue. Of course, names would be changed, and the story would be tweaked a bit because some things needed to be kept a secret—like the whole Josephine issue. But, all in all, I'd let my imagination go wild. Only a select few knew that most of it was true.

I heard the front door open and close. Footsteps stomped up the carpeted stairs, and Kyle poked his head into the room.

"You still sitting there?"

I kept my eyes on the screen as my fingers rapidly stroked the keys on the laptop. "Yep. I have a deadline to meet before next month's issue is released."

Kyle flopped down on the bed. "You need to get out of the house. Take a break for Christ's sake."

"Mmm-hmm." I kept typing as I ignored him.

"I'm serious. Not only am I worried about you, but Riley is, too."

I finished my paragraph, hit save, and shut the lid. "Fine."

Kyle followed me to the bathroom and stopped at the door. "Are you ever going to come back to the club?"

I picked up my toothbrush and dabbed a bit of paste on the blue and white bristles. "I don't know."

I shoved the toothbrush in my mouth and brushed swiftly back and front. I spat out the toothpaste, rinsed the brush, and swished my mouth with water.

I pushed past him and went to find something to eat.

"Does this have anything to do with Drake and Erik?" Kyle followed me into the kitchen.

"Let it go, Kyle." I stared into the fridge.

"Look, Drake has moved on. He has a girlfriend now."

My back straightened as I ignored Kyle's gaze. "Drake's back?"

"Yes, he is."

"This has nothing to do with Drake or Erik." It was a small lie.

Kyle pushed the fridge door shut. "Come here."

He pulled me to the breakfast nook and sat down. "Look, I know you are scared to go back, but do you think you are any safer here than at the club? At least there, all of us can protect you."

"I'm not sure about that, Kyle. I'm sure some are pissed at me for what I did to Josephine."

"Chloe, no one there knows. I haven't heard anyone talk about it. Look, you are the strongest person I know. I mean... you fought a room full of embalmers. To me that says a lot."

"I had you and Cyrus to help me, don't forget."

He took my hand in his and kissed it. "Yes, but it isn't like you to stay in hiding. All I'm asking is for one night of fun. When was the last time you and Hannah hung out?"

"Weeks ago, before all of this started."

"Don't shut her out, Chloe. I know you think if she stays away, you're protecting her from getting hurt and knowing the truth. Honestly, you should tell her. She's going to wonder why you stopped being friends."

Kyle wrapped his arms around me. "You know what you need? A barbeque. I'll invite Leo. He's back from London. I told him about you. He seemed intrigued. And, I'll have Matt come over. You can get to know them better. Maybe you could invite Hannah."

"Are you trying to hook me up with Matt or Leo?"

"I don't think you need help in that department, Chloe." Kyle pulled his phone out and stepped out back to make the calls.

I didn't know where to go from here. I'd told Hannah that Kyle was my stepbrother, and she had met my dad. However, I'd left out the small detail of what we were. How could I break the news to her? Maybe I wasn't giving her enough credit. We do have similar tastes. I wasn't sure if now was the right time. The more I thought about it, the more I realized there wasn't ever going to be a right time.

Sighing, I picked up the phone and text Hannah about the barbeque. I also apologized for not being around lately. And, I told her I had lots to tell her.

Hannah replied right away that she was excited to see me and would be here.

Kyle was still on the phone when he came back in. "Great! See you soon."

He hung up and put his phone in his back pocket. "It's a done deal. They will be here at three. I'm going to run to the store and get some stuff. Come with me."

"I want to be here in case Hannah comes early."

"Riley will be here soon. She can let her in. Come on. Get out of the house for a while. I could use your help."

"Fine. You win. But, we are taking my car. There's more legroom. You drive, though." I tossed him the keys.

There was a moment of silence between us before I asked about Drake.

"So, who is the girl that Drake is dating? Is it Taylor?"

"No. Some new girl who was hired. Her name is Sasha."

"What about Erik? How is he?"

"Same asshole as ever. He's been occupied with others. At least his new companion doesn't care who he sleeps with. You know what they say—you never kick your old habits."

"I suppose."

We pulled into the shopping center, and I grabbed a cart from the bin. "So, what do we need?"

"Everything that is required for a proper barbeque. Burgers, hot dogs, buns, chips, dip, some sides, and drinks."

"We should get plates and napkins too. I'm out."

We loaded the cart full of meat and cases of Dr. Pepper, water, beer, and extra alcohol for mixed drinks.

Kyle was right. I needed to get out of the house. This barbeque was going to be fun. It had been a long time since I was able to let loose.

We paid for our purchase, loaded the car, and headed back home.

When we pulled into the drive, I saw Hannah's car was parked behind Riley's. Kyle backed in so the trunk would be close to the door. I helped carry in some of the bags and left Kyle with the heavy things.

When I entered the kitchen, I glanced out the back door and

saw Riley and Hannah lying out by the pool. Riley's red suit was a two-piece attached on the sides. Hannah's neon yellow bikini almost glowed against her tan skin.

I opened the door and yelled for them. "Hey!"

Hannah jumped up from the lounge chair. "Chloe!"

She jogged over to me and threw her arms around my neck. "How are you?"

"I'm good." I hugged her back.

Kyle stuck his head out the door. "Hey, Hannah. How's it going?"

"It's going. How are you?"

"I'm good. Glad you could make it on short notice."

"I wouldn't miss this for the world. I was beginning to think you had forgotten about me." Her lips curled down into a pout.

Kyle came out and draped his arm around her shoulders. He squeezed her. "Awe, we wouldn't forget you. Now, if you will excuse me, I have to prepare the grill. Riley, you wanna mix some drinks?"

"Absolutely." She smacked Kyle's ass as she jogged by.

One of the perks of having a bartender as your best friend is that Riley knows how to throw drinks together. Even when she makes stuff up it tastes good.

Hannah and I followed Riley inside. I took the ingredients from the fridge for a salad. I tore up the lettuce while Hannah sliced tomatoes.

"So, what's been going on?" Hannah asked.

"Not much. Just been working on a story for my dad's magazine."

"That is so exciting, Chloe. Who would've thought your dad owned our favorite magazine? Not to mention having Kyle as your brother."

5

I laughed. "I know. Shocking, isn't it?"

"Are there any guys from the club coming to the barbeque?"

Riley and I locked eyes. We both knew Hannah hadn't a clue that we were lycans. She was going to have to be told, and it looked as if today was the day. I just hoped she didn't flip out or get upset that I hadn't told her sooner.

"Yeah, Kyle called a few people. I'm not sure who all is coming."

Hannah bounced up and down on the balls of her feet. Her boobs almost popped out of her tiny bikini top. "Well, whoever comes, I'm excited to meet them. Everyone at the club is so exotic."

Riley arched her eyebrow and grinned as she stirred the container filled with margarita mix and tequilas.

I laughed and added the tomatoes to the bowl.

Kyle came in, grabbed the hamburgers, and went back outside. We all stared at him the whole time.

"Riley, your man is hot." Hannah started to chop a cucumber.

"I know."

I expected to see a smile on Riley's face, but I could read her. She looked sad. I think I knew what the problem was. It was the same problem she'd had weeks ago. She wanted to be marked by Kyle, but he had not yet done so.

I laid my hand on her shoulder and squeezed it.

She looked at me, and her eyes glazed over. I knew she was trying not to cry.

"I'll be right back." Riley hurried out of the room.

I let Riley have her moment. I would've gone after her, but I didn't want to leave Hannah alone.

Hannah finished mixing the ingredients into the salad bowl

and wiped her hands on the towel. "All finished. What else do we need to do?"

"Pour the chips in a bowl, and I'll put the ice in the cooler."

After everything was prepared, Riley came back. "Okay, girls. Let's get our tan on."

She and Hannah went outside, and I changed into my black bikini. Music began playing out back. When I got downstairs, both Riley and Hannah had a drink in their hand as they danced.

I grabbed a drink for myself and joined them. We pumped our free hand in the air and whipped our hips from side to side with a little bounce.

Kyle shook his head and flipped a few burgers. "You girls are something else."

Riley bounced her way over to Kyle and started to grind her ass against his.

Kyle put the spatula down, grabbed the back of her hair, and planted his lips on hers.

Hannah and I watched Kyle shove his tongue into Riley's mouth with such force that she stumbled a little.

"Oh, wow!" Hannah fanned herself.

"Yeah, I have to put up with that from time to time. It's hard to sleep." I gulped my drink and sat in the lounge.

Hannah took the one next to me and, together, we watched them make out. "Where can I find a man like that? I hope some of the guys that show up are single."

I knew it was time to speak with her. I took a deep breath and prepared for the worse. But, before I could get the first word out, Riley trotted up to us and plopped down next to Hannah.

"It got really hot out here all of a sudden," Riley said.

"I'm sure it did." I sat up on the side of the chair. "Hannah,

7

we need to talk."

"Okay, about what?"

I arched my eyebrow and looked at Riley. She got what I was about to do and nodded. I didn't know how to start the conversation.

"Hannah, you and I have been friends for a long time, and we pretty much have the same tastes. So, I hope what I am about to tell you doesn't freak you out."

"Do I ever get freaked out?"

"At times, yes. But, this has to do with why I've been distant these past few weeks. There are other...beings among us, and most of them are at the club."

Hannah smiled. "Vampires and lycans. Yes, I know."

I shook my head. "They are not role-playing, Hannah. They are real."

Hannah's smiled faded. "What do mean?"

"I mean just that."

Hannah jerked her head to the side at Riley. "Are you one?"

"Yes. I'm a lycan."

Hannah glanced at Kyle, and then at me. "And Kyle?"

"He's one, too."

"Then what does that make you?"

I didn't answer her.

Her eyes widened. "Oh, my God! You're all wolves? Chloe, why didn't you tell me sooner?"

"I didn't know how. Even I'm still trying to deal with it. But, that's not all."

It took a little while to tell her everything. About my relationship with Erik, and what happened with Josephine. I had to mention the murder case I helped my uncle with, and how my blood was toxic to the embalmer creatures. Of course, I'd almost died when the queen got a hold of me, but, thankfully, Cyrus and Kyle were able to save me.

By the time I finished my story, I thought she was going to bolt. But, she didn't. Instead, she got up and threw her arms around me.

"Oh, my God! You could've been killed."

I laughed and hugged her back. "After everything I've told you, that's all you have to say?"

She wiped away her tears with a smile. "No. What's it like—being a lycan? Have you shifted?"

"No, I haven't yet."

"This is so cool, Chloe. I'm glad you told me."

The back door slid open and two guys walked out with coolers.

"Oh...my...God. Who are they?" Hannah whispered.

"The blonde is Matt, and the other is Leo," Riley replied.

"Are they lycans, too?"

"Yes."

Hannah gasped. "They're so...masculine."

Riley laughed. "Yes. That they are."

The heat from the sun didn't bother me since my blood ran hot anyway. But, when I saw Leo, the heat went straight to my groin. My breath caught in my throat, and I could barely breathe. I fell into a catatonic state. My only focus was on Leo.

Riley waved her hand in front of my face. "Hello? Anyone home? Someone sure is smitten."

She pulled me out of the chair. "Let's go say hi."

Leo locked eyes with me. My heart thumped loudly in my ears, and a thin layer of sweat glistened on my skin. I turned away to gather my thoughts as I gripped the top of the chair.

Riley placed her hand on my shoulder. "Chloe, what's

wrong?"

"Nothing is wrong. It's just that Leo makes me want to fall to my knees and submit to him."

A deep voice from behind said, "Why don't you, then?"

Chills ran up my spine, and goosebumps followed. I slowly turned around. My eyes were level with Leo's chest. I looked up from under my lashes at his honey-colored eyes. They held a shimmer of bronze. The heat between my thighs ignited with his stare. I went to my knees, bowing my head.

I heard Riley gasp. "Chloe, what are you doing?"

Leo gave a low growl. "So eager to please." His hand appeared in front of me. "Not necessary, though."

I took his hand. His touch alone made my core burn hotter. The dampness between my legs coated my bikini. I wanted him more than I had ever wanted anyone. This was so much greater than the feelings I'd had for Erik or Drake.

"You must be Chloe. I've heard a lot about you since my return." His grin widened. "Can I get you another drink?"

Leo's gaze burned through me. He smelled so good. His cologne barely covered his natural wolf scent. If this man could make my body ignite with just his stare and voice, I could only imagine what he could do to me in bed.

Beads of sweat trickled between my breasts. My throat went dry, and I couldn't speak.

Riley playfully hit him in the arm. "Yes, you can!"

After Leo walked away, Riley took me by the arms and shook me. "What the hell, girl? Snap out of it."

"He's so sexy," Hannah said.

Before I could react to that comment, Riley patted her on the back. "He is already spoken for, my dear."

"By who?"

Riley glanced over her shoulder at me with a wink. "He's Chloe's."

"How? They just met."

"Let me tell you about our ways." Riley threw her arm over Hannah's shoulders and guided her toward the back door.

As Hannah walked away, she glanced over at Leo, and then Matt. The two girls disappeared into the house.

Leo sauntered up to me with a beer in one hand and a daiquiri in the other.

When he handed me the drink, I managed to get the words "Thank you" out.

"Ah, she speaks."

The alcohol made my body tingle more. I smiled at Leo and felt my cheeks flush. I quickly turned my head, but he caught my chin with his finger.

"Don't look away. You have stunning green eyes, Chloe."

Leo made my heart melt. There was a connection, and I hoped he felt it, too. He bent down, his face inches from mine.

"I'm not much of a dancer, but if you want to...ya know."

At this point, anything was better than talking. He made me nervous, and I was glad there were no cages to dance in.

I had danced in a cage once with Drake. It was an erotic moment, but not as erotic as his lap dance. Now, I could only imagine what would happen if I danced with Leo. I couldn't resist him. My eyes scanned his body, I and took in his strong arms and those eyes that beckoned me. Something behind them shifted to a lighter shade.

I nodded and took a quick sip of my drink. I placed it on the table by the lounge, and we moved away from the pool. My hips swayed to the beat of the music. I raised my arms above my head and spun in a slow circle with my back arched.

As I danced around him, it gave me a chance to check out his masculine body. There was a black and grey wolf tattoo on his right bicep.

Leo's gaze followed my every move until I was in front of him again. He reached for my waist and pulled me against him. My hands rested on his broad shoulders.

"Party!" Riley yelled when she came back out with Hannah. Everyone paired off. Riley grabbed Kyle's hand. Matt swopped Hannah into his arms. She squealed when he spun her around.

We all jumped together and sang along to the song until it was over.

Riley and Hannah took me by the hand and led me to the lounge. "So, you and Leo, huh?"

"I don't know what you mean."

"The hell you don't." Riley laughed. "Don't tell me you didn't feel your animal when you saw him. He's the one, isn't he?"

"I don't know. Maybe. The only thing I feel is a strong sexual attraction."

We all looked over where Kyle was grilling food.

Riley laid her hand on my knee. "Trust me, Chloe. He's into you. I can sense these things. To be honest, I always wondered about Leo. He never seemed interested in any of the girls at the club."

"Is he an entertainer?"

"No, he's a bouncer. He gets hit on a lot. Just warning you."

"Can lycans be with humans?" Hannah asked.

"Isn't it clear to see? My mom was human. I'm sure if she had known the truth from the beginning, it would have saved her a lot of heartache. Why do you ask?" I picked up my drink from the table and took a couple of gulps.

Hannah glanced over at Matt. He was laughing at something Kyle had said. "I like Matt. He makes me smile."

"A few minutes ago, you were ready to jump Leo. Are you sure you just don't want to hook up with a lycan to see what it's like?"

"Chloe, if I can find a great guy—lycan or not—where is the harm in trying?"

"I just want you to be careful. It is a dangerous world out there."

"Yeah, I get it. I'm just curious."

I picked up the bottle of sunscreen and squeezed some of the liquid into my palm. I began rubbing it on my arms and legs.

"Need some help putting that on your back?"

I looked up and saw that Leo had taken off his shirt. I stared at his tight abs. Another tattoo covered his right pec. It was some sort of symbol. My mouth opened to speak, but nothing came out.

"Oh, for Pete's sake. Here." Riley snatched the bottle off the chair and handed it to Leo.

I anxiously waited for his hands to touch my skin. When he did, I closed my eyes and let out a moan.

His hands moved in slow circles along my back and shoulders. Wherever he touched me, his hand left a trail of heat behind. I wanted him to explore the rest of my body.

Leo leaned in and whispered, "Your body is on fire. Do you want it quenched?"

I heard the word "Yes" escape my throat.

The last time I accidentally said yes, Erik forcefully dominated me. The thought of that moment added to the erotic pleasure I was already experiencing with Leo. But, his idea of quenching was different, and it took me by surprise.

Leo swooped me up into his arms and threw me into the cool water. I came up for air and coughed.

Riley lunged at Leo. He stepped to the side to dodge her, and she fell into the pool.

Matt picked Hannah up, and she soon followed.

Riley splashed water at them. "Assholes!"

Matt and Leo looked at each other for a moment, and then both yelled, "Cannonball!"

They jumped in, creating massive waves. Leo came up between my legs and lifted me out of the water. His hands clutched my thighs to keep me from falling.

"Chicken fight!" Matt yelled as he put Hannah on his shoulders.

Riley played referee between Hannah and me. Our hands clasped together, and we pushed against each other. I felt tingles in the tips of my fingers. I knew if I kept going, electricity would shoot from my hands, and I could unintentionally hurt her.

I didn't know why this was happening to me. I was just having fun. Maybe it was because, with this type of game, it was all about defense.

I tried to let go, but Hannah wouldn't let me. "Hannah! Hannah let go of me!"

"No way!"

"Please, you don't understand. Let go now!"

I saw the sparks flicker, and Riley jumped in between us. "Hannah! You have to let go!"

As Hannah let go, a small flash erupted from my palm to hers. "Ow! What the—?"

I fell into the water, and when I surfaced, Hannah was cheering. "Yeah! I won!" She gave Matt a high-five. Then, he hugged her.

I swam over to Hannah and reached for her hand. There was a small burn mark on her palm. "Hannah, I'm so sorry."

She glanced down and quickly put her hand in the water. "It's okay, Chloe."

"No, it isn't. I could have hurt you."

"What happened, anyway? How did you do that?"

"It has something to do with my DNA. I can't explain right now."

Kyle called out, "Hey, kids! Food is ready!"

I watched Leo and Matt pull themselves out of the pool without using the ladder or the steps. It was as if they were shooting a swimsuit commercial.

Hannah, Riley, and I waded over to the steps. Leo and Matt handed each of us a towel.

I dried off and took a seat at the table between Riley and Hannah.

Leo sat across from me.

I was disappointed that he had put his shirt back on. Either way, he was certainly a distraction.

Kyle placed the meat in the middle of the table with the condiments and sides.

I poked a burger with a fork and placed it on the bun. When I reached for the ketchup, my hand brushed against Leo's. A tickling sensation vibrated through my body.

Leo stared at me and winked. "After you."

I squirmed in my seat and squeezed a bit of ketchup on my burger.

"Here you go, Leo." I handed him the ketchup.

We were silent for a while as we filled our plates.

Hannah broke the silence. "Chloe told me what happened to her while she was on vacation. I know what you all are."

Kyle glanced at me, and I shrugged. "You told me I should. So I did."

"I know, but...everything?"

"Yep. Why not? Can't go about this half-assed."

"Don't worry. Your secret is safe with me. I don't want people thinking I'm nuts." Hannah bit into her hot dog.

I stared at her.

"Oh! Chloe, I'm sorry. I forgot..."

I waved it off. "No worries."

"No, it isn't fine, Chloe. Your mother was in a mental hospital because of what she saw."

I took Hannah's hand. "I know you didn't mean anything by it. I'm not mad, okay?"

Hannah nodded, and we continued our meal.

After we ate, Hannah and Riley helped me clean up in the kitchen while the guys stayed outside to pick up trash.

"So, with Leo here, are you going to come back to the club?" Riley asked.

I felt my face turn red as I tried to hide a smile. "I don't know. Maybe."

"I want to come, too," Hannah said.

It was great that Hannah wanted to be a part of the group, but I was still scared for her. If she wanted to go down this path, I couldn't stop her. I could only warn her. Matt seemed like a great guy, but if anything happened to my friend or he hurt her in any way, he would rue the day. I would make him pay, and after everything that had happened a few weeks back, I was sure he knew that.

The guys came in with a collection of trash bags and coolers. Leo slipped up beside me and whispered, "You wanna go for a walk?"

I looked over at Riley and Hannah, but they were occupied with Kyle and Matt, respectively.

"Sure."

We walked out back and headed for the woods.

"How was your trip to London?"

"It was good. It wasn't a vacation or anything. I stayed at the club mostly because Cyrus needed me there. I did manage to get a quick visit with my old community."

"Are you from London?" I almost tripped over a tree trunk, but Leo caught my arm. Once I'd composed myself, we continued.

"Initially, no." Leo moved a huge branch out of the way of our path. "It's quite a long story."

"I have time as long as you do."

We came to a small stream and took a seat on a tree stump. The sound of the water rushing over the rocks was soothing. Birds sang their sweet songs in the trees above us. Some landed across the stream and dipped their heads in the water.

"My father was born and raised in Wissenhaute, Germany. It was a small community in the southern part of the country. Things took a turn for the worst and they decided to relocate to London. They settled in a wooded area called Dark Pine Forest. Once settled, my dad and a few others decided to come to the States. Some went their own way, while others stayed with my dad."

"You don't have much of an accent."

Leo smiled. "No. I wasn't born in Germany. I was born in Rhetford Falls, Vermont, where my dad and the others built a new community. My dad met my mother in Vermont. She was studying to be an English teacher."

"With your dad being German, do you speak any of the language?"

"Ein bisschen." Leo tossed a rock into the stream and watched the ripples expand to the edge of the water.

I stared at him and blinked. "Huh?"

Leo laughed. "I said, 'A little bit.' My dad has a heavy accent. When he goes on a rant, it's all in German. I found it funny when I was little."

"What did your mom think about it?"

"She thought it was sexy. I think she pissed him off at times on purpose."

"So, how did you meet Cyrus and get established with his club?"

"My family and I traveled back and forth to London for visits and meetings. When I turned eighteen, we stayed a little longer than we'd planned. At that time, we had taken in more people. Drake's family was one of them. I believe he was twelve at that time."

I did the calculations in my head to figure out how old Leo was. Since Drake was my age, that put Leo at thirty-one. Age was not an issue for me, obviously. I did date a vampire for what—a day?

"So, why did Drake's family assimilate into your community? Were they in trouble?"

"That is not my story to tell. Anyway, I met Cyrus when I was roaming the city one night. I've worked off and on for him ever since. When I found out he was putting together a club here in the States, I took it as an opportunity to transfer so I could be closer to my family."

I picked up a pebble and followed Leo's lead by tossing it into the water.

"So, Erik and Drake, huh?"

I glanced at him. "What's that supposed to mean?"

Leo shrugged. "Nothing. I know how much of an arrogant asshole Erik can be. I'm surprised you didn't choose Drake."

"Why would I?"

"He seems more like your type. At least he'd never hurt you."

I felt tears sting my eyes. This wasn't the conversation I'd hope to have with Leo. I'd thought we'd had a connection. Maybe I was wrong.

I wiped my cheek with the back of my hand. "I don't have to explain my reason to you for not being with him."

"I'm not asking you to."

The sun had descended behind the horizon. In its place, a full moon shone through the tops of the trees.

"I should get back." As I turned to walk back down the trail, Leo hurried after me.

"Wait!" He went around a large tree and jumped in front of me. "Let me finish what I was saying."

"Not sure I want to." I looked away, and, this time, he placed his hand on my cheek.

"Please stop looking away."

When I looked into those eyes, my knees weakened.

"Chloe." He spoke my name in a low, grumbly way.

It caused the hair on my skin to stand at attention.

"I know the reason why you didn't accept Drake's offer."

He stepped closer and stared down at me. I couldn't move. I realized I was taking short, panting breaths. I wanted him to kiss me. I wanted his lips, but I also wanted his hands on my

19

body again.

"Had I been here, I could have spared you the pain, and Erik wouldn't have hurt you. I wouldn't have let either one of them near you."

Leo was inches from my lips as he leaned in.

The moment was cut short when Hannah called to me.

Leo stepped away, and I let out a rush of breath that I was holding. I felt like I had run a marathon.

"Great timing," I whispered.

Leo held out his hand, and we walked back to the house.

"I need to get going and wanted to say goodbye," Hannah said.

"I'll walk you to your car."

I helped carry some leftover food and sat it carefully in the backseat. "I hope we can hang out again soon. I've really missed this."

"Me, too. Would it be okay if I go to the club once in a while without you?"

"Hannah, I can't tell you what to do. All I ask is that you be careful."

"I will. I promise." She crossed her heart.

I gave her one last hug and watched as she pulled out of the driveway. She honked and waved as she drove off.

The front door opened and Kyle, Matt, and Leo came out. Leo carried the cooler, and Matt had a bag of leftovers.

"I guess you guys are heading out, too?"

"Yeah, we're calling it a night. It was great seeing you again, Chloe. Come back to the club soon." Matt gave me a brief hug.

"I will."

Leo placed the cooler in the trunk and stared at me as he walked to the passenger's door. He winked and got in.

I hurried inside and ran up to the bedroom. I jumped around, saying, "Oh, my God! Oh, my God!" before falling onto the bed. I felt like I was on cloud nine. Is this what real love felt like? I didn't have the fierce sensation inside of my animal attacking me to be with Leo. This was the feeling you get when you see that one special someone and you're all giddy with the butterflies.

There was a knock on the door, and I sat up. "Come in!"

Riley poked her head in and then entered. She had a huge smile. It mirrored mine. "So, where did you and Leo run off to?"

"We just went for a walk in the woods. It's no big deal."

Riley flopped down next to me. "I don't believe that for one second. You are flush, girl." She reached out and took my wrist. "And, your pulse is beating twice the rate as if you just had great sex."

I fell back on the bed, laughing. "Whatever."

"You have a thing for him, don't you?" Riley pushed me in the arm. "Come on! You can tell me."

"Okay, okay. Yes. Leo is amazing. I don't think I need to go into detail."

Riley jumped off the bed. "I knew it! You're in love with Leo. Your lycan instincts are telling you Leo is the one."

"Please don't say anything to anyone, Riley. I'm not sure where this is going, and I don't want to look like a fool if I'm wrong."

Riley pulled me off the bed. "You're not wrong. He wants you, too." She tapped the tip of my nose with her finger. "I promise I will keep quiet. For now."

She skipped out of the room.

There was too much adrenaline running through me, so I

sat down at my desk and turned on the laptop to work on my story. It was midnight when I reached a stopping point.

I took a quick shower, and before climbing into bed, I checked to make sure the French doors were locked.

As I lay in bed, I imagined what the kiss would've felt like. I rolled over to stare at the empty spot next to me. I reached out and ran my hand over the cool sheet. I longed to have a warm body next to me, and I hoped Leo would be the one to fill that void.

CHAPTER 2 Chloe

I arrived at the club and parked in the employee lot. Normally, I would enter through the front, but I didn't want to upset the large crowd out front by cutting in line. I knocked on the back door and waited for someone to answer. The door finally opened, and Devin poked his head out.

"Oh, hey, Chloe. Good to see you again." He held the door open as I passed.

"Not working the front door tonight?" I asked.

"I was on my way there when I heard the knock." He glanced down at my bag. "You staying?"

"I might. It will save me a drive home if I get tired."

"I understand. Well, see ya."

I waved and went downstairs to put my things in my room. On my way back, I stopped at Drake's room. I knew he wouldn't be in there, but I knocked anyway.

A strong scent caught my attention. My head jerked to the right at the door next to Drake's room. Before I knew it, I was standing in front of it. I drew in a deep breath, and a familiar smell hit me hard. This was Leo's room.

My pulse quickened, and I stepped away with a smile. There was a reason I was responding this way.

I hurried up to the main area of the club and glanced around the familiar room. The red and white strobes moved about the room. I could honestly say I had missed this place.

I squeezed my way through the crowd and headed toward the bar.

Riley looked up with wide eyes and a smile. "You look stunning this evening. This wouldn't have anything to do with a certain male, now would it?"

She placed a beer on the bar and picked up the cash a guy put on the counter for her.

"Maybe." I took a seat at the end of the bar and watched Riley make my chocolate martini.

"Is Erik here?" I asked.

Riley tilted her head toward the VIP section. "Would you expect otherwise?"

I didn't bother to look. I didn't even know why I asked. "Suppose not."

Riley sat the drink on the bar and then focused on the other customers.

I spun around in my seat and sipped my drink. I almost choked when I saw Drake in his cage, dancing with a girl.

"And this is how it all started weeks ago," I mumbled.

I was happy to see him back. I missed being here, and I missed him.

The girl he was with was beyond beautiful. Long locks of black curls spiraled down her shoulders and surrounded her round face.

Drake picked her up and held her against the bars. She wrapped her legs around his waist and clawed at his back as he kissed her neck.

For the past two weeks, I'd wondered how Drake was doing. I knew I had hurt him, and I hadn't meant to. But, seeing him with this girl made me happy to know he had moved on.

I put the empty glass on the bar and glanced at the steps to the second floor. There he stood—arms crossed as he scoped the crowd. I couldn't take my eyes off him. Leo looked devilishly handsome in his work attire.

A rush of desire flooded my body, and I felt a connection deep in my soul—one that seemed to awaken my inner wolf. It was something that couldn't be tamed. The feeling was stronger than it was last night. I knew right then and there that I wanted Leo to be mine.

He turned in my direction and caught me staring.

I held his gaze until a group of girls gathered around him.

"Told you he gets a lot of attention." Riley tapped my shoulder and handed me another drink.

I spotted Erik leaning on the upper rail. Luckily, he wasn't looking in my direction. I was afraid of what would happen if he saw me. Maybe he already had. It would be like déjà vu, and I didn't want to repeat what happened between us. I had no feelings for him anymore.

A blonde-haired girl came up behind Erik, draping her arms over his shoulders. One hand rubbed his chest. She leaned in to say something to Erik. His hand slipped behind her neck, and he pulled her in for a kiss. They turned away and headed to their table.

"Asshole," I mumbled.

Leo slithered through the crowd in my direction. I straightened my posture and thrust my breasts out.

His smile widened as he neared. The color of his eyes shifted to a glowing bronze. "Can I talk to you in private?"

"Absolutely."

I accepted Leo's hand. The heat from his touch spread

through me like lava flowing into the crevices of the Earth's core. It all led to one place, and a twinge of pleasure pulsed between my legs.

Leo led me up the stairs to the second floor. I wanted to go in the opposite direction—mainly to his bedroom. I didn't want to encounter Erik, but I couldn't avoid him, either. So, I put on my big girl pants, held my head high, and prepared for whatever was going to happen.

I could sense Erik's gaze on me as I reached the top of the stairs. I could even feel his presence closing in on me.

I tightened my grasp on Leo's hand.

Leo glanced over at Erik and squeezed my hand to reassure me that I was safe.

We went down the hall to the office, and Leo shut the door behind us.

I expected to see Cyrus at his desk, but the office was empty. I took a seat on the couch and observed Leo as he moved around the bar. Every time he extended his arm for a glass or bottle, his muscles flexed under his tight shirt. I even ogled his thighs.

Not only was I sizing him up and down, but my animal was, too. What would it take for her to make an appearance? I knew she was just as curious about him as I was.

"Ah-hem." Leo cleared his throat to get my attention.

I was too busy fantasizing about him to notice him standing there with my drink.

"Oh, sorry." I grabbed the glass and took a quick sip. "What did you want to talk to me about?"

Leo sat next to me and rested his hand on the back of the couch. "Nothing of importance. I just wanted a moment alone with you."

"And, this is where you bring me?" I smiled.

Leo chuckled. "I am working. Otherwise, I would have taken you to my room."

My cheeks burned, and my body straightened to attention. It made my breasts stick out more, and I caught Leo looking at them a few times.

"You can relax, Chloe."

I released the tension and sat back against the couch. Even slouching pushed my boobs up.

"You know, if you had been here a few weeks ago, Josephine would be alive, and there wouldn't be a threat to my existence." This time, I took a huge gulp of my drink. A massive air bubble went down with it.

I bent over with my hand on my chest.

"You okay?"

I nodded but replied with a, "No."

After a few moments, it passed. "I'll never do that again."

Leo patted me on the back. "I won't let anything happen to you, Chloe."

His fingertips caressed my shoulder. "Actually, I was supposed to be here, but I stayed the extra week in London. There's an old lady in my community named Emma. She's like a grandmother to me She owns the only restaurant in town, and I stayed to help her."

The warmth of his body sent shivers through me. Were Leo to ask to mark me, my answer would be yes. I wanted him and no one else.

"That is sweet."

"Yeah. I'm just glad her great-granddaughter wasn't there."

"Why?"

"Because she's always had a crush on me. She used to follow

me around every time I visited."

"Awe, did you break her heart?"

"No. Because from what Emma told me, the girl still asks about me. She's the same age as you."

"Am I going to have a problem with her if I ever meet her? Because I'm done dealing with jealous women."

Leo laughed. "It will be handled accordingly. Trust me."

"So, where was the girl while you were there?"

"Away at college."

The office door opened and Matt and Kyle piled in. "I guess you took my advice, huh?"

"Don't flatter yourself, Kyle."

"But, it's good to see you back in your element, Chloe."

I laughed. "Not sure this is my element, but okay."

Erik strolled into the room behind them. "Well, here we all are. Chloe, I didn't expect to see you here."

I finished my drink and put the glass on the table. "Well, I am. So deal with it."

Erik held up his hands. "I didn't mean anything by it. I'm just surprised."

I felt the tension between Erik and me. It was the same as before, only this time, mine was hatred and his lust. Things really hadn't changed. It seemed as if he was pretending to move on by being with the blonde girl. Erik's power caressed me as it had in the past. Touching me in places he was no longer welcomed.

My body trembled, and I wrapped my arms around myself. I couldn't take any more of his taunting. I jumped up from the seat. "Knock it off, Erik!"

Leo, Matt, and Kyle gathered near me.

"Why are you all around Chloe like some protection shield?

I'm not going to harm her."

Leo stepped in front. "That's right. You're not."

I glanced down at Leo's tight, round ass. I wanted to reach out and caress him. It excited me to see Leo play the dominant role. I wondered how controlling he was in the bedroom. Visions of making love to Leo played over and over in my mind. What position we would be in. Would he be gentle or forceful? Would he even shift?

All this was too much, and drops of sweat oozed from my pores.

"Excuse me. I need some air." I stepped around the couch and chair to avoid Erik.

Once in the hall, I leaned against the wall, panting. My groin burned and tightened with the need to be with Leo. I hoped for it to be soon, because this feeling was building up inside, and I had to somehow find a release.

I ran down the hall to the stairs and squeezed my way through the crowd to the back of the club. I flung the back door open so hard it hit the brick wall. I put a crate in front of the door to keep it open and sat down.

"Chloe? What's wrong?" Riley poked her head out and pulled another crate next to mine.

I leaned against the warm brick wall. "This whole Leo thing is really getting to me, Riley. My body is aching to be with him. All I can think about is sex."

Riley placed her hand over her mouth and then removed it, smiling. "I knew it! He's your mate."

"I don't know, Riley. I'm not having the internal pains. My animal hasn't tried anything to break free."

"Maybe he's holding back. If he is, then you won't feel it."

"Why would he be holding back?"

"This isn't a good setting to release it, Chloe." She laughed.

"Yeah, I suppose. But, he could have at the house."

We sat in silence for a moment, breathing in the warm air. A hint of rain mixed with the appetizing aroma from the restaurants nearby.

Kyle never talked about his relationship with Riley, but I was curious to know if there was any progress since I hadn't the chance to ask her at the barbeque. "How are you and Kyle? I know why you ran out of the kitchen yesterday."

Riley's smile faded while she played with a piece of string on her shirt.

I laid my hand on her shoulder. "What is it, Riley? You know you can talk to me."

A tear trickled down her cheek, and she wiped it away. "You know how much I love him, but I don't know where his head is or how he feels about me anymore. It seems we are drifting apart, and that shouldn't happen if we were meant to be."

I laid my arm over her shoulders. She leaned in with her head against mine. "I don't know what to do, Chloe. I don't want to lose him."

"Have you told him how you feel?"

Riley shook her head. "No. I'm afraid to."

I'd never seen her vulnerable, and it pained me to see her hurting. "You should talk to him, Riley. It's the only way to find out what's going on and put your mind at ease. He's a great catch. Don't let him be the one that got away."

Riley pulled away with a glimmer of hope in her eyes. "You're absolutely right."

Out of nowhere, a clash of thunder and lightning struck overhead, and a gust of wind blew dirt and trash everywhere.

Riley jumped up and pulled me with her. "We should get

inside."

We ran to the office. Matt, Leo, and Drake were sitting on the sofa while Erik sat at the bar.

"What's wrong?" Leo asked.

"Oh, sorry. Nothing. Just a bad storm heading this way," Riley replied.

The lights flickered but didn't go off.

"I need to get back to work." Riley looked over at me and pointed. "We will hang out later and talk girl stuff."

I nodded. "For sure."

"Yeah, Matt and I need to get back to work, too." Kyle gave me a quick hug. "See you downstairs."

Erik and Leo glared at me with the same intent—a hunger of pure sexual desire. I couldn't feel it from Leo, but I saw the animal in his eyes. Erik, though, was his usual self. His power slithered over my skin.

I started to say something when Leo turned to me. "I need to get back, too." He glanced over his shoulder, then back to me. "Are you going to be all right?"

I nodded. "Yeah. I got this."

Leo whispered in my ear, "Stay in my room tonight. It's next to Drake's." He kissed my cheek and gave me a wink.

As he was leaving, Leo and Erik stared at each other until Leo was out of sight.

Still looking at the door, Erik said, "Leo, huh?"

"I don't know what you mean."

Erik turned to face me. "Batting your lashes. Having a dazed look on your face as you stare at his ass. You're hot for him, aren't you? Just like you were hot for Drake and me."

I wasn't going down this road. I wasn't going to let him push my buttons, but that comment was uncalled for. "You know the reason for my mixed emotions."

"Yeah, later, after I found out the truth about what you were." Erik closed his eyes for a brief moment. "Look, I don't want to fight. I just want a moment with you. We never really had the chance to talk about what happened. I need to explain my situation."

"No, you had your chance to explain, and you ignored the situation. I'm not wasting my time on you anymore."

I stormed down the hall to the VIP section and scanned the room for Leo. He was standing by the front door. One of the girls he was speaking with reached out and squeezed his arm. He backed away with his hand up to ward her off. The girl pouted and walked away.

I smiled and then spotted Hannah in the middle of the dance floor. I hurried down the steps and pushed my way through the crowd until I reached her.

I tapped her on the shoulder.

She spun around, eyes wide. "Chloe!" She threw her arms around me.

"Why are you here on a work night? You never go out until the weekend." I had to yell above the music.

"Well, I could ask you the same thing."

"I can work from home or have you forgotten?"

Hannah pouted. "No, I haven't forgotten."

The lights went out, and the blacklight came on. Glow stick bracelets, necklaces, and head-bands illuminated the room. Everyone began jumping in unison to the heavy beat.

Hannah grabbed my hand. "Let's dance!"

My body started to move, and I found myself letting go, getting lost in the crowd with Hannah by my side. It had been a long time since we went clubbing together.

I spun around a few times, but when I reached for Hannah, she was gone. A man grabbed my waist and started to grind into me. Another came in from behind. I was trapped between them. I tried pushing them off, but the crowd around us was tight. Even if I yelled, no one would hear—at least, not a human.

"Let go! Get off me!" I began pushing them, but they wouldn't budge.

The next thing I knew, the crowd parted and they were being pulled away. Kyle and Leo escorted me to the bar.

"You okay?" Kyle asked.

"Yeah, I'm good. No big deal." I stood on tip-toe and looked across the dance floor. "Hannah is here. We were dancing and got pulled apart."

"You want me to find her?" Kyle asked.

I nodded. "Please."

Kyle patted my shoulder and walked away.

Leo stood there, staring at me. "The thought of another man's hands on you..."

I laid my hands on the sides of his face. "I'm fine. No worries."

Leo kissed my palm and went back to the door.

There was a tap on my shoulder, and Riley handed me a bottle of water.

"Thanks."

I sensed someone was standing behind me, and Drake's scent hovered around me. I turned, and he stood there without his shirt on. His body glistened under the light.

"Hey, Chloe."

"Hi, Drake. How are you? How's the shoulder?"

"I'm good. Shoulder is fine." He turned to show me his back.

"I have scars, but the ladies seem to like it. They say it gives me character."

"Listen, Drake, I wanted to say I'm..."

A set of hands appeared around Drake from behind, and a head popped up around his arm. "Hey, baby. You coming back to the cage?"

Drake turned and pulled the girl under his arm close. "Sasha, this is Chloe. Chloe, Sasha."

"Hi. Nice to meet you." Sasha pulled Drake's arm. "Come on!"

I smiled and shrugged.

The way Drake looked at me led me to believe he still carried some feelings for me. I hoped he wasn't using Sasha as a replacement. To me, it seemed like a sudden relationship.

"Chloe!" Hannah bounced up to the bar. "That was wild!"

I broke a smile. "Yeah, it was something. How long have you been here?"

"I don't know. A couple of hours, maybe. Do you think I could see Matt?"

"Hannah, he's busy."

"I know. I just want to say hi."

I took out my phone and sent a message to Kyle. He sent me Matt's number, and I sent him a message. A few seconds later, he sent one back.

"He'll be here in a second."

Hannah hugged me. "You're the best."

"I know. What would you do without me?"

"Stay at home on a work night, eat ice cream, and watch Netflix. Face it, Chloe. You've opened up my eyes to a whole new world."

"Was it so bad before all this?" I asked.

Before she could answer, Matt came up behind Hannah and wrapped his arms around her tiny waist.

Hannah spun around and flung her arms over his shoulders. "Hi!"

"Hey yourself. What's up?"

"I just wanted to see you."

"You wanna hang with me up in the booth?"

Hannah jumped up and down. "Yes! I'd love to! " She linked arms with Matt and waved goodbye.

I smiled and waved back. I had created a monster.

I'd had enough for the evening and went to grab my things from my room. I was going to take Leo up on his offer and stay with him.

His bedroom had a cozy cabin-like vibe. The wall behind the bed was painted dark blue. The rest was covered in dark shiplap. His luggage lay open on the floor, with motorcycle and car magazines sprawled out on top of his clothes on a small table. A few black and dark blue T-shirts were folded on the bed. Most of them were Harley Davidson. One had a blue background with a wolf howling in front of a moon. Another said "Lone Wolf." Several motorcycle pictures hung on the walls.

A sketchbook and colored pencils lay next to the bed. I flipped through the book. There were drawings of bikes on all of the pages.

"Very talented. Wonder what other hidden abilities he possesses." I put the book back the way it was.

Something bulky, covered by a blue sheet, sat against the far wall. I lifted the sheet to find a blue motorcycle with a wolf on the side.

"How beautiful." I wanted to touch it, but I respected the

35

bike. I didn't want to put fingerprints on it.

I covered it back up and cleaned off the bed by putting Leo's shirts on his luggage.

I changed into my nightshirt and snuggled into the king-size bed. The scent of him rolled off the sheets as I inhaled deeply. I fell asleep with happy thoughts.

CHAPTER 3 Chloe

The first person I saw when I opened my eyes was Erik. He was sitting in the chair next to the bed, watching me.

"What the hell, Erik?" I looked over my shoulder and Leo was sleeping soundly.

"Good morning, beautiful." Erik smirked. His hair hung over his left shoulder, covering part of his face. He glared at me the same way he had weeks ago, in a way both sexy and seductive.

The hunger for him gnawed at my gut. I knew he was making me feel this way on purpose.

I looked away, pissed. "Stop it, Erik. How long have you been sitting here?"

Erik leaned forward and rested his arms on his knees. "Long enough to know that you must have had one hell of a sex dream. Were you dreaming of me?"

"Why are you doing this? Why can't you leave me alone?"

"I still feel connected to you, Chloe."

"Well, I don't feel connected to you."

"Really? I don't think that's true. Otherwise, you wouldn't be bothered by the feelings you still get when you're around me."

I sat up, and the comforter rested in my lap. "You killed

every ounce of feeling I had for you when you gave me your blood without my consent. And, you attacked me because I killed Josephine."

"Chloe, if you would just let me explain."

Leo stirred next to me. Half-asleep, he mumbled. "Erik, you have five seconds to get the fuck out of my room."

Erik sighed. "Very well. I have matters to attend to anyway. I'll see you around."

Once Erik left, I rolled over and gazed at Leo. He was on his back and one arm was tucked under the pillow. I took this moment to get a good look at the tattoo on his pec. Thick vines and foliage surrounded a shield. In the middle of the shield was a wolf. Above the wolf was the name Rendall—all in caps. Under the shield was a banner that had the word "Germany." It, too, was in all caps.

I was so focused on the design, that I didn't realize Leo was awake. He startled me when he said, "It's my family crest."

"Sorry. I didn't mean to stare."

"No big deal. I don't mind. Did you sleep well?"

"I haven't slept this good in so long." I stretched my arms above my head. "I hope you don't mind, but I noticed your stuff lying around, and I sorta peeked at it last night."

"It's fine. I've nothing to hide."

"Did you do those drawings?" I knew the answer, but I wanted to talk about his hobby.

"Yep. I rebuild bikes and cars. It's something I've always done with my father and brother."

"Oh, you have a brother? What's his name?"

"Seth. He's two years younger."

"Did you build that bike over there?" I nodded toward the corner.

"Yes."

"It's beautiful. Will you take me out on it?"

Leo laughed. "I don't ride that one. It is for show only."

"Oh." I frowned.

I looked deep into his eyes and desperately wanted to kiss him. It was hard to ignore his rapid pulse. It beat fast like mine.

My sexual desire for him was spreading quicker than a wildfire.

Leo pushed a strand of hair behind my ear. "Do I still make you want to submit to me?"

Leo held a dominant power over me. I could feel it in my bones. I wanted nothing more than to give myself to him completely.

I swallowed the lump in my throat. I didn't know if he was joking or if he was serious. "Yes."

His smile widened as he rolled out of bed with a massive erection straining in his tight boxer briefs.

I was curious at how big he was. Did it get bigger in animal form?

I watched him dress. The animal within me raised her head and arched her back. I wasn't prepared, and my breath hitched as the hunger inside began to stir.

Leo's eyes darted in my direction, and he held onto the dresser for support. The muscles in his arms tensed up as he tightened his grip.

"Leo, I'm sorry. Did I do something wrong?"

"No, you've done nothing wrong." He let go of the dresser and pulled on a shirt. "I have an errand to run. I will see you later."

I threw a pillow over my face and screamed. I was sexually

frustrated. I didn't know how to control myself or my wolf. Leo must have let his guard down just enough for my animal to sense him. To see him respond that way, led me to believe he was meant for me.

I jumped out of bed and quickly dressed. There was no way I was going to screw this up. I snatched my bag off the floor and hurried to catch up with Leo. But, he was nowhere to be found.

My shoulders slumped with disappointment that I'd missed him. I made my way to the car and saw a dozen red roses waiting on the seat. There wasn't a card attached, but I knew they were from Erik. They had his scent all over the petals. He wasn't going to quit until I gave in. If he wasn't going to heed my warning, maybe I should be a bit sterner.

I tossed the roses on the ground and headed home.

Kyle's car was in the driveway, but Riley's was gone. All was quiet when I entered the foyer. I checked all around the main floor of the house before going upstairs. I heard Kyle's voice coming from the guest bedroom.

"Yes, sir." He was silent for a few minutes.

"I'm sure you're excited about it. I know I would be." Kyle chuckled.

The door was ajar, so I peeked in. He was on the other side of the room with his back to me. No matter how quiet I was, I knew he could hear me.

Kyle turned and saw me in the door-way. "I will give you a call in a couple of days." He finished the call and hung up. "Hey, you're home."

"Who was that on the phone? I don't mean to be nosey, but it sounded important."

"Nothing, really. Just a job opportunity." He placed his

hand on my cheek and kissed the top of my head before he left the room.

"That's great! What's the job? Are you leaving the club and the magazine? Does Dad know?" I followed him downstairs to the kitchen.

Kyle whirled around with his hand up. "Whoa! Enough with the questions. I don't want to talk about it right now."

He began putting dishes in the dishwasher.

"Okay, fine. Where is Riley?"

"At her parents. It's our anniversary. I'm taking her out tonight. Matt is coming over to stay with you tonight." He shut the dishwasher door and turned it on. "I need to go get ready."

I followed him back upstairs. "I don't need a babysitter, Kyle. I think I can manage one night by myself."

He stopped at the bedroom door and turned to me. "Not happening. With Josephine's maker roaming around out there, I'm not leaving you alone. Now, stop being a baby or there will be no ice cream before bed."

He shut the door before I could protest his decision.

"Are you serious right now?" I banged on the door with my fist. "Kyle!"

I heard him laughing before he turned the shower on.

"You're an asshole!" I hit the door again and went to soak in the tub.

I liked Matt and all, but if I was to have anyone come to stay with me, I wanted it to be Leo. I guess he had to work. Maybe Kyle didn't even get to ask Leo.

A few minutes later, there was a knock on the door. "I'm heading out! Behave yourself tonight. I don't want a bad report when I return home tomorrow."

"Yes, Dad!"

Kyle's laugh faded as he walked away.

I placed a washcloth over my eyes. I must have fallen asleep. The water had turned cold, and the bubbles had vanished, leaving the water foggy.

When the doorbell rang, I got out and threw on a robe. As I ran down the stairs, I yelled, "Just a minute!"

Imagine my surprise when I saw Leo instead of Matt. He was dressed in a dark blue dress shirt and black slacks. He carried a duffle bag in his left hand.

"Is this a new dress code for security?"

"No."

I stood on tiptoe to look over his shoulder. "Kyle said Matt was coming over."

Leo stepped inside. "Would you rather Matt be here?"

"No." I pulled him the rest of the way in and shut the door. "So, why are you dressed up?"

"I'm taking you out."

"Are you asking me out on a date?"

"Yes, I am."

"Make yourself at home while I go get ready, then."

I ran upstairs and threw the closet door open. One by one, I sorted through the clothes. "No. No. No. Definitely not that one."

I tossed things aside and created a pile of rejects on the floor. I wanted to look sexy for Leo. Then, I found the perfect dress. A dark blue strapless that fell to mid-thigh.

"Oh, yes! Perfect. Now to find shoes."

Two rows of shoes were lined up at the bottom of the closet. The top shelf was for dress shoes, and the bottom was casual. I chose a black pair of three-inch heels with straps around the ankle.

"Now, hair up or down?" I toyed with the long strands, trying to decide how to wear it. I finally pulled the sides back and held it in place with a blue dragonfly barrette.

"Now, a little bit of lip gloss and eyeliner."

My hands shook while I tried to draw a curved line along the edges of my eyes. I didn't know why I was so nervous. It's not like I hadn't dated before. But, Leo was special, and I could feel that this was the real deal.

I took one last look in the mirror. Satisfied, I grabbed my clutch and made my way to the sitting room.

Leo was observing the pictures on the wall. His physique from behind was so tempting.

"I'm ready."

Leo spun around, and his mouth dropped open. "Damn. You look...wow!"

I twirled to give him the view from all angles. "Thank you."

"You have a lot of pictures. Is this your mother?" He pointed to one.

"Yes. And, this is Uncle Bob and Aunt Helen, my mom's sister."

"Who is this guy?"

"That's David. He's the one I thought was my biological father."

"Oh. I'm sorry to hear about them. I can't imagine the pain you must've gone through. I wished I could've been there for you."

"I had my aunt and uncle to see me through. You ready for dinner?"

"I am." He held his arm out, and I hooked mine through his.

This was going to be a night that I'd never forget.

There was a 1967 Chevelle in the driveway. I hurried over to the muscle machine and saw my reflection in the glossy black exterior. "Oh, my God, Leo! This is beautiful. Can I touch it?"

Leo laughed. "Of course."

I trailed the tips of my fingers along the edge of the silver chrome. "Man, this is a sweet ride."

"It will be."

I looked up as the heat rushed to my cheeks. "You do like your cars and motorcycles, don't you?"

"Yes, I do. Among other recreational activities." He opened the door for me. "Shall we?"

I lowered myself onto the seat. The slit in the dress exposed my thigh as I hoisted my legs in last. I didn't bother to fix it. I wanted to show Leo what I had to offer. But, I think he already knew since he'd seen me in a bikini.

The black leather interior cooled my back as I relaxed into the seat. The aroma of pine was strong. To most, it would give them a headache. For me, it was home. Leo's home. I pictured his house in the middle of a forest with pine trees and other greenery—like mine. I hoped one day to see where he'd grown up—whether it was his home in Vermont or the village in London.

Leo kept glancing at my bare thighs.

I placed my hand on my knee and slowly moved my fingers up my leg. I stopped at the top of my thigh. I meant to tease him a little, but, since my skin was so sensitive, I only ended up tormenting myself in the process.

Leo let out a puff of air and gripped the steering wheel. "You're killing me, Chloe."

I smiled. "Feeling is mutual. So, where are you taking me?"

"To one of my favorite restaurants." Leo went North on

Highway 55 and headed to the city.

CHAPTER 4 Chloe

The ringing of my phone broke the silence.

"I'm sorry, Leo. I should get this. It is my dad."

"It's cool. Go ahead."

I put the phone on speaker. "Hi, Dad. You're on speaker."

"Hi, sweetheart. How are things going?"

"I'm fine. Leo and I are on our way to dinner."

"Oh? Well, hello, Leo. You take good care of my daughter, you hear?"

"Don't worry. I will." Leo reached over and squeezed my hand.

"Dad, have you spoken to Aunt Helen?"

"Not yet. I know your uncle is still on pins and needles with her. I'm just waiting for the all-clear."

"I can't believe she is still upset that I found out about you being my father. Do you think she will ever get over it?"

"I do. We just have to take things slow. Anyway, I was just calling to check on you. You seem to be in good hands. You two have a nice night. We'll talk soon. I love you, sweetheart."

"Love you, too. Tell Suzanne I said hello."

"Will do."

I sighed and put the phone on silent. I didn't want any further distractions tonight.

"I can't believe Stephen hasn't spoken to my aunt. He's going to have to face her sooner or later."

"I'm sure he has his reasons." Leo turned onto the Landing by the St. Louis Arch. It was bumper-to-bumper traffic.

"I have an idea." He pulled in front of the casino and got out of the car.

I checked my makeup in the mirror before Leo opened the door to help me out.

He handed the keys to the valet.

"That is a bad-ass ride, man," the valet said.

Leo leaned in toward the man and lowered his voice. "This car is my baby. Take good care of her and I'll give you a nice tip when I get back."

The man nodded. "Yes, sir."

I held onto Leo's hand as we walked down the sidewalk. "I'm surprised you're letting someone else behind the wheel."

"Yeah. Me, too."

We stepped onto the old cobblestone street. It made it difficult for me to walk in heels. Leo held me against him and took it slow as we crossed to the other side.

People roamed the streets in search of a good bar to duck into for a cold beer. Some sat outside at dining tables, sipping sodas or other beverages. Loud music pulsed against the windows of all of the bars and clubs.

We finally reached our destination.

"I love the Spaghetti Factory!" I cuddled against Leo, and he held the door open.

The greeter at the podium smiled. "How many in your party?"

"Two."

"And the name?"

"Rendall."

The girl wrote the information down on a dry erase pad. "It will be about fifteen minutes. You can wait over at the bar if you like until your table is ready."

"Will do. Thank you."

I scooted up onto the bar stool and crossed my leg. My dress rode up a little farther.

Leo laid his hand on my knee. He was always finding a way to touch me, and I didn't mind. I couldn't keep my hands off him, either.

"You look radiant this evening, Chloe."

I turned my head, blushing, but Leo caught my chin with his finger. "I will break you of that habit."

We stared into each other's eyes, and I felt the heat from Leo's body surround me. He leaned in as if to kiss me, but, again, we were interrupted.

"What can I get you folks tonight?" The bartender placed two napkins on the bar.

I ordered an Amaretto Sour, and Leo ordered a beer.

The bartender popped the lid off the beer bottle and handed it to Leo. Then he prepared my drink. "What brings you out this evening?"

"It's our first date." Leo placed his hand in the small of my back and rubbed in small circles.

"Great place to start." The bartender placed my drink on the counter. "Enjoy your evening."

A man walked by and gave me a few glances. The last one was a little too long. Then, the man met Leo's gaze. Both, Leo and the man nodded and held up their drink as if to say, "Cheers," and he kept on walking.

I covered my face with my hand and giggled.

"What?" Leo took my hand and kissed it. "You're a beautiful woman, Chloe. Nothing to be embarrassed about."

The waitress called Leo's name, and we followed her to a table in the back of the restaurant. It was a small table for two. Smiling, she handed us a menu. "I'm Sarah, and I will be your host for the evening. Can I start you off with an appetizer?"

Leo looked over at me to see what I wanted.

"No appetizer for me, thank you."

Leo nodded. "I guess we will order, then. Chloe, go ahead."

"I would like the chicken fettuccini."

Sarah wrote it down while staring over her tablet at Leo. "And for you?"

"I'll take the lasagna with meat sauce and a bottle of your best wine."

I nearly choked as I sipped my drink. "A whole bottle?"

"Yeah. Why not?"

Sarah nodded. "I'll be right back."

Leo reached for my hand. "So, tell me about yourself. What do you like to do?"

"I assumed you already knew everything."

"Nope. Let's start with your favorite color."

"Well, I like black—but also red."

"Other than going to the club, what do you like to do for fun?"

"As you probably already know, I like to write. But, I used to go shopping and hang out with my best friend, Hannah. After what happened, I kept my distance. The barbeque helped me focus on what was important."

"And what was it?"

"My friends."

Sarah returned with a bottle and two glasses. She poured

the first drink for Leo to test. He gave her a thumbs up, and she poured my glass.

One of her co-workers brought out our dishes.

"Does everything look all right?"

Leo rubbed his hands together. "Looks great."

"Can I get you anything else?"

He shook his head. "No, thank you."

Leo took a few bites of his food. It looked like he was in heaven.

"How is it?" I asked.

He raised his eyebrows with a slight moan. "Mmm-hmm."

I wanted to kiss that mouth for the rest of the night. One thing was certain for me. I was falling in love with him. I knew we had just met, but Leo had stolen my heart from the first moment I saw him.

Leo fought with a string of cheese from his lasagna.

I giggled and swirled the noodles around my fork before taking a bite.

We kept our conversation light as we ate our food.

I heard my phone vibrate in my purse. Instead of putting it on silent, I should have turned it off. But, with the threat of Josephine's maker out there, I needed to stay in contact with my dad and Cyrus.

I checked my phone, and it was a message from Erik saying how much he missed me and apologizing for everything. He was miserable and tired of playing games. He wanted me back and asked to meet with him tonight at his apartment.

"What's wrong?" Leo dabbed his mouth and finished off a glass of wine.

I shoved my phone back in my purse. "Erik just won't give up."

"You want me to say something? I'll gladly take care of it."

"Thank you for the offer, but I can handle Erik. I have put him in his place before, and I'm not afraid to do it again."

"I'd pay to see that show," he laughed. "Would you like some dessert?"

"If I can have you, then yes." I threw my hand over my mouth. I couldn't believe I'd said that out loud.

Leo laughed and put the cork in the bottle. "We will finish this off later."

I finished the last of my noodles and pushed the plate away.

Sarah came back to the table. "Would you care to try any dessert?"

"No, I believe we are good."

"All right, then." She handed Leo the check, and he handed her his debit card.

A few moments later, she came back and placed the receipt and a pen on the table. "You two enjoy the rest of your evening."

"You, as well." Leo signed one of the slips and placed the other copy in his wallet with his card.

Leo stood and helped me out of the chair. I loved his hands. They were smooth and strong for someone who worked on bikes. It only meant one thing. He hadn't worked on one in a long time.

We stepped out into the warm night air and Leo walked up to one of the carriage rides. "My lady."

"Really?"

"Yep. Pick one."

I chose the white horse with a purple feather on its head.

Leo sat the bottle of wine on the seat and placed his hands on my hips to help me up. "Wait here."

He darted across the street to where a man was selling roses. Leo bought them all and casually walked back. He plopped down in the seat next to me and wrapped his arm around my shoulder.

"For you."

I brought the roses to my nose and inhaled deeply. "Thank you. They're beautiful."

"No, Chloe." He placed his palm on my cheek. "*You* are beautiful."

I leaned into his palm, and the carriage jerked forward as the driver snapped the reigns.

The driver looked over her shoulder. "Where would you like to go?"

"Don't care. Just make it a long ride," Leo replied.

She nodded. "You got it."

Leo pulled me closer. My hand rested on his thigh. I had to squeeze mine together to try to calm the ache that had been developing there all evening.

We sat in silence until the horse stopped in front of the Arch. Leo asked if we could take a moment.

"Of course. I will wait here," the driver said.

Leo jumped out of the buggy. "Come with me."

He helped me down, and we headed up the steps of the Gateway Arch. When he reached the top step, he looked out across the river, glanced straight up at the Arch, and then turned to look at the city.

"I love the city at night. All the lighted buildings towering into the sky."

We stood there for a moment, staring at each other.

I thought about how this would be the perfect time to share a romantic kiss. I think Leo read my mind.

His hands rested on my cheeks, and he leaned in.

"Finally, I can kiss you," he whispered.

Leo closed the space between us. His supple lips kissed softly. His tongue flicked between mine, and I opened my mouth to let him in.

Leo pulled away, exhaling. "Wow! You are amazing." He rubbed his thumb over my bottom lip. "I'm glad I came back from London."

"Me, too."

He kissed the tip of my nose.

"Take a picture with me." I reached into my purse and took out my phone.

We leaned our heads together as I snapped the shot.

"My turn." Leo took out his phone and took a picture of him kissing my cheek.

I laughed as he kept taking shots. After he was done, we sorted through them.

"I want that one." I pointed to the one where we were looking into each other's eyes. I could see the connection between us.

Leo texted the photo to me, along with his favorite—the one of him licking my cheek. I was smiling with a scrunched up nose.

We headed back to the carriage to finish the ride and then walked back to the casino for the car. As we waited on the curb, Leo's hands wandered to my ass as we kissed.

The car pulled up, and Leo examined it. Satisfied, he reached into his wallet and handed the man some money. "Like I said—a nice tip for taking care of her."

"Thanks, man!"

Leo opened the door, and I slid in. My heart was pounding. I had a feeling the evening was going to have a nice ending.

Leo peeled out of the parking area and headed to the interstate. After a few moments, he caressed the side of my face
and rested his hand on my thigh.

I arched my hips and let out a light moan.

"Damn," Leo whispered.

I looked over at Leo. "What's wrong?"

"I've got to get you home."

I smiled, knowing what he wanted. I reached over and moved
my hand slowly up his thigh toward the erection that strained
against his pants.

Leo shifted in the seat and grabbed my hand. "Not a good
idea, Chloe. I'm already breaking the speed limit."

I laughed. "Just thirty more minutes, and we will be there."

"Not soon enough. I swear I'm about to pull this car over."

"Oh? So, what's stopping you?"

"A very important item that I need. You're ovulating."

"Excuse me? How do you know that?"

Leo tapped his nose. "I sense these things. You are in heat."

I didn't care. I wanted him to pull over and take me any way
he wanted. In the car or on the car. My entire body was on fire.
My nipples hardened against the tight dress.

I pulled the house keys out to have them ready.

Leo weaved in and out of traffic as he sped down the
interstate. Once he hit the main road to the house, he took the
curves like a pro.

I prayed we didn't encounter any deer.

Leo whipped the car into the driveway. We both jumped out
and slammed the door. He came around the car and swooped
me up into his arms.

I fumbled to get the key in the door and finally succeeded.

Once inside, Leo kicked the door shut. He tilted me down. "Grab my bag."

I snagged the strap, and Leo ran up the steps, taking two at a time. I couldn't help myself. I laughed the whole time.

He hurried to the bedroom and put me down. I handed him the bag and stepped away. This was it. The moment I had waited for since I'd met him. I watched him rummage through the bag. He pulled out a box, opened it, and dumped all of the condoms on the bedside table.

He turned around and sauntered over to me. He knelt and lifted my left foot. He placed it on his knee and unbuckled my shoe. Then, he did the same with the right. Only, this time, when he tossed the shoe, he slid his hand up under my dress and pulled my underwear off. He placed a kiss on my knee and stood.

Leo walked behind me and unzipped my dress while he kissed the side of my neck. I shimmied out of the tight material and let it fall to the floor. My body trembled inside and out, but it wasn't from being cold or being aroused. It was nerves, and I realized why.

Leo turned me around and took my hands. "Hey. You're shaking."

"I'm just nervous." I stared down at the floor.

Leo raised my head with the tip of his finger. "Why?"

"It is my first time being with a lycan."

His smile reached his eyes, and he caressed my bare arm. "Chloe, until you are truly ready, we are just like any normal couple. I'm not going to go all animalistic on you for your first time. Do you trust me?"

"Yes."

He stared into my eyes while he unbuttoned his shirt and let it hang open. His breath was upon my lips.

My heartbeat increased as I took small, panting gasps.

"I'm all yours, Chloe. Undress me." He licked my lips in a swift, upward motion.

I parted my lips, expecting a kiss, but nothing happened. My fingers trailed up the middle of this belly to his shoulders and slipped off the shirt. He was pure muscle. I let my finger trace the outline of his pectorals and abs all the way down to the top of his pants. I stared into his eyes as I unbuttoned and unzipped his slacks. The dark material pooled around his feet, and he kicked them to the side.

I broke eye contact for a moment to see the bulge in the black boxer briefs that fit snugly around his thighs. Curious, I licked and bit my bottom lip.

"Here, let me get this." He pushed his thumbs under the waist-band and pulled the boxers down far enough to show off the base of his hard pole.

"More?" he asked.

I nodded. I didn't know how much more I could take. I ached with the need for him to fill me. My nipples were hard and swollen like my clit.

Leo pushed the briefs down farther until his erection sprang free.

I took a few steps back. "Oh, God." He was thick. I wasn't sure I could take all of him but was willing to try.

Leo reached for the square packet on the table and ripped it open with his teeth. We stared at each other and shared the sexual tension that was manifesting between us.

I scooted up on the bed and watched as he rolled the condom on. I didn't think it was going to fit.

"Do you think you can handle me, Chloe?"

"There's only one way to find out."

Leo climbed on the bed and spread my legs with his. "If it hurts, let me know. I will stop."

I nodded.

He held himself up with one hand while he wrapped the other around his shaft. He moved the tip of the head back and forth against my clit.

My body was sensitive, and chills ran through me at the slightest touch. I closed my eyes as my head fell back. "Oh."

"Look at me, Chloe. I want to see your eyes when I take you."

I forced myself to watch as he placed the head of his shaft at my entrance. Slowly, he pushed through, then stopped.

"Mmm, so tight." He pushed farther inside.

My eyes began to water. It hurt, but it felt good, all the same. He made me feel as if I was a virgin all over again.

"Am I hurting you?"

I shook my head. "No. Keep going. I want all of you. I want to please you."

"You already please me, baby. Are you sure you want me to continue?"

"Yes. I want this more than anything."

Leo lifted himself and angled his hips to gain better leverage as he made his descent. His thick cock stretched my walls as the last few inches disappeared into the depths of my body. There was a slight ache low in my belly as he filled me. He held himself there for a moment.

My head fell back against the pillow as I whimpered.

"You okay?" he whispered.

I could only give him a nod.

Leo moved at a slow, steady pace. The pain inside was replaced by pleasure. Each stroke caused me to moan a little louder. Since I was able to accept him now, I wanted more.

"Harder, Leo. Don't hold back, please."

Leo held my arms above my head as he pulled back and thrust forward in one long, hard movement. He repeated this over and over while his lips latched onto my nipples.

I arched my back and pushed my breasts forward while he sucked the nipple between his teeth. I bucked into him as I called out. "Oh, Leo! Oh, my..."

I wrapped my legs around the back of his thighs, drawing him in deeper.

Leo rolled over until I was on top. He grabbed my hips to guide me up and down. His entire shaft pushed deeper inside as he hit my sensitive spot over and over. The pressure was rising, and I couldn't hold back any longer. Explosions of erotic pleasure hit me like electric shocks. I felt Leo swell and knew he was drawing near.

"Damn, Chloe. Please, slow down. I won't last."

I wanted Leo to mark me. I was ready for his animal to come out. I scooted off and went to my knees with my ass in the air.

Leo clutched my hips and grunted with each hard thrust. Our sweaty bodies slid easily against one other. My pussy tightened around him, not wanting to let him go. In a matter of minutes, he let out a long groan as he reached his orgasm. He fell on top of me, panting with exhaustion, then rolled to the side.

I lay snug against him and wondered why he hadn't marked me. My eyes stung as I held back the tears.

Leo tilted my head up. "What's the matter? Did I hurt you?"

I shook my head. "It's nothing."

"Chloe, tell me what's wrong. Please."

"I'm not sad or hurt. It's just...well, my feelings for you are...

strong."

Leo placed his lips on mine and kissed me gently. "I'm right there with you, baby."

He propped himself up and stroked my cheek with the back of his hand. "You're mine, Chloe. No one else can have you."

"Why didn't you mark me?" I sat up to mirror him. "That is what I wanted when I went to my knees."

"I know. Is that why you're upset?"

I nodded.

Leo pulled me against him as we lay back on the bed. "I told you, not until you're truly ready. I have plans for us, baby. I will mark you, but not yet."

"Are we mates, Leo? Or, are we just into each other? I haven't felt your animal's calling."

Leo pulled my leg over his. "I'm still shielding him from you. He almost got loose at the barbeque. The moment our eyes met, it took all of my strength to hold him back."

"But, why?"

Leo moved his head back a little so he could see me. "You really want to know?"

"Yes. Please."

He let me go and scooted away. "Brace yourself, Chloe. I will give you a peek."

Leo closed his eyes and took a deep breath. When he exhaled, the scent of his wolf filled the room.

My animal stood on her hind legs, and her claws came out. It felt like knives cutting me from the inside out. I curled into a ball as I gripped my stomach. "Ow! Ahhh!"

The pain was gone just as fast as it had come.

Leo's arms enveloped me, and a calm current flowed through me. "Now, you know. And when you shift, it will be worse."

I gazed into his caramel eyes and caressed the dark stubble on his cheek. It felt like sandpaper against my palm. "We were meant to be."

Leo let out a small chuckle and kissed my forehead. "Yes. Chloe. I'm your mate. I'll be right back."

I was happy to know at last where Leo and I stood with each other. I lay there, somewhat satisfied, but still wanting more of him. My desire wasn't yet quenched. I could go all night if he would let me.

Leo came back into the room, crawled under the sheets, and pulled me next to him. "This is how you'll sleep next to me every night."

I snuggled closer at the thought. My bed was no longer cold and lonely.

"I want you still." My eyes fluttered shut.

Leo made a humming noise, and we fell asleep in each other's arms.

CHAPTER 5 Chloe

Leo's arm and leg were entwined with mine, and I couldn't move. Visions of what happened last night came to mind. I'd never been as happy as I was at this very moment.

I caressed the side of Leo's face and rubbed his lower lip with my thumb. He had such full lips, and I loved kissing them.

Leo's eyes flickered open, and the smile that made my heart go pitter-patter lit up his face. "Good morning,"

"Good morning to you, too." I gave him a peck on the lips. "Ya know, we forgot the flowers and bottle of wine in the car."

Leo ran his fingers through my hair and moved it to the side. "Under the circumstances, can you blame us?"

I giggled. "No, but my flowers are probably wilted by now."

"I can get you more." He leaned in and placed small kisses on my shoulder before rolling onto his stomach.

"I know, but those were my first set of roses from you."

The sheet hung past the small part of Leo's back. I got a peek at the beginning of his nice ass. I couldn't resist the urge to spank it.

"Oh, you're going to play that game?" Leo grabbed me by the waist and pulled me over his lap. The palm of his hand met my ass. "How do you like it?"

I laughed and each spank made me jump. "More, please."

Leo pushed me off and rolled on top. His hips dug into mine. "Is this what you want, princess?"

"Actually, yes." I raised my hips to add pressure to his erection.

Leo demanded control of my body and forced his tongue between my lips with heavy, wet kisses.

I slipped my hands along Leo's muscular back and wrapped my legs around him. "Oh, Leo. I want you. I can't get enough."

He touched my face and spoke in a panted whisper. "I'm not sure how much longer I can contain my animal, Chloe. Eventually, it is going to come out."

"Then let it."

"You're not ready for that, baby, trust me." Leo's head shot up. He tilted it to the side as if he heard something.

He pushed himself off the bed. "Kyle and Riley just got in."

"So, what?" I sat up on my elbows. "You know how many times I have to hear them having sex? Besides, this is my house."

Leo bent down and searched through his bag. He pulled out some items and clothes.

"What are you doing?"

"Getting some soap and shampoo. I need to shower."

"Could you not wear a shirt today?"

Leo stood up and placed the items on the bed. "Why?"

I pushed the covers off and crawled to him. "Because I like to look at you and know that you're mine."

I trailed the tips of my fingers up his arms to the back of his neck.

Leo bent down to meet my lips. The kiss was soft and sweet.

In one swift motion, he picked me up and placed me against the wall. It was cold against my back, but it soothed the heat escaping my skin.

Leo's hand seductively gripped my jaw, and he whispered, "If they were not here right now, I'd fuck you hard against this wall and everywhere else in this house."

He licked the side of my neck and nipped at my ear.

"Then do it. I know you want to. I can feel it." I pushed my hips forward.

Leo reached down between us and massaged my swollen clit with his finger. His breath was warm against my ear.

"The aching need and wanting it—only to not get it—is what makes it more intense later." He released me and let my legs slide down his.

When my feet touched the floor, he grinned. "I love seeing you squirm and knowing how wet you are for me."

He picked up his things and strolled into the bathroom.

"I should kick everyone out," I mumbled.

I threw on some clothes and hurried out of the bedroom. I stomped down the stairs with a vengeance. I was sexually frustrated, and they were about to get an ear full.

Kyle and Riley were sitting at the nook, eating pizza.

"Hey, lover-girl." Riley smiled.

Without looking up from his phone, Kyle said, "Did we interrupt your plans for the day?"

"As a matter of fact, you did."

Riley nudged Kyle in the arm. "Shut up. She's in love."

"I asked Matt to be here." Kyle finished what he was doing on his phone and set it down.

"Why didn't you ask Leo?" I crossed my arms.

"Because he was scheduled to work."

"What does it matter?" Riley sat back in her chair.

When Kyle didn't answer, Riley waved him off and pushed

the box of pizza toward me. "So, what did you and Leo do all night?" She lowered and raised her eyebrows several times.

"We went to dinner at the Spaghetti Factory and took a carriage ride."

"And, what was for dessert?" She smiled.

I felt my face turn red as I sat on one of the stools by Kyle.

"Where is Leo, by the way? Did you wear him out?" Riley laughed.

"Enough!" Kyle pushed his pizza away and went outside.

"What is wrong with him?" I asked.

Riley shrugged. "I have no idea. He was fine until we got home, and he saw Leo's car here."

"Does he not want me to date Leo for some reason?"

"You'll have to ask him."

Leo came around the corner and snatched up a slice of pizza from over Riley's shoulder.

"Hey, Leo. How are you this morning?" Riley asked.

"Never better." He winked.

"Leo, why didn't Matt stay last night?" Riley shoved the last of her pizza in her mouth.

"Well, Matt was going to, but he asked me to come in his place. He knew how much I liked Chloe, and he wanted us to have some time together."

"I think you should speak to Kyle. He seems upset for some reason."

"Yeah, sure. No problem." Leo picked up his plate and went outside to the back-yard.

As soon as Leo shut the door, Riley moved into Kyle's chair next to me and laid her hand on my arm.

"I have been dying to tell you. Last night...it happened."

"What happened?"

"He marked me, Chloe. Kyle and I are officially together."

I threw my arms around her. "I'm so happy for you."

"What about you and Leo? Is he the one or not?"

I nodded. "Yes."

"Did he mark you?"

"No. What is it with the males and waiting for the right time? You would think they would jump on it right away."

Riley laughed. "Yeah, you'd think."

I looked over my shoulder. "You don't think Kyle will say or do anything to ruin this for me, do you?"

Riley threw her arm around my shoulders and squeezed. "If you and Leo are meant to be, no one can stand in your way. His opinion shouldn't matter."

"But, it does matter to me, Riley. I want Kyle to get along with the man of my choosing."

"Maybe he is just being overly protective. Don't worry. It will be fine."

My phone went off, and when I saw who it was, I didn't want to answer it. But, I knew if I didn't, he would keep bothering me.

"What do you want, Erik?"

"Well, at least you took my call."

"I don't have time for this."

"Why didn't you answer my text or come to me last night?"

"Are you serious?"

"I am trying to apologize. Will you ever forgive me?"

"You're *not* sorry, and *no*, I may never forgive you."

"Chloe, I've missed you. And, seeing you the other night made my feelings for you come back even stronger. I still love you."

"You have a funny way of showing it after everything you

have done. Besides, don't you have a new sex toy?"

"You mean Meagan? Are you jealous?"

"No. I'm over you, Erik. I've moved on."

Erik laughed. "With Leo? Are you going to try the lycan thing now that Drake is taken?"

"If I was in front of you right now, I would slap you. And, I don't care who Drake is with."

There was silence on the other end. I pictured Erik's face. A crease would have formed between his eyes while he squinted. His mouth would be curling into a snarl with his fangs exposed. I was sure his free hand was balled into a fist. It was his go-to move when he was angry.

I smiled at the thought, and I had to get back at him with one last comment.

"Oh, and I didn't meet you last night because I was too busy screwing Leo. Don't call me again." I hung up the phone, pissed.

Leo opened the back door and strolled in. He started to pick up some bread-sticks but stopped when he saw me. "Hey, why the pouty lip? What's wrong?"

I shook my head. "Erik called and asked why I didn't meet him."

Leo wrapped his arms around me. "If that asshole doesn't leave you alone, I will make him."

I tilted my head up and batted my lashes. "I think you should mark me and soon."

"I second that." Riley raised her hand.

Leo grinned. "You won't give up, will you?"

"Nope."

"Try not to let Erik get to you." Leo bit off a piece of bread, and, with a full mouth, said, "Be right back."

66

Kyle came back in and grabbed a beer from the cooler on the floor. He leaned against the counter, popped open the top, and took a long drink.

"Hey, are you upset about something?" I asked.

"Nope. I'm glad to see you with someone, Chloe. Leo's a good guy. I know he will take good care of you. I just hope you are taking precautions." He tapped his nose.

I laughed. "Yes. Don't worry. You won't be an uncle anytime soon."

Leo came back with my wilted roses and our bottle of wine.

"Jeez, Leo, are you that broke you couldn't afford nice flowers?" Kyle took a swig of beer.

Leo smiled. "Haha, very funny. No, these were left in the car last night. Wine is still good, though. You want a glass?"

Kyle waved his hand. "Nah. I'm good."

Leo turned to Riley. "How about you?"

"Nope. I think it should be just you and Chloe's bottle. It was a special occasion."

He grabbed two glasses from the cabinet and poured us a drink. "I do want to propose a toast. To Chloe. This girl has rocked my world, and I couldn't ask for a better girlfriend."

"Aww." I leaned over and kissed him.

"Let's all watch a movie until Kyle and I go to work. I'll go pick out something." Riley happily bounced out of the kitchen, and Kyle followed.

Because Leo had purposely aroused me and then left me in a state of frustration, it was time for payback. So, I reached down between us and lightly stroked him. When I felt him twitch and slowly grow hard, I walked away.

"Damn it to hell, Chloe. You're going to pay for that."

"I hope so," I said over my shoulder as I left the kitchen.

We all gathered in the living room. Kyle sprawled out on the loveseat with Riley on him. Leo and I spooned on the couch.

I loved having the warmth of his body behind me and his arm over me.

"What are we watching?" I asked.

"*The Cabin*," Riley replied.

For the next hour and fifty minutes, Leo kissed and nibbled on my neck and ear. His hand slipped under my shirt and cupped my breast. He gave my nipple a pinch, and it sent a jolt right between my legs. He moved his hand down to grab my ass.

I had to bite my lip to keep quiet.

"I want you, Chloe," he whispered.

I turned my head and whispered against his lips, "I want you, too."

The movie finally ended and Kyle and Riley went upstairs to change for work.

I jumped on Leo's lap and kissed him. We were like two teenagers making out as quickly as we could while the parents were out of the room.

Leo squeezed my ass and moved me back and forth. The friction against my clit almost gave me an orgasm.

"We're heading out!" Kyle called. "We'll be staying at the club tonight. I know you two want to be alone...again."

We heard the door click shut.

Leo gave me a wicked look. He picked me up, draped me over his shoulder, ran up the stairs, and threw me on the bed.

Leo quickly undressed. His swollen cock stood at attention as it waited for me. The tightness in my belly shifted down to my aching pussy.

A deep growl came from Leo as he jumped on the bed and

straddled me. His nails extended as he took hold of my shirt and ripped it open. He slashed at my shorts until there was nothing left. The tattered pieces landed on the bed and floor.

I arched my back and gasped at Leo's domination. He licked my nipple and it hardened under his wet tongue. My body was sensitive to every touch. Even his breath against my skin sent chills through me. He kissed down my belly and over my mound to my inner thigh. His tongue slipped between my wet folds, and I nearly bucked him off as he sucked my clit between his teeth.

He slipped two fingers inside and curled them just enough to hit the right spot. He moved his fingers back and forth.

I clutched the head-board and whimpered between each panting breath. My body writhed underneath him as the pressure built inside.

"Oh, my God, Leo! I'm gonna..."

The orgasm hit hard and Leo held me down. He wasn't stopping.

"Please, Leo! I can't..."

Leo snatched a condom off the side table and ripped it open with his teeth. He quickly rolled it on and flipped me onto my stomach. His hand came down on my ass. The sting made my pussy quiver, and I was ready for him to penetrate me.

His fingers dug into my hips as he raised my ass into the air. In one swift motion, he thrust his cock inside. He wasn't taking things slow this time around. He was forceful and claimed what was rightfully his.

The sound of his body slapping against mine echoed in the room along with Leo's grunts. Each stroke caused my breath to escape in hard, panting gasps.

With one hand, Leo reached underneath me and pinched

my nipple, then slipped his finger between my legs and toyed with my swollen clit. I clenched around his shaft when another orgasm hit.

My head went back, and Leo grabbed my hair. He let out a long, drawn-out moan as he released himself. His thrusts slowed until he finally stopped.

My body went slack underneath him as he lay on top of me.

"Chloe, look at me," Leo panted.

I turned my head as far as it would go.

"I love you."

I had longed to hear those words from him. I wanted to throw my arms around his neck, but I was trapped between him and the bed.

"I love you, too, Leo."

Leo disposed of the condom and crawled back into bed. He moved my hair away from my neck and kissed down to my shoulder. "I like your birthmark."

His finger made a figure eight on my shoulder. "It's interesting. I'm so lucky to have found you. I was beginning to give up."

He placed a sweet kiss on the side of my mouth.

"Well, I'm the lucky one. From what I've been told, you're quite the catch."

"Who said that?"

"Riley. She said you have lots of girls hanging all over you."

Leo laughed. "Yeah, I don't do hook-ups. I'm in this for the long haul, baby."

We snuggled under the covers.

I laid my head on his shoulder and drew circles around his nipple.

Leo caught my hand and linked his fingers with mine. "What

do you want to do now?"

"I don't know. I just like lying here with you."

Leo kissed the back of my hand and was quiet for a moment.

"Tell me about your Dad. You know, the one who raised you."

"He was a fireman for about twenty years. He discussed changing his profession with my mom because it was so dangerous, but she talked him out of it because she knew how much he loved his job. One night, while we were having dinner, he received a call about a fire at an apartment complex. They were calling for backup, it was so bad."

I pulled away from Leo as the tears stung my eyes.

"It's okay, Chloe. No need to say more." He held me as I cried.

For so long, I had struggled to keep that horrible night out of my mind. I remembered watching the massive fire on the television with my mother as she prayed for her husband's safe return. Hours later, the chief showed up on our doorstep.

My mother fell to her knees and sobbed. For months, she blamed herself for his death. She said she should've let him retire from the station as planned. We never told anyone, but we went to grievance counseling for a while until she was able to better cope with the sudden changes.

We were financially stable, but she wanted to work to keep her mind off things. After a year, things started to get back to normal. My mother never dated after David, and every weekend, she'd visit his grave with fresh flowers.

Leo soothed my damp hair away from my face. "I'm so sorry, Chloe."

I wiped my eyes and reached for a tissue. "I haven't spoken about that night to anyone—not the details of it, anyway."

Leo pulled on a pair of shorts. "I know what you need. I'll be right back."

He returned with two small pints of ice cream and two spoons. "If my family or I get upset about something, we eat. We love our comfort foods."

I let out a small chuckle and took the spoon and container from him. "Ice cream is a good choice."

"I almost lost my mother once." Leo dipped his spoon into the chocolate.

"What happened?"

"She was out late one night, and a wolf was in the middle of the road."

"As in a four-legged wolf or like our kind?"

"Four-legged. Anyway, she swerved and hit a tree. She was in the hospital for a few days with a concussion and bruises."

I reached up and stroked Leo's face. It was nice to see this side of him. He might look like a strong man on the outside, but I could see his vulnerable side, too. He was compassionate and caring, and that was what I was looking for in a man.

It was nice to know Leo was comfortable enough to talk to me about anything. It was like we'd known each other forever. We were that in tune with one another. Things were going in the right direction with Leo, and I was happy. But, it also terrified me that something or someone could take that away from me at any moment.

No matter what, I wasn't going to let that happen.

CHAPTER 6 Chloe

A loud buzzing sound went off inside my head. I realized it was my phone and peeked out from under the cover. Still half-asleep, my hand scanned the bedside table several times before finding the phone.

Through squinted eyes, I saw it was Cyrus calling.

"Do you have any idea what time it is?" I mumbled.

"Uh, yeah. It's almost noon. I have some information for you. I'm on my way there." He hung up the phone.

I tossed the phone down and yanked the sheet back over my head. "Ugh."

I lay there for a few more minutes. It was nice and warm next to Leo. I didn't want to get up. I wanted to spend the whole day in bed with him. But, right now, that wasn't going to happen.

I flipped the cover down and rolled over to face Leo. He was on his stomach with his arms under the pillow. I trailed a finger down his spine, and he shivered.

I straddled his back as I massaged his shoulders and neck. His tight muscles relaxed under my palms.

"Mmm, that feels good. You have magic hands, baby. In fact..." He rolled over with me still on top. "Your whole body is magic."

I laughed. "Well, I am special."

"Yes, you are." Leo pulled me down and kissed me.

His erection poked me in the ass.

"Someone is more awake than we are." I nibbled the side of Leo's neck.

"He's always awake for you, baby."

I threw my leg over and sat back on the bed. "There's no time for that right now."

"Why? Are you paying me back for yesterday?"

"No. Cyrus called. He's on his way here with some information for me. I'm going to take a quick shower." I jumped off the bed and headed to the bathroom.

The hot water relaxed my achy muscles. I was a bit sore after having sex with Leo last night. It was better than working out at the gym and well worth the pain.

As much as I was enjoying the steamy shower, I had to hurry. With Cyrus, you never knew exactly when he was going to show.

I dried off and threw on my robe. "Next! I saved you some hot water."

"Thanks, but it will be a cold one for me." Leo gave me a quick peck on the lips.

I dressed, combed my hair, and put on some make-up. Leo was done by the time I finished.

He walked out of the bathroom with the towel draped low around his hips. Small water droplets slid down his belly to the V-shaped muscle.

I licked my dry lips as I watched him take the towel off and pull his black boxer briefs over his thick thighs and round ass. With his physique, he could be a stripper. I just might have to have him do a little *"Magic Mike"* routine for me.

I accidentally let out a soft moan.

Leo looked over at me as he put on his shoes. "You okay?"

"You look and smell so good." I wrapped my arms around him. "You've awakened something in me."

Leo laughed. "Baby, once this whole ordeal with Josephine's maker is over, you are not going to be able to walk for weeks."

"After last night, I can barely walk now."

Leo kissed my nose and took my hand.

Riley looked up as we entered the living room. "Hey, you two. How was your night?"

I plopped down on the couch next to her, a huge smile on my face. "I'm sure it was better than yours."

Riley stuck her tongue out.

"So, Cyrus called. He should be here any minute."

"Oh! What for?"

"I'm hoping he has some information regarding my family."

Leo nudged Kyle in the shoulder. "How's it going?"

Kyle gave a nod. "It's going."

"How was work last night?"

"A little slow."

There was a knock at the door, and I jumped up to answer it. Cyrus's back was to me when I opened the door. He turned with a smile and nodded.

"Chloe. Good to see you."

Cyrus seemed different. His posture wasn't as stiff as usual. It was as if he was a bit more relaxed.

"You, too."

I heard the rumble of a car engine in the driveway. I looked around his massive shoulders and saw a dark blue Mercedes with tinted windows. "Well, that's an interesting choice of transportation. Not teleporting anymore?"

"You haven't changed a bit. Still as mouthy as ever."

"I'm just not used to seeing you in a car."

"I had a friend bring me."

"Who?"

Cyrus's eyes narrowed. "You're doing it again, Chloe."

"Doing what?"

"Asking questions about things that don't concern you."

I felt a twinge of pain in my heart. "Sorry, I was just…"

"No, Chloe, I'm sorry. I didn't mean for it to sound that way. It's just a close friend of mine. May I come in?"

"Yeah, sure."

Cyrus swiped his thumb across my cheek to wipe away a single tear that I'd tried to hold back.

"Don't do that, Chloe. It wasn't my intention to hurt you."

Cyrus stepped away and looked up when the others came into the room. His eyes widened, and then his expression relaxed. He gave Leo a nod. "Leo. What a surprise. I thought you decided to stay in London?"

"I changed my mind, and I'm glad I did." Leo stopped beside me and took my hand.

A smile almost formed on Cyrus's face.

"So, what's this information you have for me?" I asked.

Cyrus took a deep breath. "Nothing, Chloe. I have absolutely nothing in regards to your family."

"And you couldn't tell me that over the phone?"

Cyrus shook his head. "It is the strangest thing. The only names your uncle and I could retrieve are those that belong to ones living amongst human society. Meaning you, your mom, Helen, and their mother, Mary. After that…" He held out his hands. "Nothing."

I sat down on the sofa. "This makes no sense. Didn't Aunt

Helen give you any names?"

"I'm afraid she knows nothing about her family, either."

"I'm confused. How can she not know?"

"I have a theory, but I need to gather more facts."

"Cyrus, now is not the time to be your mystical self. Tell me what you are thinking."

He scratched his head and sat in the seat across from me. "You know how I told you most mystics keep to themselves?"

I nodded. "Uh-huh."

"If your ancestors are mystics, as I suspect they are, then your family doesn't want to be found. My guess is that Helen is not one of us. And, if she is, then she has no clue."

"Cyrus, I know that I'm part mystic. But, I still need answers on how this came to be."

"Chloe, at this point, there's only one option to blow this wide open. It will cost me greatly, so I have to be extra cautious going this route. And, I'll need your help."

I scooted to the edge of the seat. "Anything. I will do whatever you ask."

"I need a personal artifact of your grandmother's. Something she may have had before Helen was born."

"I will see what I can come up with. How will this help?"

Cyrus shook his head and stood. "Just let me know when you have the item."

He glanced at his watch. "I need to get going."

"Wait! You're leaving?" I quickly sprang to my feet.

"I have somewhere to be." Cyrus headed for the door.

"You've been absent a lot. What's going on?"

"I've been busy trying to help you."

"There's something more, and you're not telling me."

Cyrus opened the door and replied over his shoulder. "And,

I don't need to." He shut the door behind him.

I glanced out the window and saw Cyrus get into the passenger side of the car. I was even more curious now.

I turned to look at Leo, Kyle, and Riley. "Did he just seriously do that?"

"Yep. So, what now?" Kyle asked.

"I'm going to call my aunt." I dialed her number as I went upstairs for some privacy.

She answered on the third ring. "Hello?"

"Hi, Aunt Helen."

"Chloe, how are you doin', sweetheart?"

"I'm fine. How are things with you?"

"All is well here."

"That's good to hear. Um, the reason I'm calling is to see if you have anything of Grandma's that is antique. It is for a project."

"Hmm, the only thing I can think of is a necklace that Mom gave your mother on her sixteenth birthday. Do you still have her things?"

"Yes. All of her jewelry is in a box downstairs. I couldn't part with anything yet. What does it look like?"

"It is a clear crystal with a silver wire wrapped around it. It almost looks like glass. Did she ever show it to you?"

"No. Not really. I'll see if I can find it. Oh, and I have one more question. Do you know your grandmother's name or your mom's maiden name?"

"No. Mom never spoke about it. When I was six years old, I asked her about my grandparents and cousins, and why we never visited them. She told me she and her mother had a huge argument way before I was born. The tension between them got worse, and when I was born, that was it. No contact."

"Your mom never said why?"

"She said I didn't need to know about it. I hoped one day they would make amends, but that day never came."

"I'm going to get answers, Aunt Helen. There have been too many secrets in this family."

"I agree, but how are you going to find the answers?"

"I have someone helping me. That is where this necklace is going to come into play. Once I get what I need, I want to have dinner with you to discuss some stuff."

"Absolutely, Chloe. I would love that."

"Okay. I'll talk to you soon."

I hung up the phone and headed to the main floor. I heard Kyle, Riley, and Leo laughing at something on the television.

I opened the door to the basement and flipped on the light. I hated the basement. Even as a child, it creeped me out. If the laundry room and wine cellar weren't down here, I would have been a happier person.

Dusty sheets covered old chairs, mirrors, tables, and dressers. My mother never got rid of anything. A yard sale sounds like a good idea right about now.

Spider webs connected the pieces of furniture in a continuous web of silk. Aside from my fear of needles, spiders were a close second.

I made high-pitched whining noises as I pinched part of a sheet and slipped it off. A job that should have taken a few minutes turned into thirty because of my phobia.

Once all of the sheets lay in a pile, I went through all of the boxes. There were maternity clothes, baby clothes, and my father's clothes. It was difficult to go through these things.

"Chloe, are you down here?" Leo called.

"Yeah, I'm here."

Heavy footsteps echoed as he descended the stairs. "What are you doing?"

"Aunt Helen said there was a necklace that Grandma gave Mom. I'm trying to find it. I never realized how much stuff my mother kept down here." I placed the clothes back in the box and scooted it under the steps.

"I was thinking of selling some of this stuff." I dusted my hands off on my pants.

Leo trailed his finger along one of the dressers. "This is nice furniture. I like this one. You should keep it. You never know when it may come in handy." He grinned.

"Okay. Maybe I will."

I looked around and found a few small boxes on a chair in the corner. The first box contained nothing but old photos. I teared up as I rummaged through them. There were albums from when my mother and Aunt Helen were little. Tons of birthday parties and school pictures.

The second box contained more pictures, but they were of my mother and David. A jewelry box with a glass see-through top was at the bottom. I opened it and sorted through the tangled mess. Nothing matched the description my aunt had given me.

"Hey, Chloe. I found something."

I put the box back and went over to Leo.

"This was in one of the dresser drawers."

He handed me a wooden box with my mother's name carved on top. I unlatched the small box and opened the lid. Inside was the necklace I'd been searching for. It was majestic.

"Oh, wow!"

I felt a small vibration tingle in my palm when I picked it up. I almost jerked my hand away, but I didn't want to accidentally drop it. I brought it closer to examine it. A mist swirled inside the crystal.

I held my hand out to Leo. "Touch this. Tell me what you feel."

He reached out and placed his finger on it. "I don't feel anything, babe. Should I?"

"You don't feel the vibrations?"

"No. Is that what you feel?"

"Yes, and that's not all. What do you see inside?"

Leo took a closer look and squinted. "I don't see anything. Why, what do you see?"

"A swirling mist."

"Wow! Apparently, only you can see and feel what this thing does. That is some mystical shit going on right there."

"I wonder if my mother saw it. Why would she keep this locked away down here?"

"Maybe your mom had the same reaction as you and it scared her. Maybe that's why she boxed it away."

"I wish I knew. Do you think Aunt Helen knows?"

Leo shook his head. "I doubt it. If she didn't mention anything like this to you, then it probably just seemed like a regular necklace to her."

More footsteps thumped down the stairs. Riley and Kyle appeared around the corner.

"Whatcha doin'?" Riley asked.

I held up the necklace and she reached out to touch it. "Wow! That's beautiful."

"I'm getting vibes from it, Riley. I don't know what that means."

"Hopefully, Cyrus will find out."

Riley, Leo, and Kyle started back upstairs. I called Kyle back to stay for a few minutes.

"What's up?"

I laid my hand on Kyle's shoulder. "You think you could get someone to help you get this dresser up to the bedroom? I want to surprise Leo."

"You're kidding, right?"

"Nope."

"You want that moved like right now?"

"Well, no, but soon."

Kyle shook and then scratched his head. "Yeah, sure."

"Thanks. You're the best." I kissed his cheek and went to go lie down for a while.

For the longest time, I lay on the bed, gazing at the white gem and the mist inside. It mesmerized me. I was anxious to see what Cyrus could find out about it. I finally sent him a message.

Are you busy?

He used to answer right away, but, lately, he didn't.

Where are you? I have what you asked for. I need to speak with you.

Still nothing.

"Damn it!" I put my phone on the table and waited to hear back.

CHAPTER 7 Chloe

There was a knock on the door and Leo came in. "You feeling okay?"

I stretched my arms and legs. "Yeah. I'm fine. Come lie down with me."

Leo shook his head. "I can't, babe, sorry. There is a bachelorette party tonight at the club, and all hands are on deck. I don't want to leave you alone. Throw some clothes in a bag. You're coming with us tonight. Besides, it might help get your mind off things."

Leo brushed his lips lightly across mine. "Meet us downstairs in five."

I nodded and got up to do as requested. I threw some clothes in a bag, along with my laptop and necklace.

Tonight, I was going to let my hair down and get wild. I searched the closet for something to wear. I found a black vinyl skirt and matching top. After I coated my eyes with black liner and shadow, I finished off with a deep red lipstick.

I grabbed my bag and headed downstairs.

Riley looked straight at me. "Whoa."

Leo and Kyle turned to see what she was gawking at.

"Damn." Leo licked his lips.

"No shit," Kyle whispered.

"What? You guys act as if you haven't seen this style before."
I laughed.

"Yeah, but not from you. I mean, yeah. We've seen you dress up for the club, but not as if you work there. Wait, are you?" Kyle asked.

I gave them a sly smile. "I might get a little crazy tonight. Come on. Don't want to be late."

I waited patiently beside Leo's car. He opened my door and put my bag in the backseat. My eyes followed his every move.

When he got in, he stared at me. "I'm not going to be able to focus on work tonight with you dressed like that."

"I'm just trying something new." I grinned.

"Who are you and what have you done with Chloe?" He laughed and peeled out of the driveway after Kyle.

"You look hot, babe. Seriously."

I smiled. "I know."

About twenty-five minutes into the drive, we saw Kyle up ahead. Leo sped up and passed him on the interstate. Leo honked, and I waved.

It didn't take long for Kyle to catch up to us. It was a race to see who would get to the club first.

Leo took a shortcut, but it didn't matter. Leo and Kyle pulled into the parking lot at the same time.

Riley jumped out of the car and slammed the door. "Are you trying to get us killed or pulled over?"

"Relax. I was just having some fun," Kyle said.

"Not with me in the car you don't."

Kyle picked Riley up and carried her to the back door.

I laughed as I stood there, holding Leo's hand. We waited to be let in.

One of the employees I'd never met before opened the door.

I kissed Leo on the cheek and headed downstairs to put my things in his room. When I came back out, Erik was coming down the hall. He stopped and whistled when he saw me.

"You look stunning this evening. What does Leo think about your outfit?"

"He certainly doesn't disapprove, but he will be very protective."

I blinked, and in that split second, Erik was in front of me.

"As he should be. What will your father think?"

I laughed. "I am a grown woman, Erik. I don't need his approval. Now, if you will excuse me."

I almost made it to the bottom of the stairs when Erik trapped me against the wall.

"This brings back a memory, does it not?" His breath was upon my lips.

I turned my head and pushed him away. "Don't you get it? I'm not interested, Erik. Leave it alone."

"I can't, Chloe. I've had time to think about everything, and I cannot express how sorry I am. I play what happened that day over and over in my head. I should've consoled you and made sure you were all right. I could've been there for you. But, I was struggling with my own demons. My anger just took over when I smelled Josephine's blood on your clothes in your bathroom."

Erik's hands rested on my cheeks. "When Cyrus told me to take the night off, I went to your house to wait for you. I wanted to talk and set things straight. I know I should've told you the reasons why I couldn't leave Josephine. I know it is my fault for what happened."

Erik clenched his jaw and then relaxed. "Knowing what is coming, I want to help protect you. I want to make this right.

85

It's not too late for us, Chloe. Please. Give me another chance."

"I'm sorry, Erik. But it's over." I moved his hands away from me and ran up to the main floor.

I leaned against the wall and felt the music pulse against my skin. Should I have accepted his apology? Maybe one day, but not now.

I looked up and saw Leo standing next to an empty cage. He waved me over. I hurried to him and threw my arms around his neck.

He backed away with a growl and his smile faded. "I smell him on you."

"It's fine, Leo. No worries." I glanced at the cage. "What's going on?"

He opened the door. "Tonight, this is yours. If you want it. Don't worry. I will guard you. No one will be able to get inside the cage. It's just you and you alone."

"Did my dad approve of this?"

Leo grinned and placed his hand on my hips. "Baby, your father owns half this club. You can do whatever you want." He nodded toward the cage. "Go on in."

He helped me inside and shut the door. "Try not to turn me on too much." He winked.

For the next few hours, my only focus was Leo. Occasionally, he would look up and watch. I could tell he was turned on by the way he licked his lips or adjusted his stance.

At one point, a guy tried to reach in and touch me. Shaking his head, Leo grabbed the guy's hand. The man stepped back and continued to watch.

It made me more aware of the people around me. Not only were there men enjoying the show, but women were, too.

Someone behind me called my name. I spun around and saw

Hannah waving.

I went to my knees so I could hear her.

"Wow! Are you stripping now?"

I laughed. "Hell no! Just dancing."

"You look amazing in there."

"Thanks. Wait there." I went to the door and tapped Leo on the shoulder.

"Hannah is here. I'm going to go say hi."

Leo looked over his shoulder and nodded as he helped me out. I gave him a quick peck on the cheek and hurried over to Hannah.

"Hey, I need a drink. Come with me." I pulled her over to the bar. Since Riley was busy, I went behind the counter to get a bottled water.

"You want one?"

Hannah shook her head. "No, thank you. Ya know, you and Leo should be in one of those cages. You two are hot together."

I patted Hannah on the shoulder. "We wouldn't make it. Too much sexual tension."

I twisted the cap off and gulped the water until it was gone. Then, I tossed the empty container in the trash.

Hannah looked up at the light and sound booth. She waved and blew Matt a kiss.

I led her to the back of the club. It was off limits to customers, but Hannah wasn't just a customer. She was my friend and a possible girlfriend to Matt. I had to find out what was going on between them.

"Are you and Matt together?"

"Not officially, no. We've kissed, but that's all. We haven't gone on any dates outside of the club."

"Are you wanting more?"

Hannah's cheeks turn a dark pink as she looked away. "I do. I have had dreams of being with him ever since we met."

"Be careful, Hannah. You are not like us, and sex with a wolf can get a little rough. You could get hurt."

"What if I become one?"

I gasped and shook my head. "Not going to happen. Besides, I think you need to be born as one. Getting bit or scratched won't work."

"How do you know? What if I inject lycan blood?"

"Hannah!" I grabbed her by the arm and took her outside. "What the hell is wrong with you?"

"Nothing is wrong with me. I look around and realize how boring my life is."

"And you think this is exciting?"

"Yes! I do!"

"I'm sure it seems that way, but everyone here keeps what they are a secret. How the hell would you explain it to your family, friends, and co-workers if you lost control or shifted? It isn't all fun and games."

I dragged her to a crate and sat down. "Hannah, what I am is an abomination. I'm not just a lycan. You witnessed that. I could be killed for what I am or captured for study."

"Your mother dated a lycan."

"But, she didn't know, Hannah."

There was no getting through to her. I hoped Matt and the others could talk some sense into her.

"What exactly are you, Chloe? What is the mystery in your DNA?"

"I'm part mystic, Hannah. "

"What is that?"

"They are like witches. Most have certain powers and some

88

use spells. I have a friend who's trying to find out about my ancestors. I'm close to getting information, but...it's a road that could lead me to danger. I know I may not like what I find, but it is something I have to do."

Hannah held my hand. "I think whatever you are, it is for the greater good."

I smiled and hugged her. "Thank you. I'm trying to stay positive."

"At least you have people to help you through it."

"Yes. I do. Please promise me you won't do anything rash."

"I promise."

"Good. Now let's get back inside."

Hannah gave me one last hug and disappeared into the massive crowd on the dance floor.

I spotted a group of girls who were dressed to the nines. One wore a sash with "BRIDE" written on it. They were gathered around Drake's cage. They were stretching their arms between the bars to get to him. For the moment, he stayed in the middle to get them riled up. Then, he dropped to the floor. I couldn't see him after that.

A man stumbled into me. He laid a hand on my waist. His other held a beer.

"Hey, baby. How 'bout a private dance? Show me what's under those clothes."

I clasped his hand, twisted it up, and applied pressure to his palm. "Don't ever lay a hand on me again or anyone here without their consent. Is that understood?"

The man nodded, and I pushed him away.

"Bravo!" Matt slipped up beside me. "You're learning, wise one."

I shrugged. "Instinct kicked in, I guess. So, who's managing the booth?"

"A new guy I've been training. It gives me a chance to be down here. I requested to work security at times. So, where did Hannah go?"

"Yeah, about that. Can we speak in private?"

"Sure. Let's go to the office."

Once inside, Matt shut the door.

It was weird not seeing Cyrus behind the desk with his fingers interlocked or his eyebrows drawn together, deep in thought.

"Chloe? What's up? Everything all right?" Matt touched my arm.

"I don't know. Just a lot of stuff going on. But, aside from me, what are your intentions with my friend?"

"What do you mean?"

I stared at him. I arched my right eyebrow.

"Oh!" Matt grinned. "I like her. She's got quite the personality. Very spunky. She makes me laugh, and she gets my jokes."

"She's into you, ya know. Like head over heels. I shouldn't be talking to you about this behind her back. But, she is my friend, and I want her to be happy but safe. You get me?"

"I get you, Chloe. I know how she feels. I see it in her eyes. I feel it when we kiss. I want to take things slow with her."

"You need to tell her that. She has this crazy notion of becoming like us just so she can be with you."

"What? I'm sorry, Chloe. I had no idea."

I held up my hand. "I think I may have gotten through to her, but, please, talk to her."

"I will."

Leo and Kyle strolled into the room.

"Sneaking off with my girlfriend?" Leo said.

"Why yes. I was giving her options."

Leo put Matt in a playful headlock. "I could take you down, ya know."

"I don't doubt that, Leo." Matt hit Leo in the arm several times as if tapping out.

I giggled, and Leo pushed him away.

"You guys on break?" Matt straightened his shirt.

"Just for a few minutes. That bridal party is too much."

"Poor Drake." Kyle laughed. "I'm sure he doesn't mind, though."

A hooded figure appeared in the doorway. The only thing visible was the person's glowing green eyes. Gold lining accented the figure's white robe.

Leo stepped in front of me. "Excuse me. You are not supposed to be in here."

The figure removed the hood to reveal a woman. A gold band spiraled around the heap of dark hair on the top of her head. Her eyeliner gave her an Egyptian look.

I stood in awe of her. She was stunning, and I was jealous of her beauty.

"My apology." She bowed. "I need to speak with whoever is in charge."

I pressed myself against Leo's back. His hand reached behind to let me know I was safe.

"Who are you?" Kyle asked.

"I cannot say. This is a personal and private issue, and I must address the one in charge."

"Well, he isn't here at the moment. I'm not sure when he will return." Leo squeezed my hand for reassurance.

The woman glided across the room to Leo. She studied me

from over his shoulders and then stepped back. "Sorry for the intrusion. Have a good evening."

Everyone waited a few minutes to speak to make sure the woman was out of earshot.

I let out a deep breath. "Holy shit!" I stepped out from behind Leo and pointed at the door. "Was that her? Was that Josephine's maker?"

"I have no idea. But, to play it safe, let's say it was," Leo said.

"I'm going to call my dad. Leo, try and get a hold of Cyrus."

My body trembled inside as I stared at the door.

Matt came up to me and was kind enough to comfort me. "We've got you, Chloe. You're going to be fine."

I leaned my head against him and let the warmth take the chill away. "Thank you, Matt."

"Anything for you, Chloe."

"I'm only getting Cyrus's voicemail." Leo put his phone back in his pocket.

I pulled away from Matt. "What the hell is up with him? He has been nonexistent for the past three weeks. I get that he's helping me out, but for him to ignore our calls is not like him."

I paced the room, and then it dawned on me. "Oh, God."

I eased myself into the nearest chair.

"What is it?" Kyle asked.

I closed my eyes and went back to the conversation Cyrus and I'd had weeks ago over dinner. "Cyrus told me he had to be careful about helping me because of what I could be. What if he is distancing himself?"

Leo shook his head. "I don't think so, Chloe. Cyrus is all about protecting you. He puts others before himself."

"That is true," Kyle agreed. "Remember the sacrifices he

made when we hunted the embalmers? He cares about you, Chloe. I'm sure he has good reason to not answer right away."

"Yeah, but when he helped last time, it was before he saw what I could do. But, I hope you're right. What about Dad? Did you get in touch with him?"

"No. I left a message. Look, there isn't anything we can do at this point. Let's just go back to work. We only have a few more hours to go. We will regroup tomorrow."

I stopped at the top of the stairs. I was no longer in the mood to dance. "I think I'll stay here for the rest of the shift."

Leo let go of my hand. "Are you sure? I don't feel comfortable leaving you alone. Not after what happened, and certainly not with Erik lurking around."

I rested my hands on his waist. "Erik isn't a threat. I'll be fine."

I stood on tiptoe and kissed him.

He rubbed my bottom lip with his thumb. "Love you."

"Love you more."

"Not possible." He leaned down and gave me a slow, soft kiss.

He pulled away and winked.

I took a seat by the rail in the VIP section. That way, no one could sneak up behind me. I watched Riley shuffle back and forth behind the bar with Taylor. Drake was headed to the private area with a couple of girls. Erik usually flaunts himself amongst the women, but tonight, he was off to the side—alone.

When a girl walked up to him, he shook his head and let her walk away.

Had he really changed? Did what happened between us mess him up? I started to feel bad for him until his blonde vampire toy, Meagan, dragged him to the back of the club.

"Chloe, right?" Sasha plopped down in the chair next to me.

I forced a smile. "Yep. How are you, Sasha?"

"I'm good. Why are you sitting here alone?"

"Just taking some time for myself."

"I saw you dancing earlier. You working here now?"

"No. Just having some fun."

She tilted her head as if she was confused.

I let out a small chuckle. It was clear that Drake hadn't told her who I was after our brief introduction the other night. I turned my chair slightly to look her in the eye. Something about her put me off. I didn't like her.

"Do you know who Stephen is?"

She nodded.

"Well, he's my father. If I want to dance in a cage, I will. I don't need permission."

Sasha sat back in the chair. Her eyes widened. "Oh! I had no idea. I'm sorry."

I held up my hand. "It's fine. You're new."

Sasha opened her mouth to say something but then didn't.

I stared at her and tried to read her body language. She picked at her long nails while she gnawed on her lower lip. I sensed she was nervous about something because I do the same thing.

I leaned forward and rested my elbow on the table. "Is something wrong?"

"No. Why do you ask?" Her eyes darted to the side.

Another mental note.

"You seemed as if you were going to say something."

"It's no big deal."

"What's no big deal?"

"Why I haven't seen you here until now, or why Drake avoids my questions when I mention you."

"Why did you mention me to Drake?"

"There's a look in his eyes when he stares at you. And, I have caught him doing it several times. Were you two ever together?"

I pulled my chair closer to hers. "Why all the questions, Sasha?"

"I'm just trying to get to know you."

I didn't know this girl well enough to give her too much information. So, I gave her a simple answer. The only one she needed to know.

"Drake had feelings for me, but I couldn't reciprocate."

Sasha didn't comment at first. "How could you not have feelings for him? He's so sexy."

"I didn't say I wasn't attracted to him. Believe me, I was. It just didn't go beyond that. I had just ended a short relationship with someone. I wasn't going to use Drake as a backup."

"Who were you with? What happened?"

This girl acted as if she was my best friend. She thought I was going to tell her everything about my love life. I leaned forward to get my point across. "It's really none of your business. It all turned out as it should."

"Well, I think Drake still has feelings for you, Chloe, and that concerns me."

"Look, Sasha, I'm with the person I'm supposed to be with. If Drake is having trouble moving on—which it doesn't look like he is—then that's his issue and no fault of mine. End of story. Shouldn't you be getting back to work?"

Sasha glanced at her watch. "Yeah. Nice chatting with you."

I just nodded and waved her away.

For the next few hours, I had a couple more drinks and watched Hannah and Matt dancing in the middle of the dance floor. For her to be here the entire night, I know she'd had a lot to drink. But, I trusted Matt would take good care of her.

Leo appeared at the top of the stairs, and I hurried over to him. "Are you off work yet?"

"Yes. Now we can retreat to my room. I've been dying to get you alone all night."

I yelped as he picked me up and carried me over his shoulder. "Leo! You're exposing me!"

He raised my skirt higher and smacked my ass. "It's a nice ass, and it's mine."

CHAPTER 8 Chloe

A knock on the door jolted me awake. Leo stirred and pulled on a pair of shorts before he answered the door.

I heard Matt's voice on the other side.

"Cyrus wants to see you two in the office."

Leo nodded and shut the door. He turned to meet my gaze and smiled. "Good morning, beautiful."

"Good morning to you."

Leo yanked the blankets off similar to the way a magician would a tablecloth. He licked his lips and a growl rumbled from within. His eyes shimmered bronze.

I started to open my legs to tempt Leo into having morning sex, but I didn't want to keep Cyrus waiting. Instead, I rolled off the bed and grabbed my bag before going to the bathroom.

I threw on some clothes, brushed my teeth, and made sure my hair was in place. When I opened the door, Leo was on his motorcycle. It was like a page out of a magazine. The mere sight of him made my heart skip a beat.

"I've never taken her out on the road, but maybe I could now that I have someone to share the freedom with." Leo kicked his leg over the bike and came over to me. He put one hand on the nape of my neck and the other around my waist. He pulled me in for a deep kiss. His tongue lapped at my mouth.

He pushed me away just as quickly as he had kissed me. "That was just a sample of what's to come." He winked and took my hand in his.

Had it not been for his arms around me during that kiss, I would've fallen to the floor. He made my legs weak, and just the kiss alone made me want him.

I grabbed my grandmother's necklace, and we hurried to Cyrus's office. He waited behind his desk.

Riley and Kyle were there, and so was my dad.

I rushed to him and hugged him. "What's going on?"

He kissed the top of my head. "You'll see."

Cyrus cleared his throat. "We're waiting on one more person."

Drake strolled in with Sasha attached to his hand.

From the look on Cyrus's face, he wasn't expecting that Drake would bring her. He came from around the desk. "Sasha, could you please wait downstairs while we have our meeting?"

Sasha frowned. "Sure." When she caught my gaze, she kissed Drake on the cheek and left.

I rolled my eyes at her childish ways as she shut the door.

"What's this about?" I asked.

Stephen pulled one of the bar stools out and sat down. "We got your message about a visitor last night."

Drake held his hands out to his sides and shrugged. "What's this have to do with me?"

"I'm assigning more protection for Chloe."

My breath caught. I should have expected this, but I didn't want it. I had to voice my concern about the situation.

"I don't think this is necessary. I mean, I don't want my house to look like the day after a frat party."

Drake looked around and shook his head. "Looks like you've

got this covered. If Sasha couldn't be here, why is Leo?"

Leo squared his shoulders and stepped forward. "I know what happened with Chloe. Kyle filled me in."

"And that still doesn't answer my question. Why can't we inform Sasha? She could help out."

Leo shook his head. "We don't know her well enough to bring her into this situation."

"What gives you the right to have a say in this at all? You've been absent for a month."

Leo smirked. "You haven't a clue, do you?" He made his way to me and placed his hand in mine.

Drake glanced down at the gesture, and I saw the hurt in his eyes. "Are you kidding me? Seriously? Him?"

"What the hell is that supposed to mean?" Leo let go and stood in front of Drake. "Why should you care? You have Sasha. Clearly, it is a mistake asking you to help us."

"Drake, don't you care about Chloe?" Riley asked.

Kyle laid his hand on her shoulder and pulled her back.

Drake's eyes darted in my direction. His jaw clenched for a moment. "Chloe knows where we stand with each other."

He broke eye contact and turned to Cyrus. "I'm out." He headed for the door.

"Drake! Don't be like that!" I started to go after him, but Leo stopped me.

"Let him go. We can do this without him."

I laid my hand on Leo's arm. "I don't need any new people to protect me. Who we have here is all I need."

My dad pinched the bridge of his nose and sighed. "Fine. I will let you discuss arrangements as you see fit. Seems as if you have everything worked out so far. Staying here last night was for the best in case she was watching the club."

"Chloe, do you have what I asked for?" Cyrus pulled on the sleeves of his jacket.

"Yes." I unwrapped the chain from around my fingers and handed it to him.

"Thank you. I will take good care of it." He placed it in his pocket and stepped onto the balcony. Then he was gone.

"I'm really getting tired of him doing that. What the hell is his problem lately?"

Stephen came up behind me and squeezed my shoulders. "Sweetheart, don't be upset."

"Why? He's unavailable lately. Whenever we call, he doesn't answer. He gives us info and then leaves. What is going on with him?"

Stephen smiled. "You know how his kind works. He is still helping the best he can, and when he can. Don't be upset with him."

I let out a sigh. "It just hurts. I don't see him as much as I used to."

Stephen kissed the top of my head. "Everything will work out. Trust me. I love you."

"Love you, too."

"How is the article coming along?"

"I'm almost finished with the first draft. When do you need it by?"

"Next Friday so we can have it ready for release."

"Guess I better get to work then."

Leo and I headed down to the main floor.

Drake and Sasha were having sex in his cage.

Leo paid no mind as he kept walking, but Drake made eye contact with me. When he did, his thrusts became harder and fiercer. It was as if he was letting his aggression out on Sasha because of me.

Normally, the situation would have turned me on. But, the only thing I felt was pity. I didn't know if it was for Drake or Sasha. Maybe both.

I turned away and ran to catch up with Leo. He was waiting at the steps.

"What do you want to do now?" he asked.

"I brought my laptop to work on my story. Do you mind?"

"Not at all. I'm gonna lift some weights." He kissed my head.

"Are you working tonight?"

"Nope. Looks like we are free to do whatever we want tonight." He grinned.

I grabbed my laptop from my bag and plopped down on the bed. I re-read what I had already written so I could get back in the mindset of where I'd left off.

I was so focused on the story that I lost track of time. I finished my paragraph and saved my work.

I was putting my laptop away when the door flung open so hard it hit the wall. I spun around, startled.

Drake barged into the room. His voice echoed off the walls. "What the hell did you say to Sasha?"

My back hit the wall as he came at me. "Excuse me? What are you talking about?"

"Sasha said she ran into you last night. What did you tell her?"

"I...I don't know what you mean."

Leo entered the room with Matt, Kyle, and Riley.

Leo stepped between us and pushed Drake in the chest. "Hey! Back off!"

"What's going on in here?" Riley asked.

Drake stepped back to distance himself from Leo. "Sasha's been bombarding me with questions about Chloe."

Matt laughed. "Sounds like your girl has the hots for Chloe."

Drake turned to Matt. "No, that isn't the case. She's asking about my relationship with Chloe, and what happened with her ex."

He turned back to face me. "So, I'll ask again. What...did... you...say?"

I gave them the rundown of our conversation. I told them that I hadn't said anything incriminating that would lead to the Josephine situation, nor had I mentioned Erik's name.

Leo paced the room. "Why didn't you tell me this?"

"And how was I to approach the subject when we were in the middle of...?"

Kyle covered his ears for a second. "Okay, okay, we don't need details. So, it slipped her mind. I'm sure Chloe didn't think anything of it."

Leo ran his hands through his dark hair and growled. "How well do you this girl? How well do any of you know this girl?"

No one answered.

"Where is Sasha now?" Leo asked.

"She's upstairs," Drake replied.

"Bring her to me. Now." Leo turned away.

I could hear him muttering something in German.

A few seconds later, Drake plowed back into the room, pulling Sasha by the wrist. He pushed her to the nearest chair. "Sit."

"What's wrong? What did I do?" Sasha asked.

Drake stepped to the side and swept his hand out. "Leo, she's all yours."

Leo took a few calm breaths and slowly approached Sasha.

He went behind the chair and bent down close to her ear. "Where are you from?"

Sasha turned to look up at Leo. "Louisiana."

"How did you know about our club?"

I could see the sweat on Sasha's forehead. I knew she was nervous about being questioned, and, under Leo's persuasion, she would break.

Leo grabbed her chin and yelled at her in German. *"Antworte mir jetzt!"*

"Hey, Leo. Calm down." Kyle patted him on the shoulder.

Sasha flinched and glanced at all of us.

Leo took a deep breath and stepped around the chair. He placed both hands on the armrest. In a calm voice, he asked, "Why are you pushing to get information on Chloe?"

Sasha shrugged. "I just wanted to get to know her."

"So, you ask about her relationship with Drake? Have you done that with all of the women here?"

Sasha blinked several times before she replied. "No, I...I was just curious about their feelings for each other."

Leo pushed away from the chair and continued to ask questions while he stared at Drake. "And, what makes you think there is?"

Sasha bowed her head. "Since he introduced us the other night, he can't seem to take his eyes off her. I just wanted to get the full story.

"Did you even ask Drake about this?"

"I asked him first." Sasha glanced at Drake. "But, he keeps avoiding my questions."

"Because there is nothing to talk about, Sasha," Drake cut in. "Chloe and I had a moment, and it didn't work out. Just let it go."

"What is your infatuation with her?" Leo continued.

Sasha jumped out of the chair. "I will not be treated this way! I'm not obsessed with her!"

"Whatever happened or didn't happen with Drake and Chloe is their business. Besides, it is over, and she is mine. So let this go and move on."

Leo stepped away and came to stand by me. "We're done here."

Drake waved his finger. "No, we are not done, and there is more to the story."

His eyes narrowed as he looked at Sasha. "Isn't there?"

"I don't know what you mean."

"Oh, for Christ's sake, Sasha!" Drake growled. "Chloe's ex! Why do you even need to know or care?"

"It's just girl stuff. We always talk about our relationships and exes."

"Yes, but that's between best friends. You don't know anything about Chloe or her situation," Drake replied.

Sasha threw her arms up. "What situation? Look, I want to be a part of the group. I'm tired of being on the sidelines. It's like everyone here is keeping a secret, and she is a part of that. If there is a problem, let me help."

"And, how do you plan to do that?"

Sasha shrugged. "I won't know unless you tell me what is going on."

I cleared my throat. "Um, Sasha? Could you give us all a minute, please?"

Sasha glared at me for a second. "Yeah, whatever." She stormed out of the room.

Kyle went to the door and peeked around the corner. He closed the door, and it gave a light click as it shut. "Guys, what are we going to do?"

"I don't know. Riley, have you had any one-on-one time with Sasha? What is your take on her?" I asked.

"Well, we did have lunch together when she first started. We had a normal 'get to know you' conversation. She asked if I was seeing anyone to make sure she wasn't stepping on my territory. I gave her the names of those who were available. When she saw Drake, I think that was it for her."

I looked at Drake. He stood with his feet apart and arms crossed as he stared at the floor. "Drake, what is your relationship with her like?"

His head snapped up. "What do you think it is like?"

He dropped his arms to his sides as he moved toward me. He stopped inches away from my face. In a whisper, he said, "By the way, did you enjoy the show earlier?"

I knew what he meant.

"I don't mean physically." I pushed him away. "I mean your communication and her actions. Is anything off about her?"

Drake smirked. "Everything seemed normal until you came back. I guess it is partially my fault for her questioning my feelings since you still make my dick hard."

Riley and I gasped.

Leo sprinted toward Drake and his fist met Drake's face. He stumbled backward and into the wall.

Drake rubbed the side of his face with a grin.

As Leo darted for him again, Matt and Kyle quickly jumped between them. "Whoa! Okay, slugger. Let's take a moment here," Matt said.

"That was uncalled for, Drake," Kyle stated.

I peered around Leo's arm. "If you are using Sasha to get back at me, you are wasting your time and hurting Sasha in

105

the process. She deserves better."

Drake belted out a laugh. "Seems like I told you the same thing with Erik. But, don't worry, kitten. I'm not using her to get back at you. I like her, and I don't use women the way Erik does."

"Enough with this!" Riley jumped in. "Drake, you need to let this shit go! I say we give Sasha a chance. Let her know about Chloe. We are all part of this club, and we can't just shut her out."

"I agree," I said.

Leo shook loose from Matt's hold. "Babe, are you sure about this? I can't help but wonder..."

I laid my hand on Leo's cheek. "I'm sure."

Leo smiled and kissed me. "Okay, then. Riley, bring her back in."

"No." I cut in. "I'll go find her and talk to her. I don't need the interruptions."

"You want me to be with you?" Leo asked.

I shook my head. "I've got this."

When I went to the main floor, everyone was setting up chairs and preparing for another night of entertainment. I spotted Devin at the bar. He looked up and waved.

"Hey, Chloe! How's it going? I didn't know you were here."

I took a seat at the bar. "I've been in and out today. Lots of stuff going on. Are you tending bar now?"

"I'm in transition. I need a little bit of a change, ya know?"

I gave a little chuckle. "Yeah, that seems to be the thing going on around here."

"You want a drink? I'll be happy to make you one."

"Sure. And, make one for Sasha. By the way, have you seen her?"

Devin took two glasses off the shelf and began mixing a drink. "I saw her go upstairs. Probably to the roof. She looked upset."

Devin's muscles tightened as he shook the shaker aggressively for a few minutes. He then poured a dark pink liquid in both glasses and topped it off with a lime wheel. "This is a Pink Flamingo."

I took a sip. "Mmm, tasty. Thanks."

"You're most welcome. You hanging out here tonight?"

I shrugged. "I'm not sure what I am doing yet. I'll see ya later. Don't work too hard."

I took the drinks and went upstairs to find Sasha. I spotted another set of stairs at the end of the hall next to the office. A sign on the wall read "Access to Roof." The door at the top of the stairs was open a crack. I used my foot to push it farther. I heard light sobs coming from the covered area.

"Sasha?"

"What do you want?" She sniffled.

"We need to talk."

"Why?"

"Because it is time you knew the whole truth of why my friends are so protective. I brought drinks."

Sasha looked at me. Her eyes were red and her mascara streaked down her cheeks.

I handed her a glass.

She accepted with a smile. "This is my favorite drink. How did you know?"

"I didn't. I just asked Devin to make something for us."

She smiled. "He's a nice guy."

"Yeah, he's okay."

I sat next to her on the sofa. The last time I was here was

when I was with Erik. I pushed that memory aside as I took a few more sips and set the glass on a small table.

"I'm going to make this story as short as I can. Questions after I'm done."

Sasha gave a single nod. "Got it."

"When I first came here a few weeks ago, I had no idea I was a wolf or that Stephen was my father. My body was going through some changes, and meeting Drake and Erik opened up a desire in me. I was confused, but I had chosen Erik. Before it was confirmed what I truly was, Erik tried to turn me. When I figured out what he tried to do, I ended it. Now, being with Erik upset his companion. She wouldn't let him go and threatened me. But, the night I left Erik's apartment, she attacked me intending to kill me. Drake tried to help me, but he got hurt in the process and almost died. In the end, she was not left standing. When Erik found out, he became aggressive because I put his life and mine in danger. Now, a mysterious woman that we assume is the girl's maker has shown up here. And, that is why I need protection."

"Oh, my God, Chloe! I'm sorry to hear that. So the scars on Drake's shoulder are from him trying to save you?"

"Yep." I reached for my glass and drank the rest in three gulps. "He tried to warn me ahead of time. He begged me not to go to Erik's that night, but I didn't listen."

"Who was the girl?"

"I'd rather not speak of it."

"I understand." Sasha finished her drink and sat back against the sofa. "So, you grew up not knowing your dad?"

"No. I had one, but that's a story for another day."

"Thanks for sharing with me, Chloe. It helps me understand things a little better."

I took Sasha's hand. "I want your relationship with Drake to work. Be patient with him. His heart is still fragile."

"I know. And, I'm sorry if I seemed rude about it. I didn't mean for things to come out the way they did."

"It's fine."

"I should get to work." Sash took our glasses.

Before she disappeared, I called out to her. "Hey, Sasha? If you ever want to hang out, just let me know."

"I will."

I leaned back and gazed at the sky. I hoped that I'd made the right decision to tell Sasha the truth. And, I hoped Drake could learn to love her the proper way.

"Chloe."

I sat up and spotted Drake.

"Is it okay if I sit?"

I held out my hand to the empty seat next to me. "Be my guest."

Drake rested his elbows on his knees and stared down. "Chloe, I want to apologize for what I said back there."

He turned to face me. "I'm also sorry for what I said a few weeks ago. I was just hurt, and I took it out on you. You didn't deserve that. I should've stayed and been the friend that you needed me to be. Instead, I bailed, and that's not me. I'm happy you found someone, Chloe. I truly am."

I took Drake's hand in mine. "Thank you, Drake. That means a lot to me. And, I'm sorry, too. I..."

Drake put his hand over my mouth and shook his head. "There is nothing for you to apologize for. So don't."

I nodded, and he let his hand fall away. "That's all I wanted to say."

"You should apologize to Leo."

"I did. I'm not sure if he took me seriously, and I don't blame him."

He got up and walked away.

"You have a great girl, Drake. Don't hurt her," I called over my shoulder.

"I don't have any intention to. Talk to you later, Chloe."

I sat there for a few more minutes and then decided to go back inside to the bedroom.

CHAPTER 9 Chloe

Leo was lying on the couch when I returned. He tossed a motorcycle magazine to the side. "How did things go with Sasha?"

"Good. How did things go with you and Drake? He said he apologized to you."

"He did." Leo got up from the couch with a sly look on his face and headed toward me.

His hand slipped behind my head, and he grasped a handful of hair. With a slight pull, he tilted my head up.

I watched as he licked his lips and leaned in. The warmth of his breath tickled my skin.

"Now, I want you to change into something sexy and meet me in the playroom." His tongue flicked between my lips.

His seductive demand took the breath right out of me. It took me a moment to respond. "Wait...what?"

"You heard me. You have twenty minutes."

"Leo, I don't have anything here."

"I'm sure you can find something." He winked and shut the door.

I didn't know what he had in mind, but it made my body respond to his request. I ran upstairs to see if I could get someone to help. Riley was too busy at the bar, and Sasha was dancing alone in a cage.

"Shit. What am I going to do now?" I mumbled.

"About what?" A voice from behind made me jump.

"Oh! Taylor, you startled me."

I didn't know her well—only from the brief conversation I'd had with her about Drake weeks ago. At this point, I had no one else to ask.

"Leo wants to meet in the playroom, but I don't have anything to wear. If you know what I mean."

Taylor nodded. "I have just the thing."

I followed her to her room, and she dumped a pile of clothes on the bed.

"I bought a bunch of stuff the other day. I haven't used any of it yet. They still have the tags. You are more than welcomed to have whatever you need."

"Oh, no I—"

"Hey, you asked for my help, right?"

I nodded. "Yes, but..."

Taylor smiled. "I know this is new to you. I'm here to help in any way I can. For you to land Leo..." She shook her head. "That, my dear, is a goal in itself. Now, don't keep him waiting. Feel free to freshen up in the bathroom."

After Taylor left, I grabbed a tiny skirt and a tube top. I didn't feel comfortable dressing in her bathroom. So, I ran to Leo's room to clean up and dress. By the time I made it down the hall, I had three minutes to spare.

The last time I was in the playroom, it didn't go so well. But, this time, I had a different kind of nervousness. I was excited to see what Leo had in store.

There was a small sign on the door that read "Private Party." I took a deep breath and pushed the door open. The room was illuminated with red lights. Music thumped through the speakers. I looked around for Leo but didn't see him. So, I called to him.

In the back of the room, a set of black curtains opened to reveal two orbs that were glowing as if they were made of bronze. Then Leo appeared wearing nothing but black leather pants.

I swallowed the lump in my throat and my heart pounded against my rib cage. The heat between my thighs ignited under his stare. He stalked in my direction. I thought about how it should be a sin for someone to look this damn sexy.

He took my hand and led me to the stage. "Dance for me."

I walked up the narrow steps and stood next to the pole. I'd never pole danced in my life. I didn't want to make a fool of myself. What if I slipped and fell? I had to shake that fear from my mind. This was an ultimate fantasy. Don't think, just do.

Leo took a seat and rested his arms on the sides of a black chair. His legs were spread to give me a full picture of his lean body.

"I can do this," I mumbled.

I hooked my leg around the pole and gripped it with one hand. I jumped up and twirled around a few times. With both hands on the pole, I squatted and came up slowly with my back arched. I stuck out my ass. I turned away from him and pulled the tube top down. Once past the skirt, I let the thin piece of material fall to the floor. I covered my breasts with my hands and spun back around. I raised my arms above my head as I leaned against the pole and slid down with my legs open.

I made eye contact with Leo as I crawled to the edge of the stage. He shifted in his seat and reached between his legs to adjust himself.

113

I slid off the stage and onto Leo's lap. I moved my hips back and forth. His erection strained against the leather pants. I took both breasts and squeezed them together.

Leo growled and stood with me in his arms. He laid me down on a small couch, and his hands slipped under the skirt and ripped off my thong. He unzipped his pants and kicked them off to the side. The tip of his cock was already wet as he hovered over me.

Leo grabbed a condom out of a bowl next to the couch. He ripped the package open and quickly rolled it on. He held his shaft as his length disappeared inside me.

He let out a low growl. "Mmm, you feel so good, baby."

I held onto the arm of the couch and looked down as Leo's hips pumped effortlessly at a steady pace. It made my eyes roll back. "Oh, God!"

Leo grabbed my ass and pulled me up. I wrapped my legs around him as he stood. His upper muscles contracted and relaxed each time he bounced me up and down as if I didn't weigh anything.

There was an ache deep within my womb, and I dug my nails into Leo's shoulder.

"Leo, you need to stop." My words came out in shallow breaths.

His thrusts came to a halt with him sheathed inside me. "Am I hurting you?"

"No. I mean...I don't know what it is."

Leo rested his forehead against mine. "Do you want to stop?"

As I looked into his eyes, not only did I see compassion and love, but also trust. The way he made me feel was something I couldn't ignore.

"No. Don't stop." I crashed my lips into his. My tongue darted into his mouth, and he sucked me in.

Leo went to the floor with me on top. We synchronized our hips with each movement. He thrust upward as he pushed me down. He swelled inside me, and it brought me close to the edge.

Leo rolled over so he was on top. He teased my body with long, slow thrusts. Each time he entered, he would stop right before he reached the sweet spot inside, and then pull back.

"Oh, Leo! More! Please!"

He shook his head. "I need to savor this moment, Chloe."

"Why?"

"To prepare for what I am about to do."

My heart raced as I looked deep into his eyes. "What are you going to do? Are you going to shift?"

"No."

He pulled out, flipped me onto my belly, and held my hips up as he plunged inside me harder and faster to the beat of the music.

"Oh, Leo!"

"When I am ready, I will let you come. Understand?"

"Y...yes."

I wasn't sure how much longer I could wait. A sudden rush of heat engulfed me, and Leo's animal made its presence known. I felt it just beyond the threshold of my mind. My wolf became alert and bowed her head to submit to Leo's calling.

The heat inside me ignited, and my skin felt like I was on fire.

"Oh, God, Leo! What's...ha...happen...ning?"

"I won't let you shift yet, but I am going to mark you."

My nails extended into sharp talons as I clawed at the floor.

If Leo wasn't going to let me shift, then he'd better hurry and finish this.

"Leo! Do something! I'm...cha...chang...ing!"

Leo's engorged shaft caused me to tighten around him.

"Now, Chloe!"

Leo bit the back of my neck, which caused my orgasm to last longer. My body shuddered violently under him.

Leo's thrusts came to a slow pulse until he stopped. He stayed in me for a moment before he released me.

I didn't even get a chance to calm down when he pulled me onto him. "Mark me, Chloe, now!"

I bit into the curve of Leo's neck. I let out a moan and wriggled my hips as he held me against him. He pushed into me one last time. I'd never encountered such sexual bliss until I met Leo. Every day, I was learning the ways of the wolf.

Getting carried away, I and sank my teeth farther into Leo's neck. It was then that I tasted his blood. I tried to pull away, but Leo's grip tightened to keep me in place. Something inside me took over, and I lapped at the wound.

With one last, hard thrust, his body stiffened under me, and he released his load. He finally relaxed and let his arms fall to the side.

I quickly sat up. "Leo, I'm so sorry!"

Leo shook his head and licked his lips. "Don't be. You were perfect."

He sat up and cupped my cheek in his hand. "You did everything just right. After a marking, wolves tend to their mate's wound. You are the most beautiful thing I've ever seen. I can't wait to see what you look like as a wolf."

I walked my fingers up the front of his torso. "Well, you're the only one who's keeping it from happening. I almost shifted, you know."

"I do, and it's like I've said—I have a good reason not to yet." Leo pulled me into a kiss. The mix of our blood aroused me.

"I'll meet you in the bedroom after I clean up in here." Leo smacked my ass, and I let out a squeal.

I climbed off him and shimmied out of the skirt. I threw it at him and laughed as I ran out of the room. I prayed I wouldn't bump into anyone on the way back.

After my shower, I looked in the mirror to see if I could catch a glimpse of my mark. There was only a slight bruise. I pulled my hair high up on my head. I was proud to show off my mark. I was now officially Leo's, and he was mine.

I wanted to go upstairs and celebrate, but I was tired. I climbed under the covers to wait for Leo but fell asleep.

CHAPTER 10 Chloe

I woke with Leo's arms around me. He was lightly snoring. I'd never heard him snore before, and it made me laugh. I trailed my finger along his jawline. His five o'clock shadow felt like tiny needles.

Leo's mouth twitched, and he opened his eyes.

He had amazing eyes. I loved the way they changed color like a mood ring. It also let me know if he or his animal was staring back at me. Right now, they were his natural color—caramel.

I scooted up to meet his lips and gave him a soft kiss before snuggling under his chin. My hand rested on his chest, and he held my hand.

"Leo, can I ask you a personal question?"

"You can ask me anything, baby."

"What is your middle name?"

Leo laughed. "It's Mychal. Spelled with a 'Y' and no 'E.'"

I sat up on my elbow with a smile. "I like it. Were you named after anyone in particular?"

"Not really. What about you?"

"My middle name is Michelle. Spelled with an 'I' and an 'E.'"

"We are quite the pair. Mychal and Michelle. I think we just picked out names for our kids." Leo smiled and caressed my arm.

The thought of having Leo's babies made my heart flutter. I knew we had been careful. But, if I were to end up pregnant now, I knew he would be ecstatic. Leo would make a wonderful father.

"We could try for one now." I grinned and slid my hand under the coves. As usual, we were interrupted by a phone call.

"I'm going to have to start turning that off," I mumbled.

I reached over to grab it off the table. "Ah, it's Hannah."

I put the call on speaker. "Hello, sunshine."

Hannah laughed. "Hello yourself. What are you up to today?"

"I don't know. Why?"

"Matt asked me out on an actual date. I need to shop for an outfit. Will you come with me, pleeeeease?"

I glanced at Leo, and he chuckled as he yanked the covers back and got out of bed.

"Sure. Maybe we can make it a girl's day out. I will invite Riley and Sasha."

"Who's Sasha?"

"Drake's girlfriend."

"Sounds like fun. Can you meet me at the mall?"

"Yep. Give me a few, and we'll be there."

Hannah let out a squeal. "You're the best bestie ever!"

I laughed and jumped out of bed and onto Leo's back. "You should have a day with the guys."

"And do what? We already hang out at a bar and drink."

"Well, I hear there is an auto show going on at the America Center. Or, you could watch football or do whatever guys do. Go shoot some hoops or play pool. Maybe try one of those escape rooms."

Leo reached behind and tickled me.

I let go and fell on the floor, laughing.

Leo held out his hand to help me up. "You are full of ideas. I will see what they are up to."

"You will invite Drake, right?"

"Ugh, Chloe." Leo grabbed a shirt from his dresser.

I tapped my foot as I stared him down.

"Okay, if it will make you happy. Stop nagging me, wife." He laughed.

I smiled and bounced over to my bag to get dressed. "Leo, why did you all of a sudden mark me? Was it because of what Drake said?"

"No, it wasn't just Drake. I've heard other guys talk about you. I'm sure you haven't met Ethan yet, but he's had his eyes on you since you came back. I knew it was the right time to claim you."

"I don't know him. In fact, there are a lot of people here I haven't met."

Leo sat on the bed to pull on his boots. "I wasn't going to say anything, but he and I got into a fight over you. I'm talking full-blown fist to the face fighting."

"You didn't look like you were in a fight last night."

Leo laughed. "You didn't see Ethan."

"Did he have a chance?"

"Nope."

"Poor guy. Sorry I missed it."

Leo came over and placed the palm of his hands on my cheeks. "No one can touch you without my permission. And, as your alpha that is something I'll never give."

He leaned down and brushed his lips lightly against mine. "I love you."

"I love you, too."

I called Riley to see if she and Kyle were still here. They were actually down the hall in the playroom.

I put my laptop in my bag and met Riley and Kyle in the hall.

"What's up?" Riley asked.

"Girl's day. Hannah needs a dress for her date with Matt."

"This is going to be fun." Riley clapped.

"Yep." I knocked on Drake's door. After a few minutes, he opened the door. He was wearing a pair of shorts and his hair was uncombed and in his eyes.

"What's going on?" Drake said in a raspy voice.

"Is Sasha with you?" I asked.

A voice answered from within the room. "Is that Chloe?"

Drake replied over his shoulder. "Yes."

There was a thud, and then a head popped up from under his arm. Sasha had a sheet wrapped around her, and she pushed Drake aside. "Hey! What's up?"

"We are having a girl's day while the guys hang. Get dressed and meet us upstairs."

Sasha's eyes widened. "Really? You want me to come along?"

"Yes. So, hurry it up."

Leo looked at Drake. "You heard her, man."

Once we reached the top of the stairs, Riley pulled on my arm. "Hold on a second." She moved my ponytail to the side. "Ah! Chloe's marked!" She jumped up and down with her arms around me.

"Way to go, bro. It's about time." Kyle held out his fist and Leo bumped him.

"Yeah, but I still haven't shifted." I stuck my bottom lip out in a pout.

Riley stopped jumping and stepped back. "Why? I mean...I thought..."

"I almost did, but for some reason, Leo has this whole plan of when and where, I guess."

Riley playfully hit Leo in the chest. "You're hindering her abilities, Leo. When she shifts, her senses will be heightened."

Leo shrugged. "We've been over this. Let it go."

We all sat at one of the tables and waited for Sasha and Drake.

Matt appeared from behind the stage. "Hey, guys. Whatcha doin'?"

I jumped off the stool and hugged him. "So, you and Hannah are going out tonight?"

"Yep. I have reservations at a nice restaurant for starters."

"She's so excited. You better not break her heart." I punched him in the arm.

Matt grabbed his arm. "Ow! That's going to leave a bruise."

"Don't be such a baby," Kyle said.

Matt laughed. "Don't worry your pretty little head, Chloe. I will treat her like a princess."

"Hey, Chloe? Dad just sent a message. He wants you and Leo to meet us at Dominic's Restaurant tomorrow at seven for my mom's birthday," Kyle said as he looked at his phone.

"Oh! I'm excited to finally meet her. I should get her a little something. What does she like?"

"Honestly, just you being at the dinner is all she would want."

"Well, looks like I'm getting a new dress, too."

"Me, too," Riley said.

Drake and Sasha finally joined us. Sasha waved and smiled, but Drake didn't look like he wanted to do this.

"Let's get going." Leo slid off the stool, and we all headed out to the employee parking.

"What are you guys planning?" I asked.

"How about an escape room?" Leo looked at the guys.

"Sounds good to me," Matt said.

"I'm in," Kyle replied.

"Sure." Drake looked at me from behind Matt.

"So, Leo, you drop us girls off at the mall. Then you can meet up with the guys." I tugged on his shirt.

"Okay. Let's go."

I sat in the front with Leo while Sasha and Riley sat in the back.

Kyle and Drake piled into Matt's car. He honked as he pulled away.

* * *

Leo pulled up at the food court entrance. Hannah was outside waiting for us.

I leaned over and kissed him goodbye. His hand slipped into my hair and grasped a handful. His kiss deepened as his tongue attacked mine.

"Excuse me, but time is of the essence." Hannah knocked on the window.

"Behave yourself while I'm gone," Leo whispered.

"You're the one that needs to behave. Try to get along with Drake."

"No promises." He winked.

I got out and waved as he drove off.

"God, I love that man," I mumbled.

"Yeah, Chloe. We all know." Riley laughed and linked her arm with mine. "It's dress time, ladies."

On our way to the upper level, we stopped at one of the displays that sold gold jewelry.

"I want to get Kyle something." Riley looked in the display case at the chains.

Sasha and Hannah went to the next display over for phone covers.

I found a pair of silver hoop earrings that I fell in love with, and I found a pretty bracelet with a heart locket. It said, "Forever in my heart." I thought it would be a lovely birthday gift for Suzanne

We paid for our items and headed to the escalators. We approached a group of guys and their heads turned as we passed by. We giggled and hurried to the dress store.

We went our separate ways since we were shopping for different dresses and met up in the dressing room. I found a beautiful blue halter dress. Riley had a sexy red, two-piece dress that showed off her toned belly. Sasha got a black tube dress, and Hannah's was a white off-the-shoulder dress.

We all stood in front of the mirror to admire our looks.

A sales employee walked over to us with a smile. "You ladies look beautiful. What is the special occasion?"

"We all have something different going on," I said.

"I have a date tonight." Hannah glowed. The smile never left her face.

"I'm sure he will be pleased with your look." She winked.

We paid for our dresses and headed to the salon to get our hair done. With it being a Sunday afternoon, it wasn't that busy. We were able to get in right away with someone. I chose to get caramel highlights to match Leo's eyes. That might sound weird, but I thought it would complement his appearance when I was next to him.

Riley had the red tips cut out of her hair, leaving it a shiny black.

Sasha got a deep violet tint to her black hair, and Hannah lightened her brown hair. It looked like strands of golden silk.

We left the salon with major makeovers and feeling sexy. We stopped at Starbucks for our favorite drinks and a snack before hitting the shoe store.

We took a seat at one of the tables by the escalator.

"This is so much fun. Thanks for inviting me along," Sasha said.

"Yeah, it was fun to get out. We should do this more often," Riley agreed.

I leaned forward and lowered my voice. "Don't look now, but those guys we passed earlier are coming this way."

And, of course, Riley and Hannah had to turn around.

"Hello, ladies. We were just wondering if you had any plans tonight. My buddy's band is playing at the Grunge tonight at seven. We're trying to get the word out and get him some exposure."

"Sounds great. We'll spread the word." Riley smiled.

"Awesome. Hope to see you there."

Once they were out of range, Sasha blurted, "They were cute."

"I think that guy liked you, Riley." I finished off my drink and tossed it in the trash.

"Whatever. Let's get our shoes and get out of here."

After an hour of trying on shoes, Hannah dropped us off at my house. She had a couple of hours to hurry home and get ready for her date.

CHAPTER 11 Chloe

Riley and I put our things in our room and then started to make dinner for the guys.

"So, what do we make for three men with huge appetites?" Sasha asked.

"How about lasagna?" I suggested. "I have two baking dishes I can use."

"Sounds good. And, I'll make dessert. Sasha, you can put together a salad," Riley said.

"Let's get to it, ladies." I pulled the ingredients out to prepare the dish.

Riley turned on the Bluetooth and played her playlist from the club. We shook our hips and bobbed up and down as we prepared dinner.

Riley's dessert was cheesecake. She placed it in the fridge next to the salad.

"Well, now we have to wait for the lasagna to cook. I'll put the bread in when it is finished. Riley, can you run downstairs and find a good wine?"

"I'm on it."

She came back a few minutes later. "There's nothing good left. I sent Kyle a message to pick up a couple of bottles. In the meantime, we could open this one for ourselves." She grinned and took the corkscrew out of the drawer.

I took out the wine glasses and placed them on the dining room table. Sasha helped with setting the table with my nice dinner plates.

"So, Sasha, do you have any siblings?"

"I have an older brother and sister. My sister is married with two kids. My brother is living the life of a bachelor."

"What about your mom and dad?"

"They still live in Louisiana. They own a bar and grill. Of course, their busiest time is during Mardi Gras."

Riley had three glasses poured. "I'd like to take a moment and make a toast. To three sexy bitches who have three of the sexiest men ever!"

I laughed. "Here, here!"

We had the bottle gone by the time the guys finally arrived.

They walked in and their jaws dropped when they saw our new look. In unison, they said, "Daaaamn."

"Like what you see?" I asked.

"Very much so," Leo said.

"What's behind your backs?" Riley tried to get a peek behind them. "Did you get the wine?"

Leo, Kyle, and Drake brought one of their hands out from behind and held up a bottle.

"Ooh, three bottles. Are you trying to get us a little tipsy?" Riley smiled.

"So, what if we are?" Kyle wiggled his eyebrows. "What smells good?"

"We made dinner."

"Can't wait. I'm starved," Leo said.

"You're still hiding something behind your back. Come on, let us see." I leaned on the counter next to Riley.

All three of the guys brought out a bouquet of roses. Leo and Kyle had red. Drake had multicolored roses with one red in the middle.

Kyle handed his to Riley. "On the way back, Leo decided to replace the ones that got ruined on his and Chloe's date. Drake and I couldn't let him show us up."

"Hey, someone has to step up and show you how to be a proper alpha to your woman." Leo patted Kyle on the back.

"Shut up, asshole."

Sasha took the flowers and kissed Drake on the lips. "I think they are beautiful. Why all the different colors?"

"You know each color means something different, right?" Sasha nodded.

"Well, it expresses my many feelings for you. I can't just pinpoint one at this moment, but I hope in time..." Drake pulled out the red rose and handed it to her. "...I can give you what you deserve the most."

Sasha threw her arms around Drake's neck.

Kyle rolled his eyes. "That was cheesy."

"I think it was sweet." Riley smacked him on the arm.

"Can we please eat now?" Leo headed into the dining room. Drake and Kyle followed.

I grabbed the main dish. Sasha brought in the salad and bread.

Riley handed Kyle the corkscrew to open the wine. "So, how was the escape room?"

"It was hard, but we made it out with five minutes to spare. Then, we went to the pool hall."

Kyle opened two bottles of wine and we filled our glasses. Leo and I sat at opposite ends of the table. Kyle and Riley sat to the left and Drake and Sasha on the right.

I smiled as I looked around the room. I pictured Leo and myself married and hosting a dinner party. Our kids would probably be running around the table, either laughing or screaming at each other.

Kyle held up his glass. We all followed. "To a great dinner prepared by the most gorgeous women in our lives. And, to great friends."

"Cheers!" I took a sip as I stared at Leo. He winked at me.

The conversation was nonexistent as we passed the food around. The only noise was the clink of silverware on the plates.

Once our plates were full, Leo broke the silence.

"How was shopping today?"

"It was fun. We all bought dresses and shoes. Then, we went to the salon."

"I can see that. You look beautiful, babe."

"Thank you. Oh, there was a group of guys that invited us to the Grunge. His friend's band is playing."

Leo leaned back in the chair and placed his hands behind his head. "You all wanna go?"

I stared at Leo. He flexed his biceps and blew me a kiss.

I smiled and let out a laugh. "Nah, it's already started. Besides, I'm tired after shopping and cooking."

As we ate, the guys talked about their escape room experience. It was nice to see Drake and Leo getting along.

"Oh, my dessert!" Riley jumped up and ran into the kitchen. She came back with the cheesecake.

She cut everyone a slice and passed it around.

"This is delicious." I licked my lips and looked up at Leo.

He stared at me for the longest time and then took a bite of cake.

"So, Drake, if it's okay with you and Sasha, you can stay here tonight. Tomorrow, I can drop you off at the club," Kyle said.

"Sounds good," Sasha said.

"And, where do you plan on putting us?" Drake asked.

"The couch in the TV room folds out into a bed."

Drake leaned on the table. "Well, what if we want to get freaky?"

I busted out laughing. "Do you know how many times I've had to hear Kyle and Riley go at it before Leo came along? We're all adults here. I think we are all going to be going at like wild dogs."

Everyone started to laugh.

"Contest for who can be the loudest," Kyle said.

I shook my head as I finished off my glass of wine. "Hell no!"

Riley got up and started to clear the table.

Kyle grabbed her wrist. "Leave that for us. You, Chloe, and Sasha chill for a bit."

"Okay." She sat down and poured the last of the wine into her glass. "You guys want to play a board game or something?"

"How about strip poker?" Kyle said from the kitchen.

Riley got up and pushed her chair in. "You would so lose, Kyle. You're not that good."

"You wanna test that theory?" He placed his hands on her hips.

"Not really."

"Fine. How about truth or dare?" Kyle slid his hands down to Riley's ass and squeezed.

Leo shut the dishwasher and turned it on. "I hate to cut this party short, but I'm taking Chloe upstairs for the night. I have my own game I want to play."

I had no time to respond as Leo threw me over his shoulder and carried me up the stairs. He stopped in the middle of the bedroom and put me down.

"Undress for me, baby." Leo pulled his shirt over his head and dropped it on the floor.

I did as I was told while holding Leo's gaze the entire time. I tossed my shirt and pants at his feet. Then, I reached behind to unclasp my bra and let the straps fall off my shoulders and the bra onto the floor. My nipples hardened under the cool air. I hooked my thumb under my panties and wiggled out of them.

Leo licked his bottom lip and cocked his head to the side. "Mmm, so beautiful, and all mine."

He shuffled over to where he was keeping his clothes and then came back. "Close your eyes."

Something silky covered my eyes as he tied it behind my head.

"Ooh, kinky." I giggled.

"Hush," Leo whispered in my ear and gave my ass a brief smack.

I jumped at the sudden impact and let out a whimper.

"You like that?"

"Yes."

Leo pinched my nipples between his fingers and thumbs. "Stay put. No peeking."

I heard Leo leave. The only sound was the pounding in my ears from the erotic rush of anticipation. I could already feel the moisture between my legs.

It seemed like forever before Leo returned. He closed and locked the door. Since I couldn't see, it helped me to focus on my other senses.

When I inhaled, the scent of roses filled the room. At a distance, the strike of a match broke the silence. My heart raced. My chest rose with each heavy breath. Something soft touched my neck and trailed down between my breasts. Then, it circled my nipple. I realized it was one of the roses.

Then, I felt heat against my nipple.

"Lift your head and straighten your back."

I did and it pushed my breasts forward. I felt a twinge of pain followed by a cool sensation on my nipple, and I gasped. Then, I felt the same thing on my other nipple.

"Do you like this?"

"Yes," I panted.

Leo's arms went behind my knees and back. In a swooping motion, he picked me up and laid me on the bed.

"On your stomach," Leo ordered.

I rolled over and waited for his next command.

The bed dipped with Leo's weight as he straddled me. Something warm dripped along my spine, and Leo massaged my shoulders and back.

"Mmm, feels so good."

"After what you did for me last night, I wanted to do something for you. I enjoyed watching you dance for me, Chloe."

"I was happy to oblige."

Leo's hands made their way to my ass. He squeezed and rubbed in slow circles. His fingers inched their way down to my inner thighs.

I found myself arching my ass into the air.

Leo chuckled. "Is there something you need, Miss Pierson?"

"Yes, but I'm also offering."

He bent down and whispered, "What exactly are you offering

me?"

My words caught in my throat. I couldn't speak.

Leo worked his way down to my tight calves and feet. "Opportunity lost, Miss Pierson."

He spanked my ass again. "Roll over."

"What?"

"I said, roll over."

I did as I was told.

Leo started with my feet and worked his way back up my legs—spreading them apart when he neared the middle.

"Oh, Leo," I whispered. "Please."

"Please what?"

His hand slipped over my mound. His thumbs circled my lower belly.

The tension rose inside. The ache for release was right there. Just one touch on the right spot and I would be in ecstasy.

Slowly, he moved to my breasts but ignored my hard nipples. My breath quickened and my body began to shake.

"Do you know why I am doing this?" Leo asked.

"'Cause you like to tease?"

"No. It's to heighten your senses. I want you to feel what I am doing without seeing what I am doing."

"God, Leo. This is torture."

Leo moved his hand between my legs. "You want a release?"

"Y-yes. Please." I thrust my hips up.

Leo covered my mouth with his at the same time his thumb slipped over my swollen bundle of nerves. He applied pressure and began moving his thumb in circles.

My body arched as the sudden jolt of an orgasm hit me. I couldn't take it anymore. My nails dug into Leo's back.

He pulled his mouth away with a loud growl and then latched

onto my nipple. He sucked hard and bit into me to draw out another orgasm.

I slinked my fingers into his hair and pulled. "Oh, God! Leo, Please, I can't...no more."

Leo lifted his head slightly with my nipple between his teeth. "Yes, you can. One more time, princess."

He switched to the other nipple and did the same thing. "Let them all hear your screams, baby."

Leo switched from thumb to finger. He gave my clit a continuous tap as he built the need inside me again.

I held my breath as I felt it rising, and then I let out a long moan as I released the tension.

Leo removed his hand and mouth as my body relaxed against the bed.

"Better?" He took the blindfold off.

I nodded and licked my dry lips.

"Here." Leo had a glass of wine next to the bed. He held it to my lips as I took a sip.

"Mmm, thank you. Now, it's my turn." I started to unbutton his pants, but he caught my hand.

Leo shook his head. "I'm fine, babe. Besides, I don't trust my animal right now. Especially after what happened when I marked you last night."

Leo got up to undress for bed and blew out the candle.

I went to the bathroom to take a quick shower. When I came out, Leo was in bed with his arms behind his head. The sheets lay low on his belly.

He smiled and threw the blanket to the side so I could snuggle against him. He draped his arm over me and kissed my forehead.

Leo whispered, *"Ich liebe dich."*

I giggled. "What did you just say?"

"I said, 'I love you.'"

"You're going to have to teach me German if you're going to start doing this."

Leo's chest shook a little as he chuckled. "I'd love to be your teacher. Will you wear a schoolgirl outfit?"

"We'll see."

CHAPTER 12 Chloe

When I woke the next morning, there was a note on the pillow with one of my roses. I smiled as I took the note.

You looked so peaceful this morning. I didn't want to wake you. I have a few errands to run. Be back soon.

Your alpha, Leo

I picked up the rose and brought it to my nose. I'd never thought I would feel this kind of love for anyone. Leo was my world. I couldn't picture life without him.

I hurried to get dressed, not knowing how long he was going to be gone. I went downstairs and saw Drake in the kitchen.

I looked around the room. "Where is everyone?"

Drake pointed out back. "Outside. We won't have many more nice days like this. I made breakfast. I kept yours in the microwave."

He pulled out a plate with two eggs, bacon, and hash browns.

I frowned. "No French toast this time, Mr. Crocker?"

Drake laughed. "No. I'm afraid not."

I sat at the breakfast nook and had my food gone in minutes. I didn't realize how hungry I was.

"You want some coffee?" Drake asked.

"Yes, please."

Drake grabbed my favorite mug and poured me a cup. He

136

refilled his cup before sitting next to me.

"Drake, can I ask you something?"

"Sure. What's up?"

"Don't get mad at Leo for this, but...well, he mentioned how his pack took in yours. May I ask why?"

Drake sat back and ran his hand through his hair. "Wow, okay. Well, another group of wolves threatened to kill us if we didn't give them our territory. I think I was twelve when that happened. Feuds like that happened quite often. It wouldn't stop. When I was seventeen, my dad left to help his comrades fight for their territory. He was killed. That is when my mother decided enough was enough and moved to California. I stayed behind, and when I turned eighteen, Leo got me a job at the club."

"I'm so sorry to hear about your dad." I consoled him by rubbing his back.

"Yeah. Leo's mom invited my mother to stay in Vermont at the new community, but she wanted away from it all."

Drake gulped back his coffee and got up to rinse the cup out and place it in the dishwasher. "Kyle told me what happened while I was in California. He also said you are part mystic."

"Yeah, I inherited it from my mom. Cyrus is looking into it for me."

"Did you guys really take on that many embalmers?"

I nodded as I took a sip. "Yep. I gotta say, I had my doubts. It was a scary situation. I would've died if it wasn't for him and Cyrus."

Drake shook his head and crossed his arms. "I shouldn't have left you, Chloe. I should've been there to help."

I laid my hand on Drake's arm. "You didn't know that was going to happen. No one did."

"But, still, I shouldn't have run out on you. A real friend wouldn't have done that."

"Drake, what's done is done. We can't change the past. Let's just move forward."

"I want to be there for you now, Chloe. I want us to be friends."

I stood up and made him unfold his arms. "We'll always be friends, Drake. That will never change."

He pulled me into a tight embrace. "You don't know how happy it makes me to hear you say that. I still love you, Chloe. A part of me always will."

I hugged him back. "I love you, too."

We both knew our meaning of love for each other was different, that it would never go past the boundaries of friendship.

The back door opened and Sasha came in. "What's going on? Why are you all over my guy?"

I stepped away and Drake stood between us. "It's not what you think. I was just..."

Sasha laughed. "I'm messing with you."

Kyle and Riley entered the kitchen. He nudged Drake with his elbow and nodded toward the basement door. The two disappeared downstairs.

Sasha hugged me. "That is the first time I've seen light in Drake's eyes. I take it you two made up?"

"Yeah, we did."

We heard a loud thud and grunting from the basement.

"Are you guys all right? What are you doing?" I yelled.

"Getting this damn dresser up the steps for you," Kyle replied.

I poked my head around the door to see them half-way up the steps. "Good job. Just think, you have one more set of stairs."

Kyle let out a growl and continued hauling the dresser up the steps.

Once the coast was clear. Sasha and Riley helped me carry the drawers to the bedroom.

"Where do you want this thing?" Kyle asked.

"On the other side of the mirror."

Drake and Kyle positioned the dresser and removed the dolly from underneath.

"Well, this came in handy. I'll take it back to the basement. Then we can head out," Kyle said.

"Sounds good." Drake followed.

Sasha turned to me and smiled. "I had fun yesterday. Thanks again for including me."

"You are a part of the gang, Sasha. Anytime you want to hang out, just ask."

She hugged me one last time and left the room.

"Kyle and I will get ready at the club and meet you and Leo at the restaurant later," Riley said.

"Okay. See you there."

The house felt empty with everyone gone. I took the opportunity to finish my story. I had four more days to get it in, and I knew I wasn't going to have much time with dinner tonight.

After a few hours, I saved my work and sent it to my dad. I sat back in the chair and stretched. I was excited about this story and all I had accomplished in such a short time.

I turned in the chair and stared at Leo's bag on the floor. I perked up when I thought of my house as Leo's home. In a way, it was.

I took the initiative to clean out my closet. I put clothes that

I no longer wanted in a bag and shoes in a large box. This gave him space to hang his nice dress clothes. I picked Leo's bag up off the floor and put his things away in the dresser.

I took his bathroom supplies and made a section in the medicine cabinet for him. As I finished up, I looked at the clock. It was well past noon. I began to worry and thought about calling him, but then my phone rang. It was Hannah.

I plopped down on the bed. "Hello, hot stuff. How was your date?"

"It was amazing. After dinner, we went to an art show a friend of his was having, and then we went back to his place. Did you know he has a loft near the club?"

"No, I can't say that I did. So, what happened?"

"What do you think? He was such a gentleman, Chloe. The way he made love to me was out of this world. I was hoping to see his other side, if you know what I mean."

"I'm sure he has his reasons, Hannah. That isn't something to go around doing. Besides, he could've hurt you."

"What do you mean?"

"I mean they are much bigger, and you are human."

"Oh, my God! How much bigger?"

I laughed. "I don't know. Like any other man, I guess it depends."

I heard the front door close and knew Leo was home.

"Hey, Hannah, Leo just got home. I'll talk to ya later."

"'K, bye."

Leo called out to me.

"Upstairs!" I ran down the hall and met him at the top of the steps. He was carrying a garment bag.

"What did you buy?"

"I got a new shirt and pants for tonight. I couldn't let you be the only one to get a new outfit."

"It took you this long to shop for one? Guys are usually in and out of a store in a matter of minutes."

Leo laughed. "No, I had other things to do, too. Why are you all smiles?"

I held my hand out to him. "I have a surprise for you." I pulled him down the hall. It was hard to do when he was full of muscle.

"What's your hurry?"

"I'm just excited."

I stopped just inside the room. "Take a moment to look around. And, not just the room itself, but inside things, too."

"Okay." Leo spotted his overnight bag and picked it up. "Why is it empty?"

I bounced on my tiptoes and interlocked my fingers under my chin. "Just keep looking. What do you notice?"

"Oh! How did you get this in here?" Leo asked, indicating the dresser.

"Kyle and Drake, silly."

He opened all of the drawers and glanced inside. "You put my clothes away, too?"

"Yes. And you have room in the closet for nice things."

Leo hung the garment bag in the closet.

I skipped over to him. "And..." I pulled him to the bathroom and opened the medicine cabinet.

Leo stood there, staring at the cabinet. "Are you saying what I think you are saying?"

"Well, yeah. Shouldn't every alpha live with their mate?"

Leo picked me up and twirled me around. "I want nothing more than to move in with you. But, there are going to be times that I have to stay at the club."

"I know. I just can't see myself without you."

Leo gave me pecks all over my face. I giggled and tried to push him away.

"Leo! Leo, stop!"

He put me down and took my hand. "I love you, Chloe. More than anything in this world."

"I love you, too. So, what other errands did you have to run?"

"Just some work stuff."

"What work stuff? All you do is stand and watch people."

Leo laughed and pulled me downstairs to binge-watch a Netflix show until it was time to get ready for dinner with my dad and Suzanne.

After a few hours, we went upstairs to get dressed. I made Leo go into Kyle and Riley's room. I wanted to surprise him with my new dress.

I put curls in my hair and did my makeup using neutral colors for my eyes and dark red lipstick.

I was slipping into my heels when there was a knock at the door. "Don't come in yet!"

"Chloe, come on! We're going to be late!"

"Give me one second!"

I spritzed on some perfume and took one last look in the mirror before opening the door.

Leo whistled when I stepped out of the room. He took me into his arms. "I love that dress on you, but I'd rather have it off."

"You look sexy, too." I leaned up and gave him a peck on the cheek.

Leo nodded down at my hands. "What's in the gift bag?"

"A bracelet for Suzanne. You ready?"

Leo held out his arm and escorted me to the car.

When we arrived, it took us a while to find a parking space. We had to park two blocks down and walk. My feet did not appreciate it.

The man behind the podium smiled. "Good evening. How many in your party?"

"We are meeting another group here under Richards."

"Ah, yes. Right this way."

We followed him to the back where everyone was waiting. They all looked up and smiled when we approached.

"There they are." Stephen stood to hug me and shake Leo's hand.

Suzanne was behind him, smiling. Her blonde hair was pulled up with a single curl on both sides of her face. She wore a dazzling blue dress that brought out the color in her eyes.

"You're absolutely stunning, Chloe. I'm so happy to finally meet you." She hugged me.

"Me, too. This here is Leo."

Leo nodded and kissed the back of Suzanne's hand.

"Oh, what a gentleman."

I handed her the gift bag. "This is for you."

"Oh, honey, you didn't need to get me anything."

"I know, but I saw it and thought it would be a nice gift."

"Well, thank you. Come sit next to me so we can get to know each other."

Leo held my chair out for me before sitting down.

Our waiter arrived and poured us all a glass of water. "Is everyone here?"

"Yes," Stephen answered.

"I will give you all a moment to view the menu, then." He

grinned and moved to the next table.

I opened the menu, but I had no idea what I wanted to order. I didn't even know what some of the items were, and I didn't want to look like an idiot and ask. I decided to go with what looked familiar.

The waiter came back to take our order. When he got to me, I cleared my throat. "Um...I will have the Caesar salad and Beef Tenderloin Spiedini."

"What sides?"

"Mashed potatoes and asparagus, please."

Once the waiter wrote it down, he went back to Stephen. "Can I get appetizers for anyone?"

"Yes, I will have the calamari," Stephen said.

Kyle and Riley ordered grilled Portobello mushrooms and salsiccia.

Leo ordered Oysters Rockefeller.

I scrunched my nose. "Really?"

Leo smiled. "You know what they say about oysters. They're an aphrodisiac."

"No offense, but I don't think you need an aphrodisiac." Kyle snickered.

Riley hit him in the arm.

"What?" He rubbed his arm, still smiling.

I felt my face turn red.

The waiter found it amusing and chuckled. "What would you like to drink with your meal?"

Everyone ordered a single glass of wine. I had Leo order for me because I had no idea what would go with mine.

Stephen ordered a bottle of Italian red wine to share with everyone.

I would hate to be the one to pay for this bill, but it was a special occasion.

As we waited, everyone chatted about events while Suzanne asked me about my life before I found out I was a lycan.

I told her stories about my mother and David, and how they had passed away.

Suzanne laid her hand on mine. "I'm so sorry to hear. Stephen has told me so much about her. He even showed me a picture. You look so much like her."

All I could do was smile.

The waiter came back with two employees, and they prepared our table with the food and drinks.

Everything was to our liking and the waiter bowed and walked away.

Stephen held up his glass. "I want to propose a toast. First, I want to say how blessed I am to have you all here this evening. To Kyle and Chloe. I love you both very much. To Riley and Leo, who have become a part of this growing family." He winked.

"And, also, to my beautiful wife, Suzanne. I love you more and more each day. I wish you a very happy birthday and many more to come."

I held the tears for as long as I could. I excused myself and headed to the powder room. I shut the stall door and silently cried. Thank God for waterproof makeup.

"Chloe? Are you all right, dear?" Suzanne called to me.

I opened the door and stared at my reflection in the mirror across from me. I looked like a mess. My eyes were red, and my nose was running.

"I'm sorry. I...it was hard to hear him say those words to you while thinking of my mother. I know it sounds silly."

Suzanne rubbed my back in small circles. "It's not silly at all. I don't want you to think I'm trying to replace your mother.

That is a role I could never play. The way Stephen has talked about Katherine...I would have some pretty big shoes to fill. I just want to be your friend."

It made me smile to hear her speak highly of my mother, and that Stephen hadn't forgotten her. And, I was glad. I knew how much Stephen loved my mother. Had he told my mother that he was a lycan, maybe they would've had a chance to be together. Instead, she walked in on him shifting. It sent her to a mental hospital for a while.

I hugged Suzanne. "Thank you."

"Come now. Let's not keep them waiting."

We headed back and took our seats.

"Everything okay?" Stephen asked.

"Yes. Now, let's enjoy this meal."

We were there for at least an hour. After drinking three glasses of wine, I was feeling a little fuzzy.

Before we left the restaurant, Suzanne opened her gift from me.

"Oh, Chloe! This is beautiful. Thank you."

"You're welcome."

After Stephen took care of the bill, we walked outside and hugged each other goodbye.

"Don't be a stranger, Chloe. Call me anytime for anything," Suzanne said.

"I will. Happy birthday."

"Thank you."

Stephen and Suzanne headed down the block and to their car.

"Where did you park?" I asked Kyle.

"One block over. We will see you at the house."

Leo and I headed to the car. His hand rested in the small of my back. I didn't even make it half-way down the block before I had to stop.

"My feet are killing me. New shoes are for looks and not walking."

Leo smiled and turned his back to me. "Hop on."

"What? No way!"

"Chloe, get on my back. Humor me."

I hiked my dress up a bit and jumped on his back. I gripped him tightly. He smelled so good. I was hoping to have the house to ourselves tonight. If not, it wouldn't stop us from having sex. We proved that last night when I knew they could hear what was going on. I was surprised no one said anything or teased me about it.

I slid down Leo's back when we got to the car.

A group of girls walked by and whispered to each other as they stared at Leo. They had the nerve to come over to him as he was getting in the car.

"Excuse me, but are you that security guy from the Rising Flame club?"

"Yeah. Why?"

"Could we get a picture with you?"

Leo shook his head. "Sorry, ladies. I'm on a date with my girl. Hit me up when I'm at the club. Have a good night."

I sat there, smiling. I waved to them as we pulled away.

"Suzanne is a lovely woman," Leo said.

"Yeah, she is."

Leo reached over to squeeze my hand. "Something wrong?"

"It was just really hard seeing Dad with her when I know he was in love with my mom. I can't help but wonder what could've been if he had told mom what he was."

"Babe, you can't dwell on the past. Your mom did find

someone else to love, and he loved her back unconditionally. That's all that matters. Right?"

"Yes. You're right."

Just then, my phone rang.

"Cyrus, what's up?"

"Where are you?"

"Um, the car. Why?"

"Where are you headed?"

"Home. Is something wrong?"

"I will meet you there."

He hung up.

"Cyrus! Hello! Ugh, I hate it when he does this."

Kyle whizzed by and honked as he sped up the road.

"You're not going to race him again, are you?"

"No, not tonight. I'm just looking forward to him getting a ticket one day."

He brought my hand to his mouth and kissed it.

"I hope it isn't when Riley is with him. He'd never live that down."

We both laughed.

Thirty minutes later, we pulled into the driveway next to Kyle. They were just getting out of the car, and Cyrus was waiting on the front porch.

"Hey, Cyrus. What's up?" Kyle asked.

"I have some information for Chloe." He looked at all of us and cocked an eyebrow. "You all look well-groomed. What's the occasion—prom?"

"No. It was Suzanne's birthday." Kyle unlocked the door, and we gathered in the sitting room.

"So, what's the story?"

"I made contact with a friend of mine." He pulled the

necklace from his pocket and handed it to me. The vibration began again in my palm.

"She was able to tap into the history of this necklace. It wasn't easy and took some time. But, I believe we found your great-grandmother."

My posture straightened, and my eyes widened. "You mean she's alive?"

Leo's arm slipped around my waist.

"Indeed. Her name is Elsie Danvers. Here are the directions, if you wish to see her."

I took the paper he was offering and stared at the scribble marks. "This is like four hours away?"

"You won't find the location on any Google map, so don't even try. When I said your ancestors didn't want to be found, I wasn't exaggerating. They are literally 'off the grid.'"

"How the hell can I just show up on her property?"

"With extreme caution. I doubt she will recognize you as a mystic. You have lycan scent all over you."

"Will you go with me, then?"

"No, Chloe. I'm afraid I can't do that. I've already dodged obstacles to get this far. I wish you the best of luck."

"Wait. It sounds like you are leaving for good. Are you?"

"No, but I need to step back, Chloe. I was able to help you in the past because I kept you anonymous. But, now, we are digging deeper into the family. The council may not like me helping you because of what you are."

He reached out to touch my cheek. "I do care about you, Chloe. I will help when and if I can. You have a large support group here."

Leo squeezed me against him and kissed the top of my head. "And, you are very well protected."

149

Cyrus nodded. "That, too. I need to go. I will keep in touch."

I slumped into the chair next to me. "How am I to manage without his help? He is the only one who can get into places and find information."

Leo squatted down in front of me. "He is right, though. And, I know you don't want anything bad to happen to him."

He stood and held out his hand. "It's late. Let's get some rest and tomorrow we'll make a trip to see Elsie."

I glanced at Riley and Kyle. "You guys want to come with me?"

"As much as I'd love to, sweetie, I can't. I have class tomorrow," Riley said.

"Yeah, me, too. I'm three classes away from finishing."

"I understand, and I'm very proud of you both. Have a good night."

"Sleep well, Chloe." Riley hugged me.

Upstairs, I put my great-grandmother's necklace on the dresser and got ready for bed. I brushed my teeth and put on my nightshirt.

"What the hell are you doing?" Leo asked.

"What do you mean? I'm getting ready for bed."

Leo shook his head. "Not wearing that, you're not. Take it off. I like you warm and naked against me."

How could I say no to him when he looked so damn good?

I took the nightshirt off and snuggled next to Leo.

"Tomorrow, when we go on this trip, do you want to stay overnight at a hotel or try and make it back in one day?" I asked.

"I wouldn't mind staying at a hotel. And whatever happens with Elsie tomorrow, know that I love you." He squeezed me.

"I love you too, Leo."

150

CHAPTER 13 Chloe

Leo's phone alarm went off. I rolled over and put the pillow over my head. I was comfortable and warm, and I didn't want to get up. The bed shifted as Leo moved around, and then he draped his arm over me.

"Time to get up. We need to hit the road. I figure we can grab something to eat on the way."

"What time is it?"

"Seven." Leo pulled the pillow from my head and kissed my shoulder. "Come on."

"I need to shower first."

"Well, get to it. I'll start packing."

I moaned as I rolled out of bed and shuffled to the bathroom. I quickly washed my hair and soaped off in about fifteen minutes. To me, that was the fastest I'd ever taken a shower. I dried my hair and stepped out of the bathroom to get dressed.

Leo zipped up his bag and looked at me, smiling. "You're so beautiful, Chloe. Now, hurry up. I'll be downstairs gathering some snacks."

I threw on some jeans and a shirt and tossed some stuff in a bag. I looked at the necklace on the dresser and picked it up. I put it on to see how it would look, and this overpowering sense of protection came over me. The white crystal seemed to brighten so I took a closer look. The glittering mist swirled inside the gem.

"That's amazing," I mumbled.

I put my shoes on and made sure I had everything before heading downstairs. Leo was talking to Kyle and Riley when I entered the kitchen.

"I'm ready to go when you are," I said.

"Be careful and good luck," Riley said.

Leo packed up the car, and we headed to the highway. We had a long drive ahead of us.

We pulled into a Denny's for breakfast. I ordered a stack of strawberry pancakes and a cup of coffee. I was deep in thought as I ate. Periodically, Leo would look up from his meal and stare at me. I could tell he wanted to say something, but he didn't.

After I finished, I pushed my empty plate to the side. "You know what bugs me?"

Leo looked at me as he drank his coffee.

I crossed my arms and leaned on the table. "That we haven't seen or heard from the mystery woman. Don't you find it weird? She seemed to not be from around here—or maybe even from this century."

"It is possible that it wasn't Josephine's maker. Maybe it truly was someone looking for Cyrus."

"I know he's been cautious lately. I don't want to get him into trouble."

"Cyrus knows when to pull back, which is why he gave the reigns to you after finding Elsie. He's good at what he does. Come on. Let's get going."

While Leo paid, I went to the bathroom and then met him at

the car. I kept playing with the necklace as I stared out of the window. I was excited to meet my great-grandmother, but I was also scared. What if she didn't accept me?

I was beginning to think this was a bad idea. I was a hybrid. What if she saw me as a threat and told others about me? What if word got out? Then I'd have to defend myself against the lord knows how many angry people.

"Babe, what's wrong?"

"I'm having second thoughts about all of this." I turned in my seat and told him how I was feeling.

"Do you want to call this whole thing off and go home? I have no problem doing so. I want you to feel safe."

"What if it's not worth getting the answers I need?"

"Are you doing this for you or for your aunt?"

I sighed and turned back to the window. "Both. If Elsie can fill in the blanks and tell me what happened all those years ago, then great. But, I don't think it is going to be something I want to hear. I may not accept her answer. I'm not even sure I'll be able to tell my aunt about it."

"So, why do it, then?"

I found myself still clutching the gem. The vibrations made me feel like nothing could hurt me, and it calmed me. This was my time, and the only chance I'd have to do this.

"Babe, just tell me what you want to do."

"I need to do this, Leo."

"Okay, then. I'm with you all the way."

For the next two hours, Leo and I talked about our childhood. I wished I had known Leo as a child. He made me laugh so hard that I had tears in my eyes. I couldn't wait for the day to meet his family. The way he spoke about his mother made me miss mine.

We pulled into a rest area to stretch our legs and eat some lunch that Leo had packed for us. We found a shaded table under an oak tree.

I handed Leo a sandwich and a soda and sat next to him with my food. We shared a bag of Doritos.

"Even though we are on a mission, I'm enjoying our little trip." I took a few bites of my sandwich.

Leo put his arm around me and kissed the top of my head. "Me, too. It's nice to get away from the club drama. But, the best part is the alone time with you."

He wiggled his eyebrows.

I laughed and pushed him away. "You're silly."

After we finished eating, I packed the food back into the cooler. I saw movement from the corner of my eye and glanced at the overflowing trashcan. There was a little tan poodle eating scraps off the ground. The poor dog was skin and bones.

"Aww, Leo, look. She's hungry."

I pulled out some lunchmeat and squatted with my hand out. "Come here, sweetie. Come on. I won't hurt you."

The dog crept toward me. I could see it shaking.

"It's okay. Come on."

It inched closer, took the meat from my hand, and then ran back to the trashcan. I sat on the ground and waited for it to come back.

"Chloe, what are you doing?"

"What's it look like?" I looked up at Leo, and he shook his head. "What? I'm helping the poor girl."

The dog came back to me and stopped a few inches away. It sat on its hind legs and whined.

"Oh, great. See what you've started?" Leo sat next to me.

I handed the dog another slice of meat. "It has no home,

Leo."

"Chloe, we can't take the dog with us."

"Why? No one seems to be missing her. For all we know, someone just left the poor thing here. And, I'm not taking her to a shelter."

I held out another slice. The dog came closer and, this time, stayed next to me as it ate. When it finished, it crawled into my lap and licked my hand.

I looked at Leo and batted my lashes. "You know, my aunt has always wanted a little dog."

"You better make sure she still wants one before you take this one to her."

I stood up and put the rest of the things in the car. The dog followed me and waited by my feet. I picked it up and cradled it against my chest.

"That's it. She's coming with us."

Leo stared at the dog and me. "You realize we have to get dog food, a collar, and a bed."

"Don't forget the chew toys."

"And the chew toys."

"Does this mean we can keep her?"

"I can't say no to you, Chloe. Especially since you have your heart set on it."

"Yeah!" I bounced up and down. "You hear that? You're going to get spoiled."

I scratched the dog's ear, and she leaned into my hand.

"Oh, God, what have I agreed to?" Leo mumbled.

I laughed and got in the car. The dog lay down in my lap and fell asleep.

"I'm going to name her Peanut." I rubbed her belly.

"Don't you think you should let your aunt name her since

you plan on giving her the dog?"

I stared at him with a smile.

"You are going to give her the dog, right?"

I shrugged. "Maybe."

Leo started the car, and we headed down the interstate until we found the nearest store for pet supplies.

We stopped at a Petco. I looked at the directions to Elsie's. We were an hour out from what I could tell. But, I couldn't understand Cyrus's instructions.

I saw Leo waiting at the rear bumper. When I didn't get out right away, he came over and opened the door.

"Are you coming?"

"Yep. I was just waiting for you to open the door for me. Or, are you finished being a gentleman?" I folded the paper and stuffed it back into my purse.

"Baby, I have yet to show you my gentle ways." He wiggled his eyebrows with a sly grin.

"I'm sure you will."

I clung to Peanut as I turned in the seat to get out. "Come on Precious. Time to go shopping."

Leo pushed the cart while I carried Peanut around the store. I didn't know what kind of food to get her, so I asked one of the workers who was stocking shelves. After I explained the situation, the worker pointed out a few bags to choose from.

Leo and I picked out a bag and he placed it in the cart.

Next, we went to pick out a collar. There were so many to choose from, I couldn't decide.

"Jeez, Chloe. Just pick one already. How about that pink one with the jewels?"

I looked at Leo as I arched an eyebrow. "Did you just seriously say that?"

Leo laughed. "I guess I did."

He pulled the collar off the hook and placed it in the cart.

Once we picked out some toys, treats, a bed, and bath supplies, we headed to the checkout. We had already spent two hours in the store.

"Hey, Leo. Do you think we should get a room for the night and visit Elsie tomorrow? She's an hour away, and from the looks of the directions, this is the last time we will be in civilization for a while."

"Yeah, it's already late in the afternoon. We'll have to find a place that accepts pets. Keep your fingers crossed."

We went across the street to a hotel. Leo pulled up to the door and ran in to see if we could stay. He was in there for a while, so I guess it was a good thing.

He came back out with a luggage cart and loaded it up. "We are good to go. I'll park the car. Wait here."

Peanut snuggled under my chin and gave me kisses as we waited. I wasn't sure if I was going to be able to part with her. She might not even want to live with my aunt once she got used to Leo and me. I don't know what goes through a dog's mind, but, what would she think if I gave her away? I couldn't do that to her.

"Babe, what's wrong?" Leo asked.

"I can't get rid of her, Leo. I just can't."

Leo smiled. "I already know that, babe. You both are too attached to each other. Come on. Let's get settled and give her a bath."

Our room was on the first floor, which was a good thing in case we needed to take Peanut outside. I didn't unpack anything since we were planning to stay here for only one night.

I headed straight for the bathroom to give Peanut a bath. She sat there and let me shampoo and rinse her without any problems.

"Oh, you're such a good girl. Yes, you are." I used one of the towels to dry her off and gave her a chew toy.

"I hate to admit it, but she is cute, Chloe. She looks better now that she's clean."

"Yes, she is." I picked her up and sat her on the bed with us.

We lay there for the rest of the day, relaxing and watching television until my stomach growled.

Peanut's ears stood up, and she arched her head.

Leo and I laughed.

"I guess we should have dinner. You want to call delivery?" Leo scratched Peanut's head.

"Yep. I want pizza."

"Pizza it is." Leo jumped off the bed. When he did, Peanut jumped up, ran in a circle on the bed, and plopped back down as she wagged her tail.

She was quite the entertainer.

I got up and went to one of the bags to get Peanut's collar and leash, and also a treat. "You want to go outside to potty?"

Peanut walked over to the edge of the bed. I put the collar on and clasped the leash before picking her up.

"We'll be back."

I walked her down the hall to the back door. She sniffed around a few bushes before doing her business by a tree.

"That's a good girl." I patted her head and gave her the treat.

Peanut decided she wanted to walk around the building. So, I let her have her way. I knew she was used to being outside. I didn't think transitioning her into an inside dog would be a problem because she stayed with me wherever I went.

It was heartbreaking to know that someone had abandoned her. She was such a good dog. But, I could tell she was happy. Her tail hadn't stopped wagging since we got to the hotel.

Peanut and I headed back inside.

Leo was sprawled out on the bed, looking sexy in just his jeans.

I put Peanut's leash on the table and sat her on the bed. She ran up to Leo and lay on his chest. Her tiny tongue lapped at his chin.

Leo laughed as he scratched up and down her back.

"I knew you two would get along." I smiled.

There was a knock at the door.

I signed for the pizza and put the box on the small dining table. I put a can of food and water out for Peanut so she could eat at the same time we did. When she finished, she ran around, trying to catch her tail.

Leo and I laughed as we watched her play.

"Let me ask you something, babe. You do plan on teaching her to sleep in her bed, right?"

"Of course."

"Uh-huh." Leo smirked. "'Cause it would be hard to make out with you if she was on the bed."

"Um, Leo." I tilted my head toward the floor. Peanut was in her bed with one of her toys, fast asleep.

I grabbed my phone and took a picture. I sent it to Riley and sent her a text.

Leo and I found her at a rest stop. I named her Peanut.

How adorable! So are you keeping her?

How could I not? Anyway, Leo and I are at a hotel. We decided to see Elsie tomorrow. I will let you know how it goes.

159

Sounds good. Have fun!

After Leo and I finished eating, we headed to the bathroom to take a shower together. We left the door open in case Peanut woke up and wondered where we were.

I leaned my forehead against the cool wall. Leo massaged my shoulders and back as he washed me off. When he finished, it was my turn to take care of him. I watched the suds slide over his abs and down his muscular thighs.

"My God, Leo."

"What?"

"You're so hot. I'm so lucky."

Leo smiled. "I was thinking the same about you."

He leaned down and slipped his tongue between my lips.

I reached behind his neck and pulled him closer. "I want you, Leo."

"Without protection?"

I nodded. "Yes. I'm okay with it if you are."

Leo's hands cupped my ass and lifted me against the wall. I hovered over his erection for only a moment before sliding down on him.

"Oh!" My eyes closed when I felt Leo push into me. Without the condom, it connected us on a deeper level. I could feel every part of him caressing me inside.

Leo leaned down and flicked his tongue along my nipple, then sucked it into his mouth.

"Mmm, oh, Leo!"

He leaned back and watched as he moved in and out of me. The muscles in his arms and abs flexed as he held me.

I dug my nails into his shoulders, and he let out a growl.

"I'm close, baby. Come with me, now."

He slammed into me harder. Our bodies moved effortlessly

against one another. I wrapped my arms around Leo's neck for support. With one last thrust, the warmth of his release spilled into me.

We held each other for a moment before he slipped out and put me down. Leo kissed me and turned off the water.

When we moved the curtain back, Peanut was sitting there, wagging her tail.

I busted out laughing. "Guess we woke her up."

"Yep." Leo wrapped a towel around me and helped me out of the tub.

We dried off, and I crawled into bed.

Leo offered to take Peanut out before coming to bed.

While I waited for Leo, I surfed the web. I went on the club's website to see what was going on this weekend. There was a band scheduled to play on Saturday. This would be the first time since I'd been going there that there would be live music. I was excited.

Leo and Peanut came back in. Peanut ran straight to her bed and lay down with her toy.

"She's a chick magnet." Leo undressed and climbed into bed.

I rolled over to face him. "Is that so?"

"Yeah, there's a group of girls here for a bachelorette party. One kept suggesting I was the stripper."

"Is that what took so long?"

Leo grinned. "I thought about it. Wouldn't hurt to make a few extra bucks."

I smacked him on the arm. "Asshole."

He laughed and pulled me against him.

I laid my hand on his belly, and he interlocked his fingers with mine.

"Ya know, I was thinking of getting another tattoo."

I raised my head so I could see his gorgeous face. "Really? Like what?"

"I don't know. Not really sure. I was thinking of adding something to the wolf. Like, maybe a forest background with a moon or something. Maybe a dragon on the other arm instead. What do you think?"

I laid my chin on his chest. "Don't really know. It's up to you."

"You should get one with me. I think it would be sexy."

"Hell no! I hate needles. You should've seen me when Nadia took blood from me for several vials. I did get a lollipop afterward."

Leo laughed. "Well, that's good. The last time I gave blood all I got was a Band-Aid and juice."

He leaned downed and kissed me slowly on the lips. "I love you, Chloe. I'll love you until my last breath. And, even then, my love will continue."

My eyes teared up. No man had ever said anything so touching. I laid my head down and snuggled against him. "I love you, too, Leo. More than life itself."

CHAPTER 14 Chloe

I woke with Leo stroking the side of my face. "You're so beautiful when you sleep. I could stare at you forever."

"Seems like you have." I caressed his face, feeling the stubble under my fingers. I wondered what he'd looked like if he shaved. Would it take away the sexiness? No. There wasn't anything he could do to make him less sexy. He should have had his own calendar.

That was a good idea. I should suggest making calendars of the men and women from the club. That would be a great sell and market the club.

"What are you thinking?" Leo asked.

I told him about my idea. For a moment, he hesitated and then rolled onto his back.

"That isn't a bad idea. You should mention it to your dad. I don't think Cyrus would mind."

Leo got up and slapped my ass. "Get up. Breakfast ends in an hour. Then, we need to get going."

"What about Peanut?"

"She'll be fine while we eat. Now, get dressed."

Leo's ass looked amazing in his jeans. Not to mention his arms and torso in his black shirt.

"Can I ask you something?" I pulled my shirt over my head.

"You can ask me anything, babe. You should know that by now."

Stepping into my jeans, I asked, "Have you thought about piercings?"

"Like what kind of piercings?"

"I don't know. Ears or lip?"

Leo placed his hands on my hips. "Tell you what. I'll get my ears done if you pierce your nipples."

For a moment, I considered it. "Hmm, tattoos and piercings, huh? I'll think about it, but how about my belly button, instead?"

"Fair enough. Now, let's eat."

We walked hand in hand to the lounge area. I grabbed two plates. One for biscuits and gravy. The other for eggs, hash browns, and bacon. I poured a cup of juice and coffee, then headed to a table by the window.

Leo was still getting food when a group of girls came in. I assumed this was the same group he talked about last night because their faces lit up when they saw him. One of the girls walked over to him and stood a little too close as she got her food.

Leo paid her no attention as he walked away and to our table.

I met the girl's gaze and waved when she caught me staring at her. Her smile faltered after that.

"Hey, I saw on the club's website that there's going to be a live band Saturday. Does that happen often?"

"Not since I've been there, no. Sounds awesome, though."

I kept glancing across the room. The same girl kept watching us. I told Leo about it.

"She just wants what she can't have." Leo finished off the last of his sausage then got up to throw away the trash.

Before he sat down, he took a handful of my hair, pulled my head back, and kissed me. His tongue explored my mouth.

"You taste good," he whispered.

He left me breathless as he sat down with a smile.

"Did you do that for show or because you wanted to?"

"Both. Are you ready to go?"

"Yeah." I threw my trash away, and we headed back to the room.

Peanut was waiting by the door. I took her out for a walk while Leo packed everything and loaded up the car. Soon, we were on the road.

Peanut stayed in the backseat on her bed and chewed on her toy the entire ride. She was a good dog. Adding her to my family put a smile on my face. I'd never been so happy. Marrying Leo and having his babies would be the next best thing. I couldn't wait for that day to come.

"Babe, you want to get the directions out? We should be getting close."

"According to the directions, we should come upon a dirt road to the right. Cyrus noted that it won't look like a road, but it is."

Leo slowed down as we watched for this so-called road. Right now, we were in the middle of nowhere.

"This might be it." Leo turned and, at a snail's pace, tried to dodge the holes and bumps in the ground.

We went as far as we could and, eventually, we had to stop. There was a huge boulder in front of us. Everywhere we looked, all we could see were trees.

"You sure about this?" I asked.

Leo got out of the car, and I followed. Peanut yelped and jumped into the front seat. I grabbed her leash and picked her up.

"This is how horror movies start." I put Peanut down to potty.

Leo pointed up. "There."

I looked where he was pointing. A house looked as if it was built into the hill. You had to look closely because it was camouflaged amongst the green vines and trees.

"How the hell do we get up there?" I walked up beside Leo.

"There's a path here."

"What if there are traps?"

"How else are you going to get up there?"

"You stay here with Peanut. I'll go."

Leo grabbed my arm. "The hell you are. You think I'm going to let you go by yourself?"

"I'm not sure how Elsie's going to take to a lycan showing up at her door."

"Chloe, what the hell do you think you are?"

"Yeah, but...I'm also a mystic." I placed my hand on his arm. "Please. I'll be fine."

"I don't like this, Chloe. Be careful."

I paced myself as I walked along the trail and I watched where and how I stepped. I made sure there wasn't anything across the path that I could snag. After an agonizingly long ten minutes, I finally reached a set of rock steps that led to the landing and wooden porch.

I looked down at Leo. I could barely see him through the thick brush. I waved to him in case he could see me. He did and waved back.

I took a deep breath and knocked on the door. I hoped she was home. To think I'd come all the way here only to find no one home would be disappointing. Which was fine. I'd just camp out in the car and wait for her to come home.

I heard the click of a lock and the door opened. I was confused when a beautiful woman answered. She looked like she was in her late thirties. For a moment, I thought I was at the wrong house. Then again, maybe this woman was taking care of Elsie. I mean, how old would Elsie be now?

"You're trespassing. Did you not see the sign?" the woman said.

I cleared my throat. "Um, I'm sorry, but I'm looking for Elsie Danvers. Does she live here?"

The woman tilted her head. "Who's asking?"

"My name is Chloe Pierson. I'm Elsie's great-granddaughter. Katherine was my mother."

"Sorry, I don't know a Katherine." The woman started to close the door.

"Please, I...Mary was my grandmother. She had two children—Helen and Katherine."

The woman stepped forward so fast that I almost fell backward. "How did you find this place?"

"I had help from a friend. I'm sorry to drop in on you like this, but I just traveled four hours to get here. Please, may I see Elsie? It is very important that I speak with her."

The woman hesitated but then opened the door wider. "You already are."

For a moment, I didn't say anything. I just started at her in awe.

Elsie laughed. "You seemed shocked. Let me guess, you expected a decrepit, wrinkly, old woman?"

"Well, yes. I mean no. Not really."

"Unless you are anything like me, you'd understand—"

"That you're a mystic," I interrupted.

167

She arched her eyebrows.

"Yes, Elsie. I know what you are. I know about vampires and wolves. I'm not exactly human."

Elsie leaned on the doorframe. "I know."

She looked past me and nodded. "Who's the lycan with you?"

"Leo. He's my alpha."

"Your alpha? Well, I didn't see that one coming."

With a flick of her hand, thick green foliage parted to expose a clear path to Leo. He held Peanut as he leaned against the hood of the car. "Call your alpha up here and come in."

"Thank you."

I waved for Leo to join me. He came up the path without any issues.

Elsie waited for us in the living room. "Please, have a seat. Would either of you like some tea? I just brewed a pot."

I accepted a cup, but Leo politely declined. He wasn't much of a tea drinker.

I glanced around at the pictures on the walls. There were no family photos—only landscape paintings. In the corner was a curio cabinet filled with glass animal figurines. The pendulum on a cuckoo clock clicked as it swung back and forth.

Elsie came in with a tray and placed it on the table in front of the couch. The teapot and cups were made of white china trimmed in gold with pink floral accents. It was very dainty. She placed a bag in each tiny cup and poured the hot water.

"I have honey and sweetener, as well." She pointed to the containers.

I took a stick of honey and placed it in the cup.

Elsie put a little bowl on the floor. "For your little munchkin. She's adorable. What's her name?"

"Peanut." Leo put the dog on the floor, and Peanut trotted over to the bowl.

"You have lots of landscaping photos." I picked up my cup and spoon and began to stir.

"Yes, I do. They are of all the places I've visited."

"No family photos?"

Elsie took a sip of tea and crossed her legs. "I don't need them. So, tell me why you are here. What was so important that you had to speak to me?"

"I'm researching my family tree. My mother and aunt have never met any of their family. I'm here to get answers as to why. I need to know what happened to cause a rift in my family."

Elsie rested her cup of tea in her lap. "My daughter, Mary, was a wild child, but she grew worse when she met Tony. She would sneak out and break curfew just to see him. As a rule, we were not to get involved with those outside of the mystic heritage. It was to protect us."

"From who? Humans?"

Elsie wiped her forehead with the back of her hand. "No, from the evil forces. The story goes that back during ancient Egyptian times, a horde of evil darkness attacked the Kingdom of Azure, killing most of the mystics there. Those who survived lived in isolation to protect themselves in case the evil ever came back to finish them off."

"And that is why you're all off the grid," Leo said.

"Yes. We don't want our kind to mix with humans..." She glanced at me. "Or lycans. It puts them at risk of exposure."

"But, as long as no one uses their powers, they should be safe, right?" I asked.

"Sometimes, a mystic cannot control his or her powers.

Certain situations may cause one to act on impulse."

"I understand that all too well," I mumbled.

"Why do you say that?" Elsie asked.

"Well, I've had to use mine on occasion. One was by accident. At the time, I didn't even know what I was."

"And, how did you find out?"

"I was attacked by a vampire. I felt all of this energy building up inside of me, and then it just leaped from the palm of my hand. Then I found out from my biological father that I was part lycan. So, over the past few weeks, I've been trying to put the pieces together."

"Your mother never knew about any of this?"

"No, and neither did Aunt Helen. My mother passed away last year."

Elsie's eyes glazed over.

"How is it that you've never heard of my mother?"

Elsie finished off her tea and placed the cup on the tray. "Marrying Tony wasn't the only thing that caused a rift in the family. When Helen was born, there was a blood test to see if she carried the mystic gene. When it turned out to be negative, we never saw Mary again or our grandchild again. We never knew she had another child."

My heart was breaking. How could I ever tell my aunt about this? I'd hoped there was a small chance that Aunt Helen was one of us. Maybe she was. If Dr. Clements found it in mine, maybe she could re-test my aunt.

I would have to broach that subject carefully.

Things just kept piling up in regards to my family, and Aunt Helen was in the dark about it all. That had to change. I knew there were risks, but she had a right to know.

"Would you like to see pictures of my mother and Aunt

Helen?"

Elsie nodded and dabbed her eyes. "I would love to."

I pulled out my phone, opened the file labeled "Family," and handed her the phone.

Elsie scrolled through the pictures, smiling. "They both look so much like Mary, and you look like Katherine."

She held out the phone, and as I leaned forward to take it, my necklace slipped out from under my shirt.

Elsie's eyes lit up, and she let out a gasp. "The necklace. You have it."

"Yes. My friend used it to help me find you."

"Is your friend a mystic?"

"Yes. He is."

"How did you get it?"

"Grandma gave it to my mother on her sixteenth birthday. I found it in a box. Can you tell me anything about it?"

"Just that I gave it to Mary on her birthday, too. It has been passed down through many generations."

"What powers does it hold?"

Elsie shook her head. "Powers? I'm not aware that it has any."

I held up the crystal. "Do you notice anything peculiar about this?"

She leaned forward. "No. Why?"

"Are you sure?"

"Chloe, it looks like a regular necklace to me. Do you suspect it has powers?"

"I think it does. I just haven't figured out what."

Elsie glanced at the clock. "You both must be famished. Let me make some lunch and we can talk some more. I'd like to hear how Katherine had a lycan baby." She laughed.

For the next several hours, we got to know one another. Elsie made sure Leo was included in the conversation. She was fascinated by him, and she was particularly interested in my mother's story.

By three o'clock, we decided it was time to head out. Leo and I had a long drive back. We were not staying in a hotel tonight.

"I'm glad I got the opportunity to sit with you and learn the truth about our family history."

Elsie hugged me for the longest time like she didn't want to let me go. "I'm happy to have met you, Chloe. You take care."

I carried Peanut to the car. I waved to Elsie as I got in.

"That was a nice visit," Leo said.

"Yes. It was."

Leo carefully backed out of the tight parking area and headed back to the road.

"So, what do you think of that story she told?" Leo asked.

"Which one?"

"About the Egyptian city being attacked."

I thought about it for a moment, and then I sat up straight. "Leo, that woman that came to the club was defiantly Egyptian. There's no way that could've been Josephine's maker."

I slouched back against the seat. "I'm more confused than ever."

"Yeah, she was awfully nice."

"It's the nice silent ones that you need to watch out for, though. Do you think she was a mystic and that is why she asked for Cyrus—or, rather, the one in charge?"

"Who knows? Just when you get some answers, new questions arise. We'll figure it out, Chloe, once we get home and have a meeting with everyone. Until then, try and get some rest."

I reached into the backseat for my small pillow and placed it between the window and my neck. It wasn't long before I had fallen asleep.

CHAPTER 15 Chloe

Leo woke me by shaking me a few times when we reached the rest stop. By the third try, I was wide awake. We were an hour away from home, and when we finally arrived, I was relieved to see that Kyle and Riley were not there. I wasn't in the mood to see anyone or explain what happened just yet. However, there was one person I did want to contact.

I went straight to the bedroom with Peanut and texted Cyrus to let him know I was home and we needed to speak.

I waited patiently for him to call, text, or drop in by surprise, but none of those things happened. I threw my phone across the room, and it hit the wall and landed on the couch. With the protective cover, it didn't even break. Which was a good thing.

I lay on the bed with Peanut and petted her as she nuzzled against my side.

There was a light tap on the door, and Leo popped his head in. "Can I come in?"

"Of course you can. It's your room, too."

Leo brought in our things and sat them next to the closet. He placed Peanut's bed on the floor. "I know, but I didn't know if you wanted to be alone or not.

"I'm sorry if I've seemed distant."

Leo climbed onto the bed behind me. "You want to talk about it?"

"What's there to talk about?"

Something distracted Peanut. She jumped up and barked at the balcony. The curtains were drawn so I couldn't see outside, but I knew someone was out there.

"I've got it." Leo moved the curtain and opened the door for Cyrus to come in.

"Ah, a watchdog, eh? She's cute." Cyrus patted Peanut's head. "I got your message. What's wrong?"

"Let's go downstairs to talk." I put Peanut on the floor and she followed us down to the sitting room.

"Cyrus, have you heard of a city name Azure?"

"No. Why?"

"I believe that is where my ancestors are from. And, I also believe the woman who came to the club the other night was from that era. But, I'm still trying to wrap my head around all of this. Did she ever make contact with you?"

"Chloe, I haven't been around much to make contact with anyone. Where is this coming from?"

"Leo and I just got back from our trip. We spoke with Elsie, and she was able to give me some answers, but it actually brought up more questions."

I explained to him about the attack in Azure, and also why my family kept it hidden all of these years.

"I will see if what she said was true. But, I don't think I will find anything to confirm it since we all know why."

"I'd hate to get you any more involved with this, Cyrus."

"Chloe, I became involved the day Stephen came to me with his idea to lure you to the club with an invitation. I became involved when we met. I became involved—"

"Okay, I get it." I held up my hands.

"I will keep you posted."

I followed Cyrus to the door and watched him disappear.

"Now what?" I mumbled.

Leo leaned against the doorframe. "Now, we just go on with our lives."

He strolled over to me and laced his fingers through mine. "Are you hungry? I can fix us some dinner."

"Yeah. I'm going to take Peanut out back for a bit." I pulled Leo down to give him a quick kiss.

"Come on, Peanut. Let's go outside."

Peanut barked and wagged her tail. I sat on the lounge chair and watched Peanut run happily around the yard. She found a small stick and plopped down on the ground to chew on it.

I turned my attention to the house. Through the window, I watched Leo move about the kitchen. I smiled, thinking about how lucky I was to have him.

I pulled out my phone and scrolled through some tattoo pictures. I found a dragonfly that I liked. It was a simple black ink design, but it was elegantly done. I continued scrolling until I found one I thought would look sexy on Leo. It was a dragon wrapped around a dagger. I saved the images to my phone.

Forty-five minutes later, I called for Peanut to go inside. She tried to bring the stick into the house.

"No. You can't bring that in."

She laid it by my foot and walked up to the door. It was like this dog understood what I was saying.

"Good girl."

I filled her bowl up with food and fresh water.

"Do you need help cooking?" I asked.

"No. Just about finished. You can set the table, though."

I placed two plates and silverware on the dining table, along with two glasses. "We need to go shopping for more wine. Between Kyle and Riley, they've cleaned me out."

"Sounds good. We could go into town tomorrow and do some shopping. We need some stuff for the kitchen. I'll make a list."

I came up behind Leo, wrapped my arms around his waist, and laid my head on his back.

He placed his hand on mine and squeezed it. "You okay, babe?"

"Yeah. I'm good."

"You want to grab that bowl of salad for me?"

I followed Leo to the dining room. "It smells wonderful, Leo. What did you make?"

"German potatoes with chicken. Go ahead and sit. I'll get the drinks."

I took a seat and waited for Leo.

"This looks great."

The chicken was so tender that I could cut it with a fork.

"I wish we had a white wine to go with this. It would be perfect." Leo kissed the tips of his fingers, and then he placed a soda on the table for me. He had a bottle of beer.

I smiled and took a bite of my potatoes.

"This is nice, Chloe."

"What is?"

He reached for my hand. "You and me. Being here alone. I never thought about settling down until I met you. Most mates choose not to be with each other."

Leo cut his chicken into small pieces and mixed it with the potatoes. "If I can be brutally honest, I'm glad you didn't

177

choose Drake. I'd have to fight him for a place by your side."

He scooped up a large portion with his fork and took a bite. "You would do that?"

Leo washed down his food with a few gulps of beer. "Yes. It is how the process works if more than one alpha is interested in a mate."

"Don't I have a say in who I choose? I mean, what if I said no and still chose Drake?" I smiled and my teeth scraped across the fork.

Leo shivered and sat back in the chair. His eyes turned to their caramel color as he smirked. "If I had not come back yet, would you have?"

The stare alone gave me butterflies. I didn't think I could ever decline this man. If I were with someone else, no matter how I felt, my feelings for Leo would be much stronger. So, yes, it was a good thing I had decided not to date Drake. I had hurt him enough, and that would probably break him.

"I don't think I could deny the magnetic attraction. What I feel for you, Leo, is more than I can handle at times. It tends to overwhelm me to where I have no control."

Leo's smile widened as he leaned forward. "I feel the same way about you, and that is what makes us an awesome pair."

After we finished our meal, Leo offered to clean up while I took a hot bath. I searched for tattoo parlors on my phone and scheduled a consult for Leo's tattoo—and possibly mine. They had an opening at one tomorrow. After fifteen minutes in the tub, I got out, dried, and dressed. I went downstairs to say goodnight to Leo.

The swishing of water in the dishwasher was the only sound. Leo was nowhere to be found. I opened the back door and stepped out. Leo, shirtless, was doing pull-ups on a tree trunk nearby. My breath caught as I watched the muscles in his arms and back bulge with each movement.

I stood there as quiet as I could be. I was mesmerized by his strength. I knew Leo liked to keep fit, and being here wasn't giving him what he needed to do that. The idea of turning the basement into a workout room came to mind.

Leo let go of the tree and dropped to the ground for push-ups. I was curious as to how many he could do, so I counted. He stopped at fifty. Then he did sit-ups. Another fifty.

He did a backward roll and pushed himself up to a handstand for a split second before landing on his feet. He turned around to stare at me. His torso glistened under the moonlight from sweat.

I swallowed the lump in my throat as my eyes roamed his body. My heartbeat increased as he strolled up to me and stopped a few inches away.

"Enjoying yourself?" He smiled.

I didn't fight the urge to touch him. My fingers trailed down between his pecs to his tight abs. I was so in love with this man. I couldn't get enough of him. I wanted him to strip me naked and dominate me right here under the stars. It felt only natural to do so.

"Leo," I whispered.

"Yes. What is it that you want, Chloe?" Leo flexed his pec muscles and leaned down toward my neck.

He inhaled a long, deep, breath. "Mmm, you want to mate."

I looked up into his glowing bronze eyes. I couldn't speak. My inner animal spoke on its own.

Leo threw me over his shoulder and took me upstairs, where he answered my animal's desire. There wasn't a spot on my body that Leo didn't caress or kiss. He satisfied me in so many ways, many of which one could only dream of.

I returned the favor by pleasuring him with my mouth for a long time. I loved to see the look on Leo's face and hear the low moans turning into a growl.

Every time Leo and I were together, our chemistry grew stronger. We knew what each other craved. We tried new things to take our desires to a whole new level. When Leo dominated me, he made me feel protected and loved. There wasn't anything we wouldn't do for each other.

CHAPTER 16 Chloe

The next morning, I couldn't find Leo or Peanut anywhere in the house or outside. I thought maybe they went for a walk in the woods. I picked up the phone to call Leo, and I noticed a message from earlier. He had taken Peanut to the vet for shots.

I heard a car door and ran to the front yard. "Leo! Why didn't you wake me to go with you?"

"I was letting you sleep. I don't like waking you unless it's necessary. You need your rest."

I laughed. "You say that as if I'm carrying your child."

"Well, we did have unprotected sex." He smiled.

I took Peanut from Leo. "How did she do at the vet?"

"She was a sweetie."

Leo and I were playing with Peanut when Kyle and Riley came home from work. Peanut was shy at first but warmed up to them quickly.

Kyle and I went inside. He plopped down on the sofa and watched Riley through the window.

"What's wrong, Kyle? Afraid she's going to want a dog of her own?" I laughed.

"It's not a dog that worries me." He held his head in his hands. "She's talking kids, Chloe. I'm not ready for that yet."

I took a seat next to him. "Did you tell her that?"

"Yeah."

"And?"

Kyle shrugged. "She didn't say anything. I want a family with her, don't get me wrong. Just not right now. We're both almost finished with school. She still yet has to decide what she wants to do."

"What about you? With you majoring in English lit, are you going to teach or something?"

"I've something in the works. I can't say what it is at the moment."

"Is it some big secret?"

"Not really."

"Kyle, you can talk to me, ya know. You've always been there for me. Let me do the same for you."

Kyle took my hand. "I will let you know soon. What about your visit with Elsie? How was that?"

I pulled away from Kyle and relaxed against the back of the sofa. "There is a lot to talk about, but we'll discuss it soon."

"Are you sure?"

"Yep. I just don't want to talk about it right now."

"I understand. I'm going to go take a shower."

Leo saw me through the window and waved me to come out. "You ready to go? Riley said she will watch Peanut for us."

"If it's not too much trouble." I looked at Riley.

"Not at all. She is so adorable. Take your time. I'll see you later." Riley and Peanut went inside.

"Let's go. I have a surprise for you." I pulled on Leo's hand.

"Oh, what is it?"

"Can't say. It wouldn't be a surprise."

We headed into Fenton and stopped at the wine store to stock up on a variety of different bottles. I was a member, so we got a discount at the checkout.

"What is the occasion?" the girl behind the counter asked.

"Empty wine cellar and a thirsty household," I said.

"Well, glad we can help replenish you." She smiled at Leo.

I rolled my eyes and gave her my card.

"Thank you for coming in. Have a nice day."

Leo glanced at her nametag. "You too, Holly."

The girl's face turned red.

I got in the car and waited for Leo to load the wine in the trunk. When he got in, I slapped his arm. "You did that on purpose."

"What?"

"'You too, Holly,'" I said in a mocking tone.

Leo laughed. "Oh, come on. I made her day."

"Yeah, I'm sure you did." I crossed my arms.

"So, now where to?" Leo started the car.

I noticed the time. "Oh, let me drive."

"Is it my surprise time?" Leo grinned.

"Just get out." I opened the door and jogged around to the other side.

"I should blindfold you." I backed out of the parking spot.

"Ooh, would you?"

I glanced at Leo and laughed. "I would if I had something."

"I could use my shirt. I know you like it when I don't wear one."

"I like it when you don't wear lots of things." I blew him a kiss.

As we made our way to the secret destination, Leo stayed on his phone. It pinged with a message. With a flick of a finger, he opened Messenger.

I heard him curse under his breath as he closed the app.

"Something wrong? Who was that?"

Leo shook his head. "It's nothing."

I knew he wasn't telling the truth. He had a crease between his eyebrows, and his lips were pressed tightly together.

I let it go for now. But, I would get to the bottom of it later. Right now, I just wanted to enjoy the day with my man.

I pulled into the shopping center and parked on the opposite end of the tattoo shop. Leo and I walked hand in hand down the sidewalk. When we approached the shop, Leo stopped outside the door.

"Tattoo? You serious?"

I nodded. "I found one I thought you would like. I know you had an idea to finish the wolf, but you can do that another time. Do you trust me?"

"Of course."

He opened the door, and a tall man with tattoos on his arms greeted us. "Hey, how's it going?"

"Hi! I'm Chloe. I called about getting a tattoo. I have an appointment with Max and Star."

The guy nodded. "Have a seat. I'll get Max. Star is finishing up with a customer."

Leo and I took a seat and waited. I heard Leo's phone go off again.

He shifted in his seat as if agitated.

"You want to get that?" I asked.

"No. We'll talk when we get home."

"That doesn't sound good." I turned away from him, worried about the messages.

Max came out from the back and smiled. "Hey. Nice to meet you. Who's the lucky person?"

Leo stayed sitting. I got up and walked to Max. I pulled my phone out and showed him the picture. "This is what I want Leo to have on his arm. Can you do it?"

"Absolutely. Send it to me so I can print it off."

I got his info and sent it.

"Give me a few minutes to get this prepared."

"I have an appointment with Star, so we'll be here."

"Cool." Max walked to the back and disappeared behind a curtain.

"Chloe?"

I turned to the sound of a woman's voice.

"I'm Star. What are we doing today?"

"I want this dragonfly on the back of my neck."

"Sure. Let me draw it up, and we'll get started."

Leo was looking at a book of tattoos. I walked over to him.

"Max will be ready for you soon."

Leo only made a humming noise as he flipped through the pages.

I laid my hand on his back between his shoulder blades. "Why do you seem upset? Did I do something wrong?"

Leo shut the book and turned to look at me. "The message was from a girl I used to date back in Vermont."

"Like, how old of a girlfriend?"

"Five years ago."

"And, why is she messaging you?"

"She's in town for a business conference. She wants to meet for drinks."

I frowned. "Has she been in contact with you in the last five years?"

"No. She found me on Facebook. Obviously, she's ignored my dating status."

"Sounds like the type that doesn't care. What did you tell her?"

"Nothing."

"Leo, remember when I told you I didn't want to put up with jealous exes?"

"Chloe, first of all, you're the one being jealous. Second, I'm not meeting her. Third, she's the one who broke it off to pursue her career. At least, that is what she said."

"You didn't believe her?"

Leo pulled me outside. "Look, I marked you. You are mine. I am yours. No ex or any other girl from here on out is getting between us. I love you."

He cupped my face in his hands and kissed me aggressively. His tongue and lips claimed my mouth. He pulled away and rested his forehead on mine. "Now, let this go so we can enjoy our day."

I nodded. "Okay."

We went back inside and Star was ready for me. I pulled Leo with me and asked to have him sit next to me. He held my hand the entire time. I squeezed my eyes at the same time I clutched him.

"Just breathe, babe. You're doing great." Leo kissed my hand.

"How long have you two been together?" Star asked.

"A little over a week," I answered.

"You wouldn't know it. I can see the connection between you two."

Leo's thumb rubbed the back of my hand, putting me at ease. I was being silly about the whole ex thing. I know it wasn't his fault. I had nothing to be jealous about. The girl had had her chance. Now, Leo was with the person he was meant to be with.

After an excruciating amount of time, my tattoo was complete. I looked at it in the mirror. "Oh, wow! That's amazing! Thank you."

"You're welcome."

Leo stood there with his arms crossed and asked about piercings.

"We do those, too. What do you want done?"

Leo and I stared at each other. I shook my head. "Enough pain for today. Maybe next time."

Max came out to get Leo. I sat and watched him draw the dagger on his arm.

"This is going to have to be in stages. We will start with this and schedule for the dragon."

Leo smiled. "Dagger and dragon, huh? I like it."

I kissed Leo on the cheek. "I'm going next door to the clothing store. When should I come back?"

"Give us a couple of hours."

For the next two hours, I shopped and bought new lingerie and some shirts. I made my way to the bookstore and got Leo a few motorcycle magazines.

When I got back to the tattoo shop, Max had just finished. Leo was standing at the mirror, looking at his new art. The dagger was all black except for the tip. It was made to look like it was dipped in blood.

"Sexy, babe." I came up next to him. "Do you like it?"

"Yes. Very much so."

He glanced down at my shopping bags. "Did you buy out the store?"

"No. I have a bag for you."

Leo opened the bag and smiled. "Sweet. Thank you, babe."

We went to the counter so Leo could schedule the next appointment and pay for the tattoos. He refused to let me pay.

We stopped at Red Robin for dinner. We both ordered a burger with endless steak fries.

"You know, I've always wanted a tattoo, but I was afraid to get one. I have had a lot of first times with you, Leo."

"And, you will have many more. I can promise you that." He winked.

I looked up and noticed Drake and Sasha.

"Look who's here," I said.

Leo looked over his shoulder. "You want to invite them over?"

"Yeah."

I got the waitress's attention. "What can I get for you?"

"That couple sitting by the door. Can you put them with us? They're our friends."

"Sure."

The waitress went over to Drake. He looked at us with a nod.

Leo moved over by me so Drake and Sasha could sit across from us. "Hey, guys! Fancy meeting you here."

"Thanks for letting us sit with you." Drake looked at the menu.

"How are you, Chloe? It's been a while since we've talked," Sasha said.

"Yeah, I've been occupied with family issues."

"Oh, is everything all right?"

I know I was still getting to know Sasha. There were things she didn't know about me. Right now, she only knew I was a lycan. I wasn't at the point that I felt I could tell her about the other side of me.

"Yeah, it's nothing I can't handle."

As we ate our meal, I told Drake and Sasha about my idea for a club calendar. They were on board with doing a shoot. I was excited to do this and promote the club any way I could. All I had to do was clear this with my dad, meet with everyone at the club, and then hire a photographer.

"So, who is working tonight if everyone I know is off?"

"Matt's working. It's a slow night anyway." Drake took Sasha's hand. "You ready to go?"

"Yep."

We paid for dinner and walked outside.

"We're going to a movie if you guys want to join," Drake said.

"Yeah, it would be a double date." Sasha linked her arm through Drake's. "Please, Chloe. It'll be fun."

Leo shrugged. "Fine with me."

I linked my fingers with Leo's. "Sure. Why not? What are we seeing?"

"That comedy about the two undercover cops caught up with the drug cartel," Drake replied.

Leo pointed to the theater across the way. "Over there?"

"Yep. See ya there."

Thursday night at the movies was a good time to go. There was hardly anyone here. We got our tickets with an hour to spare. We went into the game room. It was boys versus girls in mini bowling. I told Sasha I used to be on a league a few years ago. Leo and Drake had no idea what was coming.

Our total was 250. Leo and Drake's was 200.

We grabbed some drinks and snacks and headed to theater five for our showing. We took the top seats in the middle. Only two other couples showed.

It had been a long time since I laughed this hard. Sasha and I had tears in our eyes.

After the movie, I hugged Drake and Sasha goodbye. "See you tomorrow at the club. We'll be there early to talk to everyone about the shoot."

"Had a great time, guys. Thanks for inviting us," Leo said.

"Not a problem. Drive safe." Drake and Sasha headed to their car.

"That was fun." I grabbed Leo's hand.

I text Riley to let her know we were on our way home.

She sent back that they were cuddled on the couch with Peanut, watching a movie.

On the way home, Leo's phone kept lighting up and vibrating. Leo's hands gripped the steering wheel.

"You want me to say something to her?"

"No. I'll take care of it when we get home."

The rest of the way we were silent. I wasn't going to let this girl get to me. I was too tired even to argue. I knew Leo could handle it, but, as his mate, I had every right to step in to protect what was mine.

Once home, Kyle and Riley helped carry in the wine and take it downstairs. Leo and I showed off our tattoos, and then I took my shopping bags and the dog upstairs to get ready for bed.

I had just changed and pulled the covers down when Leo came in.

"Are you going to keep giving me the silent treatment?"

I walked over to him and hugged him. "I don't mean to."

"Come on. I'll tuck you in."

I jumped on the bed and pulled the covers up.

Leo kissed my forehead. "Sleep well. I'll be in soon."

I grabbed Leo's wrist as he turned away. "Leo, I love you."
His smile melted my heart.
"I love you, too."

CHAPTER 17 Chloe

I was packing a bag for the club when Peanut came into the room and yelped at me. I picked her up and rubbed her belly. I wanted to stay at the club with Leo tonight, but I didn't want to leave Peanut alone all night. Who would take her out?

"What am I going to do with you?" I scratched her ears.

My phone went off. It was Uncle Bob.

"Hey, Uncle. What new crime are you working on these days?"

"Several, actually. I'm not sure I could handle another weird case like the last one, but something is going on."

"What do you mean?"

"Have you watched the news?"

"No. I haven't had time. Life's been pretty busy. Please, tell me now that I'm your partner in crime."

Bob laughed. "Well, for the past couple of weeks, people have gone missing. Both men and women."

"How many are we talking?"

"At least twenty."

"Is this like the last time where the victims had no family?"

"Afraid not. I've questioned the victim's families and investigated the last place they were seen. There is no evidence

192

of foul play. It's like they just vanished."

"Why didn't you call me sooner?"

"It wasn't that bad then. Now, I'm worried."

"What can I do to help?"

"I don't think there is anything you can do. This isn't why I called, though. I was wondering if you could stop by and put a smile on your aunt's face. She's been down in the dumps lately. I don't know how to cheer her up. I've been so busy with work and all."

I looked down at Peanut. She wagged her tail as she chewed on a toy. My heart sank. I knew what I had to do.

"I'll be by in a little bit. I have just the thing to help her out."

"Okay. See you soon."

I hung up and sank to the floor in tears.

Peanut waddled over and licked my hand. I didn't want to let her go. She'd been such a ray of sunshine, and she brought happiness into the house.

I gathered up her things—only leaving a couple of toys behind—and put them by the door.

Leo came in from his run in the woods. He smelled of sweat and trees. Normally, his scent turned me on, but not at the moment. My heart was breaking, and I needed him to hold me.

"Baby, what's the matter?"

When I wouldn't answer, he pulled away, giving me just enough distance. He lifted my chin with his finger. "Talk to me."

I told him about Uncle Bob's phone call.

"Ah, and you're giving her the dog. Am I right?"

I nodded.

Leo pulled me against him. "I know how much you love

Peanut. You have such a big heart, Chloe. It's one of the reasons I love you."

I stepped away and wiped my eyes. "I'm going to go play outside with her while you get cleaned up. Everything is at the door and ready to go."

I called for Peanut, and she followed me out back. I picked up her ball and tossed it. After ten minutes of running, she plopped down on the ground.

"Giving up so soon?"

She barked and rolled onto her back.

I was going to miss this little dog.

I pulled out my phone and sent my dad a message to meet us at the club early for a meeting. He said he was already there doing inventory on the liquor and beer.

Leo opened the door and called out to me. "I'm ready to go. Car is packed, too. Are you sure you want to do this?"

"Yes. Come on, Peanut! Let's go for a ride!"

She let out a bark and ran through the kitchen and to the front door. She followed me out to the car while Leo locked up the house.

Peanut slept in my lap on the way to my aunt's house.

"Any more messages from your ex?"

"No. And, I don't care. Hopefully, she gave up."

We pulled in behind my aunt's car. They were sitting on the porch swing, and they waved as we got out.

When Aunt Helen saw Peanut, her eyes widened and a huge smile crossed her face. "Oh, look at this precious dog. Is this your new baby?"

I looked at Leo. He knew how hard this was for me, but she was going to a good home. And, it wasn't like a stranger, where I would be worried about her.

"We found her on a road trip the other day. I named her Peanut."

Aunt Helen held out her hand and Peanut licked her.

"You want to hold her?"

Helen nodded, and I passed her over.

Peanut licked Aunt Helen's chin. She laughed as she tried to move her head.

"Uncle Bob, Aunt Helen, this is my boyfriend, Leo."

"Oh, Chloe, you never mentioned you were seeing anyone. Nice to meet you, Leo." Aunt Helen's face turned a shade darker.

"Let's go inside." Uncle Bob held the door open. We all followed.

Uncle Bob raised his eyebrows and lowered his voice. "Your mate?"

I smiled with a nod.

"Well, Leo. Nice to meet you. Welcome to the family."

The two shook hands.

"Nice to meet you, too, sir."

Bob put his hand over his heart. "Sir? Oh, please, call me Bob."

Leo pointed at one of Uncle Bob's golf pictures. "First place, huh?"

"Yep. Do you play?"

Leo shook his head. "No. Never tried."

"Well, we'll have to change that, won't we?"

"Sure. I'd love to learn how to play."

Uncle Bob patted Leo's shoulder. "Come with me."

Leo followed him out back.

It was nice to see how easily Leo fit into my family. I looked out the window and saw Uncle Bob bringing out a bag of golf clubs. With Leo's passion for motorcycles and cars, it was nice to see him come out of his comfort zone to try to please my uncle.

Leo picked up one of the clubs and began swinging it. He had great form. And, I was sure that with his strength, he could drive the ball far.

Aunt Helen came up next to me. "We should go save Leo before Bob scares him off."

I laughed. "It would take something other than Uncle Bob to scare Leo off. He's not the scared type."

I followed Aunt Helen out back and she put Peanut down. She ran around the yard, barking and running in circles around Uncle Bob's feet.

I nudged Aunt Helen in the arm. "Peanut is yours if you want her."

"Oh, no, I couldn't possibly."

I put my arm around her. "As much as I want her, there are going to be times where there won't be anyone home to take care of her."

"Well, I can just puppy sit. It's no problem."

"I wouldn't want to keep moving her back and forth. Please, Aunt Helen. Would you take her?"

She looked over at Uncle Bob. He nodded with a huge grin. "Go ahead, honey. She seems to like you."

Helen hugged me. "Thank you, Chloe. I promise to take good care of her."

"I'll get her things out of the car." Leo rubbed my back.

"I'll help," Bob said.

Helen and I let Peanut get used to her new home. Leo put her toys down, and Peanut snatched up her favorite one, a purple monkey.

"I kept her bed in our room. I feed her hard food in the morning and at noon and a can at dinner. She likes to play ball before bedtime. It helps her sleep."

"Thank you, Chloe." Aunt Helen hugged me again. "I've always wanted a little dog to keep me company. You know you can visit her anytime you want."

"I know. Well, Leo and I need to get going. Call me if you have any questions."

"She had her shots. Here is the paperwork." Leo handed her the records.

I gave Peanut one last hug and quickly went to the car. I didn't want them to see me cry. That dog meant the world to me.

Uncle Bob jogged after us with the bag of golf clubs. "Leo, I want you to have these. They were my first set of clubs that my father gave me."

"Oh, I couldn't."

"Nonsense. I tried to give them to my son, but he was never interested. So, I want to give them to you."

"Thanks, Bob. I appreciate that."

"Let me know when you are available. We can meet up at the clubhouse."

"Sure."

Leo put them in the trunk and then waved as he got in the car.

Uncle Bob waved back and disappeared into the house.

Leo laid his hand on my knee as we drove off. "I know how hard it was to give Peanut away."

I leaned my head on the window. "Yes, but she seemed happy. That is all I care about."

I took Leo's hand and squeezed it. "I'm glad my uncle likes

you. He only sees his son and daughter on the holidays."

"Has it always been that way?"

"No. My cousins and I used to be really close. Abby was like a big sister to me. We did everything together. Mark was on the football team. He got a scholarship to play for several universities, but he turned them down. It upset my uncle, but it was Mark's life. He chose to go to law school in California. That's where he's been ever since."

"That's good. At least he did something he loved."

"Yeah, my aunt and uncle were not aware he wanted to go to California until after graduation."

"So, what is Abby doing?"

"She married a doctor. They live in Florida and have two kids."

"I can't wait for you to meet my family. My mother is going to love you."

"So, when do I get to meet them?"

"I'm not sure."

We pulled into Leo's parking spot, and I grabbed my bag from the backseat. We walked to the back door and waited for someone to let us in.

Matt greeted us. "Hey, guys! Stephen said we were having a meeting."

"Yep. Is everyone here?" I asked.

"Yeah. You want me to round them up?"

"Yes. Main floor. Leo, would you put my bag in the room? I'm going to find my dad."

"He's in the office," Matt replied.

As I made my way to the office, I waved to Riley at the bar. She was preparing for the night's festivities.

I stopped at the office door and saw my dad sitting behind

the desk. If Cyrus were to walk in and see his desk in disarray, he would frown. Cyrus was a very organized person.

My dad was so focused on the computer that he didn't notice me in the doorway. I gave a light tap on the door to get his attention.

"Oh, hey, sweetheart! How are things?"

"Good. You look stressed."

"Yeah. Cyrus always did the inventory and orders. I have not a clue what I am doing."

"You want some help? I used to order supplies and stuff at my old job."

"After the meeting, if you don't mind."

"Not at all. So, you liked my idea?"

"Yes. It would be great for the club. Suzanne happens to know a photographer."

"Well, let's go talk to everyone and see who is interested. We may have to do several different calendars."

Everyone was gathered on the main floor. My dad and I stood on the upper floor so we could easily address them.

"Thank you, everyone, for making it. My lovely daughter, Chloe, has something she would like to share."

I stepped up and waved. "Hey, everyone. I got an idea to help promote the club. Who would be interested in doing a photo shoot for a calendar?"

Everyone raised his or her hand.

"Wow! All right, then. So, I have several ideas in mind. One for the male entertainers, one for females, a mixture of both, and even a whole calendar of one individual. There will be many to choose from. I will leave it up to our photographer on how to do this. It will be fun and exciting to see this club succeed and get the recognition it deserves. An announcement

199

will go out once the shoot is scheduled. I'll have not only this location but several other outside locations for this. If you have any thoughts or ideas regarding the shoot, please let me or my dad know. Thanks again to all of you for your dedication."

Everyone clapped and whistled as they dispersed.

"I'm so proud of you, honey." My dad hugged me. "I never would've thought to do this. I'm sure Cyrus would appreciate it, as well."

"It's the least I could do for him since he's helped me. Now, let me take a look at your inventory stuff."

I took a seat behind the desk. "What am I looking at?"

"Oh, here." He handed me the check-off list.

"This is what we are supposed to have on hand. This is what we have. I'm having issues navigating the order form." Stephen scratched his head.

"Don't worry. I've got this. Go take a break or whatever."

"I'll just sit over here, if you don't mind."

I kept my eyes on the computer and typed away. I didn't see an issue with the site. I thought my dad was playing me so he could find a reason to put me to use around here. I wasn't going to tell him that. I knew it made him happy. It gave us a chance to do something together other than work at the magazine.

"I got your story. I must say, Chloe, it is really good. I'm not just saying that because you're my daughter."

"I know. How is Suzanne doing?"

"She's good. She really enjoyed having everyone get together for her birthday. She wants to do that more often. She suggested a family game night."

"Yeah, that sounds fun."

"How are you and Leo doing?"

"We're great. We had a little dog for a few days, but I gave her to Aunt Helen. She always wanted a dog. It helped put a smile on her face."

"That was kind of you."

"Yeah, it was hard to give her up. I was attached to her."

I looked everything over to make sure I didn't miss anything and then hit send. "All done."

I gathered the papers and put them in a folder.

"What would I have done without you?"

I shrugged. "Called Cyrus."

"Tried that. Thank you, sweetie."

"You're welcome. So, I noticed you have a live band scheduled for tomorrow."

"Yep. They're from Chicago. They're like us."

"Meaning?"

"Vampires. They're really good. Are you going to be here?"

"I may. What made you have a live band?"

"Something different. We've sold tickets to the show. Devin is going to be busy at the door."

"I'll be happy to help him."

"Would you? That would be great, sweetheart. Thank you."

"You're welcome! Now, I'm going to go get changed."

"For what?"

"I'm dancing tonight. Leo's my guard."

"Is that so? You mean you don't want to hang out and help your old man run the place?"

"Nope. Love ya!"

I heard my dad laugh as I left the office.

I hoped to find Leo in his room, but he wasn't there when I arrived. I changed into my outfit for the night and headed down the hall to the playroom. Leo was there with Drake, Matt, and a few others.

Leo waved me over. "You look amazing, babe." He kissed my cheek.

"Thank you. So do you."

I met Drake's gaze. He smiled and quickly averted his eyes.

"Chloe!" Sasha hurried over and hugged me. "You look great. Are you dancing tonight?"

"Yes. Are you and Drake performing together or separate?"

"We are doing a bit of both." Sasha tugged on Leo's shirt. "You should get in the cage with Chloe."

Leo busted out laughing, a sound that carried through the room. "I'm no dancer."

I linked my arm around Leo's. "I don't believe that for a second because in bed you know how to move."

Matt's arms went up as he retreated. "Whoa! Too much information, Chloe."

Leo looked down at me. I had never seen him blush.

"Thanks for the compliment. But, those moves are only for you, and not for anyone else's eyes."

It was my turn to blush.

"Get a room already!" Matt walked away, shaking his head.

I yelled after him. "Oh, come on, Matt! You and I both know this is normal!"

He waved me off as he disappeared through the door.

"Maybe he didn't get lucky with Hannah," Drake said.

I jerked my head in his direction. "What is that supposed to mean?"

Drake shrugged. "I don't know. He hasn't said anything about it."

"Maybe he is just being a gentleman. Besides, Hannah didn't have any complaints when I spoke to her."

Leo pulled me to the door. "Come on. We need to get upstairs."

Loud bass music thumped through the speakers at a steady rhythm. Lights flashed red and white over the dance floor. People were already gathered around the bar and hurrying to get a table before it became too crowded.

"I'll be right back." Leo kissed my cheek and went to the entrance where Kyle was standing.

I looked over at the cage that I was going to be in. I remembered when I once told Riley and Cyrus that I would never work here. Technically, I wasn't. I danced only for Leo. And, maybe for myself. Just to let off steam. If I entertained the customers, then great. But, that was all they were going to get from me.

A hand slipped around my waist and pulled me against a hard body. Erik's scent swirled around me. I tried to push him away, but he held me tight. His breath brushed lightly against my ear.

"You're stunning tonight, Chloe. What do you say we blow this joint and go back to my place?"

I took hold of Erik's index finger and pulled it back at the same time I turned around. "What part of 'leave me alone' do you not get?"

"I just want to be alone with you, Chloe. I want to talk and work things out."

A hand appeared on Erik's shoulder and pushed him aside. Drake stood there. "I suggest you listen to Chloe or suffer the consequences."

Erik turned to face Drake. "Suffer the consequences from who? You, Leo, or Kyle?" He took a step toward Drake and stopped inches from his face. "I'm not afraid of them or you."

Drake smirked. "You should be. Chloe has a massive amount of protectors. Just save yourself the embarrassment."

Drake patted Erik on the arm and looked back at me with a grin. His eyes held a sapphire glow.

I knew we'd talked about where our relationship was not going. But, his eyes held a different story. I couldn't help but think he still wanted to be with me, just like Erik. I hadn't known that, like Erik, he couldn't let go. He did have a big heart, and I was now sure that both Sasha and I were sharing it. Thing is, I'd hoped that by now, Sasha was the only one occupying that space.

Drake approached his cage, stepped inside, and pulled his shirt off over his head. Women immediately started to gravitate to him. They reached as far into the cage as their arms would allow, trying to touch him.

Erik had sauntered off to the VIP section. He kept his gaze on me and smiled.

I flipped him off and climbed inside my cage. Many different feelings were building up inside of me. Anger. Anxiety. Sadness. I let myself go and danced as hard as I could. Thrusting and swerving my hips. Flailing my arms in every direction. I didn't focus on anything except the music.

A large surge of energy hit me so hard it forced me against the cage and held me there. The heatwave came from Drake's direction.

His back faced me. He moved his hips in circular motions first to the left and then to the right. He jumped up and grabbed the bars of the cage. Slowly, he pulled himself up, and then lowered himself. The muscles in his arms flexed each time he pulled up. He let go and landed on his right knee with his hand on the floor. He was in a predator stance. He stood in slow motion and turned to face me. With his head down, he rolled his eyes up. It made me catch my breath. They were like two ice blue crystals staring back at me. His chest heaved with each panting breath.

I had never seen this type of show from Drake, but it was the sexiest thing I'd ever seen. I swallowed the lump in my throat as my heart beat faster. The longer I stared at him, the harder it was to look away. His inner being had me pinned.

My animal stood on her hind legs—stretching as she did. Sweat coated my hot skin. Drake has never been able to call to my animal. Maybe it was because of Leo that my animal was more aware now.

My vision blurred, and I fell to my knees as pain tore through my joints. The music disappeared. In its place was the drumming of my heart. It consumed my head, and I couldn't focus on anything. I had no control. The bones in my fingers popped as they grew longer. My nails dug into the floor.

"No! No, this can't...ahh...be hap...pening...again!"

I hunched over, and a set of arms grabbed my waist to yank me out of the cage, breaking the connection. Then, all went black.

CHAPTER 18 Chloe

My body jolted when the cold water hit my face. Drake and Leo stood over me. I jumped up so fast that I stumbled back into a brick wall.

"Chloe, are you okay?" Leo asked.

I pushed Drake in the chest. "*What the hell, Drake?* What was that? What did you do to me?"

"Chloe, calm down. I'm sorry. I didn't know that would happen!"

"How the hell did you call my animal?"

He shook his head. "I...I don't know."

Leo looked at Drake. A crease formed between his brows and he let out a growl. "*You what?*"

"Look, it's like I said. I had no idea."

Leo pushed Drake back and kept advancing on him. "You almost had her shift in front of everyone!"

"I know! I said I was sorry!"

Leo paced in circles. "*How?* How is it possible?"

"It's not the first time I've felt his animal, but it was the first time I responded." I was able to stand on my own two feet now but still leaned against the wall for support.

"Maybe Chloe has two mates," Riley said from the door. "It took you, Leo, to awaken her. But, somehow, it recognizes

Drake."

"That is absurd!" Leo pointed his finger at Riley. "Don't ever say that again. I marked her. She is mine. No one else's. *Got it?*"

"I understand that, Leo, but—"

Leo spun around to face Drake so fast that Drake stumbled back. "No! This thing you have for Chloe ends now! Don't ever try that shit again or I swear I'll defend my right as her alpha!"

Drake held up his hands. "Yes, I get it, Leo."

"Do you? 'Cause it seems to me you keep trying your damnedest to get close to her."

"Leo, if I were you, I would be more worried about Erik."

"What do you mean?"

"He tried to get Chloe to leave with him." Drake shoved past Leo, hitting his shoulder against Leo's as he headed back inside.

Leo's eyes narrowed as looked at me. "Is that true?"

"Yes. Right before I got in the cage, but Drake stopped him."

"Hmm, playing knight in shining armor, I see."

"Guys, I might have a theory," Riley said.

Leo and I both turned to face Riley.

"Since Chloe isn't full-blooded lycan, our rules don't apply to her. So what if you marked her, Leo? That doesn't make her yours. I think whoever gets Chloe to shift will be her true mate."

Leo and I stared at each other for a moment.

"She has a point," I said.

"I hope what you're saying isn't true. I love her and I don't want to lose her. Now, if you will excuse me, I'm going to go find Erik and put a stop to this once and for all." Leo hurried back inside.

"Chloe?" Riley's fingers grazed my arm.

I looked at her, confused and terrified. My knees gave out, and I slid down the wall.

"Does this change things? I know how you felt about Drake before Leo."

"Absolutely not! My heart belongs to Leo and no one else. I will always care about Drake and love him as a friend. Nothing else. He needs to focus on Sasha." I stood up, dusted myself off, and went back inside to search for Leo. He was nowhere to be found.

I went to the bar and had Taylor make me a drink. I told her I didn't care what she gave me just as long as it was strong.

I sat there sipping my drink when a woman slipped up beside me. She asked Taylor if she knew where she could find Leo.

"I'm not sure where he is. Sorry." Taylor smiled and walked away.

I looked over at the woman. She was my height, with long blond curls and bright green eyes. She wore a tight, blue dress that showed off her huge breasts. I knew right away who she was, and I didn't like it one bit that she was here.

I gulped the last of my drink and hurried in search of Leo. He had disappeared into the back of the club. I rushed over to him before blondie saw him.

"Did you find Erik?" I wrapped my arms around him.

"No. He's not here. I looked everywhere. That asshole better not—"

I put my finger over his lips. Standing on tiptoe, I leaned up to kiss him. "Forget him. Forget work. Let's go home."

"Chloe, I can't. This is my job."

"I'm sure my dad won't mind."

Leo laughed. "Just because your father owns the place doesn't give me the choice to come and go as I please. I need a paycheck. Why don't you go rest in my room?"

"Because I don't want to be here right now. I—"

"Leo!" a woman's voice called out.

He glanced over my shoulder, and I saw his eye twitch.

"You've got to be kidding." He seized my hand. Turning around, we headed to the back.

"Leo! Wait!"

She caught up and got right in front of us. "It's me, Allison."

"What are you doing here?"

"I wanted to see you since I'm only here for a few days. You look really good."

"Well, you saw me. Now, if you will excuse me."

Allison stepped in front of Leo. "Please, Leo. Don't be like this."

"Be like what? You start texting me after five years. You show up at my place of work wearing the dress from our first date. In case you haven't noticed, I'm taken."

"You remember this dress?"

"What are your intentions here, Allison? 'Cause I'm not interested." Leo pulled me against him. "It's not only disrespectful to me but to my fiancé, as well."

I took in a sharp breath as I glanced up at Leo. He caught me off guard with that comment. But, was it just for show, or did he mean it?

Allison ignored the fact that I was standing right there. "I just wanted to see you and have a few drinks. That is all."

"Really? 'Cause you haven't acknowledged Chloe since this conversation."

She turned toward me and smiled. "Hi! I'm Allison—Leo's

ex-girlfriend."

Leo didn't give me a chance to respond.

"Look, I'm not going to do this here. There is no need for us to hang out or even to speak to each other. You left me, remember?"

"I've lived with that painful decision every day. It's one of the reasons I'm here. I want to say that I'm sorry for everything."

"Do you even know what you're apologizing for?"

"Well, yes. I made a mistake, Leo."

"And, which mistake would that be? Leaving me or hooking up with your best friend and getting knocked up?"

Allison's posture stiffened and she held her breath.

"Yeah, you didn't think I knew about that, did you? Well, guess what? He called and told me the day after it happened."

"Leo, no! I never..."

Leo pointed at her. "Your lie ends here. I never wanted to believe him, but when you got back from your trip, you acted differently. And, a few months later, when you broke up with me, it wasn't just for a job opportunity. You didn't want me to find out you were pregnant. You knew I would want a paternity test, so you ran."

Allison's eyes widened.

"Aren't you a bit curious as to how I found out? I flew to California to surprise you and try to work things out. But, I was the one surprised when I saw your belly. Tell me, Allison. Did you ever tell him you were pregnant?"

Allison nodded, and a tear trickled down her cheek.

Leo shook his head. "We are done here. Don't ever come back here, and don't ever contact me again."

Leo grabbed my hand and pulled me out the back door and

to the car.

"Leo, slow down! Leo, stop!" I pulled my hand away.

He paced back and forth behind the car. "Fuck!"

The rage in his eyes scared me. I gave him his space and sat on the curb, waiting for him to calm down. No wonder he didn't want to talk about her. She hurt him in more ways than one.

Leo placed his hands on the hood of the car and took several deep breaths. "I'm sorry about all this. Is that why you were in a hurry to leave?"

"Yes. She asked Taylor where to find you. That's when I saw you."

Leo sighed and turned around. "Again, I'm so sorry, Chloe."

I stood up and placed my hands on his waist. "Don't be sorry. You didn't know this was going to happen. We all end up running into our exes at some point in our lives."

A slight smile crept across his face. He took my hands and kissed each palm. "Let's go home."

"What about your job?"

"I'll let Stephen know what happened."

"Are you okay to drive?"

"Yes. I just need to get out of here."

I slid into the passenger's seat, and he closed the door.

When Leo got in, he sat there for a moment, staring straight ahead. Seconds passed in silence until he spoke.

Leo scooted his seat back. "Come here. I need to hold you."

I climbed over the console and sat facing Leo. I buried my face in his neck. His arms tightened around me.

"I'm sorry she hurt you, Leo. Did you not tell anyone?"

I felt him shake his head.

It pained me to know he'd carried that burden for years. I'm sure it had messed him up. No wonder he hadn't dated after that.

"I love you, Chloe," he mumbled into my hair.

"I love you too, Leo. I would never hurt you like that."

"I know. I'm not worried that you would." He lifted his head and kissed me.

It was a slow and soft kiss. His tongue lightly brushed mine. He pulled his head back and looked down. He licked his lips and squeezed my ass.

I knew what he was thinking. I laughed and got back in the other seat. "Let's go home, Romeo."

* * *

Leo and I lay in bed until the wee hours of the morning, watching old black and white movies on TCM. It was nice holding each other. The only thing missing was Peanut. I had gotten used to her little yelps as she slept. I was sure she was snuggled against my aunt instead of in her pet bed.

Leo's phone went off, and he glanced at the caller ID. "That's weird. Matt's calling. Hello."

There was a brief silence.

"You didn't. Chloe and I are watching movies. What's up?"

Leo quickly sat up. "When was this?"

I laid my hand on his arm and whispered, "What is it?"

Leo held up a finger and flung himself out of bed. "Are you kidding me? Tell me this is a joke."

He started pacing about the room with his hand on the back of his neck. "Okay. Well, we will wait and see what Devin has to report. Call me later with an update."

"Ugh!" Leo ran his hands through his hair after he hung up.

"Chloe, we don't need this shit."

"What's going on?"

"Matt and Devin were on the rooftop, hanging out, and they saw Sasha two blocks over getting into a cab. Matt told Devin about our issue. He is following her now."

"I wouldn't worry. It could be nothing."

"Matt says she never leaves the club without Drake—ever. And, she was looking around to make sure no one saw her."

Leo climbed back into bed and turned off the television. "I knew something seemed off about her."

I stroked the side of Leo's face and kissed him softly on the lips. "Can I ask you something off subject?"

Leo snuggled against me and closed his eyes. "Mmm-hmm."

"Why did you tell Allison I was your fiancé?"

"Because in a way, you are. That is what a marking is."

"What is a wedding ceremony like?"

He didn't answer.

"Leo?"

I laid there for a while listening to his shallow breathing and heartbeat. It soothed me. I knew Leo was trying to protect me from everyone, but I prayed that this thing with Sasha wasn't what it seemed. I would hate to think I'd confided in her and accepted her as my friend only to learn she'd betrayed our trust. I was just glad I never mentioned Josephine to Sasha.

CHAPTER 19 Chloe

I heard a loud puff of air coming every few seconds from the floor. I sat up and crawled to the end of the bed. Leo was doing his push-ups.

"You're up early." I sat there and watched him.

Without missing a beat he said, "I couldn't sleep."

He finished his reps and grabbed the towel next to him. "This whole Sasha thing is bugging me."

"No word from Matt yet?"

Leo shook his head as he stood up, twisted the top off a water bottle, and took a drink.

I watched his throat move with every swallow.

"Leo, there is nothing you do that isn't sexy."

He let out a chuckle. "Funny. I think the same of you."

He leaned down and kissed me. "Something on your mind, Miss Pierson?"

I pulled Leo down on top of me. "You tell me since you can read me so well."

My tongue darted out to lick his moist lips.

Leo kissed along my neck to my earlobe and nibbled.

He pulled my shirt up over my eyes so I couldn't see, sucked my nipple into his mouth, and pulled. He released the suction and made a popping sound as he did.

"Oh, Leo. I need you. Please."

"I know you do." Leo gave me a quick peck on the lips and pushed himself off me.

"What are you doing?" I leaned up on my elbows.

"I need to get a shower. My appointment to get the rest of my tattoo done is scheduled in a couple of hours. Are you going with me?"

"I don't know. What am I going to do the whole time I'm there?"

Leo shrugged and tugged his shorts down. His cock was swollen and at attention.

"Looks like you need something." I opened my legs and trailed my hand down my thigh until I reached my center.

"You're killing me, Chloe." He spun around on his heel and hurried into the bathroom.

"Asshole!" I got up to dress and then went down to the kitchen to make a bagel with cream cheese.

I made a cup of coffee and sat at the counter to eat. My phone beeped with a text message. It was from Aunt Helen. She had sent photos of Peanut. It brought tears to my eyes, but I was glad to see how happy they were.

As I was scrolling through the pictures, I got a call from an unknown number. I normally don't answer unknown calls, but I did this one. "Hello?"

"Chloe, it's me, Sasha. Do you have a moment?"

"Of course. What's wrong? You sound upset."

"I don't want to talk over the phone. Are you by chance coming to the club tonight? If not, I can come over."

"Leo and I will be there soon. He has an appointment first, though."

"Okay. Let me know when you guys get here. This is rather

important."

"Yeah, sure. See you later."

I hung up, confused. It made me wonder if this had anything to do with her sneaking out of the club last night.

I had just finished my bagel when Leo poked his head into the kitchen.

"Hey, sexy. Let's get going."

I poured coffee into a travel mug and followed Leo to the car.

As soon as I shut the door, he peeled out of the driveway. "So, are you going to wait at the tattoo shop with me or is there something else you'd rather do?"

"I guess I'll hang out. I have my phone to keep me company."

"Or you could get another tattoo or piercing." Leo wiggled his eyebrows.

"I don't think so. By the way, Sasha called me. She needs to speak to us. She sounded upset."

"Hmm. I'm sure she has every reason to be."

"If this has to do with where she went last night, let's not think about it right now. We don't know the details."

Leo's phone pinged with a message.

"Can you get that, babe?"

I picked up the phone and read the message. "It's from Matt. He said he has news."

"Tell him we will be there later."

I sent the message and placed the phone back in the holder on the dash.

"Where do you think Erik went last night?" I asked.

"I don't know. Maybe he went home when he realized he was in deep shit."

"Erik isn't one to run from a fight though, Leo. He told

216

Drake he wasn't afraid of you."

"Are you concerned about that asshole?"

"No. I'm just saying." I laid my hand on his thigh.

Leo rubbed my cheek with his hand. "I just want to protect you. You're my life, Chloe."

"I know. And you're mine."

After three hours of sitting in a tattoo shop, we finally got to the club. A huge bus with blacked-out windows was parked in the parking lot. Another was near the building. The word "Haze" was painted on the side of the massive vehicles.

"This is the band that's playing here tonight," I said.

The back door was propped open and the road crew was unloading the truck and hauling equipment inside.

We entered the main area where the road crew was milling around the stage. They were setting up the lights and putting the drums together—which also had the band's name on it.

Matt waved and jumped off the stage. "Hey, guys. It's going to be a full house tonight. We have a sold-out show. Stephen said no one can get in unless they have a ticket."

"Have you heard their music?" I asked.

"Yeah. They're pretty good. Let's head up to the office."

We followed Matt upstairs and glanced around the office. Sasha, Drake, and Devin were already there.

Sasha let go of Drake's hand when she saw us come in. "Thanks for meeting me."

"Wait, what's going on?" Matt asked.

"Sasha has something to say," I said.

Matt stepped aside with his hand out. "Oh, not a problem. The floor is yours."

Sasha closed her eyes and took a deep breath. Then she looked at me. "You might not like what I have to say, but...I lied to you."

She turned to address the rest of the room. "I lied to all of you. I was sent here to find out what happened to a girl named Josephine. But, when I met Drake, I didn't care about the mission or want any part of it because I..." She looked down, and then up at Drake. "I fell in love with you. I kept telling the sorceress there wasn't anything to report, but last night, she wanted to meet with me. She threatened Drake's life if I didn't find out the information she needs. But, it isn't just Drake's life. It's all of us."

Drake grabbed Sasha by the shoulders and shook her. "How could you do this? How could you not tell us! I gave my heart to you, Sasha, and this is how you repay me? By putting me at risk?"

I sprinted over to them and tried to pull Sasha out of Drake's grasp. "Drake! Stop!"

He pushed her away and went to the bar for a drink.

Sasha took one step in his direction. "I'm sorry. I thought she'd leave when I told her there was nothing to be found."

I lightly touched Sasha's arm to get her attention. "Did I hear you right when you said 'sorceress?'"

"Yes, that's correct. Look, Chloe, I'm on your side. When you told me why you needed protection, I put two and two together. It didn't change anything for me. I never told a soul. I can't sit back and let innocent people die."

I thought back to the conversation I'd had with Uncle Bob and the details of his new case. Was this why all the missing people had vanished? Did the sorceress have something to do with it? I needed more information.

"Sasha, for the past two weeks, people have been disappearing. Do you know if the sorceress has anything to do with that?"

Sasha took a deep breath. "If she's been here that long, then yes. When she hunts, she takes the victims to a secluded location. After she consumes their blood, her protectors eat the flesh."

I grabbed my stomach as I leaned on a chair. "Oh, my God."

"How do we kill her?" Kyle asked.

Sasha shook her head. "I don't know exactly. But, she's not the only one you need to watch out for. Some of her protectors are not your normal lycans. They are feral, ravenous creatures. They're hard to kill."

"Are you serious?" Kyle came around the couch. "I've heard of them, but I thought it was just tales."

"I assure you, Kyle, they are real."

"Thank you for the information," I said.

"You're welcome. Whatever you decide to do, be careful." Sasha glanced at the bar where Drake was, but he ignored her as he gulped his beer. Her shoulders slumped as she left.

"What did you see last night, Devin?" I asked.

"The cab dropped Sasha off just across the river. She walked a few miles to the old Indian burial grounds to meet with someone. And, now we know who. There were at least three normal-looking lycans there, as well."

"Did you get close enough to hear what they were saying?"

"No. If I had, they would've sensed me. After the meeting, Sasha headed back here."

"How long was this meeting?"

"About twenty minutes, give or take. But, I noticed the sorceress was wearing an amulet of some sort, and she was holding what looked like a spell book."

Leo patted Devin on the shoulder. "Thanks for the information."

Devin nodded. "You're welcome. If there is anything else you need, please don't hesitate to ask. And, thanks for trusting me and telling me what's going on."

Leo pointed at the door. He spoke between clenched teeth. "I told you Sasha was bad news." He rested his elbows on the bar top and held his head.

"She came clean, Leo. She's trying to make this right."

"Of course she is, Chloe! She got caught!" Drake gulped the last of his drink and slammed the bottle on the counter.

"She didn't get caught, Drake."

"Come on, Chloe! Do you think she would've said anything had the sorceress accepted Sasha's answer and left?"

"No, but..."

"She betrayed my trust. *All* of our trust. She could've said something sooner."

"Someone should keep an eye on her." Leo straightened and turned around to lean on the bar.

Drake growled. "I will. Hell, I'll use her the way she did me. I'm sorry for all of this, Chloe. I really am."

He stormed out of the office.

I slinked my arms around Leo and laid my head on his chest.

"What is our plan?" Kyle asked.

"We need to get that amulet and spell book," Leo said. "Tomorrow we go to the caves and attack her before she can attack us."

I pushed away from Leo. "Absolutely not! That's too dangerous!"

"Chloe, we don't have a choice. We're sitting ducks if we don't. She won't expect us to show. Devin said there were only three lycans. Between Matt, Kyle, and me, we can take them down. This is our chance."

"Hell, count me in." Matt raised his hand. "Let's kill this bitch."

"Sounds good," Kyle said.

Everyone left. It was just me and Leo.

"I don't know about this Leo."

"We'll be okay. I promise." He tilted my chin up and kissed me softly. "I'm going to get ready for work."

After Leo left, I called my uncle to give him the information I'd just learned about the possible victims. I was pretty sure they were connected in some way. Unfortunately, I had to leave a voicemail. He was probably out on the golf course.

I walked down to the main floor and saw the stage set was almost completed. The instruments were in their place, but lights, cords, and speakers still had to be done.

"Chloe! Is that you?"

Smiling, a guy jogged over to me. He looked familiar. I finally recognized him when he got closer. We were acquaintances through my cousin Mark. They were on the football team together in high school.

"Trevor?"

"Yeah, it's me. How are you?"

"I'm good." I pointed to the stage. "You with the band?"

He looked over his shoulder, then back to me. "Yep. I've been with them for about two years. I do the sound and lights for the show."

"How did you get that gig?"

This was a question I shouldn't ask, I thought. But, knowing the band members were vampires, Trevor must know of their existence. I had to find out how much he knew. I had to be careful about what I said around him.

221

"The guy they used to have left the group. I was at one of their concerts and heard them talking about how they were going to find someone to fill in. I offered my services."

"And that's it?"

"Yep, pretty much. So, you work here?"

I shoved my hands in my pockets and shrugged. "Uh, well, sort of. My dad owns the club."

I realized I'd just made a mistake by blurting that out. I hoped Trevor didn't catch it, but he did.

"Didn't your dad...you know?"

"Yeah. He wasn't my biological father. I actually found out about that recently."

"Oh. Is that a good or a bad thing?"

"It's a good thing. It took me a while to process the information, but...ya know."

"How did you find out? Did your mom tell you?"

I looked down for a brief moment. "No. She passed away last year. My dad was the one who told me."

"Jeez, Chloe. I'm sorry to hear that. You doing okay?" His hand rested on my upper arm.

"Yeah. I miss her, but it's getting easier to cope with my family to get me through. I gained a stepbrother out of it."

"Oh, wow! That's cool."

"Hey, Trevor! Come on, man!" someone called out from the rafters.

"Guess I should get back to work. We'll talk later."

I nodded. "Sure."

I went to the bar where Riley was stocking the shelves. "Need some help?"

"Sure. You could help me empty these boxes."

I began putting bottles of liquor on the shelves.

"So, who was the handsome guy you were talking to?"

"His name is Trevor. We went to school together. Actually, he was two years ahead of me."

"Oh. Small world. He works with the band, huh?"

"Yep."

"So, he knows what they are?"

I shrugged. "It would be hard to work for them and not know."

"Not necessarily. If they are careful enough, he wouldn't have a clue." Riley put the last bottle on the shelf and broke the box down. "You worried about tomorrow?"

"Of course I am."

Riley opened two boxes and pulled out jars of olives and cherries. "With the information they've been given, I'm sure they will be fine. If Sasha neglected to tell us about the lycans..." She shook her head. "I don't want to think about the outcome."

"Me, either."

Riley broke down the last of the boxes. "I never got the chance to ask about your visit with your great-grandmother. How was it?"

"I'm not ready to talk about that yet."

"Okay, well, I'm here for you."

"I know." I touched my necklace and let the small vibrations comfort me. Sometimes, I didn't even notice the sensation. I had gotten used to it.

After the shelves were fully stocked, I helped Riley carry the boxes out to the dumpster. Then, I went down to Leo's room to lie down. I only meant to rest my eyes for a few minutes, but those minutes turned into a couple of hours.

I stretched my arms and legs and changed into my outfit

for the evening. When finished, I stopped at Drake's door and knocked. I wanted to see how he was doing.

He opened the door in his leather pants and no shirt.

"What do you want, Chloe?"

"I just wanted to check on you."

"You shouldn't be here. Especially after what happened between us last night."

"I'll be fine as long as you don't let it out." I grinned.

Drake chuckled and stepped into the hall. "It's better if we're not alone." He pulled his shirt over his head and shut the door.

"I trust you."

"You shouldn't."

He was silent for a moment. "Walk with me."

I followed Drake upstairs and out to the alley.

"I didn't want to say this in front of Leo, but I couldn't stop myself last night, Chloe. I usually use my animal when I perform. It gives off a sexual vibe that all the ladies respond to. I didn't know it was going to affect you. If Leo hadn't pulled you out of the cage..." He shook his head. "I'm sorry that happened. I just wished I understood why."

I didn't want to lie to Drake and pretend I didn't know why. But, I also couldn't tell him about Riley's theory. It would make things worse, and I didn't want to give him hope. I knew Drake wouldn't intentionally try anything out of spite. That was Erik's go-to move. Not Drake's.

I leaned against the brick wall by the dumpster. "Have you seen Erik since last night?"

"No, and it's not like him. He usually likes to hang around to make a point."

"Do you think something happened to him? If Josephine's

maker is back...what if she got to him? What if he's in trouble?"

"He deserves whatever he has coming to him. You actually care about him?"

"I do care, Drake. I'm still pissed at him, but that doesn't mean I want him dead or anything."

Drake reached up and placed his palm on my cheek. "One of the things that attracts me to you, Chloe, is your heart. You're such a caring person."

"I have my mother to thank for that."

He let his hand fall to his side and stepped away. "I should go find Sasha. You staying around for the concert?"

"Yeah. I'm going to help Devin until it starts."

Drake nodded and disappeared through the door.

The sound of the band warming up echoed into the street. I went inside to watch. The doors of the club were opening in an hour. Tonight, there was going to be no cage dancing. My dad wanted the customers to focus on the band.

I watched them warm up for a few minutes, and then I looked up at the sound booth.

Trevor smiled and waved at me. I did the same.

"Hey, Chloe," Devin called from the entrance. "What's up?"

"Nothing. Just checking things out before we open."

"It's going to be a full house. We've got two lines forming. One is already around the block."

"Why two?"

"One is the VIP line. We're letting them in early."

"I told my dad I'd help you out. It will get people in faster."

"That would be great."

A set of hands covered my eyes from behind. "Guess who?"

"Um, Chris Hemsworth?"

"Very funny, Chloe." Leo picked me up and held me against

the wall. His lips crashed into mine.

I moaned into his mouth. My hips pushed against Leo's erection. "Hard for me already?"

"I'm always hard for you, Chloe." He let my feet touch the floor.

"Let me see your tattoo again."

Leo pulled up his sleeve and pulled back the covering to reveal a beautiful dragon wrapped around the dagger.

"That's beautiful. The guy did a great job."

"Yep. So, what are you up to?"

"I'm getting ready to help Devin. And you?"

"I'm going to get with the guys and see where I'm going to be tonight. I love you." Leo gave me a peck on the cheek and took off.

"You two are quite the pair." Devin tugged on a strand of my hair. "Come on. We've got work to do."

After we got the line down enough for Devin to handle things himself, I went inside to watch the show. I saw Sasha sitting in the upper section by herself. I had mixed feelings about her. I was furious with her, but I also knew she'd been put into a difficult position and that she'd had no choice in the matter.

I headed over to her and sat next to her. "You okay?"

Sasha wiped her eyes. "I'm so sorry, Chloe. Really, I am."

"I'm glad you told us, Sasha. Thank you."

"Drake hates me." Sasha covered her face with her hands. In between sobs, she said, "I screwed up."

I handed her a few napkins. "You betrayed his trust, Sasha. It's going to take some time for him to trust you again. You need to make things right."

I scoped the crowd below, looking for Drake. He was dressed in a security shirt and standing next to the stage. He turned in my direction and looked directly at me and Sasha.

She didn't notice him staring.

"Excuse me. I'm going to go to the restroom." Sasha got up and hurried away.

I looked back at Drake. He turned away and disappeared behind the stage.

I sighed and sat back in the chair. I hoped that Drake and Sasha realized how much they needed each other and worked things out before it was too late.

CHAPTER 20 Chloe

I didn't want to watch the concert by myself. I went to the bar to grab a drink for me and a beer for Trevor. I knocked on the door to the sound booth and poked my head in.

Trevor turned around and smiled. "Hey, Chloe. Come on in."

"I thought you might need a drink." I handed him the beer.

"Thanks. Have a seat. You want to watch the show from up here?"

"Really?"

"Yeah. You can see how things work. Plus, you get a good view."

"True." I took a sip and sat in the chair next to him.

Trevor took a swig of his drink and turned his chair to face me. "So, tell me about this brother of yours. How'd he take the news of suddenly having a sister?"

I smiled. "He knew way before I did. It's a long story."

I stood up and looked out the window. "See the two guys on the left side of the stage?"

Trevor took another drink. "Uh-huh."

"The shorter of the two is Kyle. He's my brother. The tall one next to him is Leo. He's my boyfriend."

"Ah, lucky man."

I turned my head, smiling. My face was a few inches from Trevor's. I quickly backed away and sat down.

Trevor leaned in and stared at me. "Your eyes are more vibrant than they were in school. Those aren't contacts, are they?"

I laughed and remembered asking that very same question when I first came here. "Nope."

Trevor smiled. "Are you one of them?"

"One of what?"

He whispered, "Vampire."

"No, I'm not."

"Look, I know they exist, Chloe. You don't have to deny it."

"I'm not denying anything, Trevor. I'm not a vampire."

"Then why are you so beautiful? I mean, you look the same as you did in high school, but your features are more enhanced."

I smiled and looked away. "You thought I was beautiful in high school?"

"Yes, but Mark threatened to kill me if I ever asked you out."

"Thank you for the compliment. So, how did you find out that vampires existed?" I finished my drink in one gulp.

"I walked in on one of their orgies after a concert one night. I'm talking sex and blood. It was like I was walking onto a movie set. I couldn't believe what I was seeing. I just stood there, taking it all in. Roman, the lead singer, saw me. I hurried out of the room and left to get some fresh air. When I got back to my hotel room, Roman was waiting for me. We had a long conversation, and the rest is history."

"So, you didn't freak out?"

"No. I mean, at first, I thought they were playing around, but Roman explained that it was all real. I just went with it.

They're an awesome group of guys."

"Have you ever participated in their orgies?"

Trevor smiled. "Of course."

"Are you one of them, Trevor? Did Roman turn you?"

Trevor shook his head. "No. I'm one hundred percent human, Chloe. You have nothing to worry about."

Trevor finished his beer. "Well, time to start the show. And, this conversation isn't over, young lady."

For the next two hours, I sat back, watched Trevor work his magic, and enjoyed the concert. My dad was right. They were good.

I saw Hannah and Matt off to the side of the stage. They were jumping around to the music. I didn't know Hannah was going to be here. Otherwise, I would've hung out with them. Maybe after the break, I'd head down.

The first half of the set ended and Roman started making an announcement. Trevor and I walked down to the bar to get another drink.

"Come with me. I want to introduce you to Kyle and Leo."

With drinks in hand, we inched our way to the stage. Leo smiled when he saw me.

"Hey, gorgeous. Enjoying the show?"

"I am." I stood on tiptoe to kiss him. "Leo, this is Trevor. We went to school together."

Leo and Trevor shook hands.

"More like I was her cousin's best friend."

Leo nodded. "Good to meet you."

I patted Kyle's arm. "This is my brother, Kyle."

The two shook hands.

"Nice to meet you both." Trevor put his hand on my lower back. "I need to get back and prepare for the last set. Talk to you all later."

Leo's eyes narrowed as Trevor walked away. "What the hell is that all about?"

"What?"

"Him touching you."

"Leo, calm down. It was nothing. I'm going to hang out with Hannah. I'll meet you after the concert."

I walked away in search of Hannah. It was too crowded to spot her. I finished off my drink and set the empty glass on the counter. Riley and Taylor were hard at work. Even though I stood amid a massive crowd, I felt alone. I was trying to have a good time, but I didn't have anyone to share it with.

"You bored?" Drake leaned against the counter with a smile.

"Not really."

"You want some company?"

"That would be nice, but I think you should find Sasha and talk to her, Drake. She's hurting."

"And I'm not? I had plans for us. I wanted to..." Drake growled and turned away. "Never mind. I need some air."

"Drake, wait!" I tried to follow him, but I lost him in the crowd. When I got to the back alley, he was nowhere to be found. I went up to the roof to see if he was there, but, to my surprise, I found Roman instead.

A girl was sitting on the ledge with her legs wrapped around him. His hips thrust with such speed it was like a movie in fast forward. His head was buried in her neck.

I accidentally bumped into a trashcan, and Roman turned his head in my direction. He smiled and licked his lips.

"I'm so sorry," I said.

Roman stepped away from the girl and zipped up his pants. "Don't be."

In a matter of seconds, he was in front of me. His finger trailed my jawline. "Such a beautiful creature. Are you claimed by anyone?"

I swallowed the lump in my throat. "Yes. I am."

"Hmm. Pity. I was looking forward to tasting you, too. The more the merrier. Guess I'll have to make due until the after-party. See you later."

Roman held his hand out to the girl behind him and they walked away.

I stood there for a moment, blinking. What the hell just happened? That was really weird.

On the way back, I stopped at the office to see my dad. He was at the bar, pouring a drink.

"Hey, sweetheart. How are things going down there?"

"Fine. Shouldn't Cyrus be here to help you? This is a lot for you to handle."

Stephen smiled, poured another glass, and handed one to me. "He has other matters to attend to. Have a seat. Let's talk."

I sat down and took a sip. The drink was strong, and it made me cough. "Wow! That's too much."

Stephen laughed and took the drink from me. "How have things been? There's so much to catch up on."

I took a moment to bring my dad up to speed with what had happened with Elsie and the story of how I'd found my necklace.

He took the crystal between his fingers and rolled it around.

"It's an interesting piece. So, there's something swirling inside and it has a vibration?"

"Yes. Only I can see and feel it."

"What does that mean?"

"I'm just as clueless as everyone else."

The music began playing from downstairs. I glanced at the door.

"Go have fun, Chloe. We'll talk more later."

I hugged him and headed to the VIP section to watch the rest of the show. Half of the time I zoned out as I thought about other things. I didn't even hear the music.

My phone buzzed with a message from Uncle Bob.

If what you're saying is true, what am I supposed to do? This is out of my territory. Does Cyrus know? Can he help like last time?

I sighed and text back.

I doubt Cyrus knows. He's been MIA lately. Besides, Leo and a few others have a plan for tomorrow afternoon. I'll be in touch. Love you.

What the hell are you planning? Jesus, Chloe. You're going to be the death of me. Just be safe. Whatever it is. Love you, too.

I put the phone back in my pocket and watched the show for the next two hours. By 2:00 a.m., the club was closed to the public. Those who remained were the Rising Flame crew and the band. My dad had gone home at midnight.

We all gathered down in the playroom and waited for the real party to begin. Music thumped over the speakers while strippers began their dances on the poles. Clothes came off and a massive orgy took place.

Roman had the same girl from earlier sprawled out on the bed and chained. Four of his band members crawled on the bed toward her. Two of them clamped down on her wrists with their mouths. The other two teased and sucked on her nipples while Roman crouched between her legs.

I heard her cry of pleasure above all of the noise in the room. Some of the lycans paired off while others lay in a huge pile

233

on the floor.

I stood in awe at the situation and the raw sex that lingered in the air cause a pool of wetness in my panties.

Drake was nowhere to be found, and Sasha was in a corner by herself.

"This is so wild!" Hannah squealed. "I'm glad you let me in here."

I shook my head and plopped down on the couch next to Leo. "You shouldn't be here, Hannah. It could get dangerous."

"She's in good hands, Chloe. Don't worry." Matt pulled her into his lap.

Hannah ground her hips against him while she tongued his mouth. She sat back and pulled her top off. With no bra on, her breasts bounced freely.

Matt took one of her nipples into his mouth. He grasped her ass as he stood and carried her to the back.

Riley was all over Kyle. I looked over just in time to see her pull his cock out of his pants.

I gasped and quickly averted my eyes.

Leo laughed. "Get used to this, babe. This is how it is down here."

"Yes, I know. I've been through it before. Sort of."

"With Erik?"

"I never had sex with anyone in here but you. My first time here was when Erik brought me. Things went bad because of Josephine."

"Ah, I see. Well..." Leo put his drink down and straddled me. "Time to have our fun and make better memories."

Leo grabbed the center of his shirt and ripped it off. He gyrated his hips and began unbuttoning his pants.

My mouth hung open as Leo did a striptease. I was about to

help him out of his pants when the heavy wooden doors were flung open, the force ripping them from the hinges. My body jolted at the sudden noise.

Leo turned around at the commotion.

Out of nowhere, oversized figures darted in from the hall and attacked random individuals. They sank their teeth into their flesh and pulled away with mouths full of blood.

I screamed as I pushed myself up against the back of the couch. I fell backward and onto the floor.

Leo jumped over the couch and landed next to me. "You need to hide. Now!"

Vampires lunged forward, confronting the intruders. They hissed and bared their fangs as they tried to rip into the invaders' flesh.

The lycans shifted and attempted to pull the feral wolves off. Leo was the only one who didn't because he knew it would trigger my wolf. And, right now, I couldn't deal with that.

"Holy shit!" Trevor slid up beside me. "What the hell is going on?"

"We're under attack. Trevor, you need to hide. You're human and...oh, my God, Hannah!"

I jumped up and saw her running into the back hall.

"Trevor, run to that hallway. Find my friend Hannah. Stay with her and don't come out until this is over."

"Chloe, no! Don't!"

"I have to. I'm not human like you. Now, go!" I pushed him away and jumped over the couch.

Leo yelled for me. "Chloe, what are you doing? No!"

"I have to help fight, Leo! I can't hide what I am any longer!"

The room was in chaos. I couldn't keep track of where my friends were. Then I saw Sasha jump on one of the feral wolves

235

and slash its throat with a knife. Its flesh sizzled and smoke appeared from the wound. It slumped to the floor, motionless.

I climbed up onto the stage to get a better view. I had to slow these monsters down. I let all of my anger build up inside. My palms tingled with balls of white light. I raised my hands and released the energy across the room. The creatures stumbled backward. It gave the others just enough time to attack the best they could.

The entire room echoed with high-pitched screams. Out of all of them, I heard one familiar voice. I jerked my head to the left. One of the creatures had his teeth around Riley's neck as it held her against him.

"No!" Rage overtook my senses. I lunged at the wolf that had my friend captive. I raised my hand and released another white ball of light right between his eyes.

The wolf dropped Riley. Her limp body fell to the floor. The wolf came at me with his mouth open, baring his sharp, bloodstained teeth. I slid to the floor and kicked his legs out from under him. He fell with a thud. I wasted no time jumping on top of him. I brought my fist up and rammed it deep into his chest. I pulled out his heart, gripping the muscle in my hand. Blood oozed between my fingers.

I sat there for a moment, staring at the mess, my chest heaving with each breath. I had never done anything like this and it shocked me. I shook my hand violently to rid it of the contents. The damaged muscle plopped to the floor.

After the drumming in my head stopped, all was quiet. The killing had stopped, and the only thing I could think about was Riley. I hurried over to her. She kept gasping for air. Blood coated her mouth and the sides of her face as she coughed.

Tears spilled down my cheeks as I took her hand. "Riley.

No."

Kyle fell to his knees and took her head into his lap. "Don't do this to me! Fight, baby!"

A voice from across the room yelled for someone to go get Dr. Clements.

I felt Leo at my back. He whispered, "Chloe, your hands."

I noticed they were glowing just as brightly as my necklace. A woman's voice spoke to me and told me to use my power for the greater good and heal her. I didn't see anyone around who could've said that so clearly. I didn't know where it came from and it terrified me. But, a soothing vibration from the necklace took over. I knew what it was telling me to do.

I took a deep breath and placed my hands over Riley's neck. The warmth of the light inside me flowed like embers through a crevice. I release all that energy into Riley.

"Holy shit," Kyle and others mumbled.

Leo placed his hand on the small of my back and whispered, "Chloe, what are you doing?"

Not everyone knew I was something other than a lycan. My great-grandmother was right. In certain situations, one couldn't help but use one's powers.

I knew if word got to the wrong people, I'd be so screwed. But, I didn't care. This was one of my friend's life on the line, and I was not about to let her die.

Riley's eyes flew open and she took in a sharp breath.

Kyle held her and kissed her several times on the head. "You're okay, baby. You're going to be okay."

I felt weak, but I still had a little energy left. I looked around the room, and I saw that all eyes were on me.

"How the fuck did you do that?" Roman stumbled forward. "What are you?"

237

Riley tried to smile. Her tone was weak when she spoke. "She's something special."

I bent down and hugged her, crying into her shoulder.

Leo patted me on the shoulder and then pulled me back a little. "Give her some room, Chloe."

I let her go, and Leo helped me to my feet.

"Did we get them all?" I asked.

"Yeah, I believe so. We lost a few people, though. I'm not sure who until we see who is missing."

"How the hell did they even get in?" Kyle asked.

"Good question." Leo looked over at Sasha. She was helping others who had started to clean.

"She couldn't have done this, Leo. She was..." I stopped and thought back to when she ran off crying before the concert. I hadn't noticed if she came back. If she had let them in, where had they been hiding? And, why wait to attack?

"What is it, Chloe? What were you about to say?"

"Just that she was in here with all of us."

"I still don't trust her."

"Does someone want to fill us in on what Chloe did?" a voice in the crowd said.

I glanced at Leo and knew that because of my actions with Josephine, I had brought danger to them. They would probably no longer accept me. They might even kill me. I thought I would be able to keep what I was a secret.

If I had been able to transform into a wolf, I wouldn't have had an issue.

"They have a right to know, Leo." I squeezed his hand. "It's for the best."

He clutched my hand and nodded. He acknowledged all who waited for an explanation. "I will fill all of you in shortly."

Leo led me away from everyone. "I'll contact Cyrus and Stephen to let them know what happened. The game is on now, Chloe. Later today, we get our revenge."

"Maybe we should wait a day. After all this, we need to compose ourselves and not rush into anything. We need a clear head."

"Who's 'we?'"

"You, me—"

"Hell no! You're not coming with us, Chloe. No way."

"But, you could use me. If someone gets hurt, I can help."

"You're also the target."

"It looks like we all are, Leo."

"Chloe?" Hannah's face was streaked black from her mascara. She clung to Trevor. Her body shook with fear.

I hugged her tight and stroked her hair.

"I'm sorry, Chloe. You were right. I shouldn't have been here."

"Unfortunate circumstances, Hannah."

"I don't want to be alone. Can I stay with you at your house?"

"I'm not sure how long I'm going to be. Besides, I think it's best we stay here. I'm not sure what is waiting at home for me. You can stay in my old room."

"Thank you."

Matt carried Hannah out of the room. She buried her head in his neck to avoid looking at the slaughtered bodies on the floor.

I hugged Trevor and thanked him for watching over Hannah.

"Of course. It's the least I could do."

I pulled away, and he took my hand. "Hannah told me what you are. I think that's cool."

I managed a smile and walked away. I stepped over and

239

around mangled bodies the best I could. One person looked familiar. I bent down to get a closer look.

"Oh, my God! Taylor!"

Leo knelt next to me, and I fell into him, crying. He rested his chin on my head and cradled me.

"Come on, baby. Let's get you out of here."

I held on to him as we walked out of the room. I turned to look over my shoulder, but Leo put his hand up to block my view.

"Don't look back, baby."

Leo and I stopped in to check on Hannah. She was taking a shower, and Matt was sitting in a chair, waiting for her. He was bent over with his arms on his knees, his head in his hands.

Matt looked up when we came in. He locked eyes with Leo and then stood slowly. "What's wrong?"

"It's Taylor. She didn't make it."

"Oh, damn." Matt ran his hands through his hair. "This is going to mess Drake up."

I knew Drake and Taylor did things sexually to release their frustration. I wasn't sure how far back their arrangement went, but Drake said there was nothing between them on an emotional level. But, the way Drake wore his heart on his sleeve led me to believe he liked her more than he was willing to admit.

I think his hopes of getting back with me had gotten in the way of him committing to Taylor. Who knows, maybe it was just a "friends with benefits" relationship. But, whatever it was, we were just starting to become friends. I never really got the chance to know her. I would miss her.

Matt walked to Leo and patted his shoulder. "We should get back."

Leo nodded and turned to me. "Do you know about Drake and Taylor?"

"I know enough."

Leo rubbed my chin with his thumb. "He hasn't had any luck with the girls."

"I know. After what Sasha did, he's really going to hurt once he hears about Taylor."

"Yeah, but we'll all be here for him." He kissed me and left the room.

After Hannah finished her shower, I gave her some of my clothes to put on. Then, it was my turn. By the time I had finished, Hannah was already asleep. I kept the table lamp on and left to go to Leo's room.

I lay there for hours, staring at the ceiling and wall. I couldn't sleep. Every time I shut my eyes, I saw blood splattering the floors and walls and the feral wolves killing those I loved. One of them was Leo.

I sent a message to my uncle to let him know what had happened. This was getting bad. If those things had attacked during the concert, the secret of what we were would've been exposed all over the news.

There was a light tap on the door before it opened. A sliver of light from the hall illuminated the room.

"Chloe?"

I sat up and turned on the table lamp. "Cyrus?"

"Sorry to wake you. May I come in?"

"Yeah, sure. I wasn't asleep. What time is it?"

He slipped inside and shut the door. "It's 6 a.m. I came as soon as Leo called about the attack. How are you holding up?"

"I'm not okay, Cyrus. We lost people. Some I didn't know, but still. It is a great loss to this club. And, it's all because of me."

"Don't do that, Chloe. None of this is your fault."

"If I hadn't killed Josephine, this wouldn't have happened."

"If you had *not* killed her, it would've been you." He sat on the bed next to me. "I care a great deal about you, Chloe. You've done so much for this club. Kyle said you saved Riley's life. He told me what happened. How?"

Unable to talk about it, I choked up.

Cyrus scooted closer to me and, for the first time, held me. "Let me see what happened."

I nodded and pulled away.

He placed his hands on my temples and closed his eyes. His eyes twitched as visions invaded his mind. He then opened them.

"Oh, Chloe. How did you know how to do that?"

"I heard a voice, and it was plain as day. Like someone was standing right next to me. It told me what to do. I know I shouldn't have exposed myself like that. I know I took a big risk, but..."

Cyrus reached for my hand. "Chloe, calm down. Look, Stephen and I sat down with everyone and explained your situation and story. A majority of them were awed, and some were a little terrified. But, in the end, every single vampire and lycan supports you. None of them liked Josephine. They remembered how you stood up to her. I gave them all a choice to stay or go if they wanted. No one chose to leave, Chloe. This is their home as much as it is yours. You don't need to fear them. We're all family here."

Cyrus's words soothed my heavy heart. Here I'd feared the worst. But, everyone was willing to stick by me.

Cyrus wiped a tear that lingered on my cheek. "I'm so sorry

I wasn't here. I'm sorry I've been absent from your life these past few weeks. It's just that I've had requests from my elders that I had to fulfill. It took priority over anything else."

"I have been upset lately that you've not been around. I thought you were avoiding me or something. But, I understand. I just wish you would've talked to me."

"Chloe, you know there are certain things I cannot discuss."

"I know, but I meant it about the things that were going on with me. I know in the past you let me figure things out on my own 'cause I'm such a great detective."

I got Cyrus to smile.

"But, I depended on you. Since I've found my mother's necklace, I'm not sure what it even does or if it does anything at all. I know it glowed brighter when I healed Riley."

Cyrus nodded. "Again, I'm sorry for not being able to give you much about your ancestors. This goes beyond my time and outside my territory. Mystics hail from different parts of the world, different realms, and different eras. I would take Elsie's word in whatever she told you."

"But, Elsie didn't have a clue as to what this necklace contains. Isn't there a mystic antique dealer or something?"

"There is, but they won't be of much help, Chloe. Take whatever information you've gained and use it as best you can."

"Are you giving up?"

"I have no choice, Chloe. I'm getting dead ends for a reason. I was lucky to have found Elsie. Try and get some rest."

"Thank you, Cyrus." I leaned up and kissed his cheek.

He placed his palm on my cheek and smiled. "You're an amazing woman, Chloe. Everything will fall into place. Just like last time. Just be patient."

"Yeah, but last time you knew what was going on. Please tell me this isn't the same situation. Because if it is, I couldn't forgive you this time."

"I assure you, Chloe. This time, I'm at a loss."

As he was leaving, Leo came in and headed straight for the bathroom. I heard the shower turn on. Twenty minutes later, Leo came out and climbed into bed.

He pulled me against him and mumbled with his eyes closed. "I love you, and I'm exhausted."

I kissed him on the lips and burrowed under his arm. I hoped he was able to get enough rest for what was about to happen later in the day. Leo was going to need all of his strength if he planned on going to the caves.

I just prayed that we were not outnumbered. I wished there was a way to get a count of how many feral wolves we were dealing with now that we'd killed quite a few. Guess we wouldn't know until we get in there to observe the situation. I didn't care what Leo said. I was going with them. This was my fight. I wanted to be a part of it. I wasn't a coward. I wouldn't hide.

CHAPTER 21 Leo

I was careful not to wake Chloe as I rolled out of bed and dressed. I had several reasons. One, she is even more beautiful when she sleeps. Two, she looked peaceful. The horrible events that took place hours ago had kept her up. She'd had trouble sleeping. She would toss and turn and mumble. Now, it seemed like she was getting the rest she needed. And, three, there was no way in hell I was letting her go with me today. I'd be too busy worrying about her to concentrate on anything else.

I tied my shoes and pulled my drawing tablet out of the drawer. I yanked a piece of paper from the back and wrote her a note.

My dearest Chloe,

Don't be pissed at me, but I just couldn't let you go with us today. It's for your own protection. What kind of alpha would I be if I put you in harm's way? I might as well just hand you over to the sorceress myself. We know that isn't going to happen. Please, just stay put until I get back. Spend some time with Riley and Hannah. You could use each other's company. Have I told you how proud of you I am? The way you handled the situation last night was brave.

Ich liebe dich (means I love you...in case you forgot).

Love, your alpha, Leo

I placed the note on my pillow and slipped out of the room. I knocked on Chloe's old bedroom door to see if Hannah was there. Riley opened the door.

"Leo, come in."

I glanced around, and I didn't see Hannah. I asked where she was.

"Bathroom. So, what brings you here?"

"I just wanted to see how you both were feeling."

"I'm good. If it wasn't for Chloe, I wouldn't be here. How did she do it?"

"I haven't talked to her about it yet. It's horrible—the people we lost. And Taylor..."

"Yeah, I ran into Drake earlier and told him what happened. He's taken it pretty hard. I don't think he will be going with you guys today."

"I gathered that." I looked over my shoulder and shut the door. "Look, Chloe is determined to go with us today. I'm so against it."

"Me, too. I take it you want me to babysit?"

I laughed. "If you don't mind. I left her a note. I'm sure she would rather spend the day with you than trying to get herself killed."

"I would hope so."

"Well, I'm going to get the guys and get out of here. Do you know where they are?"

"Kitchen. Be careful. Bring my man back in one piece."

"Mine, too," Hannah said as she came out of the bathroom. "Riley told me what was going on today."

"How are you, Hannah?"

"I'm coping. Chloe tried to warn me that dating a lycan could be dangerous. I never thought how much that was true until last night."

"That is for totally different reasons, though. Anyway, I'll see ya later."

I headed to the kitchen area. Kyle and Matt were eating Cocoa Puffs. I grabbed a bowl and spoon and joined them at the table.

"Have you guys seen Drake?" I poured the cereal into the bowl.

"No," Kyle said with his mouth stuffed full.

"Negative." Matt took his bowl and spoon to the sink. He washed and dried them before putting them away.

I shoved cereal into my mouth, one spoonful after another. I was in a hurry to get out of here.

"Is Chloe up?" Kyle asked.

"No, she's still sleeping, which is why we need to get going. She's going to try and go with us."

I slurped the milk from the bowl and put it in the dishwasher. Yeah, I could've taken the time to wash it by hand as Matt had, but we were wasting time.

"Well, guys, it's time. Whose car are we taking?" I checked my phone to see if there were any messages from Stephen or Cyrus.

"We'll take mine," Matt said.

We all headed to the parking lot.

"After last night, I hope there aren't many wolves to fight. If we are outnumbered, we are so screwed." Matt fastened his seatbelt and started the car.

"Leo, I've been meaning to ask. How the hell did Chloe heal Riley?" Kyle asked.

"I don't know." I laid my head against the seat and closed my eyes. I thought about how much my life had changed in just a week. I should've said goodbye to Chloe personally instead of leaving her a stupid note. I'd taken the cowardly way out so there wouldn't be any confrontation. That was the wrong thing to do. What the hell was I thinking?

"How far is this place?" My phone buzzed in my pocket, and I checked to see who it was. It wasn't anything important.

"About thirty minutes from here." Matt turned onto the interstate. "I was so worried about Hannah last night. I'm just glad Chloe's friend Trevor was with her. I'd hate for her to have been alone."

"What I'd like to know is how those assholes got in. I still have suspicions about Sasha." I rubbed my temples.

Matt shook his head. "I don't think so, Leo."

"Why? Because she helped kill them? It could all be an act."

"Leo, let's just focus on one thing at a time," Kyle said. "Besides, I'm with Matt on this. I don't think it was her, either."

Matt pulled off the interstate and onto a highway. Three miles down, he turned right on a dirt road and parked in the brush so the car was surrounded by trees. There was a fenced-off area with a huge sign wired on the side. NO TRESPASSING.

Matt walked a little way down the fence.

Kyle went in the opposite direction and disappeared into the thick foliage. "Matt, Leo! Over here!"

There was an entryway covered by vines, shrubs, and tree roots.

We entered with caution. I took the lead with Kyle and Matt behind. At first, it was warm inside the tunnel. But, the farther we went, the cooler and darker it became. Our canine vision helped us navigate through the dark, tight spaces that we had to duck and crawl through.

We reached an area that contained water. I didn't want to go through it, but there was no choice.

"We should have brought a change of clothes," Matt said.

"Yeah, I wasn't expecting this." I inched my way into the water. It was ice cold.

We approached a fork in the tunnel and took the wider tunnel. I hoped we'd be able to find our way out of this maze.

"This is insane," Kyle whispered.

"What I'd like to know is where her protectors are," Matt replied. "You'd think they'd be guarding the entrance."

I stopped and turned around. "Why would they be standing guard? They have no clue that we know their location?"

We ducked under a low boulder and were submerged up to our chins in water.

"Just so you know, I'm refusing to go underwater," Kyle said.

"Maybe we are going the wrong way," Matt suggested.

"No, I think this is right. Now, if it were too easy, then I would say yes," I said.

We finally entered a clearing surrounded by rock. At first, I thought it was a dead end, but then Kyle tapped me on the shoulder and pointed to the ceiling.

"We're going to have to climb."

"Great," I huffed.

As I waded over to the far wall, the waterline slowly decreased until it came to our knees. I stared up at the vertical rock. There was too much condensation for me to get a good grip. I searched along the walls, looking for a better way up.

I put my left foot on a tiny rock, reached with my right hand,

and found a small crevice in the wall. I held my breath as I put my weight on my left leg. I paused for a moment and let out a puff of air. I took another deep breath and raised my right leg. My foot hit a rock that wasn't visible, but I could feel it.

"Guys follow my lead. So far this seems to be working."

I worked my way to the top and grabbed the ledge to hoist myself up. There was a hole in the wall, and I peeked through. "There's a small tunnel up here."

I sat there and helped Kyle and Matt onto the ledge. "We are going to have to crawl in there."

"Are you serious? This is nuts. I don't think this is the right cave, much less the way in." Matt said.

"We've come this far. We have to keep going."

I made my way through the narrow and winding tunnel until I came to another hole. This one led up. We sat there a moment before moving forward.

I was about to climb into the hole when a scraping and shuffling sound echoed down the tunnel above us. My body tense, and we sat in silence. The sound grew louder.

"It's getting closer," I whispered.

"Shit, shit, shit," Matt mumbled.

With nowhere to go, we scrambled back the way we'd come. I rounded a tight curve so fast I head-butted one of the rocks on the wall. Before I could let out a cuss word, Matt threw his hand over my mouth and whispered for me to be quiet.

The scratching noise stopped for a brief moment, and then it started back up. This time it was moving away.

"Let's go back and see what that was," Kyle said.

"What? No way!" I crawled after him.

Kyle was already down the tunnel and near the hole. He poked his head up.

"What is it? Do you see anything?" Matt asked.

Kyle ducked back down. "Shit. There's some weird animal up there pacing back and forth. Looks like a lizard or something."

"What the hell do we do? Try a different way?" Matt said.

I shook my head. "No. I think this is the right path."

"This isn't one of her protectors. This could be some weird creature living here and we invaded its territory. This might have only been a meeting place and not where the sorceress is hiding out. You actually think she would stay in a place like this?" Matt said.

Kyle hesitated for a brief moment. "Only one way to find out. Now, I either take it up there or lure it down here to us."

"What if there are more of these things?"

"Guess we shall see." Kyle patted Matt on the shoulder.

"Let me go first." I crawled past Matt and Kyle.

Kyle grabbed my arm. "No. Chloe would kill me if anything happened to you."

"As alpha, I'm leading this mission, and I'm going in first."

I turned around and started up and through the hole. "Here goes nothing," I muttered.

I pushed myself up to the next level and quickly, but quietly, made my way down the tunnel. It opened up a little more and gave me room to move. Halfway along, I heard a hiss like a snake. Then, a pair of yellow eyes appeared a few feet away from me.

I stopped dead cold, barely breathing. But, I stood my ground as the creature approached.

Its snake-like eyes glared at me and its tongue flickered in and out of its mouth. Its long claws clicked and scraped along the rock floor, sending chills down my back. Its scales were dark green with red specks.

I was within reach of the creature. I grabbed the head, and in a swift motion, twisted it to the side. The bone snapped in half and the creature's body went limp.

"Well, that was quick and easy."

I made the mistake of turning my back as I called for Matt and Kyle. Sharp claws dug into my shoulders, and a thousand tiny pin-like teeth sank into my arm.

"Ah! Son of a bitch!"

When Kyle and Matt appeared, three more lizards were already upon us.

Kyle reached around me and broke the lizard's neck. At the same time, the other two attacked Kyle. One dug its claws into his back. The other bit into his side.

"Oh, shit!"

Matt and I each grabbed one and tried to pry them off, but their teeth and claws were snugly caught in Kyle's skin

In between the struggles and screams through gritted teeth, Kyle managed to say, "Pocket...knife...right...side."

Matt reached into Kyle's pocket and pulled out the knife. He sliced the lizard's throat and stabbed the other one in the head. We expected blood to spurt from their wounds. Instead, some type of green ooze drenched Matt and Kyle. Somehow, I got lucky and didn't get any on me.

"How disgusting!" Kyle wiped the goo from his eyes.

"You two okay?" Matt handed Kyle his knife back. "You look like you got it bad."

"Yeah, I'm just peachy. Let's keep moving," Kyle said.

"Let me lead for a while. It will give you two a little time to heal." Matt led the rest of the way down the twisting tunnel.

Unfortunately, we hit a dead end.

"What the hell?" Matt felt along the wall in search of some kind of entrance but didn't find one.

He sat back on his heels. "Let's go back and check along the sides of the walls. Maybe we missed something. Another hole could be hidden somehow."

We turned around and checked the sides of the wall until Kyle found the hole. It was well camouflaged among the other rocks. We crawled through and found the tunnel sloping downward. A red-orange light flickered up ahead.

We made our way into another small clearing and peeked over the ledge. Torches lit the room. Two lycans were just milling around, another two were deep in conversation along the far wall near another opening, and one sat on a rock, reading.

"We are outnumbered. I was afraid of this," Matt said.

I peeked over the ledge to observe the situation. We all sat back against the wall and took a deep breath. I whispered, "They don't look like feral wolves."

"Maybe they are only feral at certain times like when they need to eat or something," Matt said.

"I hope that's not the case." I scratched my head. "All right, here's the plan. The ledge goes all the way around, so we can split up and jump down on them. Kyle, you take the one reading. Matt and I will try and take on the rest."

We made our way around the wall, careful not to knock loose rocks down, and took up position over our targets. I raised my hand and counted to three before leaping down to our enemies.

As Kyle jumped down, he rammed his knife into the lycan's neck and quickly withdrew it. The lycan fell to the ground as smoke rose from his sizzling flesh. Kyle stabbed him in the heart to finish him off.

I grabbed my target's neck on the way down and twisted it. Then, I picked up a rock next to him and smashed his head in, over and over again. The lycan didn't have a chance, and I wouldn't let him have one.

Matt—on the other hand—was having issues with his targets. One held Matt's arms behind his back while the other punched him in the stomach. Matt reared back, kicked his legs out, and hit the lycan in the jaw. He flew back and hit the ground. Then, Matt bent forward and flung the one behind him over his shoulders. He kicked the lycan in the temple before grabbing his head and twisting it.

Kyle yelled to Matt and tossed his knife to him after he was done. Matt sliced the lycan's throat and stabbed him several times in the heart. Before he could get to the last one, the lycan grabbed Matt and threw him across the room. The knife skidded across the floor and toward a small crack.

Kyle and I both dove for the knife and crashed into each other, but it was too late. The knife disappeared into the hole.

"Try and get it if you can. I'm going to go help Matt." I grabbed another rock as I jumped off the ground.

The lycan was on top of Matt with his hands around his throat. Matt gasped for breath. With one hand, the lycan punched Matt in the face repeatedly until I bashed the back of his head in. The lycan fell over as blood seeped onto the ground.

Matt lay on his back, coughing for air.

"You okay, dude?" I held out my hand to help him up.

He nodded and gave me a thumbs up.

We walked over to Kyle, who'd found a small sliver of rock. He stuck it down in the hole and tried to pry the knife out.

"Here. I see the tip of it. Can you grab it?"

I reached down and wedged my pinky against the knife. Together, we pulled it out of the hole. We rolled onto our backs, taking deep breaths.

"That wasn't so bad now, was it?" I said.

"Piece of cake," Matt replied.

"And here I thought fighting those embalmers a few weeks ago was fun." Kyle laughed.

I sat up and stared at the dead wolves. "I'm glad they didn't go feral on our asses. We would've been in deep shit."

"We were damn lucky, that's for sure." Matt patted my shoulder as he and Kyle got up.

I managed to make it to my feet and then nodded at the opening where two of the guards had been. "Well, I guess we head down that tunnel."

We came to a sealed-off room covered by stacks of rocks. One by one, we removed them.

Once the last one was gone, I peeked in and found a room full of bones. "What the hell?"

Kyle and Matt stuck their heads in.

"Shit. Are those human?" Matt asked.

"Maybe some animal bones, too." Kyle stepped inside the room. "Sasha wasn't kidding when she said they were here long enough to do this. I wonder if Chloe's uncle said anything to her about a new case involving missing people. Did she say anything to you, Leo?"

I shook my head as I stepped around the massive pile of skeletons "Nope. Let's spread out and see if there is a book here."

I glanced around and found a set of steps made of stone. I walked up the steps and a few loose rocks slipped out from under my feet. When I made it to the top, a woman in a black hooded cloak trimmed in red lay there with her hands over her chest. Her eyes closed.

The amulet lay across her chest. It was in the shape of a figure eight—the eternity symbol—with an arrow through it that pointed up and down. In the center of the top circle was a ruby.

I stared at her for the longest time. It was like she was pulling me into her web while she slept. I had the feeling of a thousand bugs crawling over me. Of course, I checked to make sure that wasn't the case. But, there was an issue.

"Guys, you need to come up here. We have a problem."

"What is it?" Kyle came up on my left side and Matt moved to my right.

Matt pointed to the woman. "That's not the woman who showed up at the club."

Kyle backed up and ran his hand through his hair. "What the hell is going on? Who the fuck is this? Are we being played here?"

I sighed and sat on one of the boulders. "When Chloe and I went to see Elsie, she told us that Chloe's family originated in the Egyptian era. I'm pretty sure that other woman is related to Chloe."

"Are you serious? Why didn't the woman say something?"

"I'm not sure. From what we learned, Chloe's mystical family has been hiding for thousands of years from some evil force. Their city was attacked and a majority of the mystics were murdered."

"Holy shit! This is too much. Do you think she's involved?" Kyle pointed to the woman.

"I don't know. But, there is one thing that concerns me. Chloe has a birthmark in the shape of the infinity symbol on her shoulder."

"Leo, I believe the pieces are starting to come together." Matt patted my shoulder.

"Yeah, and I'm afraid to see the big picture. Is there even a book of spells?"

"We should look just in case." Matt carefully looked around where the mystery woman was lying and then shook his head. "There's nothing here."

With the way the woman was positioned and what she was lying on, it seemed possible that something could be hidden underneath her.

"The book could be under her. We have to move her," I said.

"No freaking way! I'm not touching her!" Kyle backed away with his hands up.

"She won't wake up, Kyle. She's dead. Besides, we are touching the stone she's lying on and not her physically."

"Forget the book. Why don't we just kill her and be done with this whole damn mess? It's why we're here in the first place." I stepped up and felt the vibrations pulsating from the woman. I quickly stopped and tilted my head.

"What is it?" Kyle asked.

"I feel vibrations. Don't you?"

"Yeah, a little."

"Chloe feels the same thing with her necklace."

"Well, then we can't get that close. That stupid amulet is her protection." Kyle reached down and barely touched the necklace when a bright red spark hit him. He flew across the room.

"Kyle! You okay, man?" Matt and I asked together.

"Yeah." Kyle groaned as he got to his knees. "Let's not speak of that to anyone." He dusted himself off. "Let's just get this over with."

Kyle stood at the foot of the sorceress. I took the head. The heavy vibrations began and soon turned into stinging sensations that grew stronger the closer we got.

"We have to do this fast. On three. One...two...three."

Kyle and I hurried to pick up the stone she lay upon. Our palms started to sting, and then the smell of burning flesh hit our nose. Quickly, we set her down to the side and looked at our hands.

"Jesus, that fucking hurts," I said.

"No shit."

We sat down and took a moment to heal while Matt examined the inner part of the stone. "I don't believe this! There's no book here. What's the point in coming here if we can't even get near her to kill her?"

"Yeah, what do we do now, Leo?" Kyle asked.

"Let's just put her back and get the hell out of here." Matt took off his shirt and placed it over his hands.

Kyle and I did the same. This time, the stinging wasn't so bad.

Once the woman was back in place, we all stood there, staring at her.

"Should we hide the wolves' bodies? I would hate for her to wake up and see them dead." Kyle looked back to where they lay.

"And put them where? I say leave 'em. She sent us a message, so we'll leave her with one. Now, let's just get out of here and figure out our next move." I looked around the cave for a different way out. There was a slope leading up to another tunnel.

"Up there." I pointed. "Let's check it out because I'm sure

as hell not going back the way we came."

"Me, either," Kyle said.

We headed up the narrow path and down a tunnel. So far, we hadn't stumbled upon any other catacombs. The incline started to get steep as we continued until we entered a part where it was more open.

"There's light up ahead. We must be close to an entrance."

I took a step into the open space and stopped when movement in the shadows caught my attention. I jumped back into the tunnel that we had come from and held up my hand for Matt and Kyle to keep quiet.

Raspy breathing echoed through the cave, followed by slurping and the tearing of something squishy.

"What the hell is it?" Kyle whispered.

"Don't know. It's in the gap of the wall." I peeked around the rock and focused my eyes on where the sound was coming from. Something flew out of the dark and landed in the middle of the floor where the only light from the outside illuminated it.

I jerked my head back and leaned against the wall. "Holy shit! It just tossed a bone onto the floor."

"Do you think it's a feral wolf?" Kyle asked.

"I hope not."

"Do you think there is only one?"

"I think so. I don't hear any others. I'll go out and distract whatever this thing is. You come up from behind and slice its damn throat."

Kyle nodded. "You got it."

I took a deep breath. I didn't know what kind of creature I was about to face. As soon as I stepped into the light, the creature lunged from its hiding place and landed on me. I fell

259

backward onto the floor, trying to hold it off. It was one of the feral wolves. It was stronger than me.

Saliva dripped from its sharp, blood-blackened teeth as it snapped at me. Its putrid breath made me gag.

Kyle quickly ripped open its throat with his knife and caused blood to spray my face. I quickly jerked my head to the side and pushed the limp creature to the side. I rolled over, coughing. "Bloody hell!"

"Sorry, Leo. I guess I should've stabbed its back first. But, then I figured, why should Matt and I be the only ones to get drenched in foul-smelling fluid?" He laughed.

I got to my feet and gave Kyle a shove. "Asshole."

"Hey, at least I saved your life."

"Are you two finished over there? Let's go," Matt said.

We passed through a cave entrance and, in a few steps, we were outside and standing on top of a hill.

"Are you kidding me? This whole time we could've gone in this way," I said.

"But then we would've missed all the fun." Kyle grinned.

I slapped him upside the head. "Shut up, dick."

We all laughed as we found our way back to the car.

There was a burning sensation in my side. I looked down at my tattered shirt and saw blood. I took off the shirt, and, to my surprise, there were three long gashes. "Shit."

"What is it?" Kyle turned around and saw the wound. "Ouch. That looks like it hurts."

"Nah, it tickles. Of course it hurts, numbnuts."

Matt walked around Kyle and moved my arm to the side to get a better look. "Oh, man. That looks bad. Is that from the lizard thing or the wolf?"

"I don't know. Don't tell Chloe." I pressed my shirt against my side to slow the bleeding.

"Dude, we won't have to tell her. She's going to see it. There's no hiding that." Kyle walked to the car and got in the front seat.

"It's a good thing we left our phones in the car or they would be ruined." Matt got in and started the car.

I lay down in the backseat and checked my phone. Chloe had been blowing up my phone with calls and text messages. I knew she would. She was going to kill me when I got back.

"Hey, Riley left a message that they're at the house. She also said Cyrus closed the club for the week. According to his calculations, we lost ten people. Cyrus wants to hold a memorial for them later this week."

Kyle proceeded to give the names of those we'd lost.

We were damn lucky that we made it out alive. And, I'm not just talking about the cave. I'm not one to scare easily. There was nothing in life that I didn't face head on, and, let me tell you, I've seen a lot of messed up shit in my life. But, this took the cake. This was something we were not prepared for. I could've lost Chloe. Hell, she could've lost me. One thing was for sure—under no circumstances was I backing down. I would find a way to kill the sorceress. And then, when I did, I was taking a vacation with Chloe.

CHAPTER 22 Chloe

When I woke up and found Leo's note, I was beyond angry. I needed to be with him. I didn't want to sit on the sidelines and wait while they were in a dangerous situation.

I called several times and left messages, all with no reply. He probably didn't even have the phone on.

After I dressed, I stepped into the hall and listened for any kind of sound. But, there was nothing. I knocked on my old room and Hannah answered.

"Hey, Hannah. You doing okay?"

"Yeah, I was just hanging out in here until you stopped by. I didn't want to wake you. What about you? Are you all right?"

"As good as anyone could be, I suppose. Have you seen Riley?"

"She's down the hall." Hannah grabbed her things. "I need to get going. I'll talk to you soon."

I hugged her goodbye and walked down the corridor. There was a new set of doors to the playroom. I opened one and poked my head in. A few people were cleaning, and a few others were off to the side, sitting in silence.

When I stepped into the room, everyone stopped what they were doing and looked in my direction. I didn't know what to do or say. I just stood there.

A man with a mop came over to me. "Hey, Chloe. I'm Ethan. Sorry, we haven't had a chance to meet properly. I'm one of the security guards."

I remembered Leo mentioning how he got into a fight with Ethan. His wounds had obviously healed. "It's nice to meet you."

"I just want to say...what you did for Riley was unbelievable. I mean...I've never seen anything like it before."

I shrugged. "Me, either."

After a few seconds of silence, we smiled at each other.

I glanced around the room and asked if he'd seen Riley.

"She was here a moment ago. Maybe she's in back."

I thanked him, and as I headed to the back, I paused and looked down to where Taylor's body had been. I couldn't help myself. I slumped to the floor and sobbed.

A pair of arms embraced me from behind. Riley's perfume mixed with the cleaning fumes. I turned to embrace her, and, together, we mourned the loss of a dear friend. We sat there for a while without words.

Riley was the first to respond.

"Chloe, how did you do it?"

"I don't know. I just heard a voice and my hands..." I held them out and stared.

Riley took my hands and squeezed. "It's okay. Maybe some other time. I'm fine, thanks to you. Dr. Clements check me over and gave me a green light."

"I'm glad to hear. You gave me quite a scare."

"Yeah, you're not the only one. Did you find Leo's note?"

"Yes. I'm pissed that he left without me. I should be with him."

"You're safer here."

263

"Am I? After what happened, I don't think anywhere is safe."

Riley jumped up and pulled me off the floor. "Well, I'm glad you're here, and I'm ready to get out of here."

On our way back down the hall, I asked where Sasha was. I suggested we invite her over.

Riley shook her head. "I spoke to her briefly. She wants to be alone right now. Drake is still MIA. No one knows where he is."

"I feel bad for them. I hope they can work it out."

When we stepped out into the alley, I saw Trevor was loading up the truck.

"Hey, Chloe. Are you leaving?"

"Yeah, I need to get home."

"Tell your cousin I said hello."

"I don't ever talk to him. But, if I do, I'll tell him."

Riley and I continued to the car. When I slid into the front seat, my head began to pound. My eyes were growing sensitive to the light and I felt slightly nauseated. I closed my eyes and laid my head back.

On the way home, the rocking of the car caused my nausea to grow, and I thought for certain I was going to vomit.

"Are we almost home? I'm not feeling well."

"Five minutes. What's wrong?"

"Migraine."

We finally pulled into the driveway. I sat there for a moment before getting out of the car. Riley helped me inside and to the bedroom. She went to the bathroom and came back with some medicine, water, and a cool cloth.

"Here, take these."

I popped the pills in my mouth and gulped the water.

Riley placed the cool cloth over my eyes. "Get some rest,

Chloe. Try not to worry about Leo. He'll be fine. They all will."

I heard the click of the door as it shut.

A few minutes later, my phone startled me as it went off. I quickly answered, hoping it was Leo, but it was Uncle Bob.

"Hello, Uncle."

"Hello, niece," He chuckled. "I wanted to give you a call to let you know that I was recently paired up with a detective named Elliot Sawyer."

"Is that a good thing?"

"Yes. A certain someone sent him my way, if you know what I mean."

"Yeah, I get you." I rubbed my temples. It was taking forever for my headache to go away, but the meds were making me sleepy.

"Anyway, thanks for your help, Chloe."

"Any time."

I hung up and rolled over, putting Leo's pillow over my head.

Hours later, I heard the shower running. I jumped up and ran to the bathroom. "Leo?"

The shower curtain moved to the side and he poked his head out. "Hey, babe."

"You're back. Why didn't you wake me?"

"'Cause I was caked with the stench of disgusting goo. We'll talk about what happened when I get out. Meet me downstairs."

I kissed Leo. "I'm glad you're back and safe."

I hurried downstairs. Riley and Kyle were in the dining room, eating sandwiches. I took a seat across from Riley.

"Feeling better?" she asked.

"A little." I rubbed my temples. "Where is Matt?"

"He stayed at the club to get cleaned up. I hitched a ride back with Leo." Kyle tossed the last of his sandwich in his mouth.

"So, what happened today?" I took a potato chip off Kyle's plate.

Kyle shook his head as he rubbed his neck. "It was a messed up situation. There were these giant lizard creatures that we unexpectedly confronted."

Leo came in with a plate of food. "Yeah, it was nothing I've never seen before."

He bent down and kissed me before sitting at the end of the table next to me. "And, we have a problem. The woman we saw in the caves isn't the woman who showed up at the club. And, there was no spell book. At least, we didn't find one."

"Did you kill her?" Riley asked.

Kyle laughed. "We couldn't even get close enough to touch the woman. She's well protected by some magical force."

"So, what is our next move?" I asked.

Leo wiped his mouth with a napkin and shook his head. "I honestly don't know, Chloe. We are out of moves at this point. I hope the woman that showed up at the club is your ancestor."

"Wait, what?" Riley perked up.

"I'll tell ya about it later," Kyle whispered.

I was terrified now. It seemed as if things were just about to become a checkmate, and we were the king with no moves. No one to protect us.

"Chloe, maybe you should take this opportunity to learn some spells. You are a mystic, after all," Riley said.

"Not all mystics can cast spells. They just depend on the powers they inherit."

"But, you're not like any other mystic, Chloe."

Kyle leaned on the table. "Riley has a point. It doesn't hurt to try."

"There is one more thing." Leo got up and exited the room. A few seconds later, he came back with a piece of paper and a pen.

"Chloe, if I'm right about this, the sorceress and the evil spirit that Elsie spoke of are one and the same."

"What makes you say that?"

Leo drew a symbol on the paper and handed it to me. "Because the sorceress is wearing this amulet. It is the same figure eight that is on your shoulder, and I felt vibrations from it."

He reached for my hand. "Babe, I think you should try to find out about this amulet. Maybe we can find a clue as to what we are up against."

"Guess I have some work to do." I took the paper and went to the kitchen. I held onto the counter as I silently let the tears fall.

Leo placed his hands on my waist and rested his chin on my shoulder. "It's going to be okay, Chloe. We'll figure something out."

I turned and slipped my arms around him. He pulled back, wincing.

"What's wrong?"

"Nothing."

"Leo, don't 'nothing' me." I lifted his shirt and saw blood on some gauze. "What the hell happened?"

"I got into it with a feral." He pulled his shirt down and stepped away.

"Let me try to heal you." I grabbed his hand and led him to the bedroom.

Leo sat on the bed and pulled his shirt up just past the gauze.

"Nope. Take it off, mister."

I helped him slide the shirt over his head and then tossed it to the side.

"Lay down."

Leo groaned as he got comfortable.

I started to remove the gauze, but Leo grabbed my hand.

"What are you doing?"

"I need access to the wound if I am to heal it, Leo. Stop being a baby."

I peeled the tape off the sides. Then I tried to pull off the blood-soaked gauze, but it stuck to the wound. I finally freed it and gasped at the sight. The wound was seriously infected. White and green puss foamed around the skin.

"Oh, my God! Leo, this is not good. Did you clean this?"

"Yes, babe. I did."

I placed my hands above the wound and let the heat from my palms seep into him. I did this for several minutes, but there was no change.

"Leo, did you have Dr. Clements look at this when you got back?"

"No. I didn't even go inside. Kyle and I just hopped in the car so we could get home."

"We have to call her, Leo. I can't heal this. It's too far into your bloodstream. It's not like when I healed Riley. Stay here. Don't move."

Leo mumbled something. His eyes fluttered shut.

I called the doctor and gave her a quick rundown of what had happened and what the wound looked like. When I hung up, I slumped to the floor next to the bed and cried. I wanted to hold Peanut in my arms. I missed her and her little puppy kisses. She was the one thing that helped me take my mind off of things.

There was a knock on the door and Riley and Kyle came in. Riley's smile faltered when she saw me crying.

"Chloe, what's wrong?"

"I can't heal him. The wound..." I leaned against her shoulder as the tears continued.

"Should we call Nadia?" Kyle said.

I jerked my head up at Kyle. "I already did. Why didn't you make him see her when you got back?"

"Chloe, this is Leo we're talking about. It's like talking to a brick wall. I did suggest it, but he refused. At the time, it wasn't that bad."

I gradually pulled myself off the floor. "If anything bad happens to him, Kyle, I swear..."

Riley held me back. "Chloe, it's not Kyle's fault. Come on, let's go downstairs."

"No." I pulled out of Riley's hold. "I'm not leaving him."

Riley and Kyle left without an argument.

I placed a clean patch on Leo's wound and lay next to him. I watched his chest move up and down with each shallow breath. I stroked the side of his face. His dark whiskers had grown a little longer.

"I'm here, Leo. I love you."

I placed a kiss on his cheek and rested my head on his shoulder.

These past few days had been hell. I was tired of fighting. I was tired of the worry. I was tired of being afraid of losing Leo. I just wanted this all to end so we could have a normal life. But, even then, was there such a thing?

After a few minutes, I carefully rolled off the bed and went to my desk. I took out a notebook and turned on the laptop. "Let the games begin."

For an hour, I searched website after website about candle colors and their meanings. It all seemed like a contradiction. Certain colors for candles could mean good or bad things, depending on how you used them. Then, I started reading about certain spells. I couldn't make heads or tails on any of it. I jotted down a bunch of information to try to come up with a protection spell of my own. I was overwhelmed. I didn't know what the hell I was doing.

There was a knock on the door. Dr. Nadia Clements came in with Riley and Kyle.

"Hi, Chloe." Nadia smiled. "How's our patient?"

"He's still sleeping." I got up from the desk and went to the bedside.

"Rest is good for him." Nadia set her bag on the bed and opened it. She took out a pair of latex gloves and slipped them over her hands.

"Now, let's take a look." As Nadia pulled the gauze off, Leo began to stir. His eyes fluttered open.

"What the hell?"

Nadia placed her hand on Leo's chest. "Just lay back and let me inspect the wound."

Leo laid his head back and groaned.

Nadia took one look and flinched. "Leo, how long has it been since you were infected by the feral?"

"I'd say it was around...two o'clock, give or take."

"You should have come to see me immediately." Nadia tied off Leo's arm and took out a syringe to collect a blood sample. After that, she gave him a shot of antibiotic, and then washed and redressed the wound.

Nadia cleaned up the mess and handed me a bottle. "Give him one pill every six hours. If his symptoms worsen, get him to me ASAP."

"I will. Thank you."

Riley walked Nadia out, and Kyle stayed behind.

Leo struggled to sit up as he held his side. "Umpf. Son of a... bitch. That hurts."

Kyle grabbed Leo's arm and helped him to his feet. "You okay, man?"

Leo nodded. "Yeah, I'm just peachy."

"You should rest," I said.

Leo cradled my cheek in his palm. "I'm fine. I need to get up for a while. My body is feeling stiff."

Leo glanced over at the computer screen. "Doing your research?"

"I'm trying, but none of it makes sense. There are a few things I need." I wrote down the items on a piece of paper and handed them to Kyle. "Go to this address. It is a Wiccan store. Try to find these books, potions, candles, and incense."

Kyle read down the list. "Are you serious?"

"Yes. Now go." I pushed him out the door. "Time is of the essence. And, take Riley with you."

Leo was sitting on the bed, holding his side, when I turned around. I knelt in front of him and placed my hand on his knee.

"Are you okay, babe?"

"I think so."

"Do you want to lie down and watch a movie?"

"Sure."

I helped Leo back on the bed and grabbed a blanket to drape over us. I flipped through a dozen channels before we decided to watch *Thor*. About fifteen minutes in, Leo was lightly snoring.

I kissed his cheek and turned off the movie before going

downstairs to call my dad. I had to fill him in on what had happened—that is, if Kyle hadn't done so already. He was the only person I could count on right now, and I hoped there was something he could do to help.

I paced the floor and chewed on my bottom lip while the phone rang. He picked up on the third ring.

"Hello, sweetheart. How are you doing?"

I started to tell him I was fine, but I caved and the tears came again. It took me forever to explain the situation between gasping sobs.

"Calm down, Chloe. I know someone who might be able to help. Suzanne has a friend who is into Wicca. I'll give her a call."

"Thank you. I just don't know what I'm going to do if she can't help."

"Don't worry. As for Leo, I'm sure he'll be fine once the antibiotics kick in. I'll see you soon."

I sighed and checked to see if there were any messages from Cyrus. I took a picture of the drawing and sent it to him. I asked if he could find out about it. I knew he'd said all this was beyond him, but he had to know something. Time was running out. I had a bad feeling that evil was out there, watching, at this very moment.

I went through the house to make sure all of the windows were locked. I even closed the curtains. Call me paranoid, but I always trust my gut. Right now, I didn't like what it was telling me. The fact that Leo was out of commission right now worried me. I had no one to protect me.

I texted Drake and Matt to see if they could come over and stay. If anything happened, Kyle wouldn't be able to protect me all on his own. Not if the sorceress had more minions roaming around out there.

I got a reply right away from them both. They were in my driveway.

I looked out the window and saw two sets of headlights being turned off. The driveway was full of cars, and it was going to get even fuller when Kyle and my dad showed up.

I opened the door with a forced smile. "Hey, thanks for being here."

"We figured it would be best since Leo's hurt," Matt said.

"You read my mind," I said.

They followed me inside and Matt dropped his bag by the door.

"The couch in the living room pulls out, and there's a cot downstairs to bring up."

"I'll get it." Matt patted my arm and headed for the basement.

I turned to Drake and noticed the somber look on his face. It was like I didn't recognize him. The spark in his eyes wasn't there. I reached for his hand and squeezed it. "How are you holding up?"

"I'm fine, Chloe. Don't worry about me."

"I'm sorry about Taylor. I know she meant something to you."

"Yeah. I don't really want to talk about this." Drake pulled away and went to the living room.

Matt came in. He was carrying the cot. "Where shall I put it?"

"Wherever you want to sleep. I'll go grab some sheets and pillows."

I went up to the hall closet to grab the linens and two pillows and took them down to the guys.

Matt was setting up the cot behind the couch.

I heard the front door open and click shut. Kyle and Riley entered the room.

"Hey, did you find everything okay?"

"No. When I showed the list to the lady behind the counter, she looked at me weird. She didn't have everything in stock, but she was able to substitute some of the items." Kyle handed me the bag.

"Thanks. My dad knows someone who might be able to help. He's on his way."

"Well, fingers crossed." Kyle jumped on the couch next to Drake and turned on the TV.

"I need some air." Drake got up and walked out, slamming the front door shut.

"What the hell?" Kyle turned around to look over his shoulder.

"I think he's still in a bad mood," Riley said and sat next to Kyle.

I felt Leo's presence enter the room. He was holding his side. "Hey, guys."

Matt flung a blanket on the cot and tossed a pillow down. "How is the wound?"

"Hurts like a mother."

I laid my hand over Leo's. "Aren't the meds working?"

"No. It may take a while. Come out back with me." Leo tilted his head to the door.

I took his hand and followed him out back.

He carefully lowered himself onto the lounge and patted a spot next to him. "Lay with me."

I snuggled next to him and stared up at the sky. The sun had set to a point where the horizon was dark blue. There were no

274

clouds, and the stars were making their twinkling debut.

I reached under Leo's shirt and caressed his belly, careful not to hit his wound. He was so soft and smooth. I slid my leg over his and raised my head to kiss his neck.

"Did you find anything out about the sorceress's necklace?"

"No. I sent it to Cyrus. He's better at research than I am."

"You should still try in case he doesn't make it here with information."

We were lying there in silence when a noise from the woods caught our attention. Drake staggered out of the clearing and then fell.

I jumped off the lounge and ran to him. Drake's pant leg was shredded and coated with blood. "Oh, my God! What the hell happened?"

"I was chasing a deer and fell into a stupid trap."

"Is it broken?"

Matt and Kyle came running out of the house and to us. They each took a side and helped Drake up.

"Shall I call Nadia?" I asked.

"No. "I'll be fine. I just need to get cleaned up."

"You can have my room," Kyle said.

I watched Drake hobble inside the house with Kyle and Matt.

"Is he going to be okay? What happened?" Leo asked.

"He fell into an animal trap."

Leo and I went inside. I sat in the kitchen with my phone and took Leo's advice. I typed the word amulet in the search engine and clicked on images. I scrolled through the first ten pages of what were hundreds.

"You've got to be kidding. There are way too many." I closed and pocketed the phone when the doorbell rang.

Riley had already answered the door.

My dad stepped inside with a smile. I hugged him and looked over his shoulder at a woman waiting on the porch.

"Didn't Suzanne come with you?"

"She couldn't make it." He held his hand out to the brunette. "Chloe, this is Donna."

The woman smiled and nodded. "It's nice to meet you."

"You, too. Please come in."

"Your dad filled me in on our way over. I'll do what I can to help, but spells aren't something you can just learn in one night. It takes time, knowledge, and experience."

"Well, I am part mystic if that helps the situation."

"It may."

"Good. Let me get my things." I hurried into the living room for the bag and then had her follow me upstairs.

CHAPTER 23 Leo

Stephen's smile faltered when I stepped into the room. He started to say something, and I held up my hand before he could. "Before you ask, I'm fine. Can I get you a drink?"

"Brandy, if there is any."

"Sure. Follow me into the kitchen."

I took a glass and the brandy from the cabinet and poured his drink. I stood there with my hands on the counter like a bartender to see if the drink was to his liking.

Stephen took a swig and banged the glass down on the counter. "Now that's what I'm talking about."

I grinned. "That good, huh? You want another?"

He nodded. "Yep. Hit me."

I poured him another glass.

"Are you not going to drink with me?"

"Yeah, that will go well with my pain meds."

Stephen chuckled and picked up the glass. He moved it in circles and watched the liquid swish around. "I've gotta tell ya, Leo. I've never seen Chloe so scared. I know she's trying to be strong, but she's holding back. I'm glad she has support from you and the others."

"She has you, too."

Stephen gulped his drink and held the glass out for another.

"One more then I'm done. I do have to drive."

I poured him another and put the lid back on the bottle. "I have something to ask you."

I set the bottle off to the side. "After this mess is over, I need to head back to London next month for our annual meeting, and I want to take Chloe with me."

Stephen sat back in the chair. "You will bring her back, though, right?"

I shrugged and smiled. "Maybe. There's something I wanted to do while there, and I would like your permission."

Stephen's eyes lit up. "Are you asking me for my blessing?"

"Yes, sir. I want to marry her."

Stephen threw his hands in the air, then slapped them on the counter. "Yes! Of course you have my blessing. I'm thrilled."

"I'd like to surprise her. Please don't say anything."

Stephen moved his fingers across his mouth like he was zipping it shut. "I won't say a thing."

He held up his drink. "Here's to you and Chloe. I wish you both lots of happiness, and for me, lots of grandchildren."

"What? Chloe's pregnant?" Riley squealed as she came into the kitchen.

"No, she's not pregnant." I managed a laugh, but the strain shot a pain through my stomach and back from the wound. I put the brandy back in the cabinet and the glass in the sink.

"Then what was that comment about?" Riley grabbed some drinks from the fridge.

"Don't worry about it. Let's go into the family room."

Riley passed out the drinks and took a seat next to Kyle. They were watching *Van Helsing*.

I leaned against the wall with my arms crossed. It helped me cover up the fact that I was holding my wound. I felt like

I was being split in two. The pain had spread into my lower back and legs. I was determined to take my medication a few hours early. If this didn't get better by tomorrow, I was going to have to see Nadia. Something was wrong, but I didn't want to say anything to worry Chloe. She had enough on her mind.

CHAPTER 24 Chloe

Donna and I went over a few different protection spells. The thing is, I needed to make the spells my own. I wasn't quite sure how to do this. There was no way I was going to be able to pull this off.

I walked Donna downstairs. Everyone was watching a movie. Stephen looked up from his phone at Donna. "You all done?"

"For now. I need to get home." Donna glanced at her watch.

Kyle paused the movie and walked to the front door with Dad and Donna.

I noticed Leo leaning on the wall. "Babe, you should go lie down. You don't look well."

"Yeah, I think I will. I'm going to take my meds."

He held onto the rails as he slowly took the stairs one by one and disappeared into the upstairs hall.

My dad waited for me at the door. I hugged him. "Thank you for bringing Donna over. Tell Suzanne I said hello."

"Will do." He placed his hand on my cheek. "You be careful, you hear me?"

I leaned into his touch with a nod. "I will."

Kyle locked the door behind him, and then he stared at me. "I'm worried about Leo."

"Me, too," I said. "He looks bad. I mean really bad."

"If he and Drake don't heal soon, we are down two lycans."

"Maybe others at the club will take their spot."

"They might."

There was a knock at the door. Kyle and I looked at each other and shrugged. I wasn't expecting anyone to stop by—unless it happened to be Cyrus.

I opened the door, and to my surprise, the woman in the white robe smiled back at me.

My mouth gaped open, and I stumbled backward. "You."

"Hello, Chloe."

"You mind telling me who you are?" Kyle said from behind.

"That is why I am here. May I come in?"

I glanced over my shoulder at Kyle, and he gave a nod. I stepped to the side to let the woman pass.

"Kyle, go get Riley and Matt."

"You don't want Drake or Leo here?"

"No, let them rest."

Kyle hurried into the living room and came back a few seconds later with Riley and Matt. "Okay, tell us why here. And, just so you know, if you make any attempts..."

The woman held up her and smiled. "I mean you no harm. Trust me. I'm the least of your worries."

She took a seat and straightened her robe. "I know you have a lot of questions. Let me begin with who I am. My name is Akila, and I'm one of your ancestors."

A smile spread across my face, and I heard Riley behind me gasp.

Kyle laid his hand on my knee and squeezed it.

"I know this is going to be a lot to process, but what I'm about to tell you is not known in any history book or any Internet search. Which is why Cyrus had a difficult time finding information about your family or that necklace." She tilted her head down at the crystal.

"You spoke with him?"

"I did earlier, yes."

"So, what brings you here after all these years?" Kyle scooted to the edge of the couch.

"Chloe knows. Don't you?"

"You mean about being in isolation for centuries. That story is true?"

"Indeed, it is. I know you visited Elsie. She was only able to tell you some of the story."

I reached for Kyle's hand. "Yeah, so why was the city attacked?"

"One of our own became infatuated with dark magic. Her name was Talibah. She wanted to be immortal and strengthen her powers. She thought her spells were weak. She was banished from our city for practicing dark magic. Late one evening, there was a commotion, and I peeked out the window to see our city in flames. Dark shadow figures slaughtered those who ran."

I slumped back in the seat. "Oh, my God! That's horrible."

The woman stood up and paced back and forth. "I was involved with our mystic healer's son. He burst into my room and told me his mother was dead. He saw the whole thing. We were going to escape together, but evil was closing in. He told me to run to our secret place and wait for him. I watched the city illuminate the night in orange light. I waited all night, and he never came."

I placed my hand over my heart. "I'm so sorry."

"The next day, I scavenged the city for any survivors. Thick smoke and the smell of burnt flesh lingered in the air. The last home I checked was Sanura's—our healer. I found her on the floor with her throat ripped out. Her necklace lay next to her. I took it and searched the rest of the city. There were a few survivors, and, together, we sought refuge near the Mediterranean Sea. Not long after, I found out I was pregnant. And that is where the passing of the necklace came into place."

Akila knelt in front of me and took my hands in hers. "I have waited centuries for this moment. I chose wisely when I saved you. I couldn't let the family line end with Katherine." She laid her hand on my cheek.

I pulled my head back from her hand. "What are you talking about?"

"When your mother was admitted to the hospital on suicide watch, I was notified by someone very close to me. He is the link to all mystic worlds. I visited her and made her forget the bad things she'd gone through. I told her she'd had a one night stand with a man who she would never see again. And that she was happy to have a child to love and care for regardless of the situation. I gave her the life she deserved. And you, Chloe. You are a reincarnation of Sanura. And as a hybrid, you can be even more powerful."

"Excuse me? I'm a what?"

Akila clasped her hands together. "I followed Talibah here. You have the power to end this, Chloe."

I shook my head and jumped out of the chair. "Absolutely not! Nope! I'm not doing this again. I may have taken out an embalmer queen and her sidekicks, but this is something I don't want any part of."

Akila placed her hands on the side of my face. "Chloe, this is who you are. It is in your blood. This is your destiny. You even bear the mark. Otherwise, that crystal would not shine

283

so brightly around you."

"You see it?" I asked.

"No, I don't have the power, but you do. I have faith in you, Chloe. When the time comes, you will know what to do."

"Why didn't you tell me all this when you first showed up? It would've helped me out in the long run."

"As a rule, when you enter another mystic's territory, you must have permission. Cyrus is a hard man to get a hold of. Besides, you found out most of the information on your own, like I knew you would."

Akila stepped away. "My job here is done for now. I must go."

"Wait!" I hurried to her. "If what you say is true, and I'm a healer, then why couldn't I heal my boyfriend's wound? He was attacked by a feral wolf."

"Ah, yes. Talibah's creation. It's probably because the infection has spread to his bloodstream. That is something you can't reverse. Has it been treated?"

"Dr. Clements gave him antibiotics and took a blood sample."

Akila shook her head. "That is not strong enough. Where can I find this Dr. Clements?"

"She's at the club."

"I will visit her. Hopefully, I can help."

"Thank you."

Akila bowed her head and turned into a white mist before filtering out of the room.

The room was quiet for some time. I spun around to look at Kyle, Riley, and Matt. "Is this a dream?"

Riley jumped up and down. "This is amazing! A descendant from ancient Egyptian times. So awesome!"

"I'm glad you think so."

Kyle hugged me. "You finally got your answers, Chloe."

"I'm not sure I want them now."

"At least we have a name for them now." Kyle pulled out his phone. "I'm going to let Dad know."

I stared off into space, trying to let the information sink in. Was I really as powerful as Akila said I was?

"Hey. Are you going to be all right?" Riley asked.

"I don't know. Ask me when this nightmare is over. I'm going to go check on Drake and Leo."

I hesitated at the guest bedroom door the same way I did when Drake first stayed over. I creaked the door open a little. A sliver of light from the hall shone on his bare back as he lay on his stomach. The covers barely covered the roundness of his ass.

I swallowed hard as my heart sped up. Why was I reacting to him this way? Maybe Riley was right. Between him and Leo, their inner animal was fighting for my animal's affection.

"I can do this. I can do this," I whispered.

Drake lifted his head and mumbled, "Chloe, is something wrong?"

I shuffled toward the bed and sat on the edge. "I didn't mean to wake you. I was just checking on you."

Drake rolled onto his back, placing his hands behind his head. He taunted me with his biceps. "I'm healed. No big deal."

I sat there in silence for a moment, deciding whether or not to ask about his and Sasha's relationship. I wasn't sure it was a great time to discuss this after Taylor's death, but this was something that had to get cleared up.

"Are you and Sasha going to get back together?"

Drake exhaled as he sat up on one elbow and leaned toward me. "I don't know, Chloe. I do find her attractive, but after what she did..."

"Her feelings for you didn't change Drake. She loves you. You have to understand the position she was in."

"Aren't you pissed at her?"

"For a brief moment, I was. But, even though she was there for a purpose, that all changed when she met you. She was enjoying life with you and making new friends. The fact that she wasn't honest at first hurts, but what's done is done."

Drake scooted closer and his scent swirled around and caressed me. Not just on the outside, but on the inside, as well. It was his animal trying to find mine again.

I closed my eyes to control each breath. I managed a whisper. "Drake, don't."

"Sorry." He pulled back. "I was just testing the water to see if I could do it again. Why are you reacting this way to me? Why now?"

At this point, Drake had a right to know about Riley's assumption. I couldn't lie to him anymore. This wasn't going to change my mind about who I wanted.

"Riley thinks that since I'm not a full lycan, I am open to any wolf until I shift."

"So, when you shift, it will link you to that particular alpha as your mate."

"Yes. That is what we are going with."

I caught a glimpse of his erection as he flung the covers off and rolled out of bed. With his back to me, he pulled on his pants.

"Were you not going to tell me?"

"I'm sorry. I didn't know how. I didn't want..."

Drake spun around to look me in the eye. "You didn't want to what? Get my hopes up?"

He shook his head and grabbed his shoes.

"Where are you going?" I got up and went to his side of the bed.

After the last lace was tied, Drake stared at the floor. "To the club. I can't be here right now."

He looked up at me for a brief moment and sighed. "I know I don't have a shot in hell with you, Chloe. You made your decision, and I'm going to respect that. But, if Leo can't grow a set of balls and let you shift into what you need to become, then he has no right to threaten me for trying."

Drake snatched his bag off the floor and dashed out the door.

I stood there, trying to understand what had just happened. It wasn't the reaction I'd expected from him. I thought he would try and persuade me to choose him. I was wrong, and I hurt him yet again.

He was right, though. Leo was going to have to let me shift or there were going to be consequences. I could accidentally do it and claim another wolf as my mate. That would not be good.

CHAPTER 25 Drake

I didn't bother telling anyone I was leaving. I slammed the door behind me, and by the time I got in the truck, Kyle was at the door, calling for me. I ignored him as I sped out of the driveway like an escaped convict.

I hoped there weren't any cops out patrolling the roads. I wasn't in the mood to be pulled over for speeding. I'd probably lose my temper, shift in front of one, and then all hell would break loose.

I was done torturing myself with thoughts of Chloe. I'd hoped for a brief moment that she would change her mind, but it was clear how much she was in love with Leo. It was time for me to move on and have the happiness I deserved.

Right now, there was only one other girl who did love me. And as I thought about it, I realized I had a thing for her, too. Sasha was special. And, for her to come forward and tell us what happened did mean something. She could've just sat back and not said a word.

It was time to put my plan into motion. My dick hardened at the thought of her wearing those barely-there outfits. And, the way she danced erotically. Moving her hips. Licking her lips. Shaking her ass.

I reached down and adjusted myself. I was so deep in thought

288

that I didn't see the red light. I slammed on my breaks and almost skidded into the middle of the intersection. Luckily, there were no other cars around.

I gripped the steering wheel so tightly that my knuckles turned white.

"Holy shit."

I continued on and finally pulled into the parking lot of the club. We had a new back door with a keypad so we could let ourselves in. I punched in my number and flung the door open. My animal eyes searched the club for Sasha. Even though the club was closed, it wasn't going to stop us from trying to enjoy ourselves after a tragic event.

I found Sasha dancing in one of the cages. The only thing this chick had on was a black thong.

Like a wolf on a mission, I yanked the door of the cage open. "We need to talk."

Sasha raised her arms above her head and whipped her hips to the side. "Are you sure talking is what you want to do right now?"

"I have two questions for you, Sasha. One, do you still want me?"

Sasha stopped dancing and knelt in front of me. "Of course I want you, Drake. I always have."

I grabbed Sasha by the waist and tossed her over my shoulder. I felt her breasts bounce against my back with each quick step.

Once in my room, I threw her on the bed and tore off my clothes.

"I take it you're not mad at me anymore?" She grinned.

I grabbed her ankles and pulled her to me. I hooked my fingers under the thin, lacy thong and ripped it off her.

"You said two questions. What is the second?" Sasha opened

her legs to show me how wet she was.

"Not yet," I growled.

I threw her legs over my shoulder. The one thing I loved about her was her flexibility. I could put her in positions one could only dream of.

Sasha looked down and licked her lips. She watched as I plunged deep inside her. She tilted her head up and let out a moan. Her eyelids shut halfway and her lips parted.

The look on her face was so damn sexy. With each thrust, her tits bounced perfectly in unison. She raked her nails down my arms, and I lost it. I released everything I had deep inside her—filling her full of my warm seed.

It took me a moment to catch my breath before rolling off her.

Sasha snuggled her head against my neck while placing little kisses on my shoulder. Her fingertips trailed up and down my chest.

"That was quick," she whispered.

"I'm not even close to being done with you, Sasha."

She smiled and threw her leg over to straddle me. She placed my semi-hard-on inside her and began rocking back and forth. Then, she began bouncing.

I tilted my hips up to deepen my penetration as she screamed my name.

To hear my name roll off her tongue as she reached an orgasm made my dick swell. I pinched her nipples to make the sensation last.

"I want to mark you, Sasha. I want to make you mine."

Sasha slid off and arched her back as an invitation. It was her submission to me. It was the lycan way of saying yes.

I crawled behind her and grabbed her hips. I was already

hard again and excited to finally mark someone.

I held my shaft as I slowly guided myself inside of her. She was tight at first. Then she expanded to accommodate my thick girth. I stayed like this for a few seconds. I wanted to savor the moment of being deep inside her.

Sasha moaned and twisted the sheets in her hand. "Oh, my God, Drake!"

My fingers dug into her hips as I slowly pulled back and thrust forward, forcefully. Again, I held it inside before repeating.

"Harder! Please, Drake!"

I reared back and rocked back into her over and over. I kept a hard steady rhythm. "Like that, baby? Is this what you want?"

"Yes! Oh, my God! Don't stop!"

I moved the hair away from her neck as I felt her pussy clench my dick. I was about to come and knew that once I sank my teeth into her, she would, too.

"Now, Drake! Do it now!"

I leaned over her and placed my mouth over the back of her neck. My canine teeth expanded and sank into her soft skin. The taste of salty flesh filled my mouth. Sasha bucked her ass against me as she let out a long moan.

I held her tight as my cock spasmed inside her again.

After the orgasm subsided, I rolled onto my side and pulled her with me. We were still connected. Her pussy wasn't letting me go just yet. I wasn't complaining. It felt amazing being inside her.

I wrapped my arms around her and kissed her shoulder. I was finally content. My lustful need for a companion was sated. I had no regrets about my decision. This was where I belonged. This was where Sasha was meant to be. She was my heart, my love, my friend, and, soon, she would be my wife and the mother of my children.

CHAPTER 26 Chloe

I went to check on Leo. When I entered the bedroom, his body was shaking violently on the bed.

"Leo!" I turned on the light and noticed he'd taken the whole bottle of antibiotics.

"Oh, my God! What did you do?"

Leo was soaked from sweat. I touched his forehead and his temperature was way above the norm for a lycan.

I hurried into the bathroom for a washcloth. When I came back, he was not on the bed. He was standing with his head down. His chest heaved with heavy breaths.

"Leo?"

Something told me to not get close.

"Baby, look at me."

Leo's head jerked up. His beautiful caramel eyes were yellow. Saliva dripped from his canine teeth.

My body froze at the sight of him. I thought if I didn't move, he wouldn't, either. I was wrong. He inched toward me and snarled.

I held up my hands and backed away until I hit the wall. "Leo, it's me, Chloe."

He kept moving forward.

"You can fight this! You have to." I began to sob.

What I was saying wasn't getting through to him. I had no choice but to call for help.

"Kyle! Matt! Help me!"

In a matter of seconds, they darted into the room.

"What's going on? What's wrong?" Kyle stopped dead when he saw Leo.

"Well, this certainly isn't good," Matt mumbled.

"Chloe, don't move," Kyle said.

I glanced at the bathroom, thinking I could make it to there and shut the door.

"I saw that. Don't do it, Chloe."

"Kyle, you have to do something. Call Nadia. Call Cyrus. Call anyone. Please help him."

"What do you want me to do, Chloe?"

"We could tie him down," Matt suggested.

Leo took two more steps toward me, then stopped. "Chloe, help...me."

He fell to the floor and shredded his shirt, along with the bandage. White pus bubbled inside the wound and a greenish liquid seeped out. He wasn't healing at all.

Leo writhed on the floor. His back arched, causing every vertebra to pop.

"Shit! He's turning into one of those things!"

Riley ran into the room. "What's all the commotion?"

Matt grabbed her and pulled her back before she got any farther inside.

"Oh, my God!" Riley averted her eyes and tucked her head against Matt.

"Get out of here, Riley!" Kyle ordered.

Without arguing, she flew from the room.

Leo grabbed the dresser and pulled himself up. He turned

to me and darted across the room. Kyle and Matt tried to grab him, but he slipped out of their grasp.

Leo headed in my direction, and I froze in fear. It felt like slow motion as I waited for the impact of his body. Instead, he rushed past me and jumped through the French doors. Glass shattered to the floor, and Leo disappeared over the balcony rail.

"Fuck!" Kyle took out his phone and carefully stepped outside to look over the rail. "Cyrus, we have a huge problem. Leo is turning into a feral, and he just escaped from the house. You better call me back."

I sank to the floor, sobbing. "No! This can't happen!"

Matt sat next to me and held me. "We'll find him, Chloe. We won't let him become one of those killers."

I pushed him away. "Don't make promises you know you can't keep!"

Kyle called for Riley to come back. "Take her to our room and stay with her. We need to go find Leo."

"Be careful."

Riley led me across the hall. The scent of Drake still lingered in the room. I pulled away from her and stopped at the door.

"I can't."

"Why? Drake left. He won't be back."

"Yes. I know." I wiped my face and headed downstairs.

"Chloe, wait! What happened with Drake? Do you know why he left?"

"Riley, I have enough to worry about right now with Leo roaming the night. Drake is the last thing I want to discuss."

"Okay, I'm sorry. Can I get you something to drink?"

"Water." I sat on the couch and stared at the wall. The thought of Leo out there and possibly killing someone made me feel sick.

I jumped off the couch and ran to the bathroom. I fell to the floor and heaved into the toilet. Nothing was coming up, and that made it worse.

Riley came in and sat next to me.

I took the water and managed a few sips. "I can't lose him, Riley. I just can't."

I leaned against her and sobbed. My heart was breaking. I felt helpless. There wasn't anything I could do for Leo.

I sat there forever until there were no more tears to shed.

Riley helped me get settled on the couch. She lay next to me and soothed the hair from my face.

I was exhausted. My eyes were heavy and sticky from crying. I shut them and tried to relax. I needed to get some rest so I could prepare for whatever else was going to happen.

I wasn't sure how long I'd slept, but when I woke, I heard whispers in the next room and the mention of Leo's name.

My body was sluggish as I got up and made my way to the other room.

Riley, Kyle, Matt, and Cyrus were gathered in the sitting room. They all looked at me when I stumbled into the room.

"Any word on Leo?"

Kyle shook his head. "I'm afraid not. We've all looked around the woods and the city. The good thing is there haven't been any reports of any missing or dead people."

"Yet," I mumbled.

Kyle rubbed my arms. "Devin is out there right now looking for him. He's scoping out the burial grounds to see if anything is going on. As of right now, Devin thinks she moved locations because of...well, you know...waking up to find her minions dead."

"So, where could she have gone?"

"Not sure. I'm sure Devin will contact us once he finds out."

Cyrus cleared his throat and came over to me. "We need to talk."

"Is it about Akila? 'Cause she was already here. I know everything now."

Cyrus's shoulders relaxed. He wiped his forehead. "I'm sorry. I should've contacted you sooner, but—"

"It's fine. Don't worry about it. Guess I don't need information regarding that amulet after all. Akila was supposed to go to the club and speak with Dr. Clements. Do you know if she's there?"

"I believe so."

"Chloe." Riley laid her arm over my shoulder. "You look exhausted. Why don't you go upstairs and get some rest? Stay in our room. Kyle and I will sleep on the sofa."

I nodded and went up the steps. I stood in the doorway for a moment and stared at the unmade bed that Drake was in. I knew his scent would be all over the sheets. It was going to be hard to lay in it. I had no choice. My room was off limits until I got the doors fixed.

I pulled the covers over my head, and it wasn't long before I fell asleep.

Around one a.m., I jolted awake. I reached for Leo and realized I wasn't in my room and Leo wasn't here. I knew the animal inside me felt my sorrow. She paced in a circle with her head down. It was like I could hear her whining in my head.

I yanked the covers off and went downstairs for some fresh air. I opened the back door and walked over to the pool. I stared down at the dark water. Every few seconds, it would shimmer with the reflection of the moon.

My eyes stung as tears clouded my vision. I prayed that Leo would return to me.

I needed the cold water to numb the pain. So, I jumped in and let myself sink to the bottom. It felt as if all of my worries were drowning. After a few seconds, I didn't feel a thing.

When I came up for air, I realized someone was pulling me out of the pool by the hair. I tried to scream, but my mouth was quickly covered. A sharp object penetrated my neck, and within a few seconds, everything around me swirled. My vision grew hazy, and my body went limp. After that—nothing.

CHAPTER 27 Chloe

Why couldn't I move my arms? Was I dead? It was hard to open my eyes. I tried once but failed. Twice, and I was halfway there. By the third time, everything was fuzzy. I finally blinked several times for clarity. I pulled on my arms and looked up at the chains that were draped over one of many different-sized pipes.

Questions flooded my mind. Where the hell was I? How long had I been out? Would anyone find me?

I prayed that Cyrus or someone would stroll in at any moment and save me. But, I knew I was on my own.

I glanced around at my surroundings. The walls were cement with four large pipes along the side.

A moan came from the far corner. Someone else was here with me. Their knees were buckled underneath as they dangled from the chain. Pools of blood surrounded their feet and covered their tattered clothes.

"Hello? Excuse me?" I called out, trying to get their attention.

They lifted their head slightly and blood dripped down the side of their forehead and under their nose. Their complexion was pale and their lips cracked from dryness. I stared at the tortured soul and realized who it was.

"Erik! Erik, is that you?"

His body jerked with another moan.

"Erik! It's me, Chloe. Can you hear me?"

His head turned in my direction. "Chloe?" He gurgled and coughed.

So this was where Erik had been all this time. And no one had noticed or cared that he was missing from the club except me. I felt bad for him. I never wanted this for him.

"Erik, what happened? Where are we?"

"Don't...know."

He could barely speak. I could hear the dryness in his throat and mouth.

"Let me guess. Josephine's maker did this to you?"

"Mmm."

I took that as a yes.

I tugged on the chains, hoping the pipe was weak enough to break. But it wouldn't budge.

A scraping noise from the hall caught my attention. Then, a hissing sound echoed into the room. A large lizard came through the doorway. Its long talons clicked on the floor, and its tongue flicked out of its mouth as it moved in my direction.

"Oh, shit."

This was one of the things that Leo had encountered in the tunnel. I had hoped they were all dead. How many of these things did she have around here?

The animal stopped a few inches away, and then it slashed at my leg with its long talons. I was quick to move my leg out of the way. I hissed at the creature when it hissed at me and kicked it hard in the face.

Their outer shell was extremely hard, and the blunt force did absolutely nothing except to piss it off.

It snapped at my feet, and I kicked it over and over. Then, I got the idea to trap its head between my feet. I gave it a sharp twist to the side and heard the bones snap. The carcass fell to the side, and I pushed it away with my foot.

"Damn. Now I know how Leo felt."

I looked back at Erik. His eyes were closed. "Erik?"

He didn't respond.

I had to find a way out of this mess. I had to save us. It was all up to me.

My arms started to go numb. I pulled again on the pipe and rust particles fell on my head. I tried to move the chain back and forth while pulling. The pipe started to give a little. But, I had to stop when I heard another noise from the hall.

"What now?"

A silhouette appeared in the doorway and glided into the room. Green eyes were the only thing illuminated under a black cloak.

The figure stopped in front of me and glanced down at the dead carcasses. They removed the hood and glared at me with narrow eyes.

"Not very good protectors if they keep getting themselves killed," I said.

I didn't even see her hand, but I felt its impact across my face. It jarred my head to the side, and the taste of blood coated my tongue. I spit the metallic substance at her feet.

She gripped my jaw in her hand and forced me to look at her. "I want answers, and I want them now. Where is Josephine?"

"What makes you think I know where she is?"

"Because I have information that you are the one who knows."

My eyes darted to Erik. I thought for a moment that he must be the one who told her. But, the shape he was in made me think otherwise. He had been punished because he had withheld information. So, who told? Was it really Sasha?

The woman gave a small chuckle. "You think it was Erik? I'm afraid not. He refuses to tell me anything."

"Whoever it was, they're lying."

The sorceress smiled and stepped closer. "I don't think so... Chloe."

My breath caught. I wanted to stay calm. But, calm wasn't going to get me anywhere, and neither would aggression. No matter what I did, the outcome would be the same regardless. If I told her the truth, she'd kill me. If I didn't, I'd get tortured. It was a win-win for the sorceress. Maybe I should call her by her real name, I thought. That would certainly shake things up. But, I didn't want to let the cat out of the bag just yet.

"Look, I don't know who told you that I know where Josephine is, but I don't. I just recently started going to the club."

"You're lying! If I have to force it out of you, I will!"

The sorceress hissed and exposed her teeth. These were not normal vampire fangs. Every single one of them was sharp, like a shark. White foam dripped from the sides of her mouth. Her forehead transformed from smooth skin into layers of large scales. Her nails extended into claws, and she sliced at my face and arms.

Each cut burned to the point where I thought I was on fire. I bite my lip and squeezed my eyes shut to hide the pain. I didn't want to look weak in front of her, but I didn't know how much longer I could suppress the urge to let out a violent scream.

But, when the sorceress saw how quickly the wounds healed,

she stopped and stared. It seemed to infuriate her even more. "What are you? You're not a vampire!"

She slashed at me once more. "Ugh! That's not possible!"

She headed for the door and stopped for a brief moment. "I'm not done with you. When I return, I'll convince you to tell me the truth."

Once the sorceress was gone, I continued to try and free myself. Instead of concentrating on the pipe, I worked on pulling my wrist through the clasp. The edge of the metal cut into my skin and blood rolled down my arm. It was too tight.

Erik let out a groan. I glanced at him, and the whites of his eyes were black. His fangs extended from his gums. The smell of my blood had awakened him. He was hungry and weak.

"Hold on, Erik. Just a little bit longer."

I pulled and pulled on the other cuff, but this one seemed to be locked tighter around my wrist. "Shit! Come on."

"Chloe," Erik mumbled. "Chloe, I'm sorry."

"Erik, don't. I'll get us out of this. I promise."

The sound of the sorceress coming down the hall alerted me. But, to my surprise, it wasn't the sorceress. It was Devin.

"Devin! Thank God you're here. Quick, help me."

He walked over nonchalantly. He reached up and ran his finger down my bloody arm. He brought his finger to his lips and licked the blood. "Sorry, love. I'm afraid I can't do that."

"What? Why?"

He stepped back and smirked. "Because you're right where you belong." He looked over his shoulder. "You and Erik both."

"You're the one who gave me up? But, why? I thought you were on our side? What did I ever do to you?"

"Lots of questions. Let me see." He rested his chin on his

forefinger. "Why and what you did to me can be answered with one name. Josephine."

"Can you be more specific?"

Devin got in my face and clenched his teeth. "You took the only girl I ever loved away from me!"

For the first time, I saw the pain in his eyes. I thought I almost saw tears. And then it hit me. I remembered seeing them together the first time I went to the playroom with Erik. I should have known then. Especially the way he took her out of the room.

"I'm sorry, Devin. But, she threatened me too many times. You were there for one. Didn't it bother you to know she also slept with Erik and even wanted Drake? She wasn't a one-man deal."

"I didn't care. She was in my bed more than Erik's. And, thanks to Matt, I finally found out what had happened to Josephine. That night Sasha left the club, it was clear what I had to do. So, after Sasha left the meeting, I visited the sorceress. I told her I knew about someone who had answers, and, in time, I would bring that person to her. I just wanted to make people suffer first. She was on board with that idea. And, of course, I let you believe I was on your side."

"And the attack on the club?"

"Brilliant, wasn't it?"

"No! Innocent people died. People who were your friends. How could you do that?"

"They were not my friends, Chloe. Every single one of them hated Josephine."

"So, you let Leo, Kyle, and Matt go to the caves knowing there were more protectors and no spell book...because?"

"It was the only way to try and take out those who were

protecting you all at once."

I looked away, holding back the tears. I knew Matt would be torn up about this since he was the one who told Devin. What would've happened had he not? The sorceress may have shown up at the club to wreak havoc anyway.

The clinking of chains echoed in the hall.

Devin stepped aside to look at the door. "And, here comes the best part. Brace yourself, baby."

"I have a little gift for you, my dear." The sorceress stepped to the side to reveal a feral wolf.

My heart sank to the pit of my stomach. "Leo!"

The tears that I had managed to hold back now dripped down my cheek. He wasn't the same as when he'd escaped the house. He was hunched over and foaming at the mouth. His hands and ankles were in chains.

"Well, it seems I have the one thing that just might get you to talk. Seeing your reaction is priceless." She cackled.

"What have you done to him?" I cried.

"I didn't do anything to him. However, since he was infected by one of my own, he is now under my control." She un-cuffed Leo and pushed him forward. "I will leave you two lovebirds alone. Come with me, Devin. We have things to prepare."

Devin looked back with one last grin and winked.

Leo swayed from side to side as if waiting to be commanded to attack. His large claws hung down at his side. He licked his lips and left a trail of white, sticky slobber.

"Leo. Please," I sobbed. My heart was breaking at the sight of him. I didn't know if he could understand me. Even if he did, would it matter?

I relaxed my arms in the chains. It hurt, but not as much as the pain I felt on seeing Leo like this.

Leo shuffled toward me and stopped just inches away. His head twitched to the side. *"Garrr! Ugh!"*

"Leo, if you can understand me, I love you. I love you so much," I sniffled.

He brought his finger to my cheek and dragged his nail down my face. He leaned in and licked the drop of blood from the wound. He pulled back and blinked. His yellow eyes faded but then became yellow again.

It dawned on me. I couldn't heal him with my power, but maybe I could with my blood. There was hope yet.

"Yes!" I blurted. "Drink my blood, Leo. I can save you."

Leo grabbed a hold of the shackles around my wrists and broke them with a quick pull. My arms fell limp at my sides.

"Chloe, what the hell are you doing?" Erik asked.

I ignored him. My only focus was Leo and on saving his life first.

I reached up to touch Leo's face, but he snatched my hand. He twisted my arm around my back and held me flush against him. Leo sank his teeth into my neck.

My legs gave out, and Leo sank to the floor with me. He slurped the blood as it spewed into his mouth, but it didn't last long. He pushed me away and rolled over onto his side. He gurgled and spat blood on the floor.

"Leo!" I knelt next to him, but he crawled away from me.

His head jerked up and he glared at me. His eyes kept changing from yellow to bronze as if he was fighting the disease.

I thought if I could tap into my animal, I could help him find his way back. But, my animal did not recognize Leo. The contaminated blood had mutated his system.

Leo's body thrashed around on the floor as he gasped for air.

Then he was silent.

I hurried to Leo and shook him. "Leo! Leo, wake up! Oh, God! What did I do?"

I checked for a pulse and was relieved when I felt a strong heartbeat.

The sorceress appeared in the entranceway. She'd taken her cloak off, which probably meant business. Her beautiful emerald corset matched her eyes. It made her red hair look like bright flames. And, right between her breasts was the amulet.

"Well, well, I see you got loose. Oh, you naughty girl." She clicked her tongue.

Her eyes narrowed when she saw Leo. "Well, I didn't think you had it in you to kill your lover. Impressive."

She came toward me and halted. Slowly, she backed away

I took this as a sign that she felt something she wasn't supposed to.

The necklace's vibration comforted me, and it gave me the strength that I needed. Now was the time to fight, and I knew just what to say to make her strike first.

"You know what? You're right. I do know what happened to Josephine. And, let me tell you something. Your daughter was nothing but a psychotic bitch. She didn't know when to quit with the threats. I wasn't afraid of her, and she misjudged me. Like mother, like daughter, I will soon take your life as I have done hers."

The sorceress let out an ear-piercing scream. She held up her hand and threw a ball of fire at me.

My hands went up instantly to block it. The only thing I felt was a heavy ripple of heat.

"Thank you for the gift. Let me return the favor." I raised

307

both of my hands above my head and let the electricity grow. When the power became too much to contain, I released the white balls of light.

It bounced off her just as I had expected, but I only wanted to show her what she was up against. And, it did make her back up just a little.

"How can this be? I killed them! I killed every last one of them! I was the only one left!"

I paced around her in a complete circle. All the while, we stared at each other.

She cringed and narrowed her eyes, causing a crease to form between her brows. Like a flash of light, she flew at me with such rage that she broke through my protection shield. She wrapped her long, bony fingers around my neck.

I put my hands together to make a fist and brought them up fast between her arms to break the hold. Then I came down hard on her beautifully sculpted nose. She screeched as blood flowed down her chin. I then brought my foot up and kicked her in the stomach. She flew backward and hit the wall.

She lay there for a moment, motionless.

I crept up to her and nudged her with my foot.

She coughed and struggled to get to her feet. When she was on all fours, she said, "Tell me how this feels."

She rammed a sharp rock into my abdomen.

I didn't scream. I only gasp for air as she'd taken me by surprise. I went to my knees, and after a few seconds, I fell completely to the floor. I pulled the rock from my stomach. Inch by inch, the pool of blood spread away from me.

I tilted my head and saw Erik struggling against his chains as he threatened her.

"You bitch! I'll fucking kill you!"

She flung her head back and laughed. "I don't think so. You'll pay for not protecting my daughter."

A sudden chill filled the air around me. My wound had finally healed, but I was weak.

The sorceress grabbed Erik by the back of the head, and he laughed at her.

"I'm glad you think your death is funny," she said.

Erik shook his head. "Not my death. Yours."

The sorceress looked over her shoulder to see me on my feet.

I held the sliver of rock up and tossed it aside with a smile.

She pushed Erik away. "I don't understand. You should be dead!"

I leaped at the sorceress, but she caught me and threw me into the wall.

"Is that all you got, sorceress?"

The sorceress hissed, and at the same time, we lunged for each other. She jumped over me and pulled my head to the side.

Erik yanked on the chains, trying to get free as he yelled, "No, Chloe! Don't let her bite you!"

But, it was too late. She sank her fangs into me and began to drink.

The pain was excruciating. I screamed while wiggling against her.

"No!" Erik pulled on his chains and succeeded in breaking one free.

I started to feel weaker. My surroundings were fading in and out. I hoped that the sorceress would just kill me now and get it over with.

For a moment, I gave up. This was it. I had no more strength or fight left in me. If the necklace was the answer to killing this woman, I had no idea how to activate it.

That is until a voice inside of my head chanted a spell.

In that moment, my necklace began to glow and the vibrations were so strong that the sorceress pushed me away with a high-pitched yelp. Her amulet burned her skin.

As I fell to the floor, I reached for the amulet and yanked it off her neck. A bright light exploded in the room. I held up my arm to shield my eyes.

The sorceress stood there in disbelief. "No one has ever been able to retrieve my amulet. And the light. You...you must have the mark. You must be a descendant. But, how?"

A voice from behind her interrupted. "Hello, Talibah."

The sorceress turned around. She froze for a moment and then pointed at Akila. "You! How are you alive?"

"Nassor saved my life. I watched the city burn from afar."

"No!" The sorceress flew across the room, but Akila vanished as if she were a mirage.

The sorceress spun around, trying to find where she'd gone. "Come back! Come back and fight me, you coward!"

Her eyes began to glow as she stared at me. "I will finish you."

My body jolted and the light that surrounded the room entered into me. Suddenly, I had no control. Something had taken over my soul.

I smirked at Talibah. "You killed me thousands of years ago. Now, I've come to return the favor."

I held the amulet in the air and cast another spell.

"No! No!" The sorceress fell to the floor, writhing in pain.

My necklace broke open. The white fog that it contained seeped out and floated over to the sorceress's body. It mixed with the mist that was evaporating from her skin. The haze grew thicker as it swirled around the room.

Talibah's body dried up and then burst into flames. She tried to crawl to me, but her fingers turned to ash. The flames made their way through her body until there was nothing but a pile of black and grey dust.

The amulet grew silent, and the mist was gone, along with the vibrations. I tried to move but couldn't. Even lifting my head seemed like a chore.

I managed to look over at Erik. I saw his mouth moving, but I couldn't hear what he was saying. A loud ringing filled my head. I closed my eyes for only a moment but I was consumed by darkness.

CHAPTER 28 Drake

Sasha's arm and leg were entwined with mine as she lay next to me. I stroked her hair and watched her sleep. Her long, dark lashes curled up. The vision of her looking at me under those lashes made me smile.

I moved her arm away and rolled out from under her. I sat on the side of the bed for a few moments. My life had just changed with one decision, and I would remember it for the rest of my life. I threw on some clothes and went up to the roof for some fresh air. The night sky was clear, but it was hard to see the stars beyond all of the lights in the city.

I leaned against the rail and watched the last of the bars close for the night. People still sat out on the patios, drinking beer at last call.

I caught Sasha's scent before she wrapped her arms around my waist. "What ya doing up here, baby?"

"I couldn't sleep. Thought I'd get some air." I twirled around to put her against the rail. "What are you doing up?"

"I missed you." She stood on tiptoe and kissed the tip of my nose.

I looked over her shoulder and saw Devin on the phone. He walked two blocks down and turned right.

I took Sasha's face in my hands. "Baby, I need you to go back to the bedroom and lock the door. Under no circumstance do you open the door until you hear from me."

"Why? What's wrong?"

"I have a gut feeling that something is wrong. Please, just do as I say."

"Is it Chloe? I want to help."

I closed my eyes for a brief moment and took a breath. "Sasha..." I opened my eyes and stared into hers. "Please, as your alpha, I'm trying to protect you. Let me handle this."

With a nod, she took off.

I looked below to make sure there wasn't anyone around. I leaped off the building and landed in a squat. I sprinted down the sidewalk and stopped where Devin had turned. I poked my head around the corner and saw him halfway down the block. He walked up a set of stairs and entered a building.

I jogged down the sidewalk to the steps of an old, empty apartment building. I rested my hand on the door handle and slowly pushed down until I heard it click. Inch by inch, I opened the door enough to slip inside. I placed my back against the wall and listened for any sound that might give me clues as to where Devin had gone.

A heavy door closed at the end of the hall.

I snuck down the hall and stopped at the corner. There was a sign on the wall with an arrow pointing down. *Utility, Laundry, Maintenance, and Plumbing.*

I didn't know what I was getting myself into or what to expect. I cracked the door enough to listen. I heard faint voices, and one of them sounded like Chloe.

I stepped back and shut the door. "Shit. Shit. Shit."

I hurried out of the building and down an alley, taking out my phone to call Kyle. I hoped I was wrong about this.

"Come on. Pick up, asshole."

In a sleepy tone, Kyle mumbled, "Do you have any idea what time it is?"

"Yeah, and I don't care. Is Chloe there?"

I heard Kyle sigh. "Let it go, man."

"No, I need to confirm if she's there. I need to know she's all right."

Kyle's voice came in a little clearer. "Why? What's going on?"

"I don't know, but I followed Devin to an old apartment building. I could've sworn I heard Chloe's voice. Please just check on her."

"Yeah, okay. Hold on."

I paced up and down the alley several times before he answered.

"Drake, she's gone. I've looked everywhere for her. I happened to find a syringe by the pool."

"Shit! This isn't good."

"Are there any windows for you to look in?"

"I don't know. Let me figure out the layout."

I went back to the building and around back. There were two small windows. Both of them were caked with dirt and mud. I tried to peek between all of the gunk, and that was when I saw someone hanging from chains. They were barely on their feet.

I moved away from the window and leaned against the wall. "I found out where Erik has been. He's chained up. I'm sure Chloe's down there with him."

"Jesus. Okay. Matt and I are on our way. Don't do anything stupid and try to play hero."

"Don't worry. I'll wait for you at the club."

I hung up and ran back to the club. I entered the key code

to the back door and hurried downstairs. I banged on my bedroom door. "Sasha, it's me. Let me in."

She opened the door, and I pushed through.

"What's going on?"

I grabbed my knife from the dresser and placed it in my pocket. This situation called for some extra protection.

"Chloe and Erik are in trouble, and Devin is the one to blame for all of this."

"Devin? Why?"

"I don't know, but that asshole is dead."

I kissed the top of her head. "I'm meeting Kyle and Matt outside. Stay put."

She grabbed my arm. "I want to come with you. Chloe's my friend."

Drake shook his head. "I don't want to put your life in any more danger. Please, just wait here."

"Please be careful."

"I will."

As I opened the door, I turned to her and quickly kissed her again. There was something else I had to say to her before I left. "I love you."

Sasha's eyes widened, and she smiled. "I love you, too."

I hurried outside and paced in circles as I waited for Matt and Kyle. They finally pulled up, and I sprinted to the car.

"Let's do this and try not to get killed," Kyle said.

"That's my plan," I replied.

I gave Matt directions back to the building. We parked two buildings down. As soon as we entered, a loud explosion from below shook the building. A woman screamed as if she were being tortured.

"That's defiantly not Chloe," Kyle whispered.

"If that's the sorceress...what the hell is going on?" Matt said.

"Time to find out. Come on." I led the way down the corridor.

Before we got to the end of the hall, Devin sprinted around the corner. He stopped dead when he saw us.

"Where are you off to in such a hurry?" I asked.

"Thank God! Chloe's hurt," Devin said.

"So, why are you running?"

"To get help."

"Bullshit!" I balled my hands into fists. Without looking away, I said, "Kyle, you and Matt take care of Chloe. I've got this asshole."

"You sure?"

"Absolutely."

Devin glared at Kyle and Matt as they slipped by and disappeared around the corner.

I held my arms out to the side. "What are you doing, Devin?"

"What's it look like?"

"You piece of shit. You tried pinning all this on Sasha, but it was you the whole time! Why?"

"I don't have to tell you a damn thing, Drake. But, thanks to Matt, I was able to seek revenge for Josephine." Devin grinned.

"You son of a bitch!" I lunged for Devin, but he sprang toward the ceiling and clung on.

I jumped and snatched his pant leg, pulling him to the floor. I rolled over Devin and sank my sharp teeth into his shoulder.

Devin shoved his fist into my rib and quickly flipped us over. He pinned my right arm behind my back. I reached into my pocket with my free hand, pulled out my knife, and rammed it in Devin's eye. He flew off me, screaming in a furious rage.

I made it to my feet, and in a matter of seconds, slash marks appeared on my chest. Devin whizzed by me again, and, this time, he aimed for the face. I felt the sting on my right cheek. He was too fast to keep an eye on him.

But, at the right moment, I reached out and grabbed him by the throat. I felt his esophagus collapsed as I tightened my grip.

I know crushing his windpipe wouldn't kill him—the bastard didn't breathe anyway. But, it made me feel better.

"This is for trying to frame Sasha." I shoved my knife into his ribcage and twisted it.

"This is for attacking the club and betraying us all." I pulled out the knife and stabbed him in the neck.

"And, this is for trying to hurt Chloe." I thrust the knife into his heart.

Devin's eyes bulged out of his sockets. Blood spewed from his wounds and dripped from his mouth.

"Every life that we lost because of you can never be replaced. You, on the other hand, can be." I pulled the knife loose and put it in my pocket. I let Devin's limp body fall to the floor.

He wasn't dead yet. I took pleasure in bleeding him dry by ripping out his throat with my canine teeth. His body shriveled like a prune until all that was left of him was a pile of ash.

CHAPTER 29 Kyle

I hurried down the stairwell taking the steps two at a time. We searched all of the rooms until we reached the end of the hall. It was the utility and plumbing room.

I burst inside, and the first person I saw was Erik.

He looked up, shocked to see me. "Kyle! Kyle, check on Chloe!" He nodded to the other side of the room.

"Shit. What happened?" I knelt beside her.

"She killed the sorceress."

Matt pointed to the pile of dust on the floor. "Was that her?"

"Yeah. What the hell is Chloe? I've never seen anything like it," Erik said.

"That's a discussion for later," I replied.

"Can you please get me out of these chains?" Erik rattled the one chain attached to the pipes.

"Yeah, let me check the maintenance room." Matt hurried down the hall.

I laid Chloe's head in my lap. Her breathing was shallow, but at least she was alive. I noticed her necklace was broken against her chest. I rolled it between my thumb and finger.

"That necklace saved her life. A woman in white appeared from nowhere, strange words were exchanged. I mean...what the hell? It looked as if Chloe's body was taken over by another entity."

"What?" I glanced over at Erik.

"Yeah, she also...oh, dude, Leo! He's over there in the corner."

"Leo's here?" I carefully lowered Chloe's head and crawled over to Leo. His pulse was steady, and he looked better than earlier in the evening.

"Erik, what the hell?"

"Chloe fed him her blood. He was infected with something. Kyle, I've been down here for what seems like forever. What the hell has been going on?"

I sat there, shaking my head. "Our club was attacked by the sorceress's feral wolves Saturday night after it closed. We lost a few people."

"Jesus!"

"We have a new door with a keypad for us to enter so no one has to keep watch. Did Devin mention why he did this?"

"Yeah, it was to get back at Chloe for killing Josephine. He was in love with her. He had no idea what happened to Josephine until..."

"It's my fault," Matt said as he stepped into the room, carrying an ax. "I told him what happened."

"You couldn't have known, Matt. We thought we could trust him. We all thought Sasha was the bad guy."

Drake rushed in with blood covering his mouth and clothes. He took a moment to look around the room. "Damn. Leo, too?"

"Hello!" Erik yelled. "Chains!"

"Oh! Right." Matt took a quick swing with the ax. Brief sparks and a loud clang echoed off the walls.

The chain broke in two and Erik fell to his knees, rubbing

his wrist. "Thank you."

I started to pick up Chloe. Her eyes fluttered open.

"Kyle?"

"Yes. I'm here. You're safe now. It's over."

"How did you find me?"

"I didn't."

I looked over at Drake, and he knelt at her other side.

"I did. I followed Devin here."

She reached up and caressed his face. "Thank you."

Drake pulled away. "You're welcome, but it looks like you did most of the damage."

Chloe forced a smile and winced. "My shoulder burns."

I pulled the top of her shirt down to reveal her birthmark. "Chloe, you look like you've been branded."

"Is it my birthmark?"

"Yes."

"It started burning when I grabbed the amulet from the sorceress. I chanted some weird spell and, poof, she burst into flames."

Matt picked up the sorceress's amulet. "See how easy that was to get, Kyle."

I gave him an evil eye. "Shut up."

Matt laughed and placed it in his pocket.

"Come on. Let's get out of here. Hold on to my neck." I placed an arm under Chloe's legs and used the other to support her back.

"Wait! Don't forget Leo. Is he alive?" Chloe reached for Leo.

"He's going to be fine, Chloe." I carried her out of the building.

CHAPTER 30 Chloe

Leo's soap and cologne lingered in the air. The bathroom door opened, and he came out wearing a pair of jeans. His smile tugged at my heart.

I bolted out of bed and jumped into his arms. "Leo! You're okay!"

He stumbled backward and laughed. "Hey, baby."

I pulled my head back so I could see him better. "I had a horrible nightmare. You were a feral wolf, I was captured, and..."

Leo shook his head. "It wasn't a dream, Chloe. It happened."

He sat down with me in his lap.

I caressed the side of his freshly shaved face. "I was afraid I'd lost you."

"For a moment, you did. The last thing I remember was being at the house. I could feel my body changing, and that is when I bolted. I had to get away before I hurt you. Then, I saw you in chains and the sadness in your eyes."

He stroked my cheek. "Your beautiful face and voice kept me from losing control. You saved me, Chloe. In more ways than one. You may not have been able to heal me from the outside with your powers, but you did on the inside."

"What made you taste my blood?"

"That was the feral in me, Chloe. It wasn't intentional."

"Well, when I saw the change in your eyes afterward, I knew what had to be done."

"I'll forever be grateful."

Leo reached behind my head and pulled me in for a kiss. The animal in me was able to recognize him again. She stirred and waited for Leo's animal to make a move. But he didn't.

Leo pulled away and rested his forehead on mine. "I met Akila. While you were resting, we all gathered around to hear the story. I'm amazed by you, Chloe."

"Yeah, I have something to add to that story. Something I witnessed during the whole process."

"And what is that?"

"I want to wait until I speak to Akila. So, how is Matt dealing with this?"

"He hates himself for blurting things out to Devin. I told him it wasn't his fault."

"Where is he now?"

"He's out with Hannah. He needed some time away. I don't blame him. A lot of us need time to heal from this. Which leads me to Kyle."

Leo pushed me off his lap and stood up with his hand out.

"He said to send you his way once you're awake. You'll find him in his room."

"Okay." I gave Leo a deep kiss.

Kyle's door was open, and he was packing his things.

"What are you doing?"

Kyle looked up from his bag and smiled. "Hey, you look better."

He came around the bed and hugged me.

"Are you and Riley taking a trip somewhere?"

Kyle sighed and took my hand as he sat on the bed. "You remember our little chat awhile back about me looking into another job?"

I nodded. "Uh-huh."

"It's another company our dad owns. The guy running it is retiring, and I'm taking over for a while."

"Kyle, that is great!" I threw my arms around his neck.

"It's in New York, Chloe. I'm moving to New York."

I loosened my hold and let my arms slide away. My smile faded as I looked at him. "What? Why can't dad just hire someone else?"

"Chloe, this is important to me. I've been working for this opportunity for a long time."

"What about Riley?"

"She's coming with me."

I thought I was done with the tears, but one escaped and ran down my cheek.

Kyle caught it with his thumb. "Don't do that. Don't cry. This doesn't mean we stop talking. We'll keep in touch because we are both an important part of each other's lives. I'll be home on holidays and vacations. We can video chat. It's not the end of the world."

Kyle slipped off the bed and knelt in front of me.

"Look, you and Leo can start your life now. Turn the extra room into a nursery."

I smacked him on the arm. "Don't tease."

"I'm serious, Chloe. We are all ready to move on with our lives. We can't stay at the club forever."

"What about Cyrus? Does he know?"

"Cyrus has his own plans, I'm sure. Dad is still going to run the club and hire new people. We'll see what happens."

Tears rolled down my cheek and Kyle wiped them away.

"When are you leaving?" I pulled away from him.

"On Friday. Riley and I still need to pack up stuff here."

"I'll miss you."

"I'll miss you, too, Chloe."

Kyle pulled me off the bed and into a hug.

There was a knock on the doorframe. "Hey, it's time."

I looked over Kyle's shoulder at Leo. "Time for what?"

"You'll see." Leo held out his hand and Kyle followed behind.

We went upstairs to the main floor of the club. Tables were rearranged with food and drinks. Everyone was gathered around with drinks in hand.

"What's this?" I asked.

"A celebration for lots of reasons." Leo led me farther into the room.

Cyrus's voice broke out over the crowd. "Can I have your attention, please?"

The room fell silent as all eyes focused on the stage.

"Over the past few days, this club has suffered a great loss. Today, we celebrate their lives. They will be missed but never forgotten. Thus, we still plan on putting together a calendar in dedication to them. We're also celebrating those that are leaving to peruse the next stage in their life. Kyle and Riley are leaving for New York. Drake and Sasha are headed to California."

I gasped and searched the crowd for Drake and Sasha, but I didn't see them.

"And to Chloe and Leo."

I turned back to Cyrus, whose smile widened. "Chloe, you've been through a lot more than we have. It is because of you that we can put all of the bad aside and focus on the future of this club. Things are changing, but it is for the best. I've never met an individual as strong as you. I see great things for you. Now, let's eat and enjoy the rest of this day."

Everyone clapped and cheered as they disbursed to the food table.

I stayed off to the side to let the line die down. There was a tap on my shoulder. Drake and Sasha stood there hand in hand. Her cheeks were a light shade of pink.

"I'm glad you're okay, Chloe." She hugged me and then pulled away. Her hand went right back into Drake's.

"So, you two are together now?" I grinned.

Drake pulled Sasha against him as he looked down at her. He gave her the look he used to give me.

"Yes. We're official."

"As in marked?"

Drake nodded. "Yep."

"I'm so happy for you both. So, you're off to Cali, huh?"

"Yep. I'm going back for a few weeks to introduce my mom to Sasha. After that, we are off to see her parents."

"This sounds serious. When are you leaving?"

"Tomorrow."

"Oh." I looked away as my smile faltered.

"Chloe." Drake hugged me and whispered in my ear. "This isn't goodbye. We'll be back. We just need this time to be together."

I nodded against his chest. "I know."

I gently pushed him away. "It's just so hard to see everyone leaving in the same week."

"Yeah, I'm sure it is when you've grown close to us all." Drake patted his belly. "I'm hungry."

Sasha and I laughed as he hurried to the food table.

I hugged Sasha once more. "I'm sorry we didn't get a chance to hang out more. Maybe one day soon."

Sasha smiled. "I would like that very much."

"You take care of him or else."

"Don't worry. I will."

Leo waved me over to a table where Kyle and Riley were waiting. I took a seat next to him. He had a plate full of food waiting for me.

Drake and Sasha soon joined us, and then Cyrus and my dad. It warmed my heart to see us all gathered at the same table and getting along with one another. Time stood still as we ate and spoke of what was next for us. It was nice to be with everyone and not have to worry about anyone coming after me. We were finally getting to have the normal life that we deserved.

The only thing left to do was to speak with my aunt. It was time to tell her the truth. Not only about me, but about her grandmother. I wasn't sure how to go about doing it, but it had to be done.

Akila appeared from across the room.

I took this opportunity to speak with her alone, but Leo wasn't having any of that. He had to escort me. I had no problem with it.

"I'm glad you're still here," I said.

"I'll always be here for you. We are family." She smiled and held my hand as we took a seat.

"You save us all, Chloe. We no longer need to hide."

"You sure about that?" Leo leaned forward and rested his arms on his knees as he linked his fingers together. "I'm sure there are still a lot of her minions out there waiting for her return or for her to give the next order to kill. What happens when she doesn't show?"

"Most of them cannot survive without her."

"Most? What about the other percent? Won't they go rogue if no one is around to keep them in line?"

Akila shook her head. "I'm not worried about them. They will be dealt with. They are easier to take down with Talibah gone."

I touched my neck and the absence of the necklace. "It broke."

"I know."

"Did you have any idea that would happen?"

"No. In fact, I witnessed Sanura's soul entering you. That was the swirling mist you saw inside the crystal." Akila looked away. "I was wrong."

"About what?"

"You have the mark which tied you to Sanura. She waited thousands of years for the right soul to come along and take out Talibah. You're not a reincarnation of her after all."

"That's what I was going to mention. So, does this mean I'll no longer have my powers?"

"You are still a mystic healer, Chloe. Your powers are yours and yours alone. For you to have healed Leo with your blood leads me to believe you have pushed your abilities beyond their limit. I never thought it was possible until now."

"Did Matt give you Talibah's necklace?"

"He did."

"I have one more question about my powers. Weeks ago, when all of this started, I had visions of Erik's past when I consumed his blood. But, when I had Josephine's or any other creature, I did not."

"Is Erik different from the others in any way?"

"Yes. He's not a full vampire."

"It could be that anytime you consume human blood, you have visions. Maybe that is your personal power in addition to what you inherited from Sanura."

Cyrus approached, and Akila immediately stood and bowed her head. "Cyrus."

He did the same. "Akila."

"Thank you for your hospitality, and for watching over Chloe."

"It's been my pleasure."

Akila turned to me. "I must go."

Before she could perform her vanishing act, I hugged her. "Thank you for everything."

"You're most welcome. I will be in touch. There are a couple of things I need to take care of before we see each other again." She stepped away, and then she was gone.

"That is one ability I wish I had," I murmured.

"Me, too. That way, you could escape any situation." Leo laughed.

Cyrus smiled and tugged on his sleeve. "I guess this it, then."

"What do you mean?"

"You no longer need me. You have all you need, Chloe."

I shook my head. "No! No, you don't get to do this to me, too."

"I'm not leaving you for good, Chloe. I'm just saying the investigation is closed."

I put my hand over my heart. "You scared me for a moment."

"Sorry about that. Just so you know, I will be absent for a while."

"Cyrus, you've been absent most of the time. How is this going to be different?"

"You got me there. But, this isn't due to business. It is more of a personal thing."

My eyebrows arched in surprise. "Personal? Like a girl thing?"

I saw his face turn a bit red. When he didn't answer, I knew I was right.

"Who?" I bounced up and down.

I got a laugh out of him.

"An old flame. We connected during my research. She was the one who helped find your great-grandmother."

"Oh? I want to thank her. Can I meet her?"

He shook his head. "Not at this time, Chloe. I'm sorry."

"I understand. Well, at least thank her for me."

"I will."

Cyrus held his hand out to Leo. "I'm happy she has you, Leo. You two complement each other, and not just on a personal level, but a spiritual one, as well. Take good care of her."

"I certainly will. You have nothing to worry about."

I expected Cyrus to vanish like he usually did, but this time he casually walked away.

"You okay?" Leo rubbed the small of my back.

"I think so."

"You coming back to the celebration?"

"In a moment."

Leo kissed my cheek and joined the others.

I stayed behind because someone was on my mind. I searched the roof first and worked my way down to the basement. I knocked on the bedroom door, but there was no answer. I tried the handle and the door clicked open.

I poked my head in. "Erik?"

I pushed the door all the way open and stepped inside. There was no sign of him. One of the dresser drawers was partially opened. I peeked inside and it was empty. I pulled the other drawers open to find them all the same.

I searched the room for a note but found nothing.

"Erik's not here."

Meagan—the one Erik had hooked up with—leaned against the door.

"I gathered. Do you know where he went?" I closed the dresser drawers.

She came in and plopped down on his bed. "No. He wouldn't tell me. I'm Meagan, by the way."

I didn't want her to know that Erik told me her name. She might want to know what he said about her, and that might get her hopes up about whatever feelings she had for him.

"Nice to meet you. I'm Chloe."

"I know who you are." She smiled. "I begged Erik to take me with him, but he refused."

"I'm sorry to hear."

Was I? Was she another victim of Erik's ways? Did he draw her to him as he did me—and every other woman he met?

"I guess it's for the best." She sat up and dangled her feet off the bed. "How could I compete?"

"Compete with what?"

"You. He was always watching you. I guess with Josephine out of the way, he was finally able to make a life for himself. He has you to thank for that. You know, for giving him his freedom."

"I suppose. But, he's not here to tell me that. Is he?"

I went upstairs and out into the alley to call Erik, but his number was no longer working. I didn't know where Erik had gone or why. I guessed he'd finally moved on.

Chapter 31 Chloe

The rest of the week flew by. Kyle and Riley finally left for New York. The next day, I prepared for the hardest thing I would ever have to do—tell my aunt everything.

I paced back and forth across the kitchen, biting my lip. Every time I passed the dining room table, I'd rearrange the placemats.

Leo finished preparing the salad and placed the bowl in the center. "What is wrong with you?"

"It's nerves. I'm not sure how my aunt is going to react. It's not just the lycan thing, but the mystic part. About my mom and her grandmother. The whole thing."

Leo handed me the plates, and I helped set the table.

"What if she wants nothing to do with me after this?"

Leo placed the silverware next to the plates and hurried back to the kitchen. "Your aunt loves you, Chloe. She will never disown you."

I took the wine glasses off the shelf and searched the inventory for the perfect wine. "You don't know my aunt. This is going to put her over the edge."

I held up two bottles. "Which one?"

Leo pointed to the left. "The Pinot Noir." He placed the bread in the oven and shut the door. "It may take time for her to adjust."

"Yeah, but what about Uncle Bob? He's known this whole time. What if she leaves him?"

Leo placed his hands on my upper arms. "Hey, don't worry. You're starting to get creases between your eyes."

I smacked Leo on the arm even as the doorbell rang.

I stood on tiptoe to kiss Leo. Even in spiked heels, I wasn't tall enough to reach him. "I hope you're right."

I straightened my dress as I walked to the door. "Well, here goes nothing."

To my surprise, it was Akila.

"I didn't expect to see you so soon. Please, come in."

"Mmm, what smells so good?" Akila asked.

"Leo and I are making diner. I'm having my dad and Aunt Helen over. It's time I told her the truth about things."

"I see. Well, I have a surprise for you."

"Is everything okay?" Leo stepped into the room. "Oh! I... um, hi!"

Akila smiled and gave him a bow. "I'm sorry to intrude."

"You're always welcome here, Akila."

Akila smiled and held out a necklace identical to the one that had been destroyed. The only difference was that it didn't glow or have a swirling mist inside.

"I made this especially for you. Sanura's essence may be gone, but this is filled with a powerful energy source. It is a concoction that I put together."

"Thank you, Akila. I missed having it around my neck." As soon as I put it on, I felt the warmth flow around me. "Oh, you were not kidding about the energy."

"Good. That means I used just enough." Akila stepped away.

"Would you care to stay for dinner?" I asked.

"I'd love to, but I am needed elsewhere. Maybe one day soon?"

"Absolutely."

"Have a good evening." Akila shut the door behind her.

Leo squeezed my arm. "I'm going to check on the bread."

I looked at the replicated crystal dangling from my neck. I missed the vibrations, but this one had a whole new meaning. This one was made for me by an ancestor from the beginning of our kind. It was more special than the other.

I heard a car pull up and two doors shut. When I opened the door, Aunt Helen had her hand up as she was about to knock.

"Oh!" Aunt Helen's hand went over her heart, and she let out a giggle. "You startled me. How are you, sweetie? You look absolutely beautiful."

She pulled me into a hug.

"Thank you. You do, too."

She touched the necklace with the tips of her fingers. "You found it. It looks good on you."

If only she knew.

Leo stepped into the room, drying his hands on a dishcloth. "Hello, Mrs. Grady. It's good to see you again."

Helen's cheeks flushed a light shade of pink. She hugged him and kissed both sides of his face. "Please, call me Helen."

Uncle Bob stepped around Helen. "Hello, Leo. How are you?"

"I'm doing well. Dinner is just about ready. We are waiting for two more guests." Leo hurried back to the kitchen.

"You been practicing your golf swings?" Uncle Bob asked as he followed Leo.

Helen grabbed my arm and pointed toward the kitchen with her thumb. "Leo cooks?"

334

"He sure does. He's part German, too."

"Whoa. The brawn, the good looks, and a chef." Aunt Helen fanned her face with her hand.

I laughed and led her to the kitchen. "How is Peanut? Is she being good?"

"Oh, she is a delight! I have new pictures to share." Aunt Helen thumbed through her photos on the phone.

She was like a proud grandmother showing off her grandchild.

We all laughed at the silly pictures.

"Stephen and Suzanne just pulled up," Leo said.

Helen and I looked up at Leo.

He quickly tapped his ear. "I have a keen sense of hearing."

"Wait! You invited Stephen?" Aunt Helen laid her hand on my forearm.

"Yes. He is my father, after all. It's time we put the past behind us and move on. Don't you think?"

Leo kissed my temple as he walked by to answer the door.

Uncle Bob placed his hand on Helen's back. "Try and be civil, dear. Give the man a chance. He deserves that much."

Helen caressed his cheek. "I will try."

Leo came back and held up a bottle of wine. "Your dad brought the good stuff."

"Good. We'll use it instead of the Pinot Noir." I gave my dad and Suzanne a hug.

"Helen, after all of these years, you still look as lovely as ever," Stephen said.

"It has been a long time." Helen glanced at the woman next to him. She held out her hand. "I'm Helen."

"Nice to meet you. I'm Suzanne."

The two smiled and then parted.

"Dinner is ready." Leo indicated that everyone should file into the dining room.

Stephen, Uncle Bob, and Leo pulled the chairs out for us ladies like true gentlemen.

"Thank you, baby." I smiled up at Leo.

Leo opened the bottle of wine and poured everyone a glass before taking the head of the table. "I want to propose a toast to the most wonderful, beautiful, talented woman in the world. You have made my life more interesting. And, I want to thank all of you for being here to celebrate her. Now, I have prepared a meal that my mother used to make. It is a chicken schnitzel. I hope you enjoy it."

I sipped the wine and watched Leo hand out the salad and the main dish. He said he was lucky, but the truth was, I was the lucky one.

"This is delicious, Leo," Helen said. "Your mother is a great cook."

"She is. At one point in my life, I gained a lot of weight due to her special dishes."

We all laughed, and Leo passed the bread to Stephen.

"Have you heard from Kyle?" Stephen asked.

"He called this morning. He and Riley are getting settled in their new apartment."

Helen took a roll and cut it in half. "Who's Kyle? Butter, please."

I handed her the butter. "Kyle's my stepbrother. He just moved to New York. He starts a new job in a few weeks."

"Oh! I had no idea. Why didn't you tell me you had a stepbrother?"

"It never came up. There's just been so much going on lately." I finished off my wine.

"Would you like another glass?" My dad asked.

I nodded and held up my glass.

"It's nice to have all of you here," Leo said.

Helen dabbed her mouth with the napkin. "It's nice to be here, Leo. And, I'd like to say something, if I may."

Leo held out his hand. "By all means."

Helen took a sip of wine and acknowledged Stephen. "I want to say I am sorry for what I did and said to you in the past. I was only trying to protect my sister, and I couldn't stand to see her lose control like that. It made me react on her behalf without even hearing what you had to say."

Stephen smiled. "I understand why you did it, Helen. I hold no grudges. I never did. There is nothing to forgive you for. It is I who should be asking you to forgive me."

He glanced at me and nodded.

Now wasn't the right time. So, I shook my head.

Helen missed the reaction between Stephen and me as she waved her hand. "Don't be absurd. You did nothing wrong."

The rest of the dinner went smoothly and our conversation was normal. It was as if there was nothing wrong in the world or any secrets to be told. But, that was about to change.

Leo excused himself and came back with a chocolate cake with a red drizzle and shaved chocolate pieces on top. He cut everyone a slice and passed it around the table.

"Oh, Leo. Is this your mother's recipe, too?" Aunt Helen asked.

"No, actually, it's my friend's. Her name is Betty Crocker."

We all laughed and ate our dessert.

The anxiety built in my chest as the time drew near. I took a few deep breaths and pushed my plate aside.

Suzanne placed her hand on mine for reassurance.

"Let's all gather in the sitting room," Leo suggested.

Aunt Helen and Uncle Bob sat on the small sofa, while the rest of us decided to stand.

"What is going on? You're all acting strange," Helen said.

"Aunt Helen, there is something I...we need to tell you. This goes back to when my mom was with Stephen."

"Okay."

"I'm not sure how to say this, but when my mother saw Stephen turn into a wolf, it was real. He's a lycan. So is Leo, Suzanne, and even me."

The room became silent for a moment until she belted out a laugh. "Oh, Chloe. Why are you making up such nonsense?"

"Honey." Uncle Bob held Helen's hand. "You need to listen to her. What she's saying is true. Even I have witnessed all the strange shit. My last two cases did not even deal with human nature. There are other beings out there."

Helen shook her head. "No. No, I refuse to believe this."

"Sweetheart." Uncle Bob turned sideways and scooted closer to her. He proceeded to tell her about his case all those years ago that had to do with the lycan killings.

Then Stephen took over with his part to explain why Katherine's attitude changed.

When it came around to me to tell my side of things, Helen bolted up from the couch and hurried to the far side of the room.

"You're all crazy! Why are you doing this?" she wept.

"I can show you, Helen." Stephen backed away and took a deep breath. He held out his hands and forced his fingers to elongate. Pointed teeth protruded from his gums, and his eyes had a slight golden hue.

That was as far as he let it go.

Helen fell against the wall. She covered her mouth with her hand as she tried not to scream. Her knees buckled, but Uncle Bob was quick to grab her.

She pushed him away and scrambled to her feet. "You knew about this the whole time? Why didn't you tell me what happened back then?"

"I didn't know how. I didn't want you to think I was crazy, too."

Helen looked around the room at all of us.

I know she must've felt betrayed. I know I had when I found out the truth. This wasn't to get back at her. It was to protect and prepare her, should anything happen out of the ordinary.

"I can't do this. Take me home." Aunt Helen grabbed her purse and ran out the door.

Uncle Bob hugged me. "Don't worry. It will take some time for her to accept this."

"We're all here for you, sweetheart." Suzanne squeezed my hand.

Stephen sighed. "No one said this was going to be easy. The hardest part is over. Now, we just give Helen space. She'll come around when she's ready."

He kissed the top of my head.

After everyone left, Leo come up behind me and massaged my shoulders. He whispered in my ear. "I love you, Chloe."

I laid my head back against his chest. "I love you, too. Let's clean up."

Leo put away the leftovers while I loaded the dishwasher. Not much was said as we cleaned. What was there to say?

All I could think about was my aunt crying herself to sleep. She probably made Uncle Bob sleep on the couch. I know how upset she was.

An hour later, I leaned against the sink, exhausted.

"Why don't you go to bed? I'll finish up here." Leo kissed my head.

I looked up at him and licked my lips. My fingers slipped under his shirt. I felt every ripple of muscle tightening as he trembled under my touch. "It's been a while since we've had sex. Right now, I need to feel close to you."

Leo pulled my hands out from under his shirt. "Babe, you've had a long day. You need some rest."

"What I want is to be with you. I almost lost you, Leo. And, after everything we've been through these past few days..." I let my voice trail off. I couldn't finish the words.

Leo rubbed my lower lip with his thumb. "Have I told you how beautiful you look in that dress?"

"No."

"Well, you do. And, you're making it hard for me to be a gentleman right now."

"I know I'm making it hard." I lowered my hand to his erection. "And, I don't want you to be gentle."

Leo groaned and stepped away. "You're killing me, Chloe."

"I can feel your animal lurking, Leo. I want to see him. I want him to come out and play."

Leo's jaw clenched.

I didn't know why he was refusing me, and it was starting to upset me even more. I had been patient long enough. My animal needed to be free. I did the only thing I could think of.

I unzipped my dress and let it fall to the floor. The only thing I was left wearing was red lace panties.

"I'm ready, Leo. I need you. My animal needs you. Please, don't deny me this any longer."

Leo growled, picked up my dress, and took me by the hand.

"Come with me."

I followed him to the bedroom. He laid my dress on the chair. Then he turned to face me and began to undress.

"Are you going to finish your striptease from the other night?"

Leo kicked off his shoes and unzipped his pants. "No."

I watched with hungry eyes as he peeled off his tight pants to expose the rest of his toned body.

He pulled the blankets down and ordered me onto the bed.

I did as I was told, and he crawled on top of me. He reached down and pulled the covers over us.

"There will be no rough sex tonight, Chloe. But, I do want to make love to you. Slow and easy. I want to feel every inch of you wrapped around my dick."

"Jesus, Leo. The things you say."

"I want to ask you something. In a few weeks, I need to go home for our annual meeting, and I want you to go with me. I want you to meet my family."

"Oh, Leo. Yes. Of course I'll go with you."

Leo nibbled the side of my neck and kissed my earlobe. "I love you, Chloe. More than anything in this world."

"Say you love me again in German."

"Ich liebe dich."

Leo kissed me gently. His tongue parted my lips and slipped inside my mouth. At the same time, he moved his hips and entered me. I moaned into Leo's mouth as his cock filled me. He rocked back and forth slowly and steadily, as promised.

For hours, he took his time until he couldn't contain himself anymore. Exhausted, we fell asleep in a tangled mess with the sheets wrapped around us.

CHAPTER 32 Chloe

The next morning, I felt revived, almost like a whole new person. I looked over at the new doors to the balcony that Kyle had installed before he left for New York.

The aroma of food filled the room. I inhaled slowly to savor the scent. I jumped out of bed, dressed, and went down to the kitchen.

"Good morning, beautiful. Sleep well?" Leo asked.

"I sure did. How about you?" I stood on tiptoe and gave him a peck on the lips.

Leo took my hand and led me to the breakfast nook. "Slept like a baby. Have a seat. I made breakfast."

There were pancakes, eggs over easy, hash browns, bacon, and biscuits. There was also a glass of milk and orange juice.

"Are you kidding? I can't eat all of this."

Leo laughed. "It's not all for you. Some of it is mine. With my dad being German, we always had a big breakfast. Besides, you will learn soon that lycans have big appetites."

"I can't wait to see what your parents cook up for us when we visit." I poured syrup on my pancakes and cut a few pieces.

Leo kissed the tip of my nose.

I took a large bite of pancake and washed it down with milk. "You know, we have the house to ourselves. So, you can make good on your promise." I mixed the eggs and hash browns together.

"What promise?"

"The one where you have your way with me in every single room." I smiled, then shoved the fork full of food in my mouth.

"You're hard to resist."

"Well, I don't know about that. You seem to resist when it comes to letting me shift."

"Chloe, don't do this. I just want—"

I placed my finger over his lips. "I'm messing with you. I know you have your reasons, but please make it soon. It's not fair to me."

"I know. But, I have plans, and I want it to be special."

Leo's phone went off, and he checked his message. "Oh, boy."

"What is it?"

"Your uncle insisted I met him on the golf course."

I busted out laughing. "I'm sorry to hear."

The doorbell rang, and Leo answered it while I finished eating. I heard him ask Elsie how she was.

"I'm good, Leo. Thank you." She entered the kitchen.

"Elsie!" I hopped off my chair and hugged her. "What are you doing here?"

"I didn't interrupt your breakfast, did I?"

"Not at all. There some pancakes left. Would you like some?"

"Oh, no, thank you. I already ate."

Leo emptied the trash can and replaced it with a new bag.

While he took the trash outside, Elsie nudged me in the arm. "You have a wonderful man there, Chloe."

"I know."

Leo came back and kissed the top of my head. "I'm headed out to meet your uncle. Wish me luck."

"Good luck."

I put my dirty dishes in the dishwasher and started it up. "So, what brings you by?"

"A few things, actually. You know, I had never met any of our ancestors. To my surprise, Akila visited me the other day. She filled me in on what I didn't know, as well as how you freed us from Talibah."

Elsie took my hand. "I'm so proud of you, Chloe. Sanura couldn't have chosen a better person to fight that evil woman."

"Well, it's not like I had a choice."

"That is true. My other reason for being here is...I was wondering if we could visit Katherine's grave."

"Of course. I'm ready to go if you are."

Elsie nodded once. "I am."

I used to go to my mother's grave twice a month to put fresh flowers down. But, I hadn't been there for several months.

We stopped to pick up a fresh arrangement at the store, and then I gave Elsie directions to the cemetery.

"Why so glum?" Elsie asked.

"Last night, I told Aunt Helen the truth about lycans. I was going to mention the mystic part, but she got upset and ran out of the house."

Elsie glanced at me and then focused on the road. "Were you going to tell her about me?"

"I want to. She has a right to know you are alive. She needs to know the reason behind all of our family issues."

As we drove up the winding road to the site, another car came into view. It was parked off to the side.

"Aunt Helen is here. That's her car," I said.

Elsie pulled behind the SUV. "Maybe we should come back later."

"Nope." I got out of the car and headed up the hill.

My parents were buried under a large cedar tree. I could hear Aunt Helen crying as I neared the gravesite.

Elsie grabbed my arm. "I'm not sure this is a good idea."

"Yes, it is. Wait here."

I didn't want to startle Aunt Helen, so I approached her from the side. She had a wad of tissue in her hand.

"Aunt Helen," I said lightly.

She looked up with puffy eyes. The tip of her nose was red from all of her nose blowing.

"Oh, Chloe," she cried.

I went to her side and put my arms around her. She leaned into me and sobbed. After a few moments, she wiped her nose.

"I'm sorry, Chloe. I didn't mean to run out on you last night."

"It's okay. I sprang a lot of stuff on you at once. I shouldn't have done that."

Aunt Helen patted my hand. "It had to be done."

Her eyes darted past my shoulder. "Who is that?"

I glanced behind to see who she was referring to. I saw Elsie holding flowers. I thought she would've hidden.

"Well, um...she's here to pay her respects to Mom."

Aunt Helen perked up. "She knew Katherine?"

She held onto Mom's headstone as she got up.

I followed her to Elsie.

"Hello. I'm Helen. I don't believe we've met." She held out her hand.

"I'm Elsie."

"How did you know Katherine?"

Elsie opened her mouth to say something, but then closed it.

I had to save this situation. And lies were not going to cut it for me. I'd come this far. Might as well finish it off.

"Aunt Helen, I didn't get to finish telling you everything. I really don't want to do this now, but...I researched our family as I'd promised."

"You did?" She looked at Elsie. "Are you a relative?"

I took a hold of both Elsie and Aunt Helen's hands. "Aunt Helen, I need you to have an open mind."

She laughed. "Oh, honey, I think we're past that now. Don't you think?"

"I suppose."

Elsie tugged on my hand. "Let me have a moment with her. I think this should come from me."

I nodded and walked to a bench by a mausoleum.

Elsie and Helen stood in front of my mother's grave and held hands. I could only imagine how this conversation was going. Had Leo let me shift, I probably could've heard from a distance.

Helen went to her knees and Elsie followed. They held each other as they sobbed. This brought tears to my eyes. I guess the conversation had ended on a good note. At least Aunt Helen hadn't thrown a tantrum and run off.

They helped each other up, and Aunt Helen waved me over.

I got up and dusted the dirt off my pants.

Aunt Helen pulled me into a hug. "Oh, Chloe. Thank you. Thank you so much."

Elsie smiled and put her arms around us. It was one big group hug.

Aunt Helen pulled away and wiped her face. "Chloe, show

me what you can do. I want to see."

I turned my palm up to produce a white light.

"Oh, that is amazing, Chloe. Are you sure I'm not like you? Maybe it's because I didn't know about it," Aunt Helen said.

"I don't believe so, honey," Elsie replied.

Helen's brow furrowed as she looked down.

"We should re-test her," I said. "There is a doctor at the club I go to. She's the one who did my blood test. Times have changed, so maybe she could dig a little deeper to see if there is even a hint of mystic DNA."

Helen's face lit up. "Oh, Chloe, could you find out?"

"Of course."

"If there is a small chance, would I be able to do what you did?"

"Some mystics have similar powers, but as for mine...that is rare. But, I wouldn't get your hopes up just yet, Aunt Helen."

Aunt Helen laughed and draped her arms over both of our shoulders. "I suppose I shouldn't. Let's all go back to the house. There's so much to catch up on. I have tons of stuff in the attic and pictures of your great-grandchildren, Abby and Mark."

"I'd love to." Elsie smiled.

We spent the rest of the afternoon sorting through boxes and looking at old pictures of my mother, Helen, and the kids. Peanut romped around the attic and hid under the furniture.

Every once in a while, Peanut would run up to me and lick my hand. Then, she'd roll over on her back to make me rub her belly.

Aunt Helen tossed a pink hat with a ribbon on it to the floor. It caught Peanut's eye, and she jumped up, yelping at it before pulling on the ribbon.

"Hello?" a voice called out. Heavy footsteps ascended the stairs. Bob poked his head between the rails. His eyes widened when he saw all three of us on the floor all dressed up in old dresses.

"Well, this is the last thing I expected to see."

Aunt Helen jumped up and ran to her husband. She threw her arms around his neck. "Oh, Bob! I have wonderful news. This is Elsie. She's my grandmother. She's a mystic, but something tells me you probably already knew that."

"The mystic part, yes. As for being your grandmother, I had no idea." Bob nodded and smiled at both me and Elsie. "Nice to meet you, Elsie. Would you care to stay for dinner?"

"I'd love to."

"Chloe, how about you?"

"I'm afraid I need to get home to Leo. By the way, how was your little outing with my boyfriend?"

"For someone who has never played a game of golf in his life, he sure kicked my ass."

I laughed. "Yeah, he's good at everything he does."

I hugged Aunt Helen and Elsie goodbye. We made plans to have a girl's night out the next weekend. I was so happy that things had worked out.

When I got home, Leo was asleep on the couch with the TV on. I kissed his cheek and pulled the blanket over him.

I went to the kitchen to heat up the leftovers from last night. I was putting the food in the microwave when Leo strolled in.

"What are you doing? I thought we could go out to dinner tonight."

"I'm kind of tired. I just want to stay in."

He scratched his head and yawned. "How was your day with Elsie?"

I jumped into Leo's arms and wrapped my legs around his waist.

"Oh!" He laughed.

"I will tell you about it over dinner."

"That good, huh?"

I nodded and kissed him.

This was the best day ever. I hoped it only got better from here, and I was sure it would. My next journey would be to visit Leo's home. Well, at least one of them. It was a big step for us both, and I was pretty sure Leo's plans involved me shifting. I smiled at the possibility of finally becoming one with nature.

About the Author

Christine Cofer lives in a rural area of Missouri with her husband and son, along with her dog, Ozzy, and cat, Shadow. She has channeled her love for the supernatural to create a world of self-driven characters. What started out as a short story—for fun—has grown into something more. Aside from writing, she is a first degree black belt in Taekwondo and has an Associate Degree of Applied Science and works as a medical billing specialist full time

You can connect with me on:
🌐 http://www.christinecofer.com
❦ http://www.facebook.com/indie.author.my.books

Subscribe to my newsletter:
✉ https://www.christinecofer.com/subscribe-for-newsletters

Also by Christine Cofer

Chloe Pierson Series

Flesh and Desire
Untamed Desire